THE OATH OF NIMROD

GIANTS, MK-ULTRA AND THE SMITHSONIAN COVERUP

A Novel by
David S. Brody

Eyes That See Publishing
Westford, Massachusetts

The Oath of Nimrod
Giants, MK-Ultra and the Smithsonian Coverup

Eyes That See Publishing
Westford, Massachusetts

ISBN 978-0-9907413-0-5
1st edition

Cover Art by Kimberly Scott

Printed in USA

Praise for David S. Brody's Books

"Brody does a terrific job of wrapping his research in a fast-paced thrill ride that will feel far more like an action film than an academic paper."
—PUBLISHERS WEEKLY (*Cabal of the Westford Knight*)

"Strongly recommended for all collections."
—LIBRARY JOURNAL (*The Wrong Abraham*)

"Will keep you up even after you've put it down."
—Hallie Ephron, BOSTON GLOBE (*Blood of the Tribe*)

"A riveting, fascinating read."
—MIDWEST BOOK REVIEW (*The Wrong Abraham*)

"Best of the Coming Season."
—BOSTON MAGAZINE (*Unlawful Deeds*)

"A compelling suspense story and a searing murder mystery."
—THE BOSTON PHOENIX (*Blood of the Tribe*)

"A comparison to *The Da Vinci Code* and *National Treasure* is inevitable....The story rips the reader into a fast-paced adventure."
—FRESH FICTION (*Cabal of the Westford Knight*)

"An excellent historical conspiracy thriller. It builds on its most famous predecessor, *The Da Vinci Code*, and takes it one step farther—and across the Atlantic."
—MYSTERY BOOK NEWS (*Cabal of the Westford Knight*)

"The action and danger are non-stop, leaving you breathless. It is one hell of a read."
—ABOUT.COM Book Reviews (*Unlawful Deeds*)

"The year is early, but this book will be hard to beat; it's already on my 'Best of 2009' list."
—BARYON REVIEW (*Cabal of the Westford Knight*)

"Five Stars."
—Harriet Klausner, AMAZON (*The Wrong Abraham*)

"An enormously fun read, exceedingly hard to put down."
—The BOOKBROWSER (*Unlawful Deeds*)

"Fantastic book. I can't wait until the next book is released."
—GOODREADS (*Thief on the Cross*)

About the Author

David S. Brody is a *Boston Globe* bestselling fiction writer recently named Boston's "Best Local Author" by the *Boston Phoenix* newspaper. A graduate of Tufts University and Georgetown Law School, he is a former Director of the New England Antiquities Research Association (NEARA) and is an avid researcher in the subject of pre-Columbian exploration of America. He has appeared as a guest expert on documentaries airing on History Channel, Travel Channel and Discovery Channel.

For more information, please visit
www.DavidBrodyBooks.com

Preface

This novel is a bit of a break from the Templar-based themes I first explored in *Cabal of the Westford Knight* and continued exploring in *Thief on the Cross* and *Powdered Gold.* In this book I venture down the rabbit hole to examine the hundreds of accounts of giant human skeletons unearthed in the 19th century by American farmers and treasure hunters. Were all these skeletons—numbering over 1,500 by one researcher's count—fakes and hoaxes? Or was there instead a race of eight- and nine-foot tall humans who roamed the North American wilderness? If so, were these giants somehow related to the giants recounted in the Old Testament?

Of course, I can't very well write a book in the "Templars in America" series without delving into the mysteries of the Knights Templars and their possible journeys to America. In this story, I focus on the rituals and beliefs of the mysterious group whom many believe were spawned the Templars—the Freemasons. Specifically, did the early Freemasons venerate a pagan Babylonian king by the name of Nimrod and, if so, why? This inquiry takes on even greater meaning when we learn that Nimrod, like Samson and so many other figures in the Bible, was himself described as a giant.

I also weave the CIA mind-control program known as MK-Ultra into the story. This program, hatched during the early years of the Cold War, authorized experiments on U.S. citizens in an effort to unlock the secrets of the mind. These experiments included the use of hallucinogenic drugs, sleep deprivation and psychological torture—the CIA justified these attacks on its own citizens as a necessity in its efforts to fight Communism.

Readers of the first three books in the series will recognize the protagonists, Cameron and Amanda, and also young Astarte. However, this novel is not a sequel to the prior three and readers who have not read the earlier novels should feel free to jump right in.

As in the previous stories in the series, if an artifact or object of art is pictured in the book, it exists in the real world. (See the Author's Note at the end of this book for a more detailed discussion covering the issue of artifact authenticity.) To me, in the end, it is the artifacts that are the true stars of these novels.

I remain fascinated by the hidden history of North America and the very real possibility that waves of European explorers visited our shores long before Columbus. It is my hope that readers share this fascination.

David S. Brody, July, 2014
Westford, Massachusetts

"The eyes of extinct giants, whose bones fill the mounds of America, have gazed on Niagara Falls just as our eyes do now."

--Abraham Lincoln, 1848

David S. Brody

PROLOGUE

[May, 1952, Buenos Aires]

The tall, stiff-backed American college professor blew on his hands as he waited in the passenger seat of a jeep at an Argentine military base. He leaned away from the window, away from the rain blowing into the vehicle, and pulled his hat lower on his head. When Leonard Carmichael had left Boston three days earlier the long winter was finally yielding to a late spring. Now he had returned to the cold. Apparently it didn't snow in Buenos Aires, but sitting here for almost an hour in the rain and fog had numbed his extremities and frayed his patience. For one of the few times in his life, he wished he smoked.

"I think I see them coming, sir," the unnamed corporal seated in the driver's seat said. "Headlights on the left."

Carmichael nodded. When he had accepted his appointment as Secretary of the Smithsonian Institution, he had been expecting a semi-retirement spent rummaging around in the nation's attic. What he had not expected was to be thrown into the middle of the Cold War.

But when the President asks a favor, one does not say no. "I have a very important mission," Truman had explained. "A secret mission. And, unfortunately, a distasteful mission. The mission requires someone with an expertise in behavioral psychology. And I need a man I can trust." Truman had smiled. "Know anyone like that?" What the President had not said, but which Carmichael understood, was that the mission also required a private citizen so that the government could deny involvement if things turned ugly. Since Carmichael would not be sworn into his Smithsonian post until January, he fit the bill. The meeting with Truman had been three months ago.

1

Tonight's meeting would be a culmination of Carmichael's efforts since.

A black sedan pulled alongside the jeep; the driver nodded, stepped from the car and opened the rear door. As if on cue, the rain fell harder, propelled by a cold wind. Carmichael shivered. He slid out of the jeep, his knees stiff, and ducked into the rear seat of the sedan. As he closed the door, cigarette smoke and the dank smell of wet wool engulfed him. He coughed into his hand and turned to eye the man seated next to him. The German looked older than his thirty-nine years—soft-bodied, balding, a gray pallor to his skin. Hardly an archetype for the Master Race. Only his cold gray eyes marked the man as any kind of menace. Carmichael did not offer his hand. "Herr Weber, I presume."

"I am *Doctor* Weber." The man's breath reeked of garlicky meat gone bad.

Carmichael exhaled and edged away. He wanted to take the man by the throat and tell him he had forfeited the right to use that title. But that would mean he actually had to touch him. "You can guess why you are here?"

"Guess? I do not need to guess. I can *deduce*."

Pedantic little prig. Had he been a student of his, Carmichael would have boxed his ears. "Go ahead, then. Deduce."

"If you were going to turn me over to the Israelis, or put me on trial for war crimes, there would be no need for this meeting. I would be on a plane already. So I must deduce you want to make me an offer." He smiled, revealing a mouth of undersized yellow teeth that made Carmichael think of rats in an alley.

"Incorrect. I may determine, based on this meeting, that you do not suit our needs. In which case there will be no offer, and within the hour you will indeed be on a plane to Tel Aviv."

Weber eye's widened—he knew that would be a death sentence. But he recovered quickly and lifted his chin. "Well, then I will have to prove myself to you. What type of services are you in need of?"

2

That was the crux of it. Few people in the history of mankind had conducted the kind of human experiments Weber had conducted; few people had been able to probe so deep into the secrets and mysteries of the human mind and psyche. And of those few people, the rest were dead.

"You spent time at Auschwitz?"

He nodded. "I was first assistant to the chief medical officer, Dr. Wirths."

"And you worked with Mengele?"

"I assisted Doctor Mengele in many of his medical experiments, yes."

Carmichael studied the man. Millions had died during the war. Tens of millions. Brave men and women, innocent children. Yet this rodent sitting next to him—who had done more evil in one week than an army of men could do in a lifetime—somehow lived. And was now about to be rewarded.

He took a deep breath, stared out the window. When he had accepted this mission, he knew it would be distasteful. But to be sitting so close to the man, to smell the evil on him….

But there was no other way. The Soviets had already recruited Nazi death camp doctors, had already begun to experiment with mind control and brainwashing. Who knew what they might accomplish? Actually, Carmichael knew all too well—studying the mind had been his life's work. A drug or chemical introduced into the water supply, or seeded inside a rain cloud, or imbedded into the jet stream—the Soviets could incapacitate America without ever firing a shot. And Carmichael had no doubt they would not hesitate to do so. The modern world had never before seen a man as evil as Hitler, but neither had it seen one as dangerous as Stalin.

An old Bulgarian proverb popped into his head. *You are permitted in times of great danger to walk with the devil until you have crossed the bridge.* He took a deep breath and stared into the eyes of the devil sitting next to him. There was no other way across the bridge.

CHAPTER 1

Cameron Thorne exhaled. He never should have agreed to participate in this conference. A couple hundred conspiracy theorists fueling each other's paranoia at a hotel in central Massachusetts over a mid-winter weekend. Even Amanda had taken a pass. "Astarte is in desperate need of new socks," she said, kissing him on the nose. "But you have fun. And don't let them convince you that aliens built the pyramids."

The pyramid theory had been the least of it; it turns out the aliens had been far busier than that. From a seat on the side of the dais, Cam listened as the jowly, middle-aged Frenchman concluded his presentation. Finally. Jacques Autier was his name. "As I said, these reptilian aliens came to earth thousands of years ago." In his French accent he pronounced it *thew-sends*, as if from an old *Pink Panther* movie.

"The aliens came to mine our gold, but once here they crossbred with our females. These aliens were skilled lovers, apparently, and the earth women welcomed them to their beds. Even today, many of us, especially those of us who descend from the French noble families, carry this alien blood through our veins." Autier's tongue flicked out to moisten his lips, as if hinting that this ancestry accounted for his prowess under the sheets. Autier continued. "It is this reptilian blood that flowed through the ancient kings of Israel, through the Pharaohs of Egypt, through Jesus Christ, and through today's royal families of Europe."

Autier scanned the hotel ballroom, shifting his shoulders as he pulled his charcoal-colored suit coat tight around his midsection. Cam's eyes followed Autier's. Not a yawn or a fidget in the entire crowd. That was the problem with being a student of alternative history: You ended up surrounded by conspiracy theorists willing to believe pretty much anything.

Autier clasped his small-fingered hands together. "Through this interbreeding, these reptilian aliens have always

4

ruled the earth." He raised a hand as if anticipating the obvious question. "And they shall rule forever. Because if we rebel, they will kill us." He bowed his head. "Merci."

Cam clapped politely, pulling himself to his feet as the crowd rose. How was he going to follow a presentation like this?

Cam found a men's room. They were taking a twenty minute break, after which he was going to discuss European exploration of America before Columbus and these explorers' connections to the Knights Templar and Freemasons. The topic fascinated Cam, and the Freemasons and Templars were usually good fodder for conspiracy buffs. But Cam's topic didn't compare to reptilian aliens mating with humans to create a sub-species of cold-blooded earth-rulers. Not even close. The good news, he supposed, was that this crowd would hardly be likely to dismiss him as a kook.

What was that expression? *Even a bad day skiing beats a good day at the office.* Well, similarly, lecturing even at a bad conference beat practicing law for a living. He still maintained a limited real estate law practice to help pay the mortgage but, thankfully, the days of seventy-hour workweeks in a downtown firm were behind him. Between his law practice, speaker fees and his fiancée Amanda's income as a museum curator, they lived comfortably.

As Cam threw his tie over his shoulder a diminutive, chestnut-skinned man sauntered over and leaned into the urinal next to his. He turned and smiled, his brown eyes bright and playful beneath a pair of dark, bushy eyebrows which contrasted with a full head of cottony-white hair—if Barak Obama had a short, kindly grandfather, he would look like this, Cam decided. "Pardon me if I do not shake your hand," he said, enunciating every word. "My name is Randall Sid. I have attended this conference for the sole purpose of hearing your lecture."

Cam looked down at the man. Cam was only of average height, but he towered over Randall by almost a foot. Even taking into account that most elderly people lose a couple of inches, Randall could never have been much more than five feet tall. "Mine?" Cam asked.

"Indeed. And to meet you. I attended your lecture once before. You spoke at a Masonic Lodge in Rhode Island a number of months back."

Cam walked to the sink and washed his hands. "I guess I should be flattered." He smiled. "I can't even get my mother to hear my lectures more than once."

Randall grinned. He wore a gold and black argyle sweater vest over a button-down cream dress shirt and a pair of khakis. Cam wondered if he dressed like a prep school student because he couldn't find clothes in his size. Or maybe he just liked the sweater. "An attractive young lady accompanied you in Rhode Island. British. Amanda, perhaps, if I remember correctly?"

Randall spoke in the Boston Brahmin accent made famous by President Kennedy and later Charles Emerson Winchester III in the M*A*S*H television show—he omitted the letter "r" from the end of words as did other Boston speakers, but otherwise he cherished every letter of every word like a favorite pair of khakis. He seemed to enjoy the act of speaking, as unwilling to rush through a sentence as through a snifter of fine brandy.

"Yes, Amanda Spencer-Gunn, my fiancée."

He winked. "Truth be told, I came here today to see her more than I did to hear you."

Cam chuckled. Despite Randall's stilted way of speaking the man exuded an air of jovial irreverence. "I get that a lot," Cam said. Amanda was strikingly beautiful, like something out of a Grimm fairy tale—cream-colored skin, lime-green eyes, blond flowing hair and a lithe, gymnast's body. And highly intelligent, as much of an expert on the Templars and their exploration of North America as was Cam. In short, Cam liked to joke, way too good for him. But she didn't enjoy public speaking so she was happy to stay home with Astarte, the nine-year-old girl they were in the process of adopting. Cam smiled wryly. "Apparently Amanda had a desperate need to go shopping for socks."

Randall smiled again and motioned toward the ballroom. "I believe the term for this type of event is 'large tent'—there is sufficient room within for any and all conspiracy theories. Much like a Jesse Jackson campaign rally. I do not blame your Amanda for passing on it." He chuckled. "No, not at all."

Cam took his time drying his hands. He figured Randall was around eighty, but sharp and vibrant. And he obviously hadn't followed Cam into the bathroom to inquire about Cam's love life.

Randall continued. "I was observing you during this last lecture. Unless I am an even worse poker player than my friends tell me I am, my guess is you are not a subscriber to the reptilian alien theory?"

Cam shook his head. "I'm pretty open-minded—"

Randall interrupted. "Which is a fine thing to be. I have never observed anyone's brain falling out because of it," he smiled.

Cam laughed. "As I was saying, I could even be convinced aliens landed here. But reptilian aliens breeding with humans and creating a ruling class? Sorry."

Randall nodded. "Quite." He flushed the urinal and turned to face Cam; one bushy eyebrow lifted toward the ceiling. "As everyone knows, it was a race of alien giants, not reptiles, who bred with our women."

"I'm sorry, giants?"

"Are you not a Bible scholar, Mr. Thorne?"

"Not really, no."

"What's that old expression? *Fable is more historical than fact, because fact tells us about one man whereas fable tells us about a million men.* That's what the Bible is, you see, a fable. But it tells the history of mankind."

"But what does this have to do with giants?"

7

"Genesis, chapter six, verse four." He cleared his throat and spoke in a deep, sonorous manner, apparently in an attempt to be more God-like, the effect somewhat mitigated by the fact he was standing with his zipper down in front of a urinal. *"There were giants on the earth in those days; the sons of God came in unto the daughters of men, and they bore children to them."*

Cam replayed the words in his mind. "Wait, does that say the sons of God mated with human females to produce giants?"

"That is precisely what it says. You have heard of the term 'fallen angels,' no doubt. This is what the term is referring to. Angels, or sons of God, who came from the sky to breed with human women."

"But we're talking about angels. Earlier you said it was aliens."

Randall zipped his fly but seemed in no rush to end the conversation. "Indeed. The Bible calls them angels because they came from the sky. I believe it is just as likely they were aliens." He lifted his chin. "And, since the offspring of these aliens were giants, it seems to me that the aliens must have been oversized as well."

Cam nodded. He supposed giant aliens were as believable as angels.

Randall continued. "So, as I said, rather than alien reptiles breeding with our womenfolk, as Monsieur Autier would have us believe, I think it is more likely that the blood of alien giants courses through our veins. In fact, that is precisely what ancient Sumerian tablets describe." He smiled and raised himself up on his toes, his white hair bouncing with him. "Unfortunately, the giant gene appears to be a recessive one."

Cam laughed. He liked people who could make fun of themselves.

Randall finally moved away from the urinal and washed his hands. "As strange as this last tale was, I fear you are going to need to totally suspend your disbelief for what I would like to tell you next. If you will indulge me, that is."

Cam checked his watch. Why not? He had been listening to kooks and conspiracy theorists all weekend. And Randall at least seemed likeable. "I have ten minutes before my lecture."

They found a pair of easy chairs in the hotel lobby. "I am going to give you the abbreviated version," Randall said, "because the full version would take hours." His eyes had turned hard. "Are you familiar with Project MK-Ultra?"

Cam shrugged. "No."

"Very well. You allotted me ten minutes, and I intend to get my money's worth." For a man his size, Randall spoke with a remarkably deep voice. "MK-Ultra began after World War II. It was a secret government program that drugged and brainwashed American citizens—students, refugees, convicts, residents of mental hospitals, even soldiers. The program used Americans as experimental guinea pigs, but the ultimate goal was to establish methodologies to brainwash and control the minds of foreign leaders. Many people now know about the program—there were a number of Congressional hearings in the 1980s where the details were revealed." Randall paused. "But what the general public does not know is that Project MK-Ultra continues even today. We are more subtle in our methodologies—we have come to learn that *influencing* behavior is a more realistic goal than turning our enemies into sock puppets. But the result is the same."

"It continues?"

"That is what I just said."

"And you know this how?"

Randall sat forward. "I know this because I have spent my entire adult life working for the CIA, most of the time on MK-Ultra." He stared at Cam before pulling a sheaf of papers from the briefcase at his feet. "You may read all about the program here." He extended the papers to Cam. "This is a full transcript of the Congressional hearings from the 1980s. The hearings were secret, and most of the testimony was sealed. But here is the testimony in its entirety; just please do not let anyone catch you with it. It will give you an idea of what kind of misguided programs our government pursued. And still pursues."

Cam stood and checked his watch as he accepted the papers. He needed to get into the hall to give his lecture. "Why are you giving this stuff to me?"

Randall waited until Cam raised his eyes. "Because the program is targeting you, Mr. Thorne."

"Me? Why?" He was tempted to grab the man's shoulder and shake the answer from him. What in the world could they want with him?

Randall shrugged and smiled. "If I knew that, I would not have wasted my time today listening to some idiot prattle on about alien reptiles. All I know is that the Agency intends to brainwash you." He stood and, with a surprising bounce in his stride, ambled toward the lobby door. After three steps he stopped and turned. "In fact, I believe they have already begun."

CHAPTER 2

A week had passed since the conference and Cam's conversation with Randall Sid. Cam barely remembered giving his lecture that night. It must have gone okay because a number of people came up afterward to chat and ask questions. But his mind was then—and had continued to be since—focused on Randall Sid's warning. *Was it possible the CIA had already begun to brainwash him?* He didn't know how to answer that question—it seemed to him that, by definition, people who were brainwashed weren't aware of it; otherwise they would take steps to prevent it. Had they been putting something in his water? Whispering in his ear when he was asleep? Drugging his food? Hypnotizing him?

During his lecture he had glanced out to see if Randall had doubled back to listen, but nothing. Randall claimed to be CIA, or at least ex-CIA, so Cam supposed that one of the possibilities was that the little man still worked for the government. In which case he may have been lying to Cam about the brainwash stuff. But to what end?

After the lecture Cam was supposed to have stuck around for a dinner-time panel discussion on a topic related to the reptilian alien presentation: Apparently every U.S. President, including Barack Obama, could trace his lineage directly back to the British royal family. This tied in tangentially to the fact that a high percentage of U.S. Presidents and signatories to the Declaration of Independence were Freemasons. Most of the conference attendees viewed these facts as evidence that a secret cabal of power-brokers controlled and handpicked the leaders of Europe and North America. Normally Cam would have enjoyed the debate. But he had had enough. He had spent the day listening to people play strange games of connect-the-dots with history, and his head hurt. So he had slipped out a side door. If anyone asked, he would have said he had been brainwashed into leaving early.

The Oath of Nimrod

He and Amanda had stayed up late the night he returned from the conference, batting back and forth the possibility of Cam being brainwashed or otherwise targeted for mind control. In the end they decided to take some precautions—they began to drink only bottled water; Cam made an appointment with a new doctor and underwent a full physical and body scan; and they hired a security expert to sweep their home, cars and cell phones for listening and tracking devices. These precautions uncovered nothing. "As a last resort," Cam announced, "I'm not going to watch any more *Rocky and Bullwinkle* with Astarte. I'm convinced those guys are putting strange thoughts into my head."

"Miss your cartoons? Not bloody likely," Amanda had laughed. And she was probably right. The addition of Astarte to their home had given Cam the chance to rediscover many of the cartoon characters of his youth; he had spent six months in bed with a fractured back as a fifth-grader and for long stretches his only companions were the animated characters on the old UHF television channels. Lately he and Astarte had taken to prancing around the living room reciting a poem from Wordsworth, taught to them by Bullwinkle the Moose. *A host of golden daffodils....*

Cam did forego enough cartoon time to read through the materials Randall had given him, alternately fascinated and outraged at both the arrogance and callousness of Project MK-Ultra. Even the name sounded like something out of a James Bond movie. The letters 'MK' denoted the CIA division in charge of developing secret weapons and covert tools—some testimony indicated it derived from the German spelling of 'mind control'—while the word 'Ultra' signified the most secret of all CIA classifications. Under the operation the CIA conducted mind-altering experiments on American and Canadian citizens, many of whom suffered long-term physical and psychological damage. Shockingly, some of the test subjects even committed suicide.

The list of those experimented upon by the CIA—through the use of hallucinogenic drugs such as heroin and LSD, electric shock treatment, neural stimulation, sexual abuse, and/or physical torture—read like headlines from a supermarket tabloid:

- The Unabomber, Ted Kaczynski, was given high doses of hallucinogenic drugs while a student at Harvard;
- Sirhan Sirhan was subject to mind control and may have been brainwashed into shooting Robert Kennedy;
- Boston gangster James 'Whitey' Bulger was tortured, drugged and perhaps subjected to electric shock during his incarceration at Alcatraz; and
- A number of women claimed to have been brainwashed and used as sex slaves for Bob Hope and other Hollywood celebrities.

Perhaps most disturbing of all was the revelation that the CIA employed associates of the barbaric doctor Josef Mengele, the Nazi 'Angel of Death' from Auschwitz, as consultants in overseeing the MK-Ultra program and its experiments. Which would explain the Germanic 'MK' abbreviation for 'mind control.'

Officially, the program, which operated for decades after World War II, was finally shut down in the 1980s after a series of Congressional hearings detailing the abuses shocked the nation. But according to Randall Sid it continued even today.

Late one night, after Astarte had gone to bed, Cam summarized the information for Amanda. "Are you sure this stuff is accurate?" she asked, curling up next to him on the living room couch, her thick blond locks tumbling onto his shoulder. "There's a lot of so-called facts on the internet that are batty."

"This isn't coming just from the internet. What I've been reading is sealed testimony from Congressional hearings in the 1980s. The info comes from the CIA itself. It's incredible. In the sixties the CIA was worried about all the protests on college campuses." He smiled. "You know, anti-war, civil rights, all sorts of deviant ideas. So what they did was develop a new strain of the pneumonia virus and purposely spread it on college campuses where demonstrations were planned just to keep the crowds down."

"Bloody lovely. Your tax dollars at work."

"It's pretty sick. If you Google 'Church Committee' you can read some of the testimony; most of it has been declassified." He shook his head. "But, to be fair, they said the women weren't really sex slaves, just sort of like party girls."

"Oh, well that makes it perfectly acceptable."

He dropped the papers onto the coffee table. "Sure makes me proud to be an American. I mean, associates of Josef Mengele? Really? If Hitler had been alive would we have used him as a political consultant?"

As the week went by, Cam did not hear from Randall. By Saturday the whole incident had moved to the back—or at least out of the forefront—of Cam's mind as he spent an afternoon playing pond hockey with a bunch of college kids home on winter break on the lake behind his suburban Boston home. He had seen five of them shoveling a rink across the lake and figured they might welcome the opportunity to even the sides at three apiece. It didn't hurt that he brought a wide shovel with him.

Twice their age and not as skilled, Cam hoped merely to hold his own. Two-and-a-half hours and a handful of bruises later they squared off to play a final game. Coasting forward to within five feet of his opponent, Cam swung his stick as if to pass the puck. But he whiffed, his stick passing just over the rubber disk. His opponent saw the gaffe and bolted forward, ready to pounce on the puck and move in for the winning goal. But Cam had subtly positioned his skate behind the puck and, as his opponent rumbled toward him, Cam soccer-kicked the disk forward between the tall man's splayed legs. Stepping around him, Cam took three quick strides toward the empty goal. An easy shot. But out of the corner of his eye he saw a teammate move with him—he slid the puck across and watched his teammate guide it between the boots. Game over.

The opposing player skated past and tapped Cam with his stick on the shin. "Nice move." He smiled. "Not bad for an old man."

"Old, but not yet dead," Cam said.

"One more game?"

Cam smiled. "Sorry. Gotta get to the early bird special."

Drenched in sweat, he returned to find Amanda building a bonfire on their beach; a few houses down, he could see Astarte and a few friends building a snow fort in a neighbor's backyard. Venus, their fawn-colored Labrador Retriever, skidded across the ice to greet him.

"Venus spent the whole time watching you and whining. Can't you teach her to play?"

Cam smiled. "She takes the puck and runs off with it."

"Not much of a retriever then, is she?" Amanda stood on her tiptoes to kiss him. "If you want to take a shower, I'll open a bottle of wine," she said, crinkling her nose.

"Nothing like the smell of sweaty hockey gloves," he grinned. "My mom used to make me leave my equipment in the garage."

"I'm surprised the car started afterward."

Twenty minutes later he rejoined Amanda and Venus on the beach. The sun had just set. "Giants," Amanda said, peering over her wine glass at him, the flames flickering in her blue-green eyes.

Again with the giants? He tossed a snow-crusted log onto the fire. "Okay, giants. I'm guessing when they were dirty they smelled even worse than hockey players." The crackle and hiss competed with the sounds of a still-active game being played across the lake. A winter moon bathed the frozen lake in a bluish hue.

"Not possible," she said, rolling her eyes. "But we need to research them. They're in the Bible."

"Yes, apparently the offspring of angels or aliens or something mated with human woman." He recounted what Randall told him. "In that *Noah* movie, aren't the giants made of stone?"

"The stone part is from the Sumerian creation narrative, called the 'Epic of Gilgamesh,' which most scholars believe is the basis for the early Bible stories recounting the Garden of Eden and Noah's Flood. In the Bible, of course, the giants are human, not stone."

Cam smiled. "I like the stone giants better."

She rolled her eyes. "Yes, I'm certain most boys would. Stone or human, giants appear in dozens of Biblical passages and also in the Sumerian writings."

"So what happened to them?"

"The Bible says Goliath was the last of them. But what's fascinating is that they apparently lived in North America also. I've been doing some reading—there are dozens of newspaper articles documenting your early pioneers finding giants' bones. Many of them here in Massachusetts. And many accounts describe the giants as having a double row of teeth."

"Must have made it tough to floss."

She threw a handful of snow at him. "Seriously, it seems like almost every time a farmer plowed a field he stumbled upon a giant's bones." She leaned back, gazed at the evening stars and sighed. They sat in silence for a few seconds, each with their thoughts, until she said: "He turns not back who is bound to a star."

"I'm sorry, what?"

She repeated, slowly, *"He turns not back who is bound to a star."*

"Who said that?"

"Leonardo Da Vinci." She sighed again. "It resonates with me." Hugging her knees to her chest, she waited until his eyes met hers. "I feel like we are fated to do this, Cam. To study America's hidden history. As if it is our destiny or something."

"Fated to studying giants?"

"Not just giants. All of American history. So much of it is ... *flawed.*"

"And British history is all correct?"

"Of course not—our history is as buggered as yours. But I live *here* now. And this is what we do. This is the star to which we are bound." Together they had unearthed and interpreted

16

ancient artifacts which revealed a fascinating, secret history of North America; their most important research indicated Columbus had arrived centuries late to the North American exploration party.

Cam studied her. It wasn't so much that her face was pretty, which it surely was; it was that her face was so *alive* that had first captivated Cam. Her eyes danced, her cheeks glowed, her lips glistened. And when she set her mind to something, as now, her front teeth bit down on her lower lip and her jaw muscles clenched. Amanda's face radiated the energy and intelligence and passion of the person within.

"Okay," he said, "I agree, this is what we do. But before we go racing up the beanstalk, what exactly do you mean by giants? There are tribes in Africa where most of the men are almost seven feet tall."

Amanda glanced up at a lakeside white birch, a few strands of her strawberry blond hair escaping from her wool cap. "I'm talking taller than that. There's a museum in Nevada that has a skeleton ten feet tall. Even the bloody Smithsonian dug up a bunch of giant bones." She turned. "Is it really so impossible to believe that a race of giants once walked the earth?"

Cam shook his head. In fact, it was entirely possible. But that didn't make it so. The fact that the textbooks were wrong about Columbus did not mean they were wrong about giants— it just meant they *might* be. It was a possibility. Which, of course, was where all their research began. "Okay, giants it is." He smiled. "But can we eat first? I'm starving." Cam had been a diabetic since he was twelve; he led a perfectly normal life, so long as he monitored his blood sugar levels.

"What do you fancy, young Jack? We have string beans, lima beans, baked beans and wax beans. The choice is yours."

"Very funny. How about we just order Chinese?"

While Cam smothered the bonfire, Amanda walked down the lake to retrieve Astarte. During Amanda's first couple of years in the States she had dreaded winter until Cam taught her to appreciate skiing and sledding and ice skating. "If you let the New England winters keep you in the house you'll go batty," he had said. Useful advice, but not very practical—until she discovered hand and foot warmers. Someone deserved a Nobel Prize.

Ten minutes later they all met in the house. "Did you order the food?" Amanda asked.

"Yes. I got the Pu Pu Platter—we burned a ton of calories today so I thought we deserved a treat."

Astarte moaned. "Poop platter, blech!"

Cam smiled. "Sorry, no beef with broccoli tonight." It was Astarte's favorite.

"Why not?"

"Because Mum traded the cow for magic beans. So there's no beef."

Amanda rolled her eyes. "Very funny. Don't listen to him, darling."

Cam turned to Amanda and spoke as if Astarte wasn't in the kitchen with them. "I think we need to make a doctor appointment for Astarte. What kind of nine-year-old loves broccoli?"

"It's better than eating poop platter." The girl grinned. "And it's not as disgusting as Mum liking you." She stuck her finger down her throat. "Gross!"

Cam hoisted her over his shoulder and dumped her onto the couch. "What's gross is when you giggle so hard the snot comes out your nose," he said. He tickled her side until tears of laughter flowed from her cobalt-blue eyes and ran down her almond skin. But no snot, thankfully.

"Stop!" she giggled.

"Not until you agree that I am humble and loveable, just like Underdog."

"Okay, okay, you are," she shrieked, rolling away. And then grinning, "My fingers were crossed!"

Amanda watched as they sank to the floor, panting. In some ways Cam was as much of a child as Astarte. He loved to tease her, to race her, to see the world through her innocent eyes. And, of course, watch cartoons with her. She freed him up to be a kid again, to stop being the boring adult he was so afraid of becoming.

Not that Cam couldn't be a doting parent. When Astarte had come down with the flu a couple months ago, just before Christmas, Cam had spent the entire night sitting by her bed, alternately applying cold compresses and piling on blankets. And when she couldn't sleep Cam had read to her and told stories and simply held her. In the middle of the night Amanda had come in to relieve him. "I'll stay," he had said, looking away. "You go back to sleep."

She had taken his chin gently in her hand and turned his face, tears pooling in his eyes.

He had smiled sadly. "She's so ... helpless. I guess I wasn't totally ready for this parenting thing. I knew I'd grow to love her. But it's so much more intense than I thought."

"Yes," she had smiled. "Loving a child is the most unselfish kind of love. Parents expect nothing in return."

"Makes me want to call my mother, just to say thanks. I had no idea it was this hard."

As they had whispered in the dark, Astarte rolled over and vomited onto her sheets. "I'll take care of it," Cam had said. "At least I'll feel like I'm doing *something*." He had kissed Amanda's cheek. "Go back to bed."

"I'm not going to just let you do everything yourself."

"Fine," he had smiled. "Then please get some ginger ale. It'll help settle her stomach."

Upon returning Amanda had lingered by the doorway, watching as Cam, humming softly, cleaned Astarte's face and made a nest on the floor for her out of blankets while he changed her sheets. It was a side of him she had never seen before, and somehow she had fallen in love with him all over again.

That had been a tough week. And this had been another. The whole brainwashing thing was clearly worrying Cam. So it was good to have him back in a playful mood, even if it did mean Astarte laughing snot out of her nose.

Yet the brainwashing issue had not been resolved. The idea of someone—especially the CIA—trying to brainwash Cam seemed alternately ludicrous and terrifying. What did the CIA care about centuries-old history? But if they did care—and in the past powerful forces had tried to block their research—how would someone take steps to prevent being brainwashed? It was the type of thing that could paralyze you, always wondering if the decisions you made and feelings you had were your own or instead imposed upon you.

Not to mention how the potential instability might affect Astarte. They had taken her in as a foster child just over a year ago; she had been living with her recently-deceased uncle prior to that. Her uncle had been a researcher in pre-Columbian American history, which was how Amanda and Cam first met him. He doted on the girl and had shared much of his research with her.

Astarte dried her eyes with her sleeve, then surprised Amanda by saying, "I saw on your computer you were reading about giants."

Amanda nodded and plopped onto the couch next to her. "In fact, yes. And Cameron and I were just discussing them earlier."

"Uncle Jefferson said giant skeletons were found near Hill Cumorah, and that when the Nephites first came to America there were a lot of giants here." Her uncle had raised Astarte as a Mormon; Amanda knew that the Book of Mormon, which recounted the history of the ancient Nephites, was based on writings carved onto metal plates found buried in Hill Cumorah, in upstate New York.

Amanda shifted forward. "Did your uncle ever show you any bones?"

Astarte nodded. "They were part of his collection. One time on Halloween he took out a giant skull and put it over his head, like a helmet. And all the skulls had two rows of teeth."

Cam leaned against the coffee table. "Did he ever talk about artifacts found with the giants? Things like tools or jewelry or weapons or dental floss?"

Amanda cuffed him on the shoulder as Astarte responded. "He had a giant axe he said was too big for a human farmer. It was taller than him. He thought it belonged to the giants. And he showed me a broom that he said the giants used as a toothbrush," she deadpanned. "But no floss."

Amanda rolled her eyes as Cam laughed. "God help me," Amanda said, "she's picking up your sense of humor."

Amanda continued, musing, "Too bad we don't have access to your uncle's collection." The collection, like so many artifacts which seemed to contradict mainstream American history, had disappeared after his death.

The doorbell rang and Cam jumped up to pay for the Chinese food. Astarte poured drinks while Amanda grabbed silverware.

"Funny," Cam said. "The guy wouldn't take a tip. It's getting nasty out there so I gave him an extra ten."

"Odd. Same bloke as usual?"

"No. This was an old guy. Never seen him before."

"The place may have sold recently. When I was in last week there was a new staff."

They sat as Cam pulled the food from a brown paper bag. "What's this?" he asked, removing a brown C-shaped metal object from inside an otherwise-empty white cardboard carton.

"Looks like a bracelet," Amanda said.

Cam shrugged. "Maybe the new owners are giving out prizes instead of fortune cookies, like those old Cracker Jack boxes."

She smiled, leaned closer and whispered, "Or maybe the CIA is messing with your mind."

He removed a couple other food containers before peering back into the empty carton and pulling out a piece of copy paper folded in half.

Amanda leaned in. "It's a newspaper article."

Cam scanned the words, his eyes growing wider. "It's an old article about the Bat Creek Stone." The carved stone had been found in a Cherokee burial mound in Tennessee after the Civil War. Cam and Amanda had traveled to Tennessee to study it this past summer; the stone was engraved in an ancient form of Hebrew that dated back to the second century AD. A number of funereal objects found with it, including a metal bracelet, had been given to the Smithsonian but then lost before scholars could perform tests to date them. Cam turned the article so Amanda could see it.

Amanda took the bronze-colored bracelet from Cam and held it up to the light, her hand shaking slightly. *It couldn't be.* "It looks pretty old," she conceded. "Copper, maybe."

Cam shook his head. "Old, maybe. But ancient?" He turned to Astarte. "Can you get the magnifying glass for me? I think it's in the basement on the ping pong table."

He waited until she was out of earshot. "If the CIA is messing with us, it's a pretty strange ruse," he said.

Amanda bit down on her lip. "Why would they use a bracelet to brainwash you? It doesn't make sense."

"Maybe we're thinking too literally about the word *brainwash*. Maybe they're just trying to influence our behavior in some way."

"By giving us an ancient artifact?"

Cam held the bracelet to the light, exhaled and pushed his chair back. "We're just guessing. If we want answers, there's only one place to start."

Cam jumped into his SUV. The bracelet and the newspaper article rested in their original brown paper bag on the seat beside him.

He drove for two miles until the China Garden neon sign loomed ahead in the strip mall on Route 40; he turned into the lot and parked, surprised to see the parking spaces near the restaurant empty on a Saturday night. He was even more surprised to find the front door locked, with a handwritten sign taped to the glass. "Closed For Night."

A quick check of his watch—just past seven o'clock. Odd. Paper bag in hand, he began to walk around to the back of the building. The strip mall was abandoned, the bank, dry cleaner and beauty salon all closed for the night. A single streetlight illuminated the front lot. A cold wind blew some trash past Cam and a cloud drifted across the moon. His fingers tingled, a result of frostbite he suffered as a kid while skiing; the tingling now served as a warning sign, like hairs standing on the back of one's neck, a sign that his body was pumping extra blood— and presumably adrenaline—in the face of looming danger. He liked to think of the tingling as his Spidey Sense.

He took a deep breath. "This doesn't feel right," he whispered. He tucked the paper bag into a garbage can in front of the bank, figuring nobody would be emptying the trash over the weekend.

Jogging now, he circled the strip mall. A dark-colored minivan sat parked behind the Chinese restaurant. It looked empty. Cam slowed to a walk as the moon reappeared, rubbing his hands together as his fingers tingled. He leapt back as a rat scurried by. "Relax, fella, I'm not here to take your food." The rat turned to glance back at Cam with a single red eye. Cam thought about taking it as a sign that he should stop and return home, but instead took a deep breath and approached the back door.

He banged on it with a closed fist. "Hello? Anyone there?" Hearing no response, he crouched to see if he could see any light coming from under the door. Out of the corner of his eye he saw movement. A man's boot. Adrenaline surging, he tried to stand. "Stay right there," a voice hissed. He heard a pop just as a small disk jolted into his back. Hot, searing pain pulsated through his torso, blackening his senses. His back arched and his jaw clenched as his whole body violently cramped. Paralyzed, he crumbled to the pavement as the smell of his own urine assaulted his nostrils.

23

Ten excruciating seconds passed as Cam fought for oxygen, his body writhing in agony. Finally the effects of the Taser gun began to fade and Cam gulped air. But by then Cam had been hoisted into the back of the minivan with his hands cuffed behind him. Using all his strength, he pushed himself to an upright position and turned to see a young Asian man with a raised machete in the backseat next to him. Sweat glistened on the man's upper lip and his hand shook. Obviously not a pro, Cam thought. But he moved the machete closer to Cam's ear, and Cam got the message.

An older man in the front passenger seat turned as the driver pulled out of the parking lot and headed toward the highway a half mile away. "My name is Chung. Please, where is the bracelet?"

Cam blinked away the sweat from his eyes, took a deep breath and studied his captor. Fortyish, clean cut, button-down shirt, not much of an accent. Looked more like an engineer than a hoodlum. But unlike the guy holding the machete, Chung seemed calm. "I don't have it," Cam grunted.

"We know that. We searched your pockets." He wrinkled his nose. "Our hands smell like your piss. Tell us where it is. We will drive there now and get it. Then you can go."

Cam shrugged. "Sorry, can't help you." Not that he was some macho guy, trained to withstand torture, but he wasn't ready to give up the bracelet just yet. Somebody had wanted him to have it for a reason.

Chung forced a smile. "Maybe we should go back to your house? Perhaps the little girl will tell us?" He held up the stun gun, leering.

Cam glared at his adversary, thankful that Amanda had taken Astarte to see a movie. At least they were safe. For now. "It's not at the house."

"Where is it?"

Cam shrugged again. "Someplace safe."

Chung licked his lips. "Good. In that case we are in no hurry." The van left Westford, turned onto Route 3 and headed south. From what Cam could see the driver was about the same age as the machete-holder; he guessed both were Chung's sons.

24

As they drove Cam tried to reach for his cell phone, but it was in his front pocket and there was no way to get his cuffed hands around his body. Sweat ran down his armpits and his heart pounded in his ears. The further they drove, the less likely it was that help could find him. Not that anyone even knew to look for him. Maybe he should give up the bracelet....

"This bracelet," Cam said, "why is it so important?"

Chung barely turned. "The time for talking is over."

The vehicle exited the highway, cut through some back streets of Chelmsford and wound its way to a residential neighborhood comprised of medium-sized homes on half-acre lots. The minivan pulled into a garage of a split-level smack dab in the heart of middle class America. Cam half-expected 2.2 children to come out and greet them.

The three men escorted Cam through the garage and into a semi-finished room on the ground floor. A furnace hummed nearby. They sat Cam in a metal folding chair in the middle of the room and bound his hands and feet to it, the rope also securing the chair to a steel support post. Cam tried to keep things light. "Really, guys? You're going to tie me up?" He also concentrated on expanding his chest and arm muscles as the two sons tightened the rope, hoping that when he relaxed his muscles the rope would loosen and he might wriggle free. But this was getting serious. "If you tell me why you want the bracelet, I'll tell you where it is." The two younger men looked to their father for a response, but Chung continued to ignore Cam.

A single light bulb hung over Cam's head like in some 1950s Cold War movie. A door opened and an elderly woman shuffled in. Almost toothless, she leaned forward to study Cam, the smell of garlic strong on her breath. She muttered something in Chinese to Chung, who Cam assumed was her son. Chung shook his head.

The woman glared at Cam and pulled out a pair of red-handled plumbing pliers from her housecoat. She handed them to her son and barked a short command. The van driver started to say something, but Chung silenced him with a single word.

Before Cam had time to process what was happening, Chung had clasped the pliers onto Cam's left pinky finger and twisted violently. Cam heard the bone snap a split-second before he felt a searing inferno of pain that shot up his arm and released itself in a primordial scream. Panting, Cam thrashed in his chair, afraid to look down at his throbbing, mangled finger.

Chung held up the pliers to Cam's face. "We have all night. Where is bracelet?"

Cam wanted nothing more than to wrestle the pliers away from Chung and stuff them down his scrawny throat. He had gained some wiggle room under the ropes, and these guys were clearly not pros—if he could surprise his captors and make a run for it…. If not, he'd have no choice but to turn over the bracelet-

"*Yi!*"

Cam spun to see an elderly Chinese man burst into the room. Shouting in Chinese, the man waved a shotgun over his head and motioned angrily toward Cam. Chung yelled back at him, as did the woman, arguing, while the two younger men edged away. If Cam hadn't already been Tasered, abducted and tortured, he might have found the old man's appearance amusing—he wore a blue silk bathrobe and slippers, and his wispy gray hair stood at odd angles from his head.

After a few more heated exchanges in Chinese, the old man banged his hand on the steel post, raised the shotgun, and fired a shot into the far wall. Chung recoiled, lifted his hands and bowed his head as the smell of sulfur wafted through the room.

A few seconds passed and the old man pointed the barrel of the gun at Cam. His dark eyes were wild, but his wrinkled hand stayed steady. Cam tried to hold his gaze, studying him. Cam's fingers tingled. It was the delivery guy from dinner. *What the hell was going on here?*

26

"Mr. Thorne," he said in accented English. "Come me."

The old man motioned to the minivan driver, who fumbled at untying Cam's knots. Cam lifted his hand; the end of his pinky protruded at a jagged angle. Cam pushed himself from the chair, his legs weak, and staggered toward the exit ahead of the shotgun-toting, wild-haired old Chinese man.

As Cam passed near Chung, he took a deep breath, spun quickly and threw a right hook, burying his fist deep into the midsection of the man's button-down dress shirt. Chung made a gurgling sound before dropping to his knees and then rolling onto his side, his body curled into the fetal position. Cam didn't know what the old guy in the bathrobe had in mind, but whatever it was it wasn't likely to change just because Cam evened the score a bit with Chung.

A second gunshot froze Cam. "That my son, Mr. Thorne. No hurt him," the man in the bathrobe said, the blast echoing in Cam's ears. Cam turned and the men locked eyes. Chung moaned while the others eyed Cam nervously.

Cam lifted his chin and held up his mangled hand. "Then you should have taught him some manners."

The man narrowed his eyes before smiling, revealing a mouth of pointed brown teeth. He waved a hand at the old woman dismissively. "That his mother's job." He motioned toward the garage. "We go now. You drive. I no have license."

Cam drove the minivan one-handed, his left hand resting atop his head to reduce the blood flow. But it throbbed nonetheless, every heart beat sending fresh blood to assault his damaged nerve endings.

"You go hospital, get finger fixed."

Cam nodded. "Fine. But while I drive, you talk. What the hell is going on? And if you have no license, how did you deliver the Chinese food to my house tonight?" Life would have been a lot easier if they had decided on pizza instead.

"I use my son license." He smiled. "All Chinese men look same. Where bracelet?"

"Someplace safe."

"Good." The old man took a deep breath. "My name Pugh Wei. You call me Pugh."

Cam nodded. "Okay, Pugh. Back at the house, you called me Mr. Thorne. Have we met before?"

"No. Your name on caller ID when you order food. I waiting for you order."

"Because you wanted to give me the bracelet."

Pugh nodded. "Bracelet very important."

Assuming it really did come from the Bat Creek burial mound, it was incredibly important. But that was a big assumption. "How did you get it?"

"Long time ago."

Cam turned onto the Rourke Bridge in Lowell and crossed the Merrimack River. Normally while crossing the river Cam liked to daydream about Prince Henry Sinclair and other early explorers who used the Merrimack to travel through New England before Columbus. But today Pugh Wei's story, along with the pain in his finger, held his full attention. "My guess is Lowell General's going to be pretty busy on a Saturday night. And I'm not exactly dying. So we have time for a long story."

"Okay, I tell."

The story began in the minivan and continued for another half hour as they sat in the hospital waiting room, a bag of ice and a super-sized dose of Advil helping to numb Cam's pinky; an orderly gave Cam a pair of sweatpants so he could change out of his urine-soaked jeans. They must have made quite a spectacle, an elderly disheveled Chinese man in a blue bathrobe earnestly narrating a decades-old saga to another man in bright red sweatpants holding his hand above his shoulder like a cross-dressing Statue of Liberty. At least Pugh had left the shotgun locked in the minivan.

Occasionally Cam verified parts of Pugh's saga on his smart phone, or Pugh would pause to look up a word for proper translation to English, but for the most part Pugh told his tale quickly.

It began in the late 1940s when Pugh came to New York from China to attend college and learn English. When the Communists took over China in 1949, Pugh and hundreds of other "bourgeois" Chinese students were stranded here as political refugees with only rudimentary English, no support and a bleak future. A few years later the CIA rounded up one hundred of the refugees—working with a Cornell University professor by the name of Wolff, the Agency hoped to brainwash the students and return them to China as American spies. "They pay twenty-five dollars every day," Pugh said. "We go hospital in New York City and they give drugs and do experiments."

Cam sat forward. "Are you talking about Project MK-Ultra?"

Pugh shrugged. "I no know this name."

Cam's heart raced, which caused his finger to throb. Whatever they called it, it was the same program Randall Sid first told him about last week. Which was an amazing coincidence, unless you didn't happen to believe in coincidences. Cam eyed Pugh. "Did Randall Sid tell you to give me the bracelet?"

Pugh stared back at him blankly. "I not know this man." Cam wasn't sure whether to believe him or not. Pugh seemed to be telling the truth, but who knew if Randall Sid was even his real name?

A few clicks on Cam's phone quickly confirmed Pugh's story, at least the part about the New York City tests: As part of Project MK-Ultra the CIA did indeed brainwash and drug Chinese refugees at Cornell Hospital in Manhattan in the 1950s; the program was run by a Cornell neurologist named Harold Wolff, a close friend of then-CIA director Allen Dulles.

"Many Chinese people sick from drugs," Pugh continued. "And sometimes they torture us—no let sleep or put in cold room or give electric shock. We want stop going hospital." Pugh explained how, after a few months of these experiments, a bunch of the Chinese refugees met in secret and decided to send Pugh to Dr. Wolff's office to plead their case.

The story fascinated Cam. It sounded like something out of Nazi Germany. But what did it have to do with the bracelet?

Pugh continued. "I go Dr. Wolff office." Pugh stared into the distance as he related the events, as if watching the scene in his mind's eye. Cam did some quick math in his head—based on the 1950s time frame, Pugh was probably in his mid-eighties now. But many elderly folks maintained perfect long-term memories. "I wait long time. One, two, three hours. Finally I talk Dr. Wolff. I ask he stop experiment. He say we no can stop. Say we go jail if we no go hospital."

"In some ways jail may have been better," Cam observed.

Pugh nodded. "Other man in office with Dr. Wolff while I wait. Door open and I listen. He name *Len-urd Car-mike-el*." Cam punched at his smart phone. Pugh's memory was correct: A behavioral psychologist named Leonard Carmichael was the President of Tufts University until 1953, at which point he became head of the Smithsonian Institution. As a fellow behavioral psychologist, it was entirely possible he knew Dr. Wolff and worked with him.

Pugh continued. "Mr. Carmichael showing Dr. Wolff bracelet. Say is from Tennessee. Say is very important history. Show Dr. Wolff rock with writing."

"The Bat Creek Stone?" Cam pulled up an image of the artifact on his phone and showed it to Pugh. "Is this the rock?"

Bat Creek Stone, Tennessee

Pugh nodded twice. "Hie, that rock. Dr. Wolff very excited. He ask keep stone and bracelet for study." Pugh dropped his eyes. "I angry Dr. Wolff. I take bracelet when he no looking."

"You stole it?"

Pugh nodded. "He talk on phone and not look me. I take bracelet."

"So why are you giving it to me now?"

"My son want sell. He think worth million dollars." Cam doubted that. But a collector might pay six figures if the bracelet could indeed authenticate the Bat Creek Stone. Pugh continued. "But I American now. Government do bad things, but I American. And bracelet important. I see you on television." Cam had appeared on some documentaries, including one discussing the Bat Creek Stone.

Pugh held Cam's eyes. "I old man. You take bracelet."

Two days had passed since Cam's adventures with Pugh and family. They had set and splintered his pinky in the emergency room. On the way home from the hospital Cam had swung by to retrieve the bracelet from the trash can and then filed a police report, red pants and all; Chung and sons were charged with a couple of felonies that, Cam hoped, would make them think twice before going after the bracelet again. He and Amanda had discussed what to do with the bracelet but had not reached a decision other than temporarily to put it in a safe deposit box. And they found a new Chinese take-out place.

After walking Astarte to the bus stop Cam went for a three-mile run; the ten-degree temperature actually helped—his pinky turned numb so it didn't throb. As he ran he thought about an email a buddy from his hockey team sent him with a link to an article about Ronnie Lott, a football player. Lott broke his pinky and, when it wouldn't heal correctly, had it amputated at the last knuckle so he could return to the field. The email concluded: "Game Thursday. Cut off the finger, stop whining and come play!" Cam could imagine how the conversation with Amanda would go....

He sprinted the last hundred yards into a northwesterly wind and was only mildly surprised to see Randall Sid in a camel hair overcoat and fur hat leaning against a telephone pole in front of his home. Randall smiled as Cam stopped in front of him, the wrinkles around his mouth contrasting with the smooth brown skin of his cheeks and neck. "In my younger days I might have kept up with you. Even with my short legs." Clouds of gray vapor escaped Randall's mouth as he spoke. He smiled. "Especially into the breeze—I do not offer much wind resistance."

Cam walked in a small circle, fighting to fill his lungs. He said, "I used to be faster before I messed up my knee, but I was never a thoroughbred." He smiled and sucked in air. "Now I'm more of a plow horse." He breathed again. "Soon I'll probably be glue."

Randall pushed himself off the telephone pole, the movement causing another argyle sweater—this one purple and beige—to peek out from above the top button of the overcoat. "Speaking of horses, did you know I have a twin brother?"

"How would I know that? I don't even know if Randall Sid is your real name." And what did having a twin have to do with horses?

He smiled again. "Actually, it is not. Randall is my brother's name. Sid is indeed my surname, but I think that is the result of an impatient immigration official who could not understand my father's accent—I suspect the agent was a fan of the great Spanish warrior, El Cid." His hazel eyes danced beneath his dark eyebrows. With the hat covering his wrinkled forehead, he looked twenty years younger. "In any event, my name is Morgan, Morgan Sid. My brother and I switched identities. He is a jockey."

Cam angled his head. So there was the connection to horses. "Really, a jockey?"

Randall's—or, rather, Morgan's—eyes twinkled. "In actuality, no. Our father was a jockey, but my brother owned an automobile driving school." He lifted his hat. "That accounts for all the gray hair. How he survived, I shall never know."

Cam was having trouble following the conversation's thread. But there was something … captivating about the little man. "I guess I'm supposed to ask why?"

"Why what?"

"Why did you switch identities with your brother?"

"Because even though I am retired, the Agency insists on watching me. Watching us all. The obvious solution presented itself: My brother took a leisurely cruise around the world while I took residence in his condominium in the Back Bay."

"But the CIA must know you have a twin."

He scoffed. "Please. We are eighty years old—do you think they put their best man on the case? Besides, they care more about what we do outside the country than in. I'm sure my brother is being closely watched as he purchases trinkets in some of the world's finest tourist traps."

Cam nodded. "Fair enough."

"The worst part is that I had to give up my apartment in Chinatown—do you know how difficult it is to find quality Chinese food in the Back Bay?"

Cam shook his head. "I have some stories of my own…"

"Yes. Yes, indeed. But back to Randall. The ingrate had the nerve to upgrade to first class—I think his cabin is more spacious than the condominium he left me. Which reminds me, do you know how to operate a garbage disposal?"

"Look for an on/off switch under the sink."

"Aha. That just might be the trick."

Cam smiled, his breathing returning to normal. "The CIA doesn't bother you because they think you're Randall, not Morgan. But they might figure it out if you start putting banana peels in your garbage, because Randall never did."

"Precisely." The small man's normally dark facial skin had grayed in the cold. "Of course, I am more handsome than my brother, though they do not seem to notice." He said the words lightly, smiling. "But to be safe, going forward please call me Randall. Indeed, I myself have begun to think of Randall as my name. It is the only way for the ruse to succeed. Though I refuse to adopt his wardrobe—the man wears gray as if it were a pastel. And I refuse to take up smoking." He shuddered. "Filthy habit."

"What about family?"

He shrugged. "My brother's wife is deceased and his son resides in Texas. I remain an eligible bachelor." He raised an eyebrow. "Does your Amanda have a sister, perhaps? Or even a widowed mother?"

"Um, no." Cam smiled and bent over, stretching his hamstrings. "But you still haven't said *why* you switched identities with your brother."

"So I could follow you. Is it not obvious?"

Not at all. "Why me?"

"As I said, because they are trying to brainwash you. It seems in recent months the Agency is redoubling its efforts directed at researchers like yourself."

Cam exhaled. "Even if what you say is true, why should you care?"

He stepped back, feigning disbelief. "Why should I care? *I think, therefore I am*, Mr. Thorne. Now do you understand?"

"Actually, no." The sweat was beginning to dry on his body, making Cam's back itch. And now they were debating philosophy. "I wasn't questioning your existence. I simply asked why you are following me."

The little man sighed. "Because the human condition demands it. I have spent my life working on Project MK-Ultra, but I was never privy to the large picture, never understood the project's entire scope. That is how the Agency operates—everyone only sees a sliver of the mission. I often wondered *why* we were doing what we were doing. And was it working? Then some ... actuarial with an abacus for a brain decided it was time for me to retire." He snapped his fingers. "Just like that. A lifetime of work, only to awake the next morning with very little to keep me occupied."

Cam shook his head. "Again, you still haven't explained why you chose to follow me instead of taking up stamp collecting or something."

34

He raised his bushy eyebrows. "Because the scent of the chase has filled my nostrils." He did a little skip, one foot to the other. "How does one stop at the last chapter of a fine novel? How does one leave the last piece of lobster uneaten? How does one stop wondering?"

"You tell me. You're the expert on brainwashing."

"Ah, touché. Perhaps we can solve that mystery together, though I am sure *stamp collecting* is not the solution. But to respond to your question: I follow you because I require answers. The most beautiful thing we can experience is the mysterious. I spent my entire life working on the MK-Ultra project; I *must* know how it all ends." He blinked. "I simply must."

"Well, why we're on the subject, how do you even begin to justify experimenting on U.S. citizens like you did?"

Randall gave him a quizzical look. "It was not practical to experiment on, say, French citizens. The Agency is here, our scientists are here, our facilities are here." He shrugged. "And so our experiments are here."

Cam sighed. "I don't mean how in a logistical sense, I mean how in a moral sense."

Randall stared off into space as if pondering the question for the first time. "I suppose because we see our mission as one of necessity. At the time, during the Cold War, our country's very survival was at stake. Project MK-Ultra was developed to counteract the Soviets. But all weapons—especially weapons of the mind, like these—must be tested before they are deployed. And the only way to perform tests on the human mind is to perform tests on ... human minds. There are no firing ranges or pilot simulations for mind control." He shrugged again. "We could not very well *not* conduct experiments, could we? We needed to know if these drugs worked, if we really could manipulate human behavior."

"But people died."

"A few, perhaps. Out of thousands. But potentially millions of lives could have been saved."

The Oath of Nimrod

Cam kicked at a frozen piece of slush. He did not want to become one of the CIA's guinea pigs. Especially a dead one. "So you know what happened Saturday night?"

"I do. I observed the entire sordid encounter. From a distance, of course."

"Really?" Cam studied him. "Not to be insensitive, but I'm guessing your size allows you to be pretty unobtrusive."

"I am exactly five feet tall, Mr. Thorne, including my lifts. Four foot ten without them. And I weigh one hundred twelve pounds. Even at my age, I am an accomplished contortionist. I can stay out of sight behind a shrub or a trash can or even a grassy knoll." He grinned. "I once concealed myself for six hours inside a hiker's backpack." He paused. "An empty one, of course."

Cam looked up and down the street. "If they're brainwashing me, aren't they also watching me? And won't they see you here now?"

Randall glanced at his watch. "Not before nine o'clock. The Agency has grown soft since the end of the Cold War. Nary an agent will begin his day without a good night's sleep and a hot cup of coffee. In my day, the early morning hours made for ideal surveillance—nobody expects to be spied on before brushing his teeth. Oh, and by the way, you will want to keep that bracelet. You may find you will need it."

"Need it for what?"

Randall shrugged. "Barter, perhaps."

Another non-answer. And Cam still didn't know why the CIA was trying to brainwash him. He tried a different tact. "Okay, so *how* are they brainwashing me?"

"Perhaps a better word than *brainwashing* would be *behavior control*. Brainwashing has such a Frankenstein-like connotation. You saw the movie, *The Manchurian Candidate*?"

Cam nodded. "Some war hero was brainwashed and turned into an enemy assassin every time he saw the Queen of Diamonds playing card."

"It was actually an enjoyable little film. And I suppose being able to completely reprogram someone would be quite useful; that was the initial goal of the MK-Ultra program. But

36

as I told you last week, we have come to learn that the human mind is more complex than that. The Agency now influences behavior rather than puppeteers it."

"Okay, but my question still remains. How? How are they doing it?"

"In ways you never would think of. For example, have there been any significant changes in your life recently?"

"Let's see: I was almost disbarred three years ago, then two years ago I met and fell in love with Amanda and we stumbled into this whole field of pre-Columbian research and almost got killed a couple of times. And then last year we got engaged and Astarte moved in with us. Oh, and I bought a new hockey stick."

"You should consider all of those events. Could any of them have been orchestrated by the Agency?"

"Come on, Randall. The government can't make me fall in love."

"No, it cannot make *you* fall in love, Mr. Thorne." Implicit in Randall's response was that Amanda's feelings might be in question. Cam's gut twisted—everyone always said she was too good for him. Randall continued. "And it can … remove certain hurdles when an unmarried couple attempts to adopt an unrelated young girl from out-of-state."

"Are you saying Astarte is some kind of mole?" This was ludicrous.

Randall sniffed and shook his head. "I said nothing of the kind. I simply do not know how or what the Agency is doing." He raised his chin. "If I did, I would not need your assistance, would I?"

Cam fought back his frustration. "And my helping you will help me figure out how they're brainwashing me."

"And perhaps why."

"So what's next?"

Randall turned to walk away. "Tomorrow morning. Meet me at nine o'clock at the Dunkin' Donuts on Route 40. Wear a blue baseball cap, park facing the woods in the rear of the lot, leave the car unlocked, and go in and order coffee and muffins. Return ten minutes later."

Randall smiled. "Oh, and I prefer blueberry." He pronounced it blue-*burry*.

Vito Augustine sat at his computer, as he did at least one hundred hours every week. The view wasn't great through the 3M plastic covering his bedroom window—the smokestack of an old textile mill peeking out between a couple of oak trees, and on a clear day the distant peaks of the White Mountains. But it was no worse than most views in central New Hampshire, and at least he was upwind most days from the apartment complex and the stomach-turning stink that wafted from its failing septic system.

Sitting at the desk in his boyhood bedroom was hardly the job he anticipated coming out of Cornell with a master's degree in U.S. history, but he had never done well in interviews and the job paid a grand a week. And he was beginning to make a name for himself as an internet blogger. Which meant people had stopped laughing at him so much.

But not everyone—his stepfather still called him Phineas J. Whoopee. Vito had to Google it: Whoopee was a pompous, know-it-all cartoon character from the 1960s. That was actually one of Rusty's kinder jabs. Usually he called Vito a bum or a slob or a loser—as if being the manager at a car wash was such an accomplishment.

"Vito, come down here and help me shovel."

Vito walked to the door and yelled down the stairs. "I'm working."

"I don't give a shit. Get your lazy ass down here."

Vito yanked on a pair of thick socks and shuffled down the stairs.

Rusty crinkled his nose. "Maybe if you took a shower once in a while you'd find a girlfriend," he said. "What does Phineas J. Whoopee say about personal hygiene?"

Vito pushed past him to the porch where he found his boots and a shovel. It was great to have a real job, but what he really wanted was to get a place of his own. Hopefully someplace warm. But he'd have to pay down his student loans before that happened.

Rusty joined him on the porch. "Seriously, even the cold air doesn't help. You smell like old bologna."

Vito had shut him up a few months ago when he wrote a check for five hundred dollars and wrote 'September rent' on it. The jabbing resumed after a few days, but with Vito's mom laid off from the diner during the winter months, Vito's monthly contribution went a long way to keeping food on the table and heating oil in the tank.

An hour later he was back at his computer. In many ways, this was the ideal job for him: He had been given a list of television shows, documentaries and books, mostly focusing on the topic of exploration of America before Columbus, and told to blog about them. He had written his master's thesis on the danger to academia posed by the growing popularity of alternative history: A generation ago only university-trained historians, usually with a graduate degree, were considered experts. Today any enthusiast with a laptop, an internet connection and an overactive imagination could declare himself a historian and breathlessly claim to have discovered our "true" and "hidden" and "secret" history. If you listened to these kooks, everyone from the Knights Templar to the Phoenicians to the Lost Tribes of Israel to reptilian aliens had settled in America—it's a wonder the Native Americans hadn't been squeezed out. Vito blew on his hands and shook his head. Nobody asked a geologist to take out their appendix; so why did people listen to amateurs when it came to their history?

Unlike the amateurs, Vito understood the rigor and discipline needed to be a true student of history. Fluent in Latin, he prided himself on going back to original sources, of ferreting out obscure foreign-language references, of *never* using Wikipedia as a source.

Fortunately a segment of the population had not been swept up in the tide of alternative history. These were the people he was writing for. It was good, honest work—intellectually satisfying and, in a small way, helping make the world a better place. Or if not better, at least more enlightened.

His view out the window was to the north, but his thoughts often were directed five hundred miles south, to Washington, D.C. He worked for a think tank called the Heritage Foundation, a self-described conservative organization dedicated to promoting "traditional American values." From what he could learn, the foundation had been endowed in the 1970s by members of the Mellon banking family, the Coors brewing family and other wealthy conservatives. Vito wasn't technically a Heritage Foundation employee—rather, they contracted with him on a monthly basis to write his blog. A middle-aged woman named Mrs. Conrad had flown up to Cornell to interview him, and a payroll services company on K Street sent him his monthly paycheck and reimbursed him for the few out-of-pocket expenses he had, but otherwise he had almost no contact with his employer. Other than an occasional email from Mrs. Conrad directing him to focus his blog on a particular broadcast or publication, he was completely on his own.

On his own in a physical sense, but not a virtual one. After a slow start, he had gained readership to the point that as many as a thousand people a day visited his blog. Most of them came to read his critical reviews on the various alternative history shows and documentaries on television. The shows were all garbage, but one of the unfortunate consequences of the dumbing down of America was that people believed everything they saw or read—half the country still thought fluoride in the water supply was part of some Communist plot because of the *Dr. Strangelove* movie.

The readers of his blog, at least, had not been completely dumbed-down. They may not be as educated as Vito, but at least they knew enough to turn to his blog for answers. In the end, that was the essence of his job: preventing reasonably intelligent Americans from becoming as misinformed and deluded as most of their neighbors.

He began today's entry, discussing a documentary that had aired the night before about the so-called "beehive" stone chambers of New England and New York. He introduced the subject matter and pasted an image for those who had not seen the show, this chamber from a site called "Calendar 2" in Vermont.

Calendar 2 Chamber, Vermont

He wrote: "Many of these chambers were Colonial root cellars. Others were Native American sweat lodges—stone huts used for ritualistic purification ceremonies. Those who think they were built by Europeans exploring America before Columbus are either idiots or racists. Sorry to be blunt, but there is no third choice."

Vito smiled. He had quickly learned that blog posts required a different tone than academic papers—his audience wanted name-calling, passion, maybe some blood. As long as he didn't libel anyone, he could pretty much say anything he wanted.

The documentary had made a big deal about the fact that many of the chambers had openings too narrow to fit a wheelbarrow, which the host argued negated the possibility of a Colonial root cellar. Vito countered. "It may be that a modern wheelbarrow, purchased at the local hardware store, would not fit through the doorway of a particular chamber. But here's a thought for the geniuses who insist the chambers are pre-Columbian: *In the olden days farmers made their own wheelbarrows.* That's right, they made their own. And they made it any size they wanted."

Vito went on for a while, rebutting the evidence that the chambers often faced the rising eastern sun and were therefore some kind of pagan ceremonial structures. "And, yes, most chambers open to the east. But that does not mean they were built as structures from which to observe the summer and winter solstice sunrises. Here's another thought: They were built this way so the morning sun would shine in and keep the interior warm. It's simple, folks. Occam's Razor: *The simplest theory is usually the correct one.*"

He concluded. "As I watch these shows, and listen to the so-called experts, it strikes me that perhaps I should amend my original statement. The people promoting these theories may be neither idiots nor racists. They may instead be charlatans, the twenty-first century equivalent of carnival hucksters. If someone's willing to pay them, they're willing to parade out all sorts of historical frauds and hoaxes. As circus owner David Hannum famously said, 'There's a sucker born every minute.' And, no, dear reader, it was not P.T Barnum who spoke these wise words."

Vito reread the last sentence. He was tempted to add, "And that's why you need someone smart like me to tell you what *really* happened." But it seemed unnecessarily redundant. *And also repetitive, duplicative and superfluous.* Vito grinned. He loved his job.

"I've been thinking about it. I think we should get the bracelet tested," Amanda said as Cam settled onto the chairlift next to her. Cam had been so unnerved about being brainwashed that Amanda suggested they drive up to New Hampshire to ski for the day while Astarte was in school. Amanda worked part-time as a museum curator but had Mondays off; Cam could make some calls from the car and catch up on his cases when they returned late afternoon. She had loaded the car while Cam showered after his jog.

Cam smiled at her as he kicked the snow off his skis and closed the safety bar. She knew there was no way he was going to give the artifact to Chung. "What the hell. I've still got nine good fingers."

So much in their lives had changed, but that unassuming, crooked smile was the same one that had first charmed her. He really had no idea how ruggedly good-looking he was, which made him all the more attractive. He wasn't handsome in the traditional sense, but his face was strong and solid—sort of like the actor Liam Neeson. She leaned over and kissed him. "Just don't let them hurt these lips."

He smiled again. "Next time I get tied up and tortured, I'll be sure to tell them that." Cam looked out over the White Mountains. "We can get the bracelet tested," he said, "but we both know it won't matter to the so-called experts. They'll dismiss it even if the dates come back to the second century. You know, provenance and all."

"Piss on provenance. Unless your friend Pugh is lying, that bracelet was found with the Bat Creek Stone. So it's either a 19th century fake or it's the artifact that rewrites history. One or the other."

"Pugh has no reason to lie. But like I said, the archeologists will still say there's no way to prove it's the same bracelet that got pulled from the ground. They'll say Pugh flew to Cairo or something and bought it in the antiquities market."

"So who cares what the archeologists say? The bloody lot of them are wrong more often than they're right anyway. If a nuclear bomb wiped us all out tomorrow, and a thousand years later a team of archeologists dug up our churches, what would they conclude?"

Cam shrugged. "We hadn't invented cushioned seats?"

She smiled. It was good to have him joking again. "Assuming all the prayer books and other writings were gone," she continued, "they'd say that since the churches all faced the rising sun in the east, we must have been sun worshippers."

"Of course," Cam said. "That's why we go to church on Sun-day."

"And our most important holiday is just after the winter solstice, celebrating the rebirth of the sun." Not the birth of the son, as in the child. But the rebirth of the sun, as in the orb in the sky. She continued. "And because of all the crucifixes with Jesus nailed to them they'd likely conclude we sacrificed humans on the cross, probably as an offering to our sun god."

Cam raised an eyebrow. "The red wine would be to get people drunk before sacrificing them."

She continued. "And our religion of sun-worship would be confirmed when they found a picture of the Pope parading around with his monstrance."

"Monstrance?"

"The thing they use to display the Eucharist. It's sun-shaped." She removed her mitten and pulled out her phone. "Here it is."

Pope with Monstrance

Cam leaned in. "That's either a sun or the Pope was playing with his Spirograph."

She cuffed him playfully with the mitten. "It's a sun. So looking just at the evidence inside the churches, our future archeologists actually wouldn't be far off—much of Christian ritual is in fact based on old pagan sun worship. You couldn't really blame them for being wrong."

"But wrong they'd be."

She nodded. "And I *can* blame them for being arrogant. They take snapshots in time and act like they have the whole bloody picture."

They had had this conversation before. Life was more complicated than a few snapshots—what if some future archeologist happened to uncover the remains of a Halloween party? Who knows what kind of crazy conclusions they would draw. Or a skateboard: The obvious deduction would be it was an early iteration of the automobile.

Amanda pulled her mitten back on and changed the subject. "So what does this fellow Randall have planned for tomorrow?"

Cam shrugged. "Don't know. He sort of talks in riddles. I'm not sure if it's because of his age or his training."

Amanda removed her goggles and turned her face to the sun. People often told her she had beautiful skin, but it came with a cost—she burned like a marshmallow over a flame. But a few minutes shouldn't do too much harm, and the warmth felt glorious. Perhaps, deep down, all humans truly were sun worshipers....

Eyes closed, she said: "This Project MK-Ultra your government dreamed up. I mean, it's so bloody ... *frightening*. Mind control experiments on your own citizens? What were they thinking?"

"I think they would argue their motives were pure, trying to win the Cold War and all that. And Randall made a good point—the only way to experiment with mind control is to experiment with mind control. As he said, there are no firing ranges where you can test mind control weapons. But I agree with you. It's like trying to justify torture—the ends don't justify the means."

"I still can't imagine why they are targeting you of all people." She smiled. "Other than your hockey equipment, you're hardly a threat to national security."

"Hopefully Randall can help us figure that out."

The chairlift approached the top of the mountain. "You want to go left or right?" Amanda asked.

"Doesn't matter," he smiled. "Either way I'm going to be eating ski bunny dust." She had only skied for a few years, but her gymnastics training made balance sports like skiing easy for her.

Grinning, she chose the expert trail on their left and skated toward it. "Have it your way, then. See you at the bottom." She looked over her shoulder. "Speaking of bunnies, meet me at the gondola."

"Thanks for that," Cam said as he carried their skis back to the car.

Amanda bumped up against him. "Do you mean the skiing or the gondola ride?"

He grinned. "Both. But especially the gondola." One of the nice things about midweek skiing was having a gondola car to themselves. Somehow they had been able to wriggle out of their snow pants and long underwear and still manage to be dressed again when the doors opened at the top of the mountain twelve minutes later. Not exactly their most languid session, but Amanda had a wild side that kept things fresh and, well, wild.

She grinned back at him. "Why do you think I chose Loon? Waterville doesn't have a gondola."

"Aha."

She continued. "What do you think they did back in the days of the rope tow?"

He laughed. "That's going to be a tough image to get out of my head."

They had packed sandwiches for the ride home and left in time to meet Astarte at the bus stop. "I was thinking," Amanda said, turning serious, "we should call Georgia. See what she knows about this MK-Ultra stuff."

Cam nodded. "Good idea." Georgia Johnston was a CIA agent they had met at the same time they first met Astarte and her uncle. Later they had worked with her to unravel the mystery of a replica Art of the Covenant found in the Arizona desert. Along the way they had become friends.

"I think she's back to her day job as a political consultant." When not actually on mission, Georgia's cover was working as a political strategist. And it wasn't just a cover—she was one of the best political strategists in the country.

Cam knocked the snow off the skis and laid them diagonally across the bed of their SUV. By the time he started the engine Amanda had already dialed Georgia's number. On the fourth ring it went to voice mail. "You've reached Georgia

Johnson, director of political outreach for Senator Webster Lovecroft...."

Amanda hung up. "We'll try again later. I didn't know she was working for Lovecroft."

"Me either. Has he officially announced his candidacy?"

"No, but everyone knows he's going to run," she said. "There's still a year before the first primary."

"Hopefully she can do better for him than she did for Romney."

"That wasn't really her fault. She gave good advice, told him he needed to show his personal side and stop being so bloody stiff. And she did a great job making the whole Mormon thing irrelevant. If the candidate doesn't follow her direction, what can she do?" American politics fascinated Amanda—even today the idea that any child in the country could rise to the Presidency was foreign to the European way of thinking.

"Good point. This guy Lovecroft is a lot like Romney. Good-looking, conservative, unblemished record."

"Except he's a fundamentalist Christian, not a Mormon."

"Which should help him."

"And he's tall like Romney. What is it with you Americans and your tall Presidents? Since Kennedy I think they've all been at least six feet."

"Carter was just under, but you're right. Some people think that's a big reason why Dukakis lost back in '88."

She smiled. "Well, if he had been taller he probably wouldn't have fit into the tank for that silly photo-op. So you've got a point on that one. Anyway, Lovecroft is six-ten, I think."

Cam nodded. "Almost one of your giants."

"If so, he's a *gentle* giant. I read he's one of the kindest blokes you'll ever meet. He spends his free time volunteering at a homeless shelter."

"So tell me more about him," Cam said as they wound their way south on the interstate. If Georgia liked him, he was worth considering.

"Give me a second." Amanda punched at her phone and read for a few minutes. "Fascinating candidate. Chair of the Senate Intelligence Committee. Fundamentalist Christian, like I said. Believes in the literal word of the Bible. But he seems to walk the walk, as you Americans say. Works with the poor, gives a ton of money to charity, a real 'What Would Jesus Do?' type of bloke."

She paused again, reading and summarizing. "This one reporter spent a day with him. Says he's religious, but not preachy. If you want to be Catholic or Jewish or Muslim or an atheist, that's fine with him. 'Lots of roads lead to Heaven,' he likes to say. Tries to model himself after Abraham Lincoln, and not just because he's tall."

"Can he win?"

She bit her lower lip. "Perhaps. He's not a traditional candidate. And he has some radical ideas. Says here he wants to gut the food stamps program so it only covers the basic food needs."

"So no using your food stamps for manicures and lottery tickets…."

"But then he wants to take that money and make all state universities free. He says educating the poor so they can find a job is smarter, and cheaper, than feeding them."

"Makes sense. Give a man a fish and he eats for a day; teach a man to fish and he eats for a lifetime."

"And he wants to increase the minimum wage to fifteen dollars per hour."

"Fifteen? No way will business groups support that."

Amanda again read in silence for a few seconds. "Lovecroft's idea is that the government will pay the difference. So you earn, say, nine dollars per hour at your job at Wal-Mart and then the government gives you another six through tax credits or subsidies or whatever." She sipped from a can of Diet Coke. "The idea is to give the poor an incentive to work. As it stands now, it almost makes more sense to go on welfare than accept a job at minimum wage."

Cam drummed on the steering wheel. "You know, these are the types of proposals that if the Democrats made them they'd be shot down in a second. But coming from the far right, they might have a chance. Republicans will trust him not to give away the store."

"I'm guessing that's why Georgia is working for him. People are tired of the gridlock in Washington."

"And they're even more tired of the hypocrisy."

"Well, apparently Lovecroft's favorite saying is that going to church doesn't make you a Christian any more than standing in a garage makes you a car. He seems genuine—again, like Abraham Lincoln."

"Georgia must think he has a good shot or she wouldn't work with him." Cam motioned to the phone. "Let's try her again."

This time Georgia picked up on the second ring. "I hope you're calling to ask me to come up and babysit Astarte," she sang. In her early sixties, she had no children of her own.

"No, just calling to chat."

Georgia laughed. "I've been working in Washington forty years, Amanda. *Nobody* calls just to chat."

"Guilty as charged," Cam responded. "We need to pick your brain."

"I hope it's something racy. I'm stuck out here in Kansas with Lovecroft and his folks. Nice people. *Too* damn nice. They go to church and then go home and actually do what the pastor tells them. It's freaking me out." She laughed. "I need someone to swear at me or something. Maybe even pound some tequila. Half the state is dry."

"We'll take a rain check on the tequila," Amanda said, "but I'm happy to call you a stupid bitch."

For some reason Amanda was able to get away with saying things most people could not. Maybe it was the accent. Or maybe it was because people sensed she really didn't have a nasty bone in her body. When Georgia stopped laughing, Cam said, "We were hoping you could tell us what you know about Project MK-Ultra?"

Georgia repeated much of what they already knew. "They say the operation has been shut down, but I don't buy it. Nothing at the Agency ever gets shut down. It might get renamed or reorganized, but they don't call Langley the home of spooks for nothing—nothing there ever dies."

Cam recounted his encounter with Pugh and his family. "So do you think it's possible the bracelet he gave me really is from the Bat Creek Stone mound?"

"That predates this stupid bitch's time at the Agency, but I did look into the Bat Creek Stone as part of my prep for the Jefferson January mission." January, Astarte's uncle, collected ancient artifacts he believed proved explorers came to America long before Columbus, just as the Book of Mormon said. "I remember reading something in the file about a bracelet going missing. I can check it for you if you want."

"Yes, thanks," Cam replied. "Hey, you don't by chance know an agent by the name of Randall ... no, wait, I mean Morgan Sid. He's around eighty, just retired." Cam described their meeting, knowing he could trust Georgia not to blow the old man's cover.

"No, sorry. Over twenty thousand people work for the CIA, and that doesn't include shadow agents like me. But I'll look into that bracelet for you. And I'll ask around about MK-Ultra, see if it's still active." She paused. "But you have to do me a favor in return."

"What?" Amanda asked.

"Come visit. These people are driving me crazy. The other day a woman paid for my coffee because I was fumbling in my purse. And when you come, bring something to drink." She laughed. "Something strong."

Randall Sid—the name by which he insisted on thinking of himself in order to ensure his identity-switch ruse succeeded—spent the afternoon pacing his brother's condominium, memorizing lines for tonight's Masonic ceremony. Both he and his twin were longtime Freemasons, members of a Lodge in the Boston suburb of Arlington. Randall enjoyed the camaraderie and sense of history that came with being a lodge Brother; his brother, on the other hand, had devoted his entire adult life to the Craft. He was a 33rd Degree Mason and past Grand Master who had memorized every ritual and recitation and rarely missed a Lodge event. Which meant Randall needed to memorize every ritual and recitation and rarely miss a Lodge event.

What an absolute waste of both time and brain cells. And at age eighty, both were in short supply.

Duping his Lodge Brothers had been Randall's most difficult challenge so far; many of them had been his brother's friends for decades. His first task had been to refine his accent. He had struggled for years to rid himself of his East Boston twang, even going so far as to take diction lessons after college when he had first joined the Agency because he was convinced his accent made him sound like a buffoon. But his brother still spoke like a, well, like a driver's education teacher. Randall could not bring himself to refer to their Arlington lodge as 'All-ington,' but nor could he employ words like 'indubitably' and hope to pass for his twin. A couple of them eyed him quizzically at the first Lodge meeting after the switch, and one of them even questioned him, but he terminated the conversation with a smile and, "You think I wouldn't trade places with my brother and be on that cruise right now?" After a few weeks the odd glances had ceased.

To the outside world, Freemasonry was cloaked in mystery and intrigue. It was equally mysterious to Randall, but for different reasons. Freemasons essentially founded the United States, and over the country's history many of its top politicians, industrialists, inventors and philanthropists had also been Masons—in short, Masons had done more to build this country than any other group. And yet American society had diverged far from the core beliefs and values of Masonry. Freemasonry was a true meritocracy—at tonight's initiation ceremony the new candidates would enter the fraternity as equals, stripped of their clothes and jewelry and clad only in a rough robe. A janitor and a judge would stand side-by-side, each rising through the ranks based solely on their merits. In fact, the current Master of Randall's Lodge was a plumber, while his deputy, called the Senior Warden, was a world-renowned surgeon. Yet outside the Lodge the country had moved away from meritocracy, a development that could if unchecked undermine the foundations of the United States. Men were born with head starts based on wealth and status, and achieved success based on family connections and patronage. Sure there were exceptions to this, but not nearly enough. To Randall, the true mystery was why powerful Masons had not done more to arrest this slide away from meritocracy. Randall, for example, had never risen above a certain level at the CIA because he had not attended an Ivy League college. Didn't the country's leaders see that moving away from meritocracy undermined the very foundation of American society?

Back to tonight. Randall would need to take over his brother's duties of administering the oath of initiation to the new members. The Masonic Brothers—clad in tuxedos and aprons and white gloves, with many carrying swords—would serve as witnesses as the initiates stammered through their initiation oaths. Many initiates would pause, their eyes widening, as they vowed not to reveal secrets of the Craft, under penalty of death:

I promise and declare that I will not at any time hereafter reveal or make known any part or parts of the Trade secrets of Free Masonry. The penalty for breaking this great oath shall be the loss of my life. That I shall be branded with the mark of the Traitor and slain according to ancient custom by being throttled, that my body shall be buried in the rough sands of the sea where the tide regularly ebbs and flows twice in the twenty-four hours, so that my soul shall have no rest by night or by day.

The Oath of Nimrod

It was quite an oath, and most initiates would perspire and laugh nervously as they allowed themselves to be led around, blindfolded and with a cord tied around their neck, before being lowered into a shaft from which they would be figuratively 'resurrected' by their Lodge Brothers. Thus reborn, the initiates would retire to the basement bar for cognac and cigars—usually too much of both. By then Randall's accent would no longer matter.

There would be one less initiate tonight than originally expected. During last week's Lodge meeting, after the candidates had been vetted and questioned, Randall emptied the mahogany ballot box only to find a black marble mixed in with the dozens of white ones. *A blackball.* As was required, Randall instructed the Brothers to line up a second time—he again handed each Brother a white marble and a black marble and, again, one-by-one they filed past the box to cast their votes regarding the candidate in question. Again the candidate was blackballed. Apparently, Randall learned later, one of the Brothers had witnessed the candidate berate a teenage umpire in a youth baseball game and believed him to be unworthy of Masonic membership and, as was his right, blocked the man's candidacy.

The blackball left four initiates for tonight's ceremony. Randall had been involved in hundreds of Masonic ceremonies, and hundreds of times he had memorized the various recitations without paying much attention to the words— Freemasonry was an ancient craft with rituals and customs dating back to the early days of the Old Testament. But for some reason today he focused on the title of the initiation oath: 'The Oath of Nimrod.' Other Lodges Randall had attended no longer used this historic name for the initiation oath, but Randall's home Lodge continued to cling to the old English traditions.

Nimrod? Why Nimrod?

"Well," he said to himself, "it seems I have another mystery to solve."

It probably would have been easier to conduct research on the internet, but there was something particularly gratifying about prying open the pages of an old book, the smell of leather and dusty paper filling one's nostrils. Fortunately his brother possessed an extensive library of Masonic literature; Randall found a seven-volume history of Freemasonry written in 1898 and pulled the last volume from the shelf. Opening it slowly so as not to crack the leather binding, he searched for 'Nimrod' in the index and was directed to a short chapter at the beginning of volume one.

He sat in his twin's leather recliner angled to face the television set. Skimming through the thick prose of the hundred-year-old tome, Randall slowed down and reread words that, at first glance, seemed to make little sense: The prose identified "Nimrod, King of Babylonia" as "the first Grand Master" of Masonry. How could this be? Randall had always been taught that Solomon was the first Grand Master and that the earliest Masons had been Hiram Abiff and the other builders of King Solomon's Temple, circa 800 BC. So what was this about Nimrod?

He read further. King Nimrod, a great-grandson of Noah, ruled in Mesopotamia, which is present-day Iraq, in approximately 2000 BC. Randall found an image, an ancient copper portrait of the powerful king:

King Nimrod of Babylon

While king, Nimrod constructed the Tower of Babel, which, according to the Bible, God destroyed because he found it hubristic. But the construction itself was an engineering and construction marvel, made possible through the efforts of thousands of craftsmen Nimrod organized and trained. These workmen, known as "operative" masons, were the ancestors of those who later built King Solomon's Temple and who eventually became the "speculative" (non-working) masons of modern Freemasonry.

Randall gathered a few other volumes and spread out at the kitchen table. So what happened to Nimrod? One source in the 1700s listed Nimrod along with Moses, Solomon, Nebuchadnezzar and Augustus Caesar as the greatest of the Grand Masters. Why had this once-revered figure been shoved into the shadows of Freemasonry? It was a long fall, from first Grand Master to complete obscurity; Randall, who considered himself a history buff, knew nothing about Nimrod. So, again, why had modern Freemasonry tried to erase Nimrod from its history?

The more Randall read about Nimrod, the more he understood.

First and foremost, Nimrod was a pagan. Nimrod and his people rejected the God of Abraham and instead worshipped Baal and a pantheon of other gods and idols. As part of this worship they often sacrificed children to Baal. Tellingly, the main root of the word 'Beelzebub,' meaning devil, was the word 'Baal.' In fact, Nimrod himself was also known by the name 'Belus,' a name later shortened to 'Bel' and then 'Baal.' So not only was Nimrod a pagan, he later apparently became identified as the pagan god Baal himself.

The second reason for Nimrod being scrubbed from the Masonic historical record, and this was closely related to the first, was that Nimrod openly challenged God's authority and revolted against him. This revolt explained why God found the Tower of Babel so offensive and destroyed it—the edifice was meant by Nimrod as a direct challenge to God's primacy and divinity. In fact, the name 'Nimrod' derived from the word 'marad,' meaning 'we will revolt' (against God).

Third, Nimrod descended from Noah's son Ham. Abraham, on the other hand, descended from Noah's son Shem—it was Abraham's line that became the 'Semites,' the ancestors of today's Judeo-Christian peoples. In other words it was Abraham's line (which included Solomon) whom God declared to be the 'chosen people' of the Bible, while Ham and his line, as Noah's least favorite son, were considered of inferior stock.

Perhaps, Randall mused, *this aversion to Ham is why Jews do not eat pork.* Or perhaps he was getting giddy and needed a short break. He stepped onto the rear deck of the condominium and breathed in the winter air before making himself a cup of tea and returning to his work.

A likely fourth reason the Masons distanced themselves from Nimrod was that Nimrod was a giant, one of many giants in the Bible portrayed as villainous or evil, Goliath being the most notable. In fact, according to many ancient sources, Noah's flood was intended by God to wipe the evil giants off the planet. Randall smiled and nodded: *The heroes were always the short ones.*

Finally, of course, the name Nimrod had in modern times taken on the meaning of 'dimwit.' Plenty of boys were given the name Solomon in modern times but Randall had yet to meet a man named Nimrod.

The bottom line to all this: It would have been self-defeating for the Freemasons to glorify as their founder a God-hating, child-sacrificing, devil-worshiping, dimwitted giant. Masons had enough trouble fending off accusations of being the anti-Christ as it was. Just yesterday one of the Lodge Brothers had emailed Randall an image of Washington, D.C., in which some people saw an owl—a symbol for Molech, a pagan god closely associated with Baal—imbedded in the street design around the Capitol building. Supposedly this was evidence the Masons, who the conspiracy-theorists believed secretly ran the government, continued to worship the old pagan gods.

Washington, D.C. Owl Image

Randall had examined the image on his computer; to him, it looked more like a cat than an owl. But the fact that so many people believed it might be true meant the Masons had a problem. One that Nimrod only added to.

He gently closed the leather-bound books, coughing a bit as dust filled his lungs. All this explained why a couple hundred years ago the Masons began to rewrite their history to erase Nimrod from it. What it did not explain, and what Randall found even more fascinating, was why and how Nimrod had taken on such an important role in Freemasonry to begin with. What, exactly, had his Masonic forefathers found so appealing about this pagan giant?

Dozens of novels had been written focusing on Freemasonry's dark secrets, but none of them touched on any of this Nimrod ugliness. Sometimes truth was indeed stranger than fiction.

CHAPTER 3

The next morning, as instructed, Cam wore a blue baseball cap and parked facing the woods at the Dunkin' Donuts near his Westford home. The possibility of being brainwashed was a constant irritant, like a pebble in his shoe. Was it possible Randall was playing him and was still part of the CIA? If so, was Randall doing the brainwashing? Cam grabbed a Diet Coke from the fridge before buying Randall his coffee and muffin.

Randall awaited him, scrunched on the passenger seat floor of Cam's SUV. But he was not alone. On the floor next to him rested an underinflated full-size blow-up doll.

"All right, I'll bite. Who's your friend?"

"His name, actually, is Robert." Without further explanation Randall blew into the doll's thigh, inflating him further. Under his wool topcoat Randall again wore an argyle sweater vest—this time blue and gray. Robert wore only a windbreaker and blue baseball cap.

Cam waited, figuring eventually Randall would tire and offer an explanation. He sipped his Diet Coke.

Half a minute later Randall closed the air valve. "That should do." He turned on the floor, lifted himself and, using the side-view window which he had apparently adjusted earlier, slowly surveyed the parking lot. Another half minute passed. "When I give the word, Mr. Thorne, I would like you to slip out of this vehicle and, staying low, make your way into the woods. If anyone happens to question you, pretend you are making water."

"Making water?"

Randall ignored him. "Wait five minutes and then circle around through the woods to the gas station on the far side of this strip mall. Anyone watching your car will see our friend here in the driver's seat. My car is a maroon Ford Taurus. Enter the driver's side. You will be driving."

Cam did as told and, feet wet from the snow, found the Taurus and climbed in. Randall, again, sat curled on the floor of the passenger seat.

"That doll really going to fool anyone?"

"Robert accompanied me for twenty years as I drove the highways around Washington, D.C."

"I thought you lived in Boston."

"Yes, but I spent half my time in Washington. Stupefying highway rules—many roads are restricted to multi-passenger vehicles. Hence, Robert. And he only needs to fool someone, as you say, for a few minutes today. Until we are safely out of the parking lot."

"Okay, where to?"

"Proceed to Route 3," Randall proclaimed. "I will take my seat once we are on the highway,"

"Where we going?"

"Rhode Island." He reached up and took the blueberry muffin from the bag Cam had dropped on the passenger seat. "What do you know about the Vinland Map? The one at Yale."

Cam had read about the map—purportedly a Viking map depicting an area of North America southwest of Greenland that they called Vinland—but never actually examined it. "I think the parchment dates to the 1400s. But the map itself is maybe a hoax, maybe real, depending on which ink test you believe."

"And what does your common sense tell you?"

"Didn't some guy pay a million bucks for it?"

"Indeed. And in 1959 that was a considerable sum."

"Wasn't he an art collector?"

"Correct again. Paul Mellon was heir to the Mellon banking fortune. He purchased the map and donated it to Yale."

"So I guess I'd assume it was real. You don't get that rich by pissing away your millions on forgeries. And if he was an art collector, presumably he had experts look at it for him."

They stopped at a red light. Randall waved his hand at Cam. "Drag the map up ... or whatever the correct term is ... on that phone of yours."

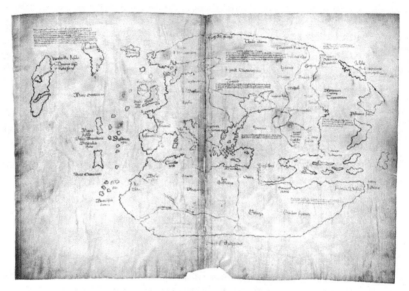

Vinland Map

It had been a while since Cam had studied the map. It really wasn't all that impressive—a crudely drawn map of Europe, taped together in the middle, with Greenland and also the three regions of Vinland (Helluland, Markland, Vinland) displayed in the upper left. The map did nothing to settle the debate whether Vinland was located in Newfoundland or further south—the depiction of Vinland at a rough location southwest of Greenland hardly constituted a 'newfound' clue, as it were.

Cam accelerated through the intersection. "Putting everything else aside, why would a forgery be so crude and rough? Wouldn't it be more valuable if it actually added to the debate in some way? I mean, it doesn't tell us anything we don't already know."

"Now you are allowing common sense to factor in," Randall said. Curled on the floor under the glove compartment in his top hat, he peered up at Cam like a garden gnome. "From what I have observed with academic types, common sense is not one of the tools they regularly employ."

Cam nodded. "Okay, but since neither of us are academics—"

"Neither *is*," Randall interjected. "The word *neither* is a singular noun."

Cam chuckled. Something about a little old man on the floor correcting his grammar struck Cam as amusing. "Like I said, since *I'm* not an academic, I can use common sense. And if I were going to go to the trouble of forging a medieval map, I'd try to make it as valuable as I could. I'd add a detail showing where Vinland really was located."

"Your analysis is sound. And the ink tests support both possibilities—authenticity and fraud. Yet the experts conclude the map is a fake."

Cam shrugged. He had spent the past couple of years being told by experts that all sorts of artifacts were fakes. As if nobody had anything better to do with their time than to carve ancient scripts on boulders in the middle of the woods, or to take medieval parchment and make a fake map out of it. "In my experience in doing this research, the experts are wrong as often as they're right. Especially when it comes to ancient history. They defer too often to the archeologists. And the problem with archeology is that only a micro-fraction of the earth has been excavated." Cam shrugged again. "Their conclusions are, by definition, limited to where they happen to dig."

Randall waited for Cam to glance down at him. "I assume you are going to support this statement with some examples," Randall said. Despite Randall's haughty mannerisms, he seemed open-minded and interested in Cam's opinions.

"Sure," Cam said. "Until just a few years ago every text book in the country said that civilization as we know it began in Mesopotamia six thousand years ago. Now a new site in Turkey called Gobekli Tepe doubles that, to twelve thousand years ago. So the historians, listening to the archeologists, were wrong by a factor of two."

"But you are talking about archeological conclusions. I was talking about an artifact, in this case a map, being considered fake."

"Don't you see how one frames the other? The archeologists define the history, and then artifacts are made to fit that history." He shook his head. "Do you know it is accepted protocol on an archeological dig to throw an artifact away if it doesn't fit the established time line? It's called an anomaly."

"I did not."

"What a great profession," Cam continued. "So as a lawyer, I could say to the jury: 'Since we already *know* my client is innocent, we are going to simply disregard his fingerprints on the murder weapon as an anomaly.'" He sighed. "For archeologists, the only evidence that is valid is the stuff that fits their conclusions."

Randall smiled. "Are we approaching the highway? The fact that I can still at my age contort my body does not mean I enjoy doing so."

"We're just about to turn onto the ramp."

Randall climbed up and buckled the seat belt; the shoulder strap passed across his windpipe so he slipped it behind his back. "I like the idea of these ancient civilizations." He raised a dark eyebrow. "How tall were the men?"

"You would have been a giant, Randall." Cam thought of Amanda, home doing research on giant skeletons.

"Ah, to never have to hem my pants," Randall sighed.

Cam drove in silence, his mind on the Vinland map. "Getting back to the whole idea of making the evidence fit your conclusion, the same thing happened with the location of Vinland. The archeologists found a Viking site in northern Newfoundland called L'Anse Aux Meadows. And here's their logic: *Since it's the only site we've found, it must be the only site there is.* And then they try to take all the evidence and make it fit that conclusion."

"Allow me a supposition: You are going to provide evidence which rebuts this particular conclusion."

They drove south. Cam pulled his sunglasses from his jacket pocket; it was one of those cold, cloudless New England days where the sun reflected off the snow-blanketed landscape. "Since you asked, I will. You've heard of the Icelandic Sagas?"

"I have, but for today's purposes assume I am ignorant." He smiled. "We both know otherwise, of course."

"Okay. The Sagas recount the journeys of Leif Eriksson and his crew to Vinland around 1000 AD. They describe Leif and his crew spending a snowless winter in Vinland, with the cattle grazing. And they also talk about the crew finding grapes and making wine and getting drunk, which is where the name 'Vinland' or 'Wine-land' comes from. But if you look at the L'Anse Aux Meadows site, grapes don't grow that far north and even in Al Gore's worst global warming nightmare Newfoundland is *not* going to have a snowless winter."

"Perhaps the climate was different then."

"Not enough for grapes and snowless winters. L'Anse Aux Meadows was a trading post, linking Vinland and Greenland. Archeologists found butternut shells during their dig up there—butternuts, like grapes, don't grow that far north. So how did they get there? The obvious explanation is Leif and his gang brought them from New England. From Vinland."

Randall took a bite of his muffin, wiped a crumb from his mouth and raised his bushy eyebrows. "And how do the so-called experts explain away these trifling details?"

Cam sniffed. "So Leif Eriksson's father was Eric the Red, who discovered Greenland. And he named it 'Green'-land even though it was pretty much all ice. So, the experts say, since Eric was lying when he put the 'Green' in Greenland, *ipso facto* his son Leif must also have been lying when he put the grapes—the 'Vin'—in Vinland." Cam exhaled. "Like father, like son. Case closed."

"And the butternut shells?"

Cam rolled his eyes. "Floated up there. Against the currents, no less. Like magic." Every time he discussed this he got angry. The archeologists couldn't explain away the grapes or the snowless winters or the butternut shells so instead of opening their minds to other possibilities they invented ridiculous explanations.

Randall chewed and nodded. "Hardly examples of academic rigor. Based on what you've told me, it seems that Vinland is likely located somewhere in New England."

"No doubt."

"And this is important because?"

"Because you asked me about it."

"Yes. But why does it matter in the greater scheme of things? Who gives a rodent's rear end where Vinland really is?"

Cam took a deep breath. "Because if Vinland is further south—say Cape Cod or Narragansett Bay—then all these other sites and artifacts we've found scattered around New England become more believable. The way it is now, the academics say the Vikings touched their toe on northern Newfoundland and then scurried home for five hundred years. Therefore nothing else can be authentic."

"Frightened away by the Eskimos, no doubt. You know how timid the Vikings were."

Randall knew more about this than he was letting on; he was testing Cam, trying to get a sense of him. Cam drove in silence for a few seconds. "So if the Vinland Map is at Yale, why are we going to Rhode Island?"

"Certainly."

"I'm sorry, what?"

"Certainly. We are going to Rhode Island."

Cam gripped the steering wheel. "This conversation is like that old Abbot and Costello routine," he muttered. "So, who's on first?"

Randall grinned. "Certainly."

"All right, you win. Where in Rhode Island are we going?"

"The University of Rhode Island, Narragansett campus. Proceed south on Route 95."

A straight answer, at least. "Why?"

He half-expected Randall to answer "Left field." Instead he got something equally obtuse, along with another sly smile: "Like father, like son."

Normally Amanda liked to join Cam when he was doing field research, but today she was happy to be left alone. His absence gave her a free day to dive deeper into some of the source material in her giants research.

Sipping a hot chocolate at a writing table looking out over the frozen lake, Venus at her feet, Amanda surfed the net and scratched out notes on one of Cam's old legal pads. Apparently the discovery of giants' bones occurred frequently in Colonial America—she found dozens of accounts of early pioneers and farmers reporting oversized skeletons. At some point she would try to verify these finds, but for now the thing she found most fascinating was a recurring detail among the reports: Many of the so-called giants possessed a double row of teeth. She reviewed her notes:

- Martha's Vineyard, Massachusetts, circa 1893: Complete skeleton of 7-foot male giant with "complete row of double teeth on upper and lower jaws."
- Hadley, Massachusetts, date unknown: 7 foot skeleton with "double rows of teeth and skull of remarkable thickness."
- Deerfield, Massachusetts, 1895: Nearly 8-foot skeleton with "head as big as a peck basket with double teeth all round."
- Lompock Rancho, California, 1833: 12-foot skeleton with "double rows of upper and lower teeth."

- Santa Rosa Island, California, circa 1800: Giant found "distinguished by its double row of teeth."
- Chesterville, OH, 1829: Giant with "skull that could have easily fit over a normal man's head and additional teeth compared to modern man."
- Seneca Township, OH, 1872: Three "at least 8-foot tall skeletons" found; "all had double rows of teeth."
- Ironton, OH, 1892: Giant found with "all double teeth."
- West Hickory, PA, 1870: 8-foot giant with "teeth all in their places, and all of them double."
- Lake Delevan, WI, 1912: 18 giant skeletons ranging in height from 7.5-10 feet tall, most with "a double row of teeth."

Amanda stared out over the lake. She tried to take herself back to the 1800s, to a time before modern communication. Most of these towns would not even have had libraries. It was possible that, independently, scores of citizens would locate bones and—out of boredom or ignorance or greed or mischievousness—fabricate stories about giant skeletons. After all, even back then, most people knew about giants from the Bible. And it would not be surprising if these giants shared qualities with the Biblical giants, such as a sixth finger. But what was the likelihood that so many of these individuals would, independently, ascribe to their make-believe giants a second row of teeth? This was a detail that would have been beyond their scope of knowledge, beyond the universe of anything they had heard before. This was not only a coincidence, but a statistically impossible one at that. And as Sherlock Holmes famously observed, when you have eliminated the impossible, whatever remains, however improbable, must be the truth…

David S. Brody

Yet despite the scores of newspaper articles and books written about the giants, there didn't seem to be any remaining skeletons. Many of the bones were given to the Smithsonian and have simply disappeared. Others have been lost to history. The whole thing seemed queer—shouldn't at least some of the bones have survived?

She decided to approach the problem from a different angle, scientifically. Was there any kind of biological or environmental reason giants could *not* have existed in ancient times? A couple of hours of research and another hot chocolate later Amanda felt fairly certain the answer was no. In ancient times, especially before the great flood, the earth's ozone layer was much thicker, protecting the earth from harmful radiation and allowing for longer and healthier life. The dinosaurs were the most obvious example—a giant humanoid would have seemed puny during the Jurassic period. Moving into more modern times, even within the past ten thousand years there is strong evidence of species shrinkage. Most mammals at the end of the last Ice Age were at least fifty percent larger than today—giant beavers, in fact, grew to the size of today's black bear. As for the question of whether a humanoid's physiology would support a giant's weight, Amanda read reports of a 1,100 pound man living in New York in the 1990's—using a formula she found in a book, 1,100 pounds would approximate the average weight of an eleven-foot giant. So at least up to eleven feet, the science seemed to work. Which is not to say giants might not have been taller—multi-ton elephants, after all, seemed to defy physiology by standing on two feet.

Of course, if there were giants, there needed to be many of them so they could procreate. That was the problem with the Sasquatch and Loch Ness sightings—how could there be just one? But in the case of the giants, there were scores of reports of them clustered across the continent. So, again, at least the science seemed to work.

This "clustering" also rebutted another argument against giants: that the giant bones were skeletons of normal humans suffering from some kind of pituitary gland malfunction, causing a condition called "gigantism" (made most famous by the professional wrestler, Andre the Giant). Many of the graves contained multiple giant skeletons, which indicated a cluster of genetically-similar giants rather than a random medical condition.

So what next? There were a few museums around that claimed to have giant bones, but most of them seemed to be run by Creationist groups bent on proving the literal accuracy of the Bible—the consensus was these were fakes. And there were some pictures of giant skeletons on the internet, but many of them were doctored, which called into question the whole lot of them. It seemed the best place to look was Washington, but of course the Smithsonian wasn't about to let Amanda go traipsing through their archives. She sat back. Without some actual bones she was at a dead end.

Webster Lovecroft tapped lightly on the office door of Georgia Johnston. He had been at his desk since 6:30 but knew better than to bother his staff before they'd had their first cup of coffee. They worked hard for him, many for little or no pay. The least he could do was treat them with dignity and consideration.

"Oh, Senator, come in," she said. He had given her the largest office in the strip mall space they rented in Wichita; both she and his election staff had objected, but he spent most of his time in Washington or on the road so he had little use for a fancy office.

He ducked in, closed the door and waited to be asked to sit. "I don't mean to pry," he said, "but I overheard you yesterday afternoon on the phone." He tapped on the wall between their two offices. "Not the best construction, I'm afraid."

She flushed a bit and smiled. "And I tend to talk loudly on the phone." She was what would have been described as 'full-figured' when he was growing up in the 1950s. Today, unfortunately for women like her, that fullness had gone out of fashion. But she was not unpleasing to look at.

"Yes, me too." He grinned. "But at least we know how to use the darn thing. Most of the staff think a phone's only good for texting and checking emails. They don't realize you can actually *talk* into it."

"We are a couple of dinosaurs, I suppose," Georgia said.

Which reminded him: He had a meeting later in the morning with a major campaign donor who wanted to show him some old dinosaur bones, plus some oversized human skeletal remains.

Lovecroft refocused. "Anyway, as I said, I couldn't help but overhear you say how you think we're all a bit too nice out here in Kansas." Smiling, he raised a hand to stop her from explaining. "I know you come from the rough and tumble world of the CIA, and things must seem pretty tame around here." Originally had not been thrilled with having a CIA operative on his staff, but she was a skilled political consultant and her CIA duties did not interfere with her day job. "Every time I come from Washington to Kansas it is a bit of a culture shock. And that's what I came to talk to you about. Do you think the country sees me as too ... I suppose the word is genteel ... to win this election?"

Georgia sipped from her coffee as she stared back at him. He valued her opinion—most of all because she was one of the few people around him who never seemed afraid to tell him the truth. Betty would have been honest with him, but cancer had taken her seven years ago at age fifty-four and he had remained single since. God might take him unexpectedly as well, and he didn't want to waste time on his social life when there was important work to do. Not that he wasn't lonely once in a while....

"I think that might be an issue at some point, but it is not at the top of my list," Georgia said. "Before you can win an election you have to win a primary. And some of your positions, frankly, scare the ... tar out of the right wing."

He appreciated her not swearing in his presence; vile language undermined civil discourse. "We've talked about that, and my positions are non-negotiable. We need to do something to end the cycle of dependence among the poor of this country. I think getting them off of welfare and into school is the key. Same thing with gun control—I'm a big hunter, as you know, but I don't need an assault rifle to take down a deer." He shrugged. "The right wing is just going to have to make some concessions."

"And I think they will. The nation is ready for a Christian President, one with true old-fashioned Judeo-Christian values. That's why I came to work for you. Your message transcends politics and class and race; your message resonates with inner-city voters as much as it does in the Bible Belt."

"You don't think voters will see me as too pious or soft or nice?"

She shrugged. "You played Big Ten college basketball and your National Guard unit was deployed in the first Iraq war. You have plenty of macho in your resume." She smiled. "And women find you attractive."

Lovecroft felt his face redden; he shrugged and crossed his arms in front of his chest. "Well," he stuttered, "women seem to be attracted to power." It always surprised him to hear that others considered him handsome. He thought of himself as grotesque, though of course all of God's creatures were beautiful in their own way. Not only was he obscenely tall, but his hands and feet were proportional to a man almost eight feet tall rather than seven—his custom-made shoes were size 22. Betty had never minded, and he had become adept at hiding his hands by folding his arms while in public, but he often felt others' eyes lingering on his snowshoe-sized shoes.

His size had bothered him more when he was a young man. While in college at Perdue he had read something Henry David Thoreau wrote, about an encounter on a Massachusetts road from Concord to Littleton with an abnormally tall young man. Thoreau called the man the Littleton Giant. The words had seared themselves into Lovecroft's memory: *There is at once something monstrous, in the bad sense, suggested by the sight of such a man. Great size is inhuman.* Monstrous. Bad. Inhuman. Such was the judgment rendered by an American icon, a man young Lovecroft admired and respected, a writer known to see the beauty and goodness in all that God created. Only decades later, when Lovecroft had truly taken God into his heart, was he able to think of himself as more than some kind of monster. He was one of God's creatures, made in God's image—though perhaps while God was peering into one of those carnival mirrors as he did so....

"It's more than that, Senator. Trust me." Georgia's words jarred him back. Yes, they were talking about women finding him attractive. Not monstrous. Attractive. She held his eyes.

The comment wasn't inappropriate, or even flirtatious— merely matter-of-fact. He smiled back at her. He knew it didn't hurt on the campaign trail to be considered good-looking. The term they used today was 'eye candy,' which wasn't a bad expression though he doubted it often was used in reference to a sixty-three year old politician with half a dozen grandchildren.

"But speaking of macho, there is one thing showing up on the polling which may be problematic for you."

"Continue." He liked that Georgia was blunt and to the point.

"Your comments on Cuba. Some interpret them to mean you favor an invasion. I'm not sure most Americans would support that."

He shifted in his seat. Even within his own mind he was unsure of his feelings about Cuba. As a man of God, how could he sit idly by while a Godless regime ruled less than a hundred miles from Florida? In the early 1990s, when anti-Christian discrimination in Cuba had been at its worst, Lovecroft—a young Congressman at the time—had called for a modern-day Crusade to overthrow Castro and allow Christianity to flourish again on the island. Things had improved since Castro's resignation, but Christians were still discriminated against. With the wisdom of experience he now realized his call for a modern-day Crusade had been a bit over-the-top. "I of course do not insist that everyone in Cuba be a Christian. But I do insist that every Christian in Cuba be free to worship without penalty."

"And if you are asked, let's say during a debate, if you still support an armed invasion, what would your answer be?"

He sighed. There was no sense sugarcoating it. "If diplomacy failed, then I would support military action." He sat up. "No man or woman should be denied the right to worship. It is a fundamental human right. As a country, we must stand up for these rights." He turned up his palms. "Surely you would agree we have gone to war with far less justification."

She nodded and scribbled some notes, her eyes not meeting his. Obviously it was not the answer she wanted to hear. "Well," she said, "my advice would be to emphasize the diplomacy part of your answer. And perhaps remind voters of the historic ties between Cuba and Russia, and the dangers a revitalized and aggressive Russia seems to be presenting."

"Fair enough. Always diplomacy first." He changed the subject. "There's one more thing I wanted to talk to you about, a related subject." This, in fact, was the real reason for his morning visit to her office. "My polling is showing that many Americans are uncomfortable with my belief that the Bible is the true word of God."

"I've been thinking about that also. It's not ideal, but you can't very well back off that position now—"

He interrupted. "Nor would I want to."

"Of course not. I think the key is to present it as your personal faith-based belief, but one that you have no desire to impose on others."

"Which, in fact, is true." He exhaled. "I was afraid you were going to suggest I tone things down. Other advisors have done so."

She shook her head. "No, like I said it's too late for that. And it's the Fundamentalist Christians and Bible literalists who are your strongest supporters. They're the ones writing checks, cheering you on at rallies, giving your campaign a grassroots energy that no amount of advertising or debating can provide." She sat forward. "No, you'd be stupid to run away from your base. The people who believe in the Bible are the ones who are going to elect you President."

He nodded. Yes, the people who believe in the Bible.

He ground his back teeth together. Unfortunately that meant every word of the Bible, even the parts which might prevent him from being elected.

Randall directed Cam to the University of Rhode Island campus in Narragansett. Ten miles due east, across Narragansett Bay and the island of Jamestown, stood the Newport Tower. "You ever see the Newport Tower?" Cam asked.

"Perhaps twenty years ago I visited Newport for a tennis tournament. While walking through a nearby park an acquaintance pointed the Tower out to me and informed me it was a Colonial grist mill." Randall shrugged. "I recall thinking it did not resemble any Colonial structure I had ever seen. But it was a fleeting thought, gone within seconds with the summer breeze."

"Your thought may have been fleeting, but it was spot on." Cam often now caught himself using British phrases and terms. "If we have time, we should cross the bridge and go see it. I can't promise the Templars built it, but I can tell you for sure it wasn't the Colonists."

"I have a feeling the Smithsonian agrees with you."

"Really? I've never heard of them studying it."

Randall raised an eyebrow. "Precisely."

"What?" Cam asked.

Randall didn't miss a beat. "What is on second base."

Cam laughed and parked in front of a warehouse at the edge of campus. Randall pointed to a fenced-in yard containing dozens of boats. "All these vessels have been repossessed for unpaid taxes and are awaiting auction." He turned to Cam. "A boat is a hole in the water into which one pours one's money."

He smiled ruefully. "In my case, an ocean liner is a hole in the water into which my brother pours my money."

Cam had been here before, but he didn't know if Randall knew that. He tested him. "So you still haven't told me what we're here to see."

"The Narragansett Rune Stone."

He continued to play dumb. "This is where it is?" Cam knew that the boulder, carved with a runic inscription, had been taken from Narragansett Bay during the summer of 2012, hoisted from the water under the cover of darkness. It had been recovered by the police a year later—apparently an abutting waterfront homeowner with a large forklift and an even larger ego had aspired to add it to his trophy collection.

"Well," Randall said, "the police could not very well drop it back in the ocean once they recovered it."

Randall led Cam toward the warehouse, pushed the door open and flicked on a light. The warehouse was empty, apparently arranged somehow by Randall. The boulder—approximating the size of a row boat—sat on a platform in the middle of the warehouse, the marks from the forklift visible on its front edge. It had not moved since Cam saw it a few months earlier.

Cam and Amanda had first examined the runic engraving a couple of years ago while the boulder was in the water, but it had required wading out to their chest at low tide and peering at the inscription between wave action. According to experts, the water levels had been lower six hundred years ago so the boulder would have sat on the shoreline. The boulder's location relative to the ocean level was one of the strongest arguments for the carving's authenticity—who would bother wading out in the surf, chisel at neck level, to carve a hoax that few people would ever see? Had it not been for some clambers walking the shoreline during a rare astronomical low tide, it is doubtful the carving ever would have been discovered.

Now, out of the water and cleaned of the sea growth that had covered the inscription, the nine runic letters were clear. At least the forklift had not damaged the carved area.

Narragansett Rune Stone, Rhode Island

"It seems our scribe was a man of few words," Randall said.

"You ever try to carve into meta-sandstone?" Cam smiled. "Even you might choose to use a single word where two would do fine."

Randall raised an eyebrow. "Doubtful."

Cam jumped onto the trailer, unable to resist again examining the boulder for more carvings or markings. "See, you can do it." He peered under and around the rock: nothing but the two lines of runic writing on the top.

"But it pains me to do so. Perchance, do you have a translation?"

"You don't?"

"Of course I do. But I want to hear yours."

"I've heard two different translations. *Four victorious near the river* is one. And *Refuge from ice, here* is another. Apparently runic translations are as much art as science. I prefer the second: there's a sheltered cove close to the boulder's original location. The style of the runes ties it back to the Kensington Rune Stone in Minnesota and the Spirit Pond Rune Stones up in Maine. Both are late 1300s."

"And you believe it is authentic?"

"I do. That 'X' rune on the left side of the second line, the one with an extra fork at the top, is unique to North America— it doesn't exist on any runic inscriptions in Scandinavia or Europe. But it exists on the Kensington Rune Stone in Minnesota and the Spirit Pond Rune Stones in Maine, in addition to this."

Randall nodded. "What about the local man who claimed to have carved it as a teenager in the 1960s?"

"His story doesn't really add up. He says he was trying to carve the word 'Skraelings,' which is what the Norse called the Native Americans, but the first letter isn't even an 'S.' And other people claim they saw the carving in the 1950s."

Randall smiled knowingly. "You are wise not to believe everything you read. Do you believe this artifact is related in any way to the Vinland Map?"

"Sure. All the rune stones, along with the map, are evidence of exploration before Columbus. Especially if you believe Vinland is around Cape Cod or Narragansett Bay— then this carving and the map are pieces to the same puzzle."

"And do you recall the name of the gentleman who donated the Vinland Map to Yale?"

"I think you said his name was Mellon."

"Correct. Paul Mellon, heir to the Mellon banking fortune."

Cam jumped off the trailer and waited for Randall to continue. Randall paused dramatically until Cam met his glance—if it had been a movie Cam would have expected eerie music.

Finally Randall swallowed and spoke, enunciating even more clearly than usual. "Would you think it more than a coincidence if I told you the man who stole the Narragansett Rune Stone was Paul Mellon's son?"

Cam sniffed. "So that's what you meant when you said, 'Like father, like son.'"

"Precisely."

Astarte hated the third Tuesday of every month. That was the day the weird lady from the government came to school to meet with her and ask her dumb questions. Last time she asked if Cameron had ever touched her private parts. So awkward.

"Astarte January, please come to the principal's office." There it was. She sighed and stuffed the last of her turkey sandwich in her mouth.

"Astarte's in trouble," Meghan sang as Astarte stood up.

Meghan was supposed to be her best friend. But when they were with a group it was more important for Meghan to be cool than to be nice. Astarte ignored her. "See you guys later." She handed Julia the chocolate chip cookie she wouldn't have time to eat. Meghan loved cookies, but not as much as she liked being cool.

The secretary brought Astarte into a small room next to the principal's office. Mrs. Beliveau, wearing a fluffy pink cardigan like the mean Professor Umbridge in the *Harry Potter* books, sat at a table waiting for her. She had thick glasses which made her eyes look really big. "Good afternoon, Astarte." She always pronounced it wrong, with the accent on the last syllable so it sounded like one of these fancy French words she heard on the cooking shows.

"Hello Mrs. Beliveau." She was always smiling, but Uncle Jefferson told her anyone who shows their teeth all the time was just looking for a chance to take a bite out of you.

"And how are things going with Mr. Thorne and Ms. Spencer?"

"Good."

"That's all, just good?"

Astarte shrugged. What was she supposed to say? Of course she missed Uncle Jefferson. But he was dead now. "Her name isn't Ms. Spencer anymore. It's Ms. Spencer-Gunn. She added the Gunn part."

"I see." She said it like it was somehow important.

But Astarte knew it was just because Mum recently found out her family name, before she was adopted, was Gunn. And when they got married it would be Amanda Gunn-Thorne. Then they would formally adopt her.

"Speaking of names, it's been fourteen months now that you've been living with them. Do you call them Mom and Dad?"

The only reason this woman was asking questions was because she wanted to make trouble. "I call them Mum and Dad-Cam."

"Dad-Cam?"

She nodded. Mum was different than Mother or Mom, and Dad-Cam wasn't the same as just plain Dad. They weren't her actual parents so it seemed right to use different words. But that didn't mean Astarte didn't love them. "It's just a name. He's still my father."

Mrs. Beliveau raised an eyebrow. "Do you call him Dad-Cam because, perhaps, he takes pictures of you?" She reached out and covered Astarte's hand. "Perhaps in the bath tub?"

Astarte forced herself not to pull away. "I don't take baths. I take showers." The woman always treated her like she was still in kindergarten.

"Yes, of course. But what about my question?"

Astarte sighed. "I call him Dad-Cam because his name is Cam and he's my dad. He takes pictures of my soccer games."

Mrs. Beliveau seemed disappointed in the answer. "Well, then. Do you have enough food? Enough clothes?"

"Yes, lots."

"And do you still go to the Mormon church?"

That had been the only argument she'd ever had with her new parents. At first they'd made her go to a Unitarian church. But she didn't like it so eventually they let her go back to the Mormon temple every Sunday. "Yes. Mum made me promise I wouldn't believe the stuff about men being better than women. Then she let me go back."

"I see." She focused her big eyes on Astarte for a few seconds. "And you're sure Mr. Thorne never touches your private parts?"

She resisted the urge to roll her eyes. "No. I mean yes, I'm sure."

"He never touches you at all?"

She didn't say that. "He kisses me goodnight. And gives me hugs. And sometimes we have tickling contests."

Mrs. Beliveau sat forward. "And where does he tickle you?"

"Last time was on the living room couch."

"No, I mean where on your body?"

This woman really wasn't very smart if she didn't know where the tickle places were. "All over, of course. It's a tickling contest."

"I see." Mrs. Beliveau sat back. "All over. Indeed."

After his morning meeting with Georgia Johnston, Webster Lovecroft made a few phone calls and read a report updating the status of the nuclear program in Iran. At 9:30 his driver, a thick-necked retired state policeman named Gus, knocked. "It's a ninety minute drive to Emporia."

Lovecroft nodded. He wasn't looking forward to folding himself into the SUV again. Even with the seat pushed back he couldn't straighten his legs. At least they didn't have to drive all the way to Kansas City.

He grabbed his briefcase, a bottle of water and an apple—then doubled back to get a water for Gus as well—before settling into the front seat. He smiled at Gus. "Speed limit. And please no stops and starts. I'm going to try to read and you know I get car sick."

Gus took a last drag on a cigarette before closing the door. "Okay boss."

The Oath of Nimrod

Lovecroft pulled out the notes he had made last week from the conversation he had with the donor, a guy named Metevier who owned a chain of nursing homes. According to Metevier, three giant skeletons were unearthed from a Native American burial mound in eastern Ohio in 1872. Each measured well over eight feet tall and each had a full second row of teeth both on the upper and lower jaws. Most of the bones were lost, but apparently Metevier's great-grandfather preserved one of the skulls and it had been passed down to Metevier.

Native American burial mounds had long fascinated Lovecroft. His grandfather on his mother's side, whom he called Agiduda, was a Cherokee elder who taught him the history of the Cherokee people. The Cherokee had originally migrated from Texas to the Great Lakes area; at some point the Iroquois drove them southeast to Appalachia before most of them were forcibly resettled via the "Trail of Tears" onto reservations in Oklahoma in the 1830s. Whether in the Great Lakes Region or Appalachia, the Cherokee practice was to bury their dead in earthen mounds. Pioneering American farmers often dug up these mounds, hoping to find burial treasure or other valuable objects. Many others were excavated by federal officials or university dig teams in the name of science. Others still were simply plowed over. As a result, few mounds remained.

None of this was particularly relevant now. But what was relevant was that Agiduda insisted that giants once lived in North America, and often interbred with the Cherokees. One summer he took young Lovecroft to North Carolina to see Judaculla Rock, a soapstone boulder covered with carvings. According to Cherokee legend the carvings were the work of a giant and provided instructions for entering the spirit world. The giant, named Judaculla, was believed to have come from across the Atlantic because he had Mediterranean features, which made Lovecroft wonder whether the markings might be some kind of map or astronomical chart tracking Judaculla's journey westward across the ocean.

Judaculla Rock, North Carolina

Whatever the meaning of the Judaculla Rock carvings, the idea that a giant had carved it always seemed perfectly reasonable to Lovecroft. The Bible recounted many incidents involving giants in the Middle East—as the word of God this point was beyond debate. And if giants existed in the Middle East, why not in North America also?

After examining the Narragansett Rune Stone, Cam and Randall grabbed sandwiches and sodas for the car ride home. Randall was an enigma, and he blindsided Cam once again. "What did you think of the speaker last week, Jacques Autier?"

"I told you, I'm not buying the reptilian aliens thing."

Randall sat back in his seat and smirked. "You might not want to be too hasty in rejecting the reptilian theory. The truth often comes down to us through our legends, our myths, our stories. Consider a few facts." He held up one finger. "First, the serpent in the Adam and Eve story. A reptile, yes? Today the Church would have us believe the serpent represents the devil or temptation. But look closely at the story: God warns Adam and Eve they will die if they eat the forbidden fruit, commonly portrayed as an apple. The serpent appears and tells them it is okay, go ahead and have a taste, nothing will happen." Randall smiled. "You know the rest. They eat the apple, but do not die. So who was correct, God or the serpent?"

Cam began to object. "But they are punished—"

"But they do not die as God promised. Let us dig a bit deeper. The apple symbolizes curiosity. God wanted blind obedience, whereas the serpent urged humankind to explore and think and learn. Which brings me to fact number two..."

He held up two fingers. "The snake, or serpent, is the symbol for knowledge. Consider the icon of the American Medical Association—a snake encircling a rod. I have never considered the snake as particularly intelligent, have you? The owl, yes. A fox, perhaps. But the snake?"

Cam shrugged and Randall continued. "Fact number three. Crocodiles were venerated by the Egyptian pharaohs throughout the ages—crocodile fat was used in their anointing ceremonies. This is not particularly surprising, given the strength and power of the animal. But did you know this reptilian veneration continued in Europe, among the royal families? This, I suggest, is an odd practice given that crocodiles do not even exist in Europe."

Cam nodded. "Continue." It was a long drive home, and he found this kind of information fascinating.

Randall showed four fingers. "Fact four. Mary Magdalene. I know you are familiar with the legend that she fled Jerusalem, pregnant with Jesus' child, and made her way to southern France—it is this line that became the French royal family known as the Merovingians just before the Dark Ages. What you may not know is that the Merovingians—which translates to 'Vine of Mary'—trace their ancestry back to a union between a descendant of the Jesus-Mary bloodline and a sea monster."

"A sea monster?"

"Yes. In other words, the Jesus bloodline interbred with some kind of reptile to form the French royal family that ruled for almost three hundred years." Randall sat back. "So, as you can see, perhaps there is more to these reptilian theories than meets the eye."

"Good stuff," Cam said. "Thanks for the history lesson."

Randall checked his watch. "So, I ask you again: What did you think of Monsieur Autier?"

He put on his blinker and switched lanes. "Maybe I was too quick to dismiss his reptilian research."

Randall looked at him sidewise and sighed. "Please focus. I did not ask what you thought about Monsieur Autier's research. I asked what you thought about *him*."

Cam shifted in his seat. "Okay, I thought he was a pompous ass."

Randall clapped his hands together. "Splendid." He sat taller in his seat. "And what if I were to tell you that Monsieur Autier's research—specifically, his theory that alien reptiles bred with human women to create a quasi-race that rules the world—was based on the work of an English gentleman by the name of Laurence Gardner? *Sir* Laurence Gardner, if we are to be accurate."

"I've heard of Gardner, I think. But I've never read any of his stuff."

"But you did not answer my question."

Cam sipped from his bottle of Diet Coke. "I suppose I would say—despite what you just told me about reptilian legends—that Sir Laurence should stick to polo or grouse hunting or whatever it is English noblemen do these days. It's a long way from legend to reptilian aliens ruling the world."

Randall nodded and pursed his lips, apparently weighing a decision in his mind. "What if I told you Sir Laurence had done extensive research on the Ark of the Covenant, the Jesus Bloodline and the Holy Grail. Would you be inclined to take his work seriously?"

"I think you know the answer already. Probably not, no."

Randall checked his watch. "This conversation—the portion of it subsequent to when I asked you to please focus—has taken less than four minutes. In that time I have explained to you my life's work, and exactly how Project MK-Ultra functions." He turned to Cam. "You see, Jacques Autier is my creation. His real name is Jack Arthur. I hired him, trained him, even taught him that horrid French accent. I created him for the sole purpose of undermining Sir Laurence's research. And I have succeeded. By the time Sir Laurence died in 2010 his work had largely been discredited. Few people remember his writings on the Ark of the Covenant or the Jesus Bloodline or the Holy Grail, much of which relates to exploration of America before Columbus. Instead, he is the nutty nobleman who believed reptilian aliens ruled the world."

"But how did just one aspect of his work come to define the man?"

The response was almost predictably obtuse. "Precisely."

"Wake up, boss, almost here."

Lovecroft opened his eyes, disoriented. He must have dozed off. "Okay, thanks, Gus." He sipped some water, replaying his dream in his head. Grandfather Agiduda stood tall and powerful, wearing his Cherokee traditional garb, preaching from a pulpit in an ornate church like a modern-day clergyman. He had been reading passages from the Bible. Genesis 6:4; Numbers 13:33; Deuteronomy 3:11; 1 Samuel 17:1. All these passages spoke of giants. Lovecroft shook his head and took another sip of water. Apparently his grandfather was trying to tell him something.

He pulled himself from the car and approached a sprawling clapboard and brick ranch-style home surrounded by a white stockade fence; in the distance a few horses drank from a small pond. Mr. Metevier did well, hopefully not at the expense of his elderly patients. Lovecroft didn't often visit people in their homes—most constituents were uncomfortable hosting a U.S. Senator in their living room. But Metevier's collection was in his basement, so here they were.

His host, a heavy-set, middle-aged man wearing a blue blazer and a pair of gray slacks, met him in the driveway. "Senator," he boomed, "it is an honor to welcome you."

They made small talk as Metevier escorted the Senator down a wide, carpeted staircase to the basement. "Just came back from a ski trip in Utah. I have family out there," he said. "When we bought this house, the basement wasn't finished. I excavated it out to give us nine-foot ceilings, then I took this center room and enclosed it in concrete. It's a safe room for me and my wife, but mostly I use it to store my collection."

Lovecroft politely turned away as his host punched a series of numbers into a keypad. A steel door slid open electronically and the men entered a rectangular room the size of large bedroom filled with museum-style display cabinets. Recessed lighting brightened the room and a climate-control system hummed in the background. Metevier pointed to the far wall. "Back there is a living area—beds, kitchen, bathroom, food and water, other supplies. Hopefully we never have to use it. But this is my pride and joy."

He showed the Senator a number of dinosaur bones. Dinosaurs were a tricky thing for Bible literalists like Lovecroft: Could dinosaurs have existed alongside humans during the past six thousand years, when God created the earth? Here, as in all things, a careful reading of the Bible provided the explanation: The Bible referred to dinosaurs in the Middle East as dragons or behemoths or leviathans. Other types of dinosaurs existed in other parts of the world. For example, his own Cherokee tradition of a thunderbird—a giant flying reptile—reflected the type of dinosaur that lived in North America. Like all creatures, the dinosaurs were taken onto Noah's Ark. But the sudden change in environmental conditions post-Flood wiped most of them out.

Metevier then showed him some artifacts from Burrows Cave and the Michigan Stone Tablets collection—artifacts that many believed to be fake but which some felt proved European explorers had visited North America long before Columbus. Lovecroft had done some reading on these artifacts—common sense told him many cultures would have tried to cross the Atlantic over the centuries. "If these are fake," Metevier said, "they are some of the most elaborate fakes I've ever seen. Take a look at this Map Stone from Burrows Cave."

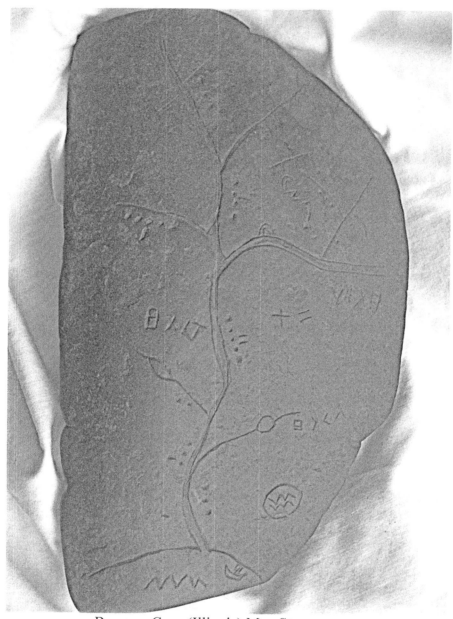

Burrows Cave (Illinois) Map Stone

Lovecroft peered closer as his host explained the artifact.

"The carving marks the journey up from the Gulf of Mexico—you can see the little boat in the water at the very bottom of the stone, next to the zigzag mark for waves in the water. They go up the Mississippi River, to the Ohio and eventually into southern Illinois. Each dot marks a day's journey. What's interesting is that if you look at the bottom of the Mississippi, where it empties into the Gulf of Mexico, you can see that the river bends slightly to the east. That's not the way it runs today—today it makes almost a ninety degree turn to the east toward Lake Pontchartrain before eventually turning south again. The difference is about fifty miles." He crossed his arms. "So why the mistake? The rest of the map is accurate."

Lovecroft smiled. "I presume you are going to enlighten me."

"Yes. From what I've read, this map shows the historic course of the Mississippi, from about two thousand years ago, before it redirected itself."

"And does that match up with the estimated date of the Burrows Cave artifacts?"

"Perfectly. The artifacts are believed to date back to the first century after Christ." He pursed his lips. "And from what I've learned about this Russell Burrows, he wasn't educated enough to know the ancient course of the Mississippi River."

Lovecroft nodded. It didn't prove the artifacts' authenticity, but it was a compelling argument.

Together they stared at the Map Stone for a few seconds before Metevier escorted him to the center of the room. As much as his host appreciated the other artifacts in the room, his tone now turned reverential. Alone inside a square glass display case rested a giant humanoid skull. "There it is," he whispered.

Lovecroft exhaled. It truly was massive, more than twice the size of a normal skull. "Very impressive."

"I've had some anthropologists look at it. They say it's proportional to a person nine feet tall." He removed a key from his pocket. "I can take it out if you'd like."

"Won't that damage it?"

"I don't take it out very often." He grinned. "But I don't often have a United States Senator visiting either."

"You said there were originally three skeletons. Where are the others? And where are the bones that go with this one?"

Metevier shrugged. "All lost. Probably just decayed. Dust-to-dust, as they say." He unlocked the case and carefully removed the skull. "Luckily my great-grandfather was a scientist and knew how to preserve bones. But back then not many people knew about bacteria and humidity and other things that cause bones to decay."

Lovecroft nodded. He had spent a summer in college on an archeological dig; he knew that certain soil conditions and burial practices would preserve a body for thousands of years but that once out of the ground the skeleton would quickly decay.

Metevier handed him the skull. "Look at the double rows of teeth," he said.

Lovecroft's face began to flush. He focused instead on the skull's sloping, angular forehead.

"You can actually fit it over your head, like a mask. Go ahead, try it."

Lovecroft was feeling increasingly uncomfortable. "No, thanks." They were handling the head of an actual person, studying it like it was part of some kind of freak show. The Cherokee believed all bones should remain buried with the body, but especially the skull, which is where the soul resided—without the skull, the soul could not travel to the afterlife. In fact, his grandfather taught him that Native Americans scalped their enemies to destroy the skull and therefore prevent the soul from coming back to exact revenge. Had this soul been suffering in some kind of purgatory for the past 140 years? He took a deep breath. "Fascinating. Truly fascinating." He glanced at his watch. "I wish I could see more of this collection."

Metevier took the hint. He gently placed the skull back in the case and turned to his guest. "Of course, I've had this tested. It's the real deal. No chance of it being fake."

They began to walk back toward the door. Lovecroft hoped Metevier would not be offended by a blunt question. "As you know, I believe the Bible is the word of God. Which means I believe in giants. You said you just came back from Utah so I am assuming you may be Mormon: May I ask if your interest in giants is tied to your religion, whatever that religion may be?"

Metevier nodded. "Fair question, and good assumption. And, yes, that was my original interest. But the truth is the truth, no matter what you believe. What's that expression? Everyone is entitled to their own opinions, but they're not entitled to their own facts. Facts are facts."

"Yes," Lovecroft smiled. "As John Adams said, facts can be stubborn things."

Metevier gestured back toward the giant skull. "And it is a fact that these giants existed. No offense, but what I don't get is why you folks in Washington keep trying to cover it up."

"Us folks in Washington?"

"Yeah, the Smithsonian. They must have some of these giant bones. So why not let people see them?"

Lovecroft nodded. It was a fair question, and someone should ask it.

But preferably not until after the election.

Cam hadn't returned from Rhode Island yet, and Astarte had gone home on the bus with a friend, so Amanda was alone in the house as the winter sun began to set in the late afternoon. She had maxed-out on her giant skeletons research, the voice inside her head in a repeating loop:

Fee-fi-fo-fum, I smell the blood of an Englishman.
Be he alive, or be he dead, I'll have his bones to grind my bread.

She finally played some Eric Clapton on her iPod to clear her head and tried to catch up on some reports for the museum she worked for. For a long period of her life listening to Clapton made her sad. There was a longing and loneliness in his songs that mirrored her own life—his song "Layla," lamenting his unrequited love for Pattie Boyd, wife of one of his best friends, George Harrison, used to bring her to tears. But that had changed when she met Cam—she had found what so many others sought, and Clapton's music reminded her how fortunate she was.

But even Clapton couldn't settle her. That small voice in her head—the one that nagged you when you forgot your wallet or left the stove on—called to her. She had learned to listen to that voice, to tune into it. *John Emmert*, it said to her. Amanda looked through her notes: Emmert was one of the Smithsonian archeologists who had been called in to examine and investigate many of the giant skeletons found in the late 1800s. Nothing particularly noteworthy about that. But there was something else about the name that rang a bell, something important….

She did a quick Google search and almost fell off her chair as an image of the Bat Creek carving popped up next to his name: Emmert was the archeologist who first discovered the Bat Creek Stone in Tennessee. Eyes widening, she stared at the screen. Could this be a coincidence? From Emmert to the Smithsonian until eventually the bracelet found its way into a bag of Chinese food. At some level it made sense: Emmert's job was to excavate Native American burial mounds. So of course he would be called in when giant skeletons were found. But even so….

She moved to the big chair overlooking the lake and called Venus to join her. The temperature had crept up to thirty, which brought all sorts of activity to the frozen surface. Ice fisherman, skaters, dog-walkers, snowmobilers. Amanda watched them, content to sip her tea with Venus' head on her lap and wonder about ancient giants. A glint of light caught her eye and she focused on a pair of men not far off the shoreline.

They looked queer, somehow out of place just standing there with no poles or sticks or other implements of winter recreation; one of them even looked to be wearing dress slacks. She slid behind the curtain and angled her binoculars toward them: A pair of Asian men, one middle-aged and the other in his twenties. The older one held a pair of binoculars also, aiming right back at her. Her heart thumped as she made the obvious association to Cam's abductors. "Venus, here girl," she called.

Amanda threw on her winter coat and some gloves and grabbed her cross-country skis and Venus' leash. She jogged to her Subaru in the driveway, secured the skis on the ski rack and navigated her way to the other side of the lake to the public beach. There, she stepped into her skis and, Venus by her side, powered her way to the middle of the lake. She checked her watch—seven minutes had elapsed since she left the house. The men had not moved.

She approached to within fifty yards. Now what? For one thing, nobody knew where she was. She sent a quick text to Cam: "2 strange men on lake looking at our house. I'm on X-country skis with Venus checking it out."

Maneuvering herself so the setting sun was at her back, she circled around and skied directly at the men, her smart phone in hand. As she approached, and as the men squinted back at her, she snapped a couple of quick pictures.

"Hey," the older man yelled. "What you doing?"

She ignored him and began to ski away.

"Hey, stop!" The two men ran after her on the snow-packed surface. A couple of ice fisherman heard the commotion and jogged toward them from the shoreline. The younger Asian man didn't seem to have his heart in the pursuit, but the older one had an angle and surprised Amanda by closing on her quickly. She probably could have outdistanced him, or perhaps even turned Venus on him, but the idea of being spied on really cheesed her off. Plus these were the guys who tried to snap Cam's finger off. As her assailant moved to within six feet, she turned toward him, took one last powerful stride and, emboldened by the approaching ice fishermen,

94

lowered her shoulder into his chest. It had probably never occurred to him that she would turn on him, and the surprise attack sent him sprawling to the frozen surface.

Venus lunged at him, growling, her teeth bared. "Down, Venus," Amanda said. She caught her breath, kicked off her skis and put her ski pole into the man's chest as he scrambled to right himself, shoving him back down. He swatted it away, but she whipped the other pole around and caught him on the ear. That quieted him.

"I know who you are," she hissed. "If I see you here again, I'm going to take this pole and poke out your eye. Got it?"

He nodded, his eyes wide with fear behind a pair of snow-crusted glasses. As she lifted the pole again, threateningly, Venus yelped and lunged as the younger man bound toward them. Neither man was huge, but both outweighed her by a good forty pounds. The younger guy kicked Venus aside and charged Amanda, his head down as if ready to make a football tackle.

Acting on instinct, she waited until the last possible instant before dropping to her back, lifting her legs and planting her feet into the man's midsection. Using his own momentum against him, she flipped him up and over her. He landed on his back—the impact on the ice and the sound of his breath escaping combining for a thud-thud sound that echoed across the open space of the lake. Venus scurried over and barked, her face inches from the prone man's neck. But the man only moaned, his weight shifting side-to-side as he writhed in pain.

Amanda lifted the stick one more time to subdue the older man, snapped close-up pictures of both men and stepped back onto her skis as the ice fishermen arrived.

"She crazy lady," the older man said.

Her heart raced but she fought to keep her voice calm. "Yeah, well, this crazy lady just kicked your ass." She faked a swing of the pole; the man recoiled, covering his face. One wary eye on her assailants, she nodded at the ice fisherman, powered three strong strides and was on her way. "Venus, come!"

Halfway across the lake her cell phone pinged. Cam, probably. Well, she'd have a story to tell over dinner. In fact, she'd ask him to pick up something on the way home. Anything but Chinese.

As they approached Westford on their way home from Rhode Island, Randall Sid—who was beginning to think of Randall as his real name, sort of the way people started to dream in a foreign language after immersing themselves in it— instructed Cam to drop him off on a side street a half-mile away from the Dunkin' Donuts. "After I jump out, circle the block two times. If I do not phone you, after the second pass leave the area and return in an hour to retrieve your car." Randall was pretty certain they had not been followed, but in his business 'pretty certain' was often as close to 'dead wrong' as your crotch was to your underpants.

"In the meantime," Randall continued, "I have something to discuss with you."

"Okay."

"Use caution around Astarte."

"How so?"

"She is an obvious vulnerability. A young girl, not your natural daughter, residing in your home." He shrugged. "It is almost too easy."

"Are you saying the CIA would make up stuff? About me?"

He shrugged again. "I am merely pointing out it is an obvious play if they wish to discredit you. Folks tend not to trust child molesters."

Cam exhaled. "Great. These people have no boundaries, do they?"

"If they do, we have not reached them yet." He pointed. "Now, pull over here and circle the block as I instructed."

Randall hid in the woods while Cam made his passes. No tail. Randall waited a few more minutes to be certain and cut through the woods along a rail bed and some snowmobile tracks back to the strip mall. He studied the customer parking lot from behind a tree.

In addition to Cameron's car, there were nine others. He memorized them and waited, daydreaming about finishing up this MK-Ultra business and then taking a trip somewhere. Not a cruise like his brother—that would be torture, stuck aboard a floating fiberglass palace with nothing to do but await the next buffet spread. He preferred to travel someplace exotic, try new foods, see new sites, meet new people. Asia was usually a good choice for him, which was one of the reasons he so enjoyed living in Chinatown—there, he has merely short, not grotesque. Perhaps Indonesia, where the average height was just over five feet....

Six of the vehicles in the parking lot departed in the first ten minutes as people scurried in and out of the donut shop and the convenience store and ATM enclosure next door. Another left a few minutes later. That left two vehicles. One was a pickup truck with a plow on the front—not likely that an Agency operative would drive that. The other was a dark-colored SUV with Massachusetts plates. No bumper stickers, no car magnets, no decals. He waited another twenty minutes: no activity. There was nothing in the strip mall that would occupy someone for more than a half hour, and the employees all seemed to have parked in the rear lot. Perhaps he had underestimated his former employer.

Game on. Indonesia would have to wait.

Sticking to the woods, Randall circled around to the far end of the strip mall, following the footsteps Cameron had made earlier in the day. He went into the convenience store first—a couple of housewives with kids, and a trucker buying cigarettes. The ATM room was empty. That left Dunkin's. A twenty-something guy in a Red Sox cap sat in the corner reading the newspaper, chatting up one of the counter girls. That explained the pickup truck. Which meant the SUV belonged to a clean-cut man in a business suit sipping on a cup of coffee with his laptop open in front of him. From the looks of the debris in front of him, he had been there a while.

Randall approached the counter and ordered another blueberry muffin. "Do you have WiFi in here?" he asked.

"No, sorry," the girl replied.

Odd place for a business man to set up shop for a day. He glanced a second time at the man. Thirty-something and far too intent on whatever was displayed on his computer screen. It was to make room for agents like this that Randall had been put out to pasture. The idiot had probably tracked Cameron here and then been fooled by the Robert-doll ruse. Now, six hours later, he was just hoping Cameron would return for his SUV so he could pick up the trail again. This promised to be entertaining.

Randall walked to the far end of the donut shop and found a framed Board of Health permit. Next he went out to the parking lot and dialed the number of the tow company printed on a sign warning against using the lot for day-long parking. "Hello, my name is Jeremy McDonough," he said, using the name from the Board of Health permit. "I am the proprietor of the Dunkin' Donuts on Route 40 in Westford. I'd like to request a tow from our lot—a car has been parked here illegally all day." He described the SUV and hung up.

Ten minutes later a tow truck arrived. The agent had situated himself so he could see Cameron's vehicle through the window, but not his own. As the truck began to pull away, Randall walked over to the agent. He smiled and motioned over his shoulder. "I am sorry to interrupt what I am certain is important work. But I believe that is your vehicle being towed."

David S. Brody

Randall had not chosen Cameron Thorne randomly; there were a half-dozen other New England researchers the CIA had targeted and Randall could have chosen to focus on any of them instead. But Thorne was special: He lived in Westford.

Randall's walk through the woods back to the Westford Dunkin' Donuts, across a stream that emptied into a pond in the distance, had brought back a flood of memories. Randall had stopped for a few minutes, eyes closed. In his mind he had added sixty degrees and subtracted sixty years. And once he began to remember he could not forget.

In his car now, he and Cameron having re-traded vehicles, Randall circled those same woods and found the entrance to the campground within. A sign greeted him: *East Boston Camps.* So it was still here. Unbelievably, after more than sixty years. Did immigrant kids from East Boston still board yellow school buses every July—bathing suit, toothbrush and a few changes of clothes stuffed inside a duffel bag—for a summer in the country as he and his brother had done? He counted the years back. He had been fifteen, so the year must have been 1949. World War II was over and the Cold War had not yet begun. Or if it had, Randall had not yet learned of it.

He followed a pitted, snow-covered road along the railroad tracks and then into the woods, climbing slightly—his were not the first tracks, so the woods were apparently in use even in winter. A few seconds later, as if in confirmation, a woman walking a dog rounded the corner ahead. She smiled and waved, strands of red hair flowing from beneath a white wool cap. Randall's heart jumped, then he smiled. Red hair. Of course. *Hello Consuela. It has been a long time since I have thought of you.* Actually, that was not true. *Correction: I think of you every day. But it has been many years since I have allowed myself to really remember.*

A few hundred yards later a gate blocked his way, so he parked and continued on foot. He crested a hill; ahead, in a clearing, a cluster of clapboard cabins sat on a rise above a now-frozen pond. Amazingly, the site had changed little. Perhaps an extra building or two, and of course a winter scene greeted him rather than a summer one, but the cabins and picnic tables and basketball hoop and beach area were just as he remembered them. How odd—in life memories rarely seemed to match reality. He chuckled, almost a giggle, really. *Yes, how wonderfully odd.* A quote from Mark Twain popped into his head, and he voiced it aloud: "When I was younger I could remember everything, whether it happened or not."

He walked down the slope toward the beach and leaned against a majestic oak. He watched his breath rise and dissipate in the light wind for a few seconds before closing his eyes and allowing the years again to fade and his memories to replace them.

He had met her the first time here on the beach. "Are you here for sailing?" she asked. "My name is Consuela. I'm a counselor." Long red hair, a bright smile, freckles dotting her nose and upper cheeks.

He was alone, his brother having chosen to work on some craft project. "Yes," he stammered. "I would like to learn to sail." It seemed like something successful people did, and he intended to be successful someday.

"Well, looks like you're the only one today. Help me put up the sail. How old are you, twelve or thirteen?"

"Fifteen," he mumbled.

She put a hand on his arm. "Now that I look more closely at your face, I can see you are a young man. I am sixteen but everyone thinks I'm younger too." It was a lie, though a kind one. Her breasts had budded and Randall had a tough time keeping his eyes from dropping.

"Consuela is a funny name," he had blurted out.

"It's Cuban."

Randall's parents were from Cuba originally. But they looked nothing like Consuela. "You don't look Cuban."

"Have you ever been there?"

"No." Westford was as far from East Boston as he had ever been; forty miles, according to a map on the wall in the dining hall.

"So how do you know what I'm supposed to look like?"

He shrugged.

"Well, you happen to be correct. I'm Jewish, so I don't look like a lot of other Cubans."

He didn't know any Jews, though he knew a lot of them died during the war. "Sorry about that."

"About what?"

"About ... being Jewish. The war and all."

She shrugged. "My family has been in Cuba for almost fifty years." She pulled a pack of gum from her shorts pocket. "Want a piece of Juicy Fruit?"

They sailed together every day that week, alone in a Sailfish, talking and laughing and jumping into the pond to cool off. One night, sitting by the fire, she sat beside him on a log, laced her fingers into his and fed him a golden brown toasted marshmallow with her free hand. To this day nothing had ever tasted so good.

"What do you think about Communism?" she asked as they floated on a windless day in the middle of the pond.

He shrugged. "I don't trust the Ruskies." It wasn't the sort of thing they talked about in East Boston.

"Well," she continued, "there are other kinds of Communism. In Cuba, my parents are friends with a man named Fidel Castro. He is fighting to make life better for the poor. As it stands now, only the rich can go to school or get proper medical care. Castro wants to change that."

He knew he should care about this—Consuela was going back to Cuba, and he must have cousins there even though he'd never met them. "Well, if it helps the people it must be a good thing." She had smiled and kissed him, which made him realize he would have agreed that letting leeches crawl over his body was a good thing if she had suggested it.

The six weeks flew by. At fifteen, he was content to just hold hands and steal an occasional Juicy Fruit-flavored kiss. But on their last night she snuck into his cabin, took his hand and led him to the beach. "Take off your clothes," she whispered. Naked, they swam out to the raft, staying underwater to evade both the other counselors and the mosquitoes. On the far side of the raft she wrapped her legs around his hips, opened his mouth gently with her tongue and introduced him to the wonders of love-making.

An hour later, their bodies wrinkled and blue, they swam ashore, dressed and huddled together under a beach towel. "Are you coming back next summer?" he asked.

She frowned. "I doubt it. Your government doesn't like Castro, and since we support him my parents almost didn't let me come this summer." She turned to him. "Will you come visit me?"

He was fifteen—the most money he ever had was when he told some high-roller at the track that Princess Polly had a bum leg; the guy won big on a long-shot and gave Randall a five dollar bill. He had bought a new bike with it, but he couldn't very well ride it to Cuba. "I'll try."

"No. You have to promise."

"Okay. I promise."

"And I promise to write."

And she had written, off and on, for the next couple of years. Then their lives moved on and Consuela slowly faded to a distant but cherished memory. Until six years later, a few days after his twenty-first birthday. A letter arrived in his mailbox, unstamped. On the inside a piece of Juicy Fruit gum was taped to a short note on lavender-scented paper. "You promised to come to Cuba," was all it said. The dot above the 'i' was in the shape of a heart.

"I'm sorry, you did what?" Cam ran his hand through his hair, unable to stop pacing around the living room while Amanda sat on the couch.

Amanda did her best to downplay the incident, her voice flat and calm. "There were plenty of people out there. So I went out to snap a photo. When one of them confronted me, I knocked him on his arse."

"Amanda, that's crazy! You could have been hurt."

"Cam, look, I appreciate your concern. And maybe it was a bit careless. But the ice fishermen were there to help if necessary. And I'm fine. Plus I've got the pictures. It's not as if you wouldn't have done the same thing."

Cam stared out at the dark lake, his eyes on the area he imagined the altercation occurred. "I don't mean to be sexist, but—"

She cut him off. "Just stop, Cam. Yes, you do mean to be sexist. If one of your hockey player friends had done what I did you'd high-five him and buy him a pint."

Cam sighed. "Yeah, but I'm not engaged to any of my hockey buddies. How would you feel if Astarte went out there to confront those guys?"

He had a point. Sort of. "I'd bloody freak. But Astarte is a child."

He plopped onto the couch next to her. "You sure you're okay?"

She smiled and kissed him lightly. "Never better. I may try out for one of those roller derby teams."

"Let me see the pictures."

She scrolled through them on her phone.

"That's them. Chung and his son."

"You mean Chung and his son knocked on their asses."

"Yes. But I have a feeling that's not for good."

"I already gave the pictures to the police. In the morning I'm going to court to get a restraining order. The police think the judge might even revoke their bail." They had been charged with abducting and assaulting Cam.

"Okay. And I'll call Pugh and tell him what happened."

"Sounds like he doesn't have much control over his son."

"Not much. But he does have a decent inheritance he could threaten to withhold."

She bit her lip. "I think they see this bracelet as a jackpot. So they're willing to risk the inheritance. Do you really think it's valuable?"

"I don't know. It might be worthless. On the other hand if it really does prove ancient explorers were here, it'd be worth a fortune."

"Even with the whole question of provenance?"

Cam thought about it. "The Burrows Cave artifacts sell for big bucks and most of the world thinks they're fakes. Plus there are thousands of them, not just one. Assuming Pugh's story holds together, and the bracelet tests out, there would be hundreds of collectors who'd love to get their hands on it. Hell, some baseball card just sold for two million. What would you rather have?"

She smiled. "A beach house, if you want the truth."

"Well, in the end it doesn't really matter what its worth. *They* think it's valuable, and that's what motivates their behavior."

"By the way, I found a lab in Lexington that will do metal-testing for us."

"Okay," Cam said. "I'll drive the bracelet in tomorrow after court. Randall thinks we should get it tested right away."

"There's no reason for you to come to court. The detective will be with me. You go to the lab first thing."

"Okay." Cam recounted his day. "Turns out that guy I heard lecture last week was a fake, a creation of Randall Sid."

"The reptilian alien guy? Why?"

Cam shrugged. "It was part of a plan to discredit some British researcher named Laurence Gardner. And it worked. Gardner did some good work, but because of all of Autier's lectures and publicity everyone now just thinks of him as the kook who thinks Prince Charles is half-crocodile. That's what MK-Ultra does. More than brain-washing, it changes reality. Or at least the perception of reality."

"I've read some of Gardner's stuff. He's a good researcher. But why would the CIA care about some Brit's research on the Jesus Bloodline?"

"It must tie into something here, something they want to control."

"Yes, probably the Templars and our Prince Henry research. Maybe we should take a closer look at Gardner's work."

"Speaking of controlling things, it also turns out there is one rich family, the Mellons, who are connected to both the Vinland Map at Yale and the Narragansett Rune Stone."

"Coincidence?"

Cam shook his head. "Randall doesn't think so."

But there was something about the Mellon name that rang a bell. She stabbed at her smart phone for a few seconds. "There," she said. "Bunny Mellon was her name."

"Who?"

"Remember the whole John Edwards scandal? Some rich socialite gave him over a half million dollars to pay off his mistress when he was running for President. Bunny Mellon was her name. Used to be friends with Jackie Kennedy."

"Isn't she a bit old for John Edwards?"

"Exactly. Apparently he charmed her. Used to call to sing to her on her birthday." She punched a few more keys. "Born in 1910, she just died at 103."

"Well, I guess you can't take it with you. How is she related to Paul Mellon? He's the guy who bought the Vinland Map for a million bucks and donated it to Yale."

"Bunny is his second wife."

"So she's the mother, or maybe stepmother, to the Mellon who stole the Narragansett Rune Stone."

"Interesting family. Sounds like they have unlimited money to throw around."

"And what they can't buy, they steal. I'm going to keep digging. So far the Mellon family is like Where's Waldo— every time I turn the page I see them." He asked about her giants research.

"I'll get to the specifics in a minute, but the big thing I learned is that John Emmert was involved in documenting many of the giant skeleton finds."

"Emmert, the guy who found the Bat Creek Stone?"

She nodded.

"So if the Bat Creek Stone was a fake, then it follows the giant skeletons could all be fakes also."

"Since when do you think the Bat Creek find is a fake?"

"I don't. I'm just making the connection."

"I suppose that's one way to look at it. And no doubt the skeptics will make that argument. But you won't believe what I found, Cam. This is too vast to be a hoax or a ruse." She took a deep breath. "There are fifteen hundred different accounts of giant skeletons found in America. The giants are written about in The New York Times, The Washington Post, Scientific America, dozens of reputable newspapers." She handed a printout to Cam. "Here's the New York Times from 1902."

David S. Brody

GIANT SKELETONS FOUND.

Archaeologists to Send Expedition to Explore Graveyards in New Mexico Where Bodies Were Unearthed.

Special to The New York Times.

LOS ANGELES, Cal., Feb. 10.—Owing to the discovery of the remains of a race of giants in Guadalupe, N. M., antiquarians and archaeologists are preparing an expedition further to explore that region. This determination is based on the excitement that exists among the people of a scope of country near Mesa Rico, about 200 miles southeast of Las Vegas, where an old burial ground has been discovered that has yielded skeletons of enormous size.

Luiciana Quintana, on whose ranch the ancient burial plot is located, discovered two stones that bore curious inscriptions, and beneath these were found in shallow excavations the bones of a frame that could not have been less than 12 feet in length. The men who opened the grave say the forearm was 4 feet long and that in a well-preserved jaw the lower teeth ranged from the size of a hickory nut to that of the largest walnut in size.

The chest of the being is reported as having a circumference of seven feet.

Quintana, who has uncovered many other burial places, expresses the opinion that perhaps thousands of skeletons of a race of giants long extinct will be found. This supposition is based on the traditions handed down from the early Spanish invasion that have detailed knowledge of the existence of a race of giants that inhabited the plains of what now is Eastern New Mexico. Indian legends and carvings also in the same section indicate the existence of such a race.

The New York Times
Published: February 11, 1902

New York Times, 1902

107

Cam scanned it. "Not much wiggle room with a headline that reads, 'Giant Skeletons Found.'"

"And this is the New York Tribune, from 1897."

SKELETONS OF MOUND BUILDERS FOUND

St. Paul, Dec. 11 (Special).—An interesting relic of prehistoric times has been discovered on the banks of the Chippewa River, in Northern Wisconsin, just between Maple and Potato creeks. A party of hunters discovered three mounds at this spot, whose curious appearance and symmetrical construction at once indicated that they were the work of the Mound Builders. The skull and leg bones of a human being were found close to the bottom of the mound, and were taken out in fairly good condition. The skull was as large around as a half-bushel measure, and Dr. McCormick estimated the height of the man, judging by the bones of the leg, to be at least nine feet and six inches. The skull and chest of another skeleton, much smaller than the first, probably a woman, was found beside the other.

While excavating there was picked up a slender rod of copper, finely moulded, and as rigid as a piece of steel. The rod is about double the thickness of a shoemaker's needle, and nearly thirteen inches long. So finely tempered is the copper that the strongest man could not bend or break it.

New York Tribune, 1897

Cam scanned this as well. "Nine feet, six inches."

"The thing is, most of the articles quote Smithsonian officials who have come to verify the discoveries."

"Officials like John Emmert."

"Yes, but not just him, many others. Again, we're talking well over a thousand reports." She showed him an image on her computer. "Someone plotted all the giant skeletons on a map. Every pin is a different discovery."

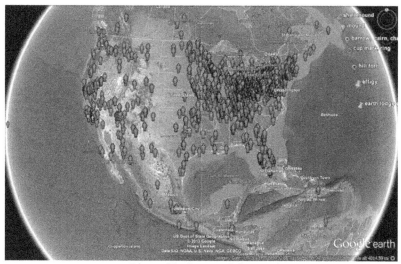

Giant Skeletons Mapped

"Wow. That's pretty widespread."

"There's got to be something to this. You don't find reports of mermaids or unicorns in the New York Times. Just giants."

"Any beanstalks?"

She cuffed him. "Jerk."

Cam continued to peer at the map. "So what happened to them all?"

"That's the bloody mystery. Many of the bones were put on display back in the 1800s and, over the years, turned to dust. Many were given to the Smithsonian and disappeared. And until recently there were still a number on display in museums across the country. But in 1990 Congress passed NAGPRA, the Native American Graves Protection and Repatriation Act, that required the bones be given back to the tribes for reburial." She shrugged. "There may be a few skeletons still in private collections, but whatever was in the museums has been reburied."

"Okay, I'll buy that. But if there are so many of these giants, how come nobody has found any recently?"

"Well, actually, they have. A farmer in Minnesota just found a giant skeleton. But no archeologist will touch it because of NAGPRA, so it's just sitting there."

"But what about, say, in the 1980s, before NAGPRA? You said most of these were found over a hundred years ago."

"The giants were almost all found in burial mounds, not regular graves. In the 1800s people used to dig up the mounds, hoping to find artifacts buried with the bodies. But most of the mounds have all been dug up. You're not likely to find a giant in a regular grave."

Cam nodded. "And if you do find one you'd be breaking the law if you disturbed it."

"Yes. It's a bit of a Catch-22. You can't prove the giants existed unless you have bones, but it's against the law to touch the skeletons."

"So it's like they never existed."

"Well, I'm sure the Smithsonian has plenty of records."

Cam sniffed. "Like I said. It's as if they never existed."

CHAPTER 4

Vito rolled out of bed, threw on some sweatpants and logged on to his computer. He checked the time: 10:51 AM. He had been up late watching a documentary about the Oak Island Money Pit in Nova Scotia.

"Vito," his mother called up the stairs. "You awake?"

"Yup, Mom."

"Honey, you going to take a shower? I want to run the dishwasher."

Her way of reminding him to bathe. "Go ahead. I'll shower later." He pulled down his t-shirt collar and smelled his armpits. Today was Wednesday; he was pretty sure he had showered Saturday afternoon. And in the winter he didn't sweat much. "Can you bring me up a Mountain Dew?" He didn't like coffee but Mountain Dew had a ton of caffeine in it.

He went right to his blog. Seventeen new entries. One of them was from a researcher who took issue with being labeled 'either a racist or an idiot,' but the others were all supportive. "Thanks for debunking the crap on television," was a common refrain.

His mother knocked lightly on his door before opening it. "Here's your soda, Vito." She walked over and put it on his desk.

"Thanks, Mom." She had aged since he went to college. She used to be a bit of a local beauty, which is how she first attracted Rusty after the divorce, but within a year of them getting married she had gained twenty pounds. And lately her skin had turned a yellowish hue. "You need to cut back on the Jack and Coke, Mom." Rusty was a putz, but at least he treated her okay. For now.

She ignored him. "How is work going?"

"Good. I got sixteen more posts today from people. Listen to this one: 'Great work, Vito. I love your blog. We need more people like you to keep the so-called experts honest!' Pretty cool, huh?"

She smiled. "I'm sorry, Honey, but I still don't get what it is exactly you do."

He turned to look at her. Even the whites of her eyes had yellowed. "I'm a debunker, Mom. People say stuff on TV or in books that is wrong, and I correct them." He lifted his chin. "It's like what Mahatma Gandhi said: 'Even if you are a minority of one, the truth is the truth.'"

"Oh." Their Siamese cat rubbed against her leg. "But why do they pay you for that? Not that I'm complaining. Me and Rusty appreciate the money. And it sure is nice to have cable again."

He lifted his chin. "Because they value the truth, Mom. Because they love America." He turned back to the computer. "Make sure the cat goes with you. Last time she peed on my clothes."

She nodded and bent over to lift the animal. "Okay. Let me know if you want a sandwich."

Vito turned back to his computer and checked his email. That girl Tammy had sent him more racy pictures—she wasn't great looking, but it's not like he had a harem down the hall. Maybe he'd take a road trip to Buffalo some weekend.

He saved the pictures and kept reading: A message from Mrs. Conrad instructed him to check out some articles and interviews featuring a Massachusetts researcher named Cameron Thorne. "Don't post anything yet," she wrote, "but prepare two separate blogs, both of which should be in the 300-word range. I will let you know which to publish." Odd, but whatever. "The first should compliment Thorne's research and declare him the preeminent scholar in the field of pre-Columbian research. And the second should blast him out of the water."

While Amanda went to the county courthouse in Lowell with one of the Westford policeman to get a restraining order against Chung and sons, Cam swung by the bank and removed the bracelet from the safe deposit box, carrying the artifact in a maroon velvet bag with a drawstring that originally housed a bottle of private stock Captain Morgan spiced rum. Once back to his vehicle he placed the bracelet in a Ziploc bag and nestled the bag inside a cardboard box filled with Styrofoam worms. It seemed like an artifact that might change American history should be handled with more care, but short of putting the seatbelt around the box he wasn't sure what else he should do.

The lab in Lexington was a half hour drive away. To avoid the last of the morning rush hour traffic, Cam navigated his Chevy Equinox through some back roads to Route 225, a country highway which would take him through the idyllic towns of Carlisle and Concord before dumping him onto Route 2 for the final leg into Lexington. During the battles of Lexington and Concord, Minutemen from Westford had walked the same route, arriving too late to take part in the history-changing skirmish. Cam hoped to avoid any hostilities today as well.

Randall had called the night before to tell him the CIA might be tailing him.

"What should I do?" Cam had asked.

"Just ignore it."

It was like telling someone not to think about a pink polar bear. Cam's eyes darted from the rear view mirror to the side view mirror, only occasionally surveying the road ahead. But it turned out the trouble was in front of Cam, not behind.

As he crossed into Carlisle, traffic ahead of him slowed. A box truck sat disabled on an uphill curve, its bearded, burly driver standing in the street directing alternating lanes of traffic around it. He waved the cars ahead of Cam past, motioned Cam to stop and walked back to his truck. But instead of dealing with the oncoming traffic he jumped into his cab, spun the wheel and angled the presumably-disabled truck across both lanes of the road.

The Oath of Nimrod

Cam sensed danger immediately, his fingers tingling as if to confirm his fear. He threw his SUV into reverse and began to spin around, only to see a dark van screech to a sideways halt behind him. An Asian woman glared at him from the passenger seat. *Chung's mother.* Three men poured out of the van. They must have followed him from the bank and called ahead to set up the roadblock. He was blocked and surrounded.

Tearing the Ziploc bag from the cardboard box, Cam leapt from his vehicle and sprinted toward the woods lining the road. Chung and his sons broke after him, followed by the lumbering box truck driver. As Cam hurdled the snow bank he cursed, remembering he had left his cell phone in the cup holder. So much for calling for help.

He sank to his knees in soft snow as he fought his way to the woodlands bordering the road, stuffing the bracelet into his jacket pocket for safe keeping. Outracing his pursuers deep into the woods shouldn't be a problem. But then what? Presumably they had weapons, and presumably they had chosen this spot to ambush him because they had scouted the area and likely planned to use those weapons under the cover of the forest.

He scanned the landscape; he had been here before. The woods surrounding him were part of town preservation land. Just off the road sat a turtle-shaped rock formation he and Amanda had visited a few times as part of their stone structure investigations, and a nearby trail led to a mysterious stone chamber known as the Acton Potato Cave. Not that any of that would help him now. But there was one thing that might....

Following a cross-country ski trail he ran deeper into the woods, perpendicular to the road. A hundred yards in, the trail came to a T. Cam sprinted to the right another thirty yards, his boot tracks clearly visible in the snow, before leaping up to grab a low-hanging branch. Hanging down, he hand-walked his way to where the branch met its trunk and dropped into the deep snow a couple of body lengths off the trail. Crouching low, he edged his way back toward the T just as Chung and his two sons ran by, following his footprints. Cam waited a few seconds for the box truck driver. *He must have stayed on the road.* Still in the woods, Cam continued to double-back toward the T. When he reached the T, Cam followed the opposite trail stem, which angled parallel to the road alongside a small pond. Cam sprinted another fifty yards before again leaving the trail; he forced his way through the snow and underbrush, this time to peer across the pond back toward the street. *There.* Just as he remembered.

By now his pursuers would have realized he had doubled-back, but Cam had a decent head start. Taking advantage of some cross-country ski tracks on the pond, Cam raced across the frozen surface, fought through more underbrush and emerged at the mouth of a stone tunnel, built by a farmer in the early 1900s to allow for his cattle to cross safely under the street and drink at the pond. Ducking under the massive stone lintel, Cam crab-walked through the tunnel, the frigid groundwater almost up to his ankles, and emerged on the far side of the road. He peered around the cow tunnel toward the street. Chung's mother and the truck driver had pulled their vehicles to the side of the road and also apparently rolled Cam's SUV into a ditch, presumably as a cover story in case the police arrived—only four or five minutes had passed and with traffic flowing again apparently the police were not rushing to the scene. The tiny Asian woman and the burly trucker now stood on the far shoulder, peering into the woods, their backs to Cam.

Cam surveyed the situation and took a deep breath. Now was as good a time as any. Using the tunnel structure to partially conceal himself, he pulled himself up the road embankment and crept toward the box truck, careful to keep his footsteps quiet. He peered through the driver's window. No keys. *Damn.*

One more chance. And no reason to keep quiet now. Sprinting again, he spanned the short distance between the box truck and the dark van, his wet feet thwacking along the pavement. The old woman turned. "Hey! There he is!"

Cam ignored her and pulled open the van's front door. *Jackpot.* Leaping in, he turned the keys—the motor fired. Exhaling, he spun the van around and sped away. Tapping the horn twice, beep-beep, he stuck his hand out the window to wave goodbye.

Unfortunately he feared it was not likely their final farewell.

Cam fruitlessly searched the van for clues before dumping it at a shopping plaza. He took a taxi home, called a tow truck to retrieve his SUV and phoned Amanda to update her on his morning run-in. "Are you at the courthouse?" he asked.

"Yes. We got the restraining order. I'm still with the Westford detective. Should I tell him what happened?"

"Sure. But I don't want to press more charges yet. We can talk about it when you get home."

Amanda returned late morning. "I made sandwiches," Cam said. "I never made it to Lexington so I thought we could drive in together now." More than ever, he wanted to get the bracelet tested.

She grabbed a couple of Diet Cokes from the fridge and smiled. "You just want me along to fight off the bad guys."

"Speaking of which, I want to make sure we're not being followed again."

"By the CIA or by Chung?"

"Either. Both. Whatever. I'll meet you at the town beach in twenty."

Cam kissed Amanda, threw on his coat and boots and went out the back door. Venus pawed at the door behind him. "Sorry, girl, you have to stay." Following the shoreline he walked along the lake to a spillway where the lake emptied into a stream that ran, eventually, to the Atlantic. In order to leave their neighborhood and drive to the town beach, Amanda would need to cross over the spillway. Cam crouched low behind a dock and made himself comfortable.

Five minutes later Amanda drove past in her Subaru. Cam waited, watching to see if anyone followed. He checked his watch. Seven minutes and nothing. Clean so far. He jogged across the lake.

"So we're okay?" she asked as he jumped into the passenger seat.

"One last thing. Maybe they have some kind of tracking device on the car. I think it's time for a car wash."

Amanda drove to a self-serve wash in Chelmsford, where Cam turned up the pressure to full and blasted the under-carriage of her car with a soap-filled stream of hot water. "Unless they have top of the line equipment, that should fritz any GPS device."

"Where to now?"

"Lexington. But take the highway this time."

"You know," Amanda said as they headed south, "Chung and his family really are a bit inept. They've come after us three times, and three times they've failed."

"Well, the first time was only because Pugh showed up."

"Even so. What's that old expression? *A hero is only as heroic as his adversary is admirable.*"

"I've never heard that."

"That's why in great literature the villain is always so … daunting. The white whale in *Moby Dick,* Moriarty with Sherlock Holmes—"

Cam interjected. "The Penguin, the Joker, the Riddler, King Tut…"

She turned and smiled. "Batman is hardly great literature, but you get the point. In our case, I feel like we've bested Elmer Fudd."

Cam weighed her words, balancing them against Randall Sid's warning the CIA was playing mind control games with him. "Do you think this is all some sort of … game?"

She shrugged. "I don't know."

He held up his broken pinky. "This didn't feel like any game."

"And it felt pretty real out on the ice yesterday also," she said, shrugging. "But still…."

They rode in silence for the better part of a minute.

"Maybe I'm just being paranoid," Cam said.

"It's not paranoia if they really are after you," Amanda responded.

He nodded. "So who are *they*? And what do they want?"

Evgenia Samsanov-Johnson pulled her collar up and wrapped her scarf around her lower face as she rode the escalator up from Washington D.C.'s Union Station subway station. "Just snow already," she muttered as the cold, wind-driven rain whipped against her skin. Winter was fine, but this wind and freezing rain shit was miserable. Turning to the left, she stepped off a curb and splashed muddy slush left over from the last storm onto her long black skirt. "Goddamn it. I hate this city."

Actually, that wasn't true. Climate aside, she loved Washington. Where else could a woman in her mid-twenties without an advanced degree find a job that paid almost six figures without taking her clothes off? And the city was alive, vibrant, powerful. The center of the universe in many ways.

Head down, she angled up Massachusetts Avenue into the residential section of Capitol Hill. There were other neighborhoods closer and with an easier commute to her office in Virginia but they were too antiseptic for a six-foot tall, biracial woman who grew up in inner city Detroit. Capitol Hill, at least once you got a few blocks away from the Capitol itself, had some soul—Black families that had lived on the Hill for generations, a large gay and lesbian population, group houses filled with students and interns, young families pushing strollers, even a few senior Congressional staff. Evgenia didn't happen to fit into any of these categories, but the Hill had been home to her ever since she came to Washington from Detroit three years ago.

Ah, Detroit. Where in the winter actual snow fell from the sky. As also, famously, did octopi, thrown from the rafters by zealous hockey fans during Red Wings games. She had pretty much grown up watching her father play and the octopi fly at Joe Louis arena, the only place in America where if you drove a golf ball due south it would land in Canada. Not that she was allowed in the locker room with the other kids—she was relegated to the back of the press box with her mother, a former ice girl who worked her way up to a position as marketing director for the team. That was her mother's official position, at least; unofficially she was the African-American mistress to the smooth-skating Russian defenseman. Her dad's wife and kids stayed back in Moscow, where he returned in the offseason. But to his credit he acknowledged Evgenia, visited regularly, and in his own way even parented her a bit.

Most importantly, he taught her to play chess.

And playing chess is what she did for the CIA. Not chess in the traditional sense, on a square board using onyx pieces. But chess in a virtual sense, on the streets of America using flesh-and-bone pieces.

What she thought of as chess her coworkers referred to as puppeteering in their office suite in Langley, Virginia. Evgenia and a half-dozen others, euphemistically called masters, pulled the strings. Presumably they all had undergone the same series of rigorous personality, psychological and intelligence tests she had. The entire operation was overseen by a man they called Dr. Jag. Someone above him picked the targets, the puppets. Dr. Jag then assigned a master to each puppet, guided the masters and provided whatever support and assistance might be necessary.

Last week Dr. Jag had assigned Evgenia a new puppet. Some geology professor from Maine researching early exploration of North America. She recalled the conversation:

"New assignment for you, Evgenia." He dropped a red manila file on her desk. Always red, for some reason. "Name is Antonopoulos, Stefan Antonopoulos. Friends call him Ant."

"Ant? That's the best they could come up with?"

Dr. Jag shrugged. "It's Maine."

She rolled her eyes. "That mean he has six legs? If so, I'll need more strings. And a raise."

"Nice try." A tall, angular, middle-aged man, Dr. Jag stood in front of her desk, his hands folded behind his back like a math teacher, the oversized blue blazer he wore every day speckled with flakes of dandruff and strands of cat hair. She and the other strategists assumed he was a bachelor; he must have left the office to care for his cat, but nobody ever saw him do so. His glasses rested unevenly on his nose, and she had to resist the urge to reach over and clean the smudges off with a tissue. "You know the drill," he continued. "Step on the ant." He liked to talk tough like that, but Evgenia bet he had never so much as kicked a dog.

"You mean discredit him?"

"Yes. He's doing some pretty compelling work showing exploration of America before Columbus, based on a bunch of stone carvings. Discredit him, and his research."

"Why do we care?"

He tilted his head at her. "Really? You're still asking questions like that? *We* don't care. The people we work for do." He motioned out the window; they were ensconced in the center of the CIA complex in Langley. "And they want him discredited." He smiled at her, showing a row of straight but yellowing teeth. "We work on a need-to-know basis…"

She finished his sentence. "And I have no need to know." The compartmentalization and secrecy had bothered her at first; it drove her crazy sometimes that she was not allowed to see the big picture, the entire mission. Dr. Jag would give her an assignment—last week it had been to entice a foreign diplomat into investing in a start-up internet sales company—but never told the reason why. She didn't know if the end game was to bankrupt the diplomat and then later buy his loyalty or rather provide him with a financial windfall so he would be more resistant to being purchased by some enemy nation. And she would never know. Once she completed her task she never saw the file again. But, in her three years at the Agency, she had come to see that the system worked. Someone high above her pay grade kept track of all the moving pieces. And the

Agency, bloated as it was, did some of the best intelligence work in the history of the world.

Pointing at the Antonopoulos file, Dr. Jag added: "I will say that this assignment came down with a little more urgency than usual—"

"So you put your best agent on it," she interjected. Smiling, she flipped open the folder and studied the professor. Classically handsome face, features you'd see on an old statue in Athens or Rome. Mid-thirties, wife, three young kids, nice smile. One of the top-ranked amateur tennis players in New England. "Okay. So what are his buttons?" Every puppet had buttons to push, some weakness or flaw or character trait that could be exploited and eventually used against him. Sometimes money, sometimes women, sometimes a desire for fame or power or glory.

"He's pretty solid; by all accounts a genuinely nice guy. I'd say if he has one weakness it's that he's obsessed with getting tenure. Top of his class at Bates, came back to teach, would be the youngest guy ever to become a full professor. Enjoys being the smartest guy in the room, and never had any reason to doubt he was. But some of the old-timers don't like his research, especially the history faculty. So tenure's not a sure thing."

"Why?"

"A lot of them came up during the 'Columbus-first' era. They've spend a lifetime debunking anything before 1492. So if they're proven wrong, they've all got egg on their face. Lots of it."

She nodded, glanced at his photo again. *Too bad women weren't his weakness.* "So is he? Smart, I mean."

"Apparently so."

"So what's the play?"

"He's coming to town for a conference. He's meeting a woman from Baltimore who has a stone artifact her mother found in Vermont in the late 1970s. It has strange carvings on it that Antonopoulos thinks might be important." Dr. Jag pushed his glasses up his nose. "You'll need to contact the woman—name is Rachel Gold—and tell her we're investigating this professor. Tell her he has a history of 'borrowing' these artifacts and then selling them to collectors after authenticating them. Overseas, which is why the CIA is involved."

"Does he?"

He grimaced. "Of course not. Tell her you'd like to come with her when she meets the good professor so you can witness him taking the rock. Tell Antonopoulos you're college friends or something. The Rachel woman grew up in Connecticut, where the mother still lives."

"Then what?"

"See how it plays out." Dr. Jag dropped three more folders—older ones, faded red—on her desk. "These are a few older cases. Same kind of deal. Researchers trying to prove ancient explorers came to America. One guy, Fell, was a linguist; Whitewood was an archeologist; Glynn was just a guy who loved history. We discredited them all. Take a look through, maybe you can get some ideas how to go after Antonopoulos."

She glanced at the folders. "Why do I need new ideas? What about just sticking with him selling other people's artifacts?"

Dr. Jag shrugged. "If you think you can make it work, fine with me. There's an incident documented in the file where our professor took some liberties with an artifact that had been lent to him—he claimed it was given as a gift."

Evgenia considered the option. It wasn't the most artful ruse, but sometimes the best plans were the simple ones. And he already had a prior incident—effective lies were always build on a foundation of truth. "I could set up a fake email exchange in which he offers to sell the artifact."

"I think you'll need more than that. In the end you'll need to actually put the money in the good professor's account if we're going to make this stick."

"Do I have it? Money, I mean?"

"It is the one thing, my dear, the Agency never seems to lack," he said as he walked away.

A week had passed and she had set into motion a plan involving Antonopoulos. It was a straightforward assignment and not all that difficult; she would be playing chess against a man who didn't even realize the game was on and who only possessed a single piece on the board—himself. It was impossible to control or even predict Antonopoulos' every move, but it was only a matter of time before she used her superior forces to position him into a corner and limit his options. She kicked at a chunk of slush in her path. The problem was that he seemed like a nice guy who had done nothing wrong. And she, on behalf of their government, was in the process of destroying him.

She trusted there was a good reason for it. Or at least hoped there was.

The phone rang as Cam stood in front of the stove, stir-frying chicken and vegetables. Astarte had an indoor soccer game tonight so they were having an early dinner. He turned down the burner.

"Mr. Thorne, we have preliminary metallurgy results on that bracelet you dropped off." Cam had paid extra for expedited turnaround. He pictured a young woman in glasses and a lab-coat, her hair pulled back in a bun. But maybe that was just from watching too much television.

Cam swallowed. "Okay, shoot."

"Well, first of all it's not copper like you thought. It's yellow brass."

"What does that tell you?"

"By itself, not much. But what is informative is the zinc content in the bracelet. It's at twenty-seven percent. For modern objects, the zinc content is usually much higher. And in ancient times it was lower. It has to do with the cementation process, and the price of the various metals. I can explain in more detail if you'd like—"

"No, that's okay. So can you date the bracelet?"

"We find brass artifacts with this concentration of zinc occurring twice in the historical timeline: First, in the Mediterranean area in the first and second centuries AD."

Cam's throat tightened. *Holy shit.* "And the second?"

"In the nineteenth century this mixture was common here in the U.S. for industrial uses—things like brass plumbing fixtures and chandelier ornaments. I've never seen it used for jewelry, but I suppose it's possible."

"Wait, so the bracelet could be either first century Mediterranean or nineteenth century American?"

"Yes," she concluded.

Cam mulled it over. The science had narrowed things down from two possibilities to ... two possibilities. Either the bracelet was an authentic ancient Jewish artifact brought to America two thousand years ago or it was one of thousands of cheap trinkets found buried in Native American graves during the pioneering era.

But there was one piece of data Cam possessed that the metallurgist didn't: Polished wood found in the burial mound with the bracelet had been carbon-dated to the second century AD. In and of itself, the wood didn't prove anything—the body could simply have been buried with old wooden artifacts or tools or wood scraps. But together with the bracelet, and of course the inscribed tablet itself, the evidence had become almost irrefutable. As if preparing for a closing argument, Cam summarized the bullet-points in his head:

- The script carved on the stone was an ancient form of Hebrew, prevalent in the early centuries after Christ;
- The geological testing showed the carving was at least many centuries old at the time the artifact was removed from the ground in the late 1800s;

- The carbon-dating showed that the wood found in the burial mound was almost two thousand years old;
- Cherokee oral history spoke of ancient explorers arriving from across the Atlantic;
- Now, metallurgy testing confirmed the Mediterranean area circa AD 100-200 as one of two possible origins of the bracelet.

Cam pictured himself in front of a jury, arguing the case. It was becoming almost impossible to reach any conclusion other than the burial mound objects being almost two thousand years old.

He stared at the phone in his hand and shook his head. Somehow ancient Jews had made it to Tennessee. And nobody knew.

Evgenia barely had time to throw on a pair of jeans and some dry socks, never mind shower. It would have been a great night to sit in front of the TV and watch the Capitals game, but duty called. Maybe the game would be on in the bar. Or maybe this Stefan Antonopoulos would be as handsome as his picture and she wouldn't care about the game.

She and Rachel had met last night at the Hawk & Dove for a dry run. The girl was nervous and frightened. The last thing Evgenia needed was for her to freak out when they met with Antonopoulos. But by the end of the evening Evgenia had convinced her things would be fine. "We're not even sure he's really a crook. And even if he is, it's not like he's violent or anything. But we've had a couple of reports, so we need to look into it. And this way your mother is protected in case the artifact really is valuable."

Evgenia arrived at ten past seven, watched in satisfaction in the bar mirror as a number of heads turned as she passed. It was nice to feel attractive, though she knew her look was singularly non-traditional, a combination of her mother's wide nose and high cheekbones and her father's thin Slavic face. Every once in a while people told her she looked like a taller version of Lisa Bonet, the daughter on the old *Cosby Show* sitcom. She was fine with the comparison, as the actress had a futuristic, multi-racial look that Evgenia imagined would be the norm centuries from now. In that future, she often wondered, would society still insist on using ill-fitting labels to describe people like her? She was not African-American or Black or Eurasian—none of these fit her. She was, simply, multi-racial.

She found Rachel in a booth upstairs on the mezzanine level. The place used to pride itself on being a dive bar, but recent renovations had purged it of most of its soul. Which was fine for tonight—they didn't need some drunk spilling a pitcher on them. Evgenia's first inclination had been to meet at the Irish Times pub near Union Station—she had fallen in love with the place the first time she saw the welcome sign: *Give me your thirsty, your famished, your befuddled masses.* But it was too centrally located and one of her Agency coworkers might inadvertently blow her cover. The Hawk & Dove, on the other hand, was on the back side of Capital Hill where only Congressional staff members hung out, plus the mezzanine afforded them extra privacy.

She slid into the booth next to Rachel and turned to face her. "Hi again," Rachel said. Big brown eyes, dark curly hair, a nose that looked like it used to be longer but for a surgeon's knife. Not bad looking. Based on their conversation last night, a theater major from George Washington University who now worked in advertising.

"You doing okay?"

Rachel exhaled. "Yes."

"Just use your theater training. You're playing a part."

"But there are no lines. That's what's making me nervous."

"But the part you're playing is yourself. You're just here to give him the artifact. He'll take the lead, I promise." She smiled confidently at Rachel. "You have the rock?"

126

Rachel patted a black leather saddle bag on the seat next to her. "Right here." She wrestled a rectangular, light gray stone from the bag. It was bigger than Evgenia thought it would be, the size of a gift box in which you'd find a fancy bottle of champagne.

"What does that thing weigh?" Evgenia asked, accepting the rock.

Rachel shifted her shoulder. "Too much. Maybe thirty pounds."

Evgenia stood, leaned the artifact upright against the cushioned booth and snapped a few pictures with her smart phone. Four rows of writing dominated the front face of the stone, with a spiral design carved below the bottom row. Evgenia didn't recognize the first three rows of script but the fourth row looked like Hebrew.

Vermont Rune Stone

Rachel talked as Evgenia examined the rock. "My mother found it on vacation in Vermont when she was a kid. She forgot she even had it until my Bubbie was cleaning out her attic."

"How did you hear about Professor Antonopoulos?"

"My Bubbie saw him on a TV documentary and called my mother."

Evgenia handed the stone back. "Okay, put it away for now. Just play it cool; like I said, let him take the lead. I'm pretty sure he'll want to take the rock with him." She grinned. "Wouldn't be much of a thief if he let you keep the goods."

Rachel smiled nervously. She said, "I also brought my mom's diary entry from when she found it. Is that okay?"

"Perfect. Those kinds of details just make the story seem more real."

Rachel frowned. "It *is* real."

"I know. The artifact is real, but this set-up is not. So the more we can get him to focus on the artifact instead of us, the better."

"Okay, here he comes."

Rachel took a deep breath and gave a shy wave; Antonopoulos nodded, shook the moisture off his jacket and strolled over. He smiled at Rachel and shook her hand, then did the same as Rachel introduced him to Evgenia. "I think I've been here before," he said as he slid into the booth opposite them. "But it's changed." He smiled again. Kind but not flirtatious. "I miss the smell of old beer."

Evgenia studied him. Just as handsome as his picture, and he moved the way her father and his teammates did, coiled and powerful but with an athletic grace. *Plus he liked dive bars.* But not as tall as she expected, maybe only five-foot eight.

She sighed. She needed a vacation, a beach someplace where she could look at men and dance a bit. Washington was a tough place to be a single woman—many of the single men were gay, and most of the straight ones were dweebs or scared off by her height. And, of course, she hated the weather. Maybe this well-paying job wasn't such a great deal after all....

"Evgenia says they just renovated," Rachel responded. "Anyway, thanks for coming all the way into the city."

"And thanks for coming down from Baltimore. I'd go a lot further than that to see this rock of yours." He shrugged. "Plus

I needed a break. I'm up in Bethesda for a conference. A bunch of rock nerds together for three days. I *really* need a drink."

He motioned to a waitress, the wedding ring on his left hand catching the light from an overhead fixture. Rachel ordered a glass of wine, Evgenia and Antonopoulos a Sam Adams. He smiled at Evgenia. "If they're down to the last bottle, I call dibs."

"Doubtful. There's lots of Bostonians down here. I'm sure they have a few cases."

"Actually," he said, "I read that Sam Adams is brewed in Cincinnati, not Boston."

She smiled. *There. The smartest guy in the room.*

He took out a small reporter's pad and pen. "Rachel, do you mind if I take some notes?"

She shrugged. "Fine with me."

"So can you tell me again when and where your mother found this? Any detail you can provide will be helpful."

"Well, I guess I can start with this." She slid a piece of copy paper across the table. "This is a copy of my mom's diary from the day she found the rock. She was thirteen. It was 1978." Antonopoulos studied the paper while Rachel talked. "Basically, it just says she was with her family on vacation in Vermont. They were playing in the woods. She saw this rock, with writing on it, sticking out of the dirt."

"Do you know where in Vermont?"

"We had a beach house up on Lake Memphremagog, near the Canadian border."

Antonopoulos looked up. "Interesting. There are some fascinating artifacts found in that area. Many researchers believe the Templars had a settlement there in the 1400s."

"That's what my Bubbie said when she called my mom. She saw you on TV. She said the Templars carved this stone."

"This could be a really important find. Really important." He smiled and rested his eyes onto Rachel's. "So how many drinks do I have to buy you before I get to see the stone?"

Evgenia watched the interaction. Even this last comment wasn't said flirtatiously. At some point Antonopoulos must have learned it was dangerous to be as handsome as he was and also be on a campus full of young women. What he didn't realize was that treating women in an asexual manner possessed him with the one quality women found irresistible—it made him seem impossibly hard to get.

Rachel flustered. "Oh, sorry." Using both hands, she hoisted the rock across the table. "Here it is."

Antonopoulos pushed his beer aside to study the stone. Using a closed pen, he pointed at the carvings. "These are runic letters, from Scandinavia. Just like English, the characters change over time—these look to be medieval to me."

"So what does it say?" Rachel asked.

He frowned. "I don't know; I'll need some help translating it." He moved the pen. "And this, as I think you know, is Hebrew. And the spiral at the bottom is also very interesting—it's an ancient Goddess symbol." He sat back. "This is the first artifact I've ever seen that has Hebrew, runic and a Goddess symbol all together." He shifted forward again and peered at the stone, a bit of sweat on his upper lip. "This combination points strongly to the Knights Templar—as religious monks, they were versant in Hebrew; many of them also spoke runic; and we believe they were secretly Goddess worshipers, which explains the spiral."

Antonopoulos pulled a jeweler's glass from his jacket pocket and began to examine the artifact more closely.

Evgenia studied him studying the stone for a few seconds and said, "I like a man who carries his own magnifying glass," She was curious to see if he'd respond to her any more amorously than he had to Rachel.

He didn't look up. "Actually, this a loupe. It has multiple lenses, unlike a magnifying glass."

Again, more interested in the rock than in flirting with her. In fact, Evgenia was probably a distant fourth—behind the artifact, his loupe and his beer.

He looked up at Rachel and set his jaw. "Rachel, is there any chance I can keep this for a few days?" he asked, one hand still on the stone.

Evgenia caught her eye. *Don't be too easy.*

"Well, I don't know…"

"Rachel, this could be very important. This could change history. But I need to study it under a microscope." He again rested his eyes on Rachel's. This time he added a shy smile and reached out to touch her hand. *So he did know how to flirt.* "I promise I'll take good care of it."

Normally Amanda attended all of Astarte's soccer games, but she begged off tonight and let Cam bring her. Cam had relayed Randall's warning about Astarte creating a point of vulnerability for Cameron that the CIA might try to exploit. But bugger that. It was important Astarte and Cam spend time alone together, just the two of them. Thankfully Astarte liked sports, so that gave Cam and her something to share—Cam was a devoted parent, but he was not big on makeovers and manicures.

Cam hesitated at the door. "You sure you're okay alone?"

Amanda took a deep breath. They could not very well stop living their lives. "The police are patrolling regularly. And I have Venus."

She locked the doors, put on the outside lights, made sure her phone was charged and by her side, and took the opportunity to do more giants research. The subject fascinated her. Plus it took her mind off of being home alone.

She had recently read that a race of pygmies, showing a genetic divergence from all other human populations going back 60,000 years, lived in the rain forests of central Africa. So why couldn't a race of giants have existed at one time also?

Tonight she planned on approaching the research from a different angle—from the mouth. Using the online site of the Journal of the American Dental Association, she did a search using the word 'hyperdontia,' the medical term for extra teeth. The articles were dry and thick with medical terminology, but eventually she found an article from the 1970s written by a dentist who removed a full second set of teeth from a young man attending Harvard Divinity School. Two aspects of this case made it remarkable: First, it involved a full set of teeth, whereas most cases of hyperdontia involved only a few teeth. And second, the dentist noted in the medical history section that the patient's height was six foot, ten inches tall.

Was this second set of teeth caused by some recessive gene that randomly appeared every so many generations? If so, could it be because of interbreeding in the past with one of the ancient giants? Or perhaps she was just being loony....

Venus barked at the door, announcing Cam and Astarte's return. "How was the game?"

"Great," Astarte said.

"Did you win?"

Astarte furrowed her brow. "I'm not sure. Dad-Cam, did we win?"

Cam smiled. "Depends how you keep score. Astarte won if you're counting smiles. The other team won if you're counting goals, six to four." Amanda had been a competitive gymnast as a child—it was a cutthroat world where nobody counted smiles. But Cam had convinced her youth sports should be about fun and learning life skills, not just winning. "As long as she is trying hard and getting exercise and being a good teammate, who cares who wins?" he said. "There'll be plenty of time to keep score as she gets older."

Astarte stuck out a purple tongue. "We got popsicles after the game. I had grape."

"I can see that." She kissed Astarte on the cheek. "Go take your shower and put on pajamas. I'll make you a snack."

She also kissed Cam, lingering for a few seconds. "You taste like lemon. Did you have a popsicle too?"

He smiled. "I worked hard. We did the wave in the bleachers."

They sat at the kitchen table; she told Cam about the divinity student with the extra set of teeth. "Interesting," he said. "Six-ten is not really gigantic, but it's getting there."

"If there had been interbreeding, say, two thousand years ago, the height would have decreased as the giant genes became diluted."

"Makes sense. Why do you use the two thousand year old date?"

"That's sort of a middle date for when the giants would have lived," she said. "Most of the skeletons were found in burial mounds. Some of the mounds are older than that, some younger. But around two thousand years ago was the peak." That was later than the latest Biblical reference to giants by a millennium, not a huge amount of time in evolutionary terms.

"Two thousand years ago is around the date of the Bat Creek burial mound."

She nodded. "I know Emmert didn't find giant bones in that particular mound, but he did find giant skeletons in other burial mounds in the area."

"Meaning?"

She shrugged. "I'm not certain. I suppose, meaning that the giants coexisted with other civilizations in North America."

"And if so, they may have interbred. Which would explain your divinity school student with the double rows of teeth."

Amanda stood suddenly. Cam's observation triggered something. "Be back straightaway." She rushed to retrieve her laptop and opened to the dental journal article as she returned. Her eyes raced across the page, her heart rate increasing. "Here it is."

Still standing, she looked down at Cam. "The article says the divinity school student was one-eighth Cherokee."

Vito was just about to call it a night and watch an old Star Trek episode when the email came in from Mrs. Conrad. "Regarding Thorne," it read, "slam him. And make it personal. I would like to see it before you post it. Top priority."

Excellent, he was hoping she'd ask him to post the critical commentary rather than the complimentary one. It made him feel ... powerful. Or at least relevant. And Tammy from Buffalo seemed to like it when he posted strong, aggressive opinions. To hell with Star Trek. He had work to do.

Not that he had anything against this Cameron Thorne guy. But obviously he had done something to piss off the government, so he probably deserved whatever he got. Vito flexed his fingers and pulled up the draft of what he had already written—it was critical, but not personal. Vito closed his eyes, thought of all the times the cool kids in school had teased him, mocked him, made him feel insignificant. He thought of his stepfather doing the same thing. This guy Thorne was just like them, successful and smart and good-looking....

And arrogant. So fucking arrogant.

Vito clenched his teeth and began to type.

CHAPTER 5

As was their morning routine, Cam and Venus walked Astarte to the bus stop while Amanda cleaned up after breakfast. Cam returned and left again on a run while Amanda read the morning news and caught up on email. One of those emails was a Google Alert, notifying her of a new blog post discussing the Newport Tower. But this wasn't just any blog post, and it didn't limit itself to the Newport Tower.

By the time she had finished, her hands were shaking. "What a flaming load of rubbish," she hissed. Taking a deep breath, she reread the article. It began:

Disgraced Massachusetts attorney Cameron Thorne, who apparently can no longer make a living as a lawyer since having his law license suspended, now spends his time promoting fake history—for a fee, of course—to an unsuspecting public.

As if that weren't bad enough, the article went on to accuse him of using Amanda as part of his ruse.

Ever notice how all those fake history documentaries on TV use a narrator with a British accent, as if we Americans are so easily swayed by the Queen's English? Well, Thorne takes it one step further: He parades out some British tart in a short skirt, who Thorne claims is his 'fiancée,' as a mouthpiece. "Tallyho, we Brits were crossing the pond long before Columbus," she parrots as Thorne nods sagely while counting his money.

Amanda felt like smashing something. And it got worse:

David S. Brody

But perhaps Thorne's cheapest trick is his use of a nine-year-old Native American girl he claims to be in the process of 'adopting' (note to self—contact the Massachusetts state authorities on this one). Thorne bases many of his claims of pre-Columbian exploration of America on—you guessed it— Native American oral history. Of course, this history (how convenient for him that it is 'oral' and therefore can't be verified) was passed on to Thorne through his intimate relationship with Native Americans. Proof of this 'intimacy,' apparently, is that they are allowing him to foster-parent one of their orphaned children. One can only hope that Thorne does not dress up this poor girl in braids and a headdress, put her in a teepee with a peace pipe in her mouth, teach her to greet visitors with a, "How, White Man," and charge admission. (Speaking of White Man, ever notice how make-it-up-as-they-go historians like Thorne always try to sell us on other white Europeans coming to America? They never talk about Asian or African explorers. Simple ignorance, or outright racism? You be the judge.)

The post concluded:

The reason Thorne resorts to these theatrics, of course, is that none of the revisionist history this huckster is peddling is true. The artifacts he relies on are amateurish fakes (note #2 to self—check with Massachusetts authorities regarding the legality of using fake artifacts as a pretense for collecting speaker fees), and the so-called 'evidence' he provides to support his theories is a laughable compilation of random and unrelated occurrences cobbled together by a disgraced lawyer trained to twist and bend facts to best serve his needs. Do yourself a favor: If someone invites you to go listen to this charlatan speak, stay home and watch old episodes of the Flintstones cartoons instead—Fred and Barney are at least as smart as Thorne, and the idea of cavemen and dinosaurs coexisting is closer to the truth than anything Thorne and his traveling circus would have you believe.

Cam burst through the door just as Amanda finished reading. "Well," he proclaimed, "that was a great run. What a beautiful day."

She sighed, stood and greeted him with a hug. "I'm afraid it's about to take a turn for the worse."

Cam made Amanda tell him what was going on before he got into the shower. It was actually a relief—from the look on her face he was afraid something had happened to Astarte. The blog was just words. As a lawyer he dealt with this kind of stuff all the time. It was easy to be nasty when you didn't have to look someone in the eye. They called it 'keyboard muscle'— anonymity and distance made everyone brave. Cam doubted this Vito Augustine guy, whoever he was, would have the balls to say anything to his face.

But that didn't change the fact that this post was now live, and based on the number of comments already it looked like half the world was reading it. And once something was live on the internet, it was there forever. Some museum curator posted a mistake-filled critique of the Westford Knight carving in the late 1990s and fifteen years later critics still relied on it as 'proof' the carving was a hoax.

"So what are you going to do?" Amanda asked.

Cam grabbed a bottle of water from the fridge. "Not sure yet. I have to tip my hat to the guy—he did a good job going right up the line of committing libel but not crossing it."

"Not crossing it? He accuses you of using Astarte as some kind of carnival freak."

"Actually, he's careful not to. He says something about hoping I *don't* use her that way. It's the same result. But legally, it's different."

"He implies you are some kind of ... sexual predator."

"He implies, but he doesn't actually say it. Randall warned us about this."

"And he calls you a racist." Amanda was pacing the kitchen, her cheeks flushed.

"Actually, he just poses the question and asks his readers to decide."

She kicked a stool and splashed some water on her face. "Well," she exhaled, "what about the other stuff?"

He was as angry as she was, but it wouldn't help to have both of them kicking furniture. "All of it is true: You are British, my law license was suspended, and I do collect speaker fees." He smiled. "And Fred and Barney are smarter than me."

She didn't even crack a smile at his attempt at humor. "How can you be so calm? This guy just attacked you, attacked *us*."

He stepped forward and folded her into his arms. "Believe it or not, I'm used to this stuff. It happens all the time. Maybe not as personal as this, but the same kind of hyperbole. Lawyers use words as weapons. This guy Vito Augustine would have made a good attorney."

She exhaled into his chest and, after a few seconds, pulled away. "Well I'm not used to it, Cameron. And I don't take kindly to my family being attacked."

"Look, I'm pissed too. But it's not like I can track him down and go kick his ass. Not that it's not tempting."

"I suppose not."

"But I think there's more going on here than just some jerk with a blog deciding to take shots at me. As far as I know, I never even met the guy. So why come after me? There are plenty of guys who register higher on the crazy meter than I do—I'm not the one claiming reptile aliens populated the earth." He paused, tried again to lighten the mood. "And I'm not the one claiming giants used to roam around North America."

Amanda slapped him on the chest.

"Anyway, like I said, I have to believe there's something else going on here."

"Are you thinking this relates to the CIA brainwashing stuff? Is this their way to get under your skin somehow?"

"I don't know. It sounds a bit like the Jacques Autier thing to discredit Laurence Gardner. And it does seem odd for the blogger to hint at some kind of inappropriateness involving Astarte, as Randall predicted. I'll run it all by Randall, see what he thinks."

Amanda pulled her phone from her jean's pocket. "While you do that, I'm going to call Georgia. Maybe she can sniff around a bit also."

Georgia answered the phone on the first ring, walked over to close her office door and lowered her voice. "Well, hello. This was shaping up to be another boring day in Happy Land. Can you liven it up?"

"Perhaps too much," Amanda laughed.

"Hell, hearing a foreign accent is the most exciting thing that's happened to me all week."

Amanda laughed again. But it sounded forced.

Georgia continued, "Before we get to the new stuff, let me tell you what I've found out about your bracelet. Yes, it disappeared back in the 1950s. Yes, they do think it's important. No, they don't have any idea where it is."

"Thanks. What about the MK-Ultra program?"

"Answers there are a bit fuzzier. When I first started poking around, I got nothing. Then I got a call back, asking if my query had anything to do with the Lovecroft campaign." She laughed. "So I lied and said of course it did, figuring that was what they wanted to hear. Turns out the program is still active, but it's wrapped up pretty tight. Still working on mind control and behavior modification. But that's as far as I got. I mentioned Cam's name but no bites."

Amanda sighed. "Thanks. Can you look into something else for me?" She described how a blogger had trashed Cam;

Georgia found the site and skimmed through it as Amanda spoke. "Cam thinks it's too random and too harsh and too personal to be legitimate. He wonders if someone put the blogger up to it."

"And you think maybe it's part of MK-Ultra." Georgia scratched down the blogger's name. *Vito Augustine.*

"Yes." Amanda also described how the Chinese restaurant owners came after Cam again, and how metallurgy testing showed a good chance the bracelet from the Bat Creek mound was authentic. "But everything feels a bit … odd. Or off. The blog post seems unduly harsh; the Chinese blokes seem inept; this Randall Sid chap dropping into our life seems too random."

"Not to mention the bracelet showing up in your Chinese food in the first place. I agree. It's not the way the world usually works." She doodled for a few seconds. "What are you guys working on now?"

"The bracelet, of course. And Cam and Randall went to see the Narragansett Rune Stone this week; apparently there's a connection to the Vinland Map and the Mellon family." She paused. "And I've been doing some research on giants."

"Giant whats?"

"Just giants. Large humans. You know, Goliath and such." Amanda summarized her research into the skeletons. "Turns out many of them have six fingers and a double row of teeth."

"The six finger thing comes from the Bible, so I guess that's not surprising. But I've never heard of the double teeth."

"That's precisely what makes it intriguing. It's such a random characteristic, yet we find it in hundreds of different accounts from all over the continent."

Georgia sighed. "Intriguing, yes. But a reason for the CIA to come after you guys? I don't see it. But I'll dig around a bit more. I'll start with this blogger and see where it leads."

"Thanks, Georgia. How's the campaign going?"

She enjoyed discussing politics with Amanda, who often had a unique and fresh perspective on American elections. "Putting the boredom aside, the word I would use is refreshing.

Lovecroft is much different than other candidates—in some ways he's the anti-candidate. He honestly doesn't care if his positions are unpopular; he's a little like John McCain in that respect. But I think that's why voters like him. There's no bullshit with him."

"Can he win?"

Originally Georgia had given him only a twenty percent chance. But recently she had doubled that. Normally her job as a political operative, her 'cover' if you will, did not overlap with her career in the CIA. Recently, however, her bosses in Langley had begun to take an interest in Lovecroft's candidacy. Usually the CIA stayed out of American politics, but she was getting the sense that many of the nation's power elite, including senior members of the CIA, were rallying behind Lovecroft as a necessary remedy to what ailed the country— and it didn't hurt that they already knew and trusted him through his work as Chair of the Senate Intelligence Committee. Reading between the lines, Georgia wouldn't be surprised to learn the Agency was working to sway the election. Within the CIA, few seemed to take heed of Woodrow Wilson's warning that the history of liberty mirrored the history of a limitation on governmental power. For most senior Agency officials, the ends always justified the means.

She couldn't reveal all this to Amanda, so she settled for, "Yes, I think he can win. From what I hear from Washington, there's a growing belief that we need someone like him as our next President to get us out of the political gridlock we are in. As long as nobody asks him about Cuba...."

"I'm sorry, Cuba?"

"He made a statement years ago about leading a Crusade to free the Cuban Christians. Probably not the smartest thing he's ever said."

"Well, he's a bit conservative for my taste, but I see what you mean about him being likeable. Reminds me of Maggie Thatcher in some ways. Not my cup of tea, but the right person at the right time."

Someone knocked on Georgia's door. "Sorry, but I have to run. I'll look into that blogger for you. Hugs to Cam and Astarte."

Georgia hung up as a few others of the Senator's campaign staff arrived with coffee and pastries for the morning briefing. But she was distracted. Explaining things to Amanda had caused a few of her suspicions to coalesce in her mind: Was the CIA running an active mission to sway the Presidential election? If so, was she herself one of the operation's stage puppets? Had, for the first time, the lines between her cover and her mission been blurred?

Stefan Antonopoulos wiped the muffin crumbs off his fingers and carefully placed the Vermont carved stone beneath the microscope. One thing about being at a geology conference was that there were plenty of scopes around; nobody batted an eye when he pulled one out at the breakfast table. He had been dying to examine the stone last night but he got waylaid in the hotel bar and he was too professional to examine the artifact after a few tequila shots....

He began by focusing the microscope on an uncarved portion of the stone. The bedrock from which the stone originated had probably been exposed by a retreating glacier during the end of the last Ice Age and had, therefore, been weathering in an outdoor environment for at least ten thousand years. This weathering—primarily caused by wind, rain and freeze-thaw cycles—had, as would be expected, scoured the surface of the stone, wearing away soft or brittle minerals from its surface.

The telling part of his examination would be an inspection of the carved grooves. They, too, would exhibit weathering patterns, depending on how recently the grooves had been carved and therefore how long the carved areas had been exposed to the elements. In short, the more the carved areas resembled the uncarved areas in a mineralogical sense, the older the inscription would have to be.

Adjusting the focus, Antonopoulos honed in randomly on one of the lines of carved runic characters. This was always the most exciting part of his work, not knowing what the scope would reveal. Involuntarily, his eye widened, his eyelid rubbing against the scope's eyepiece. He dried his hand on his pants and took a deep breath to slow his breathing. The groove was almost pristine—smooth, free of soft minerals and barely pitted. In fact, the grooved area looked nearly identical to the face of the stone. Which meant the carving must be centuries old.

Antonopoulos sat back and took another deep breath. "Hey, Linda, can you come take a look at this?" he said, calling over a respected middle-aged geology professor from the University of Vermont. "Do those carved areas look old to you?"

She, like Antonopoulos, examined the face of the stone before turning to the grooved areas. She lifted her head. "Really old. The groove I looked at was pretty weathered. Not much left in there."

"That's what I thought." He looked back at the stone; granite this hard was known to resist weathering. His heart began to race. "Is the rock native to Vermont?"

She pushed her chair away from the table and grabbed her coffee cup. "Barre Gray granite, named after Barre, Vermont. Doesn't get any more native than that."

"How old would you guess that carving is?"

She laughed. "You're not going to get me to go on record with that, Stefan." She looked him in the eye. "But I wouldn't leave that artifact lying around."

What to do, what to do? Randall paced around his brother's condominium, the same thirty-minute morning news cycle repeating itself for the third time. It might snow, there would be traffic, the government did not have enough money, and another politician was going to jail. He turned off the television.

The sheer drudgery of life was the worst part of retirement. It was not staying alive that was the difficult thing, it was *living* while doing so that was proving to be the challenge. After his morning yoga routine to stay fit and limber, what? Lately Randall even looked forward to spending extra time at the Lodge—Monday night's initiation ceremony and subsequent cognac and cigar session didn't break up until well past midnight and, he was happy to report, none of the new initiates had invoked the name of Nimrod and run off to sacrifice children to Baal. His recent mission with Cameron Thorne helped fill his day. But Randall rarely slept more than four hours a night and with his brother away there was nobody to handicap the horse races with or compete against on a crossword puzzle.

It was not supposed to be like this. Was not supposed to end like this. Consuela was supposed to be here with him. Or him in Cuba with her. But he had chosen duty, chosen his career, over love. Often he indulged in an imaginary conversation with Consuela: *Had you chosen otherwise,* she invariably said, *then you would not have been the man I fell in love with in the first place.* He sighed. Would she really have let him off the hook like that, or was this imaginary conversation simply the self-serving musings of an old, sad man? The answer did not really matter. He had made his choice. Daily, his loneliness attested to it.

Tomorrow, at least, he could kill an hour with his weekly walk to Copp's Hill Burying Ground to the gravestone of Mr. Prince Hall, an early Boston resident and abolitionist who founded a Masonic Lodge for Boston's black community. Randall made the regular trek to the North End for three reasons: first, Hall was a hero of his; second, Randall loved Italian pastries; and third, he had made a vow almost sixty years ago to visit the grave weekly to look for a single yellow rose meant as a secret signal to him. He had long given up any expectation of seeing that rose, but he could not bring himself completely to give up hope. Or the pastries....

But Copp's Hill would be tomorrow's activity. Perhaps today he would take the subway to Suffolk Downs and watch the simulcast races from Gulfstream and the other warm-weather tracks. He and his brother had practically grown up at the track—most of their father's career was spent riding there and their mother worked one of the betting windows. His parents made an odd couple—he was slight and lighter-skinned and soft-spoken while she was a tank of a woman with dark skin and a booming voice. Once, as kids, they had held a color swatch from a paint store up to their parents' faces and decided Dad was maple while Mom was ebony. Their parents had always told them they came from the Dominican Republic—apparently for immigration reasons—but while in high school Randall discovered they were actually from Cuba. Funny how the discovery meant nothing to his twin brother but completely altered the course of Randall's life....

A life that was winding down. Eighty may be the 'new seventy,' but either way it was still old. He wondered about his legacy. What meaningful thing had he done, what accomplishment would cause his death to headline the day's obituary page? There was nothing, unfortunately. He went to work, did his job, came home and ate Chinese food. What had happened to his dreams?

The phone rang, rescuing him from his melancholy. "Good morning, Cameron."

"Not really."

Well, this might be interesting, at least. "How so?"

"I just emailed you a link. Read it and call me back."

Randall sat at his computer and did as instructed. *Yes, this was getting interesting.* He phoned Cameron. "I was always partial to Fred Flintstone. He was a loyal member of the Water Buffalo Lodge, which of course was meant to poke fun at us Freemasons."

"Well, I'm the one being poked fun at now."

"Yes, I can see that."

"Do you think this is related to the CIA targeting me, or is it just random?"

"Nothing is just random. So, yes, I think it comes from the Agency."

"Why?"

Randall stared out his window at the Hancock Tower rising up out of a field of Back Bay brownstones like a single oak in a pasture. His brother had the better views, but his own Chinatown apartment was only a block away from dim sum. Really, it was no contest—one could not eat a view. He turned away from the window. "Why indeed? That is always the question with mind control, with PsyOps. What is the ultimate goal?"

"So you think this blog post is trying to get me to react in some way?"

"Precisely. It is designed to trigger some kind of behavior modification. It will be our task to determine what that modification is. That will put us one step closer to solving this mystery."

Cameron tried in vain to push him for more answers for a few more minutes before they hung up. He was looking for answers Randall either did not have, or did not care to share.

Stefan Antonopoulos returned to his hotel room from the morning seminars and gently laid the Vermont stone onto the bed. He had barely heard a word of the day's lectures, his mind totally focused on the artifact. But instead of gleeful anticipation, there was a throbbing in his gut. *Something didn't feel right.* He had read something recently about a second brain in the stomach that warned of impending danger. He needed to listen.

He was supposed to check out and catch a flight back to Portland late this afternoon. He stared at the artifact for a few seconds before making a decision. He phoned his teaching assistant. "I'm going to need you to cover class tomorrow morning. I'm stuck in Washington. I'll fly straight to Boston Friday night to give that lecture." Calls to his wife, his travel agent and the hotel front desk completed his task.

And marked the beginning of a new one.

So what next? A young woman claimed her mother found a carved rock almost forty years ago in Vermont. That and a few pages from a teenager's diary was all he really knew about the find. What was that old expression: *When something seemed too good to be true, it usually was.*

But why? Why would a young woman go to the trouble of trying to interest him in an artifact that might be fake? He hadn't offered any money for it, and even if he did it wouldn't be enough to change anyone's life. He grabbed his coat. He wasn't going to figure anything out sitting in this hotel room.

He tried Rachel's cell while walking through the hotel lobby. Straight to voice mail. He sent her a quick text: *Want to update you on exam of artifact. I'm staying in town extra day. Please call.* He really knew nothing about her, other than she was from Baltimore. Pausing in the lobby, he Googled her: A gazillion hits. He narrowed the search to Baltimore, but that still left thousands of possibilities. Why couldn't she have had a unique name ... *like Evgenia.*

He replayed the evening. Evgenia lived in Washington. And she knew the bar had just been renovated, which meant she probably lived on Capital Hill. Okay, that was a start. Something to do while waiting for Rachel to get back to him. How many six-foot-tall African-American women named Evgenia could there be in one neighborhood?

Antonopoulos ducked into the Bethesda Metro station a block from his hotel, his fingers and toes numb from the brisk wind. He had left his heavy winter clothes in Maine, mistakenly figuring the D.C. winters would be mild. He had the rest of today plus the first half of tomorrow to try to figure things out, then he'd have to fly north. Just as he was about to take the escalator down, his phone rang. The number came in as 'private.'

"Hello."

"Hi Professor. This is Rachel Gold returning your call."

He made small talk for a minute before getting to the point. "Rachel, I noticed some interesting things on this carving. Did your mother clean the rock in any way?"

Rachel laughed. "Actually, that's a funny question. When she found it in the attic it was covered with dust and cobwebs. My mom is a bit of a clean freak so she put it in the dishwasher."

Antonopoulos bit his lip. Would that explain the pristine condition of the carved grooves? Maybe. Or maybe he was being paranoid. He kept his tone light. "So that's it. I couldn't figure out why the rock was clean enough to eat off of."

"Knowing my mom, she probably used the 'Heavy Wash' setting."

"Okay, thanks again for your help. I'll be in touch."

He hesitated at the top of the escalator. Was Rachel lying? Maybe he had seen too many movies, but he had the sense last night that she wasn't being totally honest with him. And why did her number come in as private? On the other hand, the dishwasher could explain the clean grooves. And a private number combined with a hunch someone was lying to him was a pretty flimsy reason to stick around Washington.

He took a deep breath and went with his gut. Rachel was in Baltimore, but her friend Evgenia was in Washington. Glancing at a subway map, he plotted his course to Capital Hill.

Cam needed to get some legal work done, and he knew if he sat around at home he'd just fixate on the blog post and the CIA mystery. So he drove to his uncle's law office located in an old Colonial near the Westford Town Common, where Cam subleased space. He returned some calls, plowed through a couple of Purchase and Sale Agreements, and researched a case involving a dispute between neighbors over use of a shared driveway. Nothing particularly momentous, but at least nobody tried to attack him.

Mid-morning he took a break to watch a video someone had emailed him. It was a parody, making fun of fellow researcher Scott Wolter, a Minnesota geologist. Purportedly put out by a group of Mormons, the video, entitled "America Revealed," criticized Wolter for not considering that the Book of Mormon offered an explanation for the mysterious artifacts he had uncovered in his research and discussed on his television show, "America Unearthed." The video was of high quality and humorous, but the tone struck Cam as unnecessarily personal. The video attacked Wolter as much as it did his research, portraying him in a buffoon-like manner. It reminded Cam of the blogger attack. Was Wolter under attack also? Was this another example of MK-Ultra trying to discredit a researcher, this time by trying to make him look like a bumbling idiot? It sure seemed that way.

Cam considered ferreting around more, trying to learn where the video originated. But that was the problem with conspiracies—if you believed there was a conspiracy beneath every rock, then you spent all your time, well, looking under rocks. Closing his browser, he returned to his law work and finished up around noon. He phoned Amanda as he walked to his car. "I'm heading home. Want me to pick up sandwiches?" He held the phone close to his ear as a winter wind whipped across the Common and sent swirls of snow dust spinning in the sunlight. They hadn't seen Chung for a couple of days, the police were still patrolling, and Cam had the sense Chung may have given up—a boatload of money didn't do you much good if you were locked in jail. Even so, he didn't like Amanda being home all day alone.

"Greek salad for me, please. And here's something to think about while you're driving."

"Thanks. Because my mind is so totally empty right now..."

"Yes, well, Roger that. But make some bandwidth for this: There simply must be some intersection point between everything that's happening, some common thread that ties the bracelet to the CIA and to the blog post and to our research and maybe even to the Mellon family."

"Agreed. But what?"

She sighed. "Yes, that's the crux of it. I feel like we're trying to construct a jigsaw puzzle but all the pieces in the middle have been removed."

He reached his car. "I'll keep thinking about it. I also want to look into any connections between the Mellon family and the CIA. As you said, there needs to be some common thread. See you in twenty with takeout."

"Oh, Cam, one more thing." She paused for effect. "Please make sure there's nothing in the bag besides lunch."

Cam spent a couple hours after lunch surfing the internet at the kitchen table, Venus at his feet, reading everything he could about the Mellon family. The internet was an amazing research tool, allowing him to explore dusty corners of history that twenty years ago would have been hidden from even the most serious of researchers. By mid-afternoon his eyes were bleary but he had filled almost four pages of a legal pad.

Amanda brought him a Diet Coke and took the seat opposite him. "Forty minutes until Astarte gets home. Care to join me on a trip down the rabbit hole?"

"Depends what's down there."

She smiled. "All sorts of things. Shape-shifting aliens, human sacrifice, MK-Ultra, your boy Laurence Gardner."

"Makes Lewis Carroll seem downright unimaginative."

She took a deep breath. "I Googled reptilian aliens and Gardner, just to see what popped up. There were dozens of sites—some of them fringe but a couple of them legitimate—talking about this. Some guy wrote a book about something called the Boys of Montauk. Supposedly these boys were raised out on Long Island to be used for human sacrifice by a group of reptilian, shape-shifting aliens who secretly control the world."

"Let me guess: They claim Gardner is one of these aliens."

"Not just him, but George Bush Senior, the British royal family, Henry Kissinger."

"Pretty much the usual suspects for conspiracy theorists."

"Anyway, I watched a video in which a woman calling herself Starfire claims she witnessed Gardner and others shift from their human form into giant reptiles and feast on the young boys."

"Feast, as in eat?"

"Yes, as in devouring the boys' internal organs." Amanda erased the image with a shake of her shoulders. "The point is that Starfire maintains she was brainwashed to serve as den mother to these boys by the CIA. She even names Project MK-Ultra, says MK-Ultra doctors drugged and brainwashed her."

"Really? She names MK-Ultra? That's pretty specific."

"And very public. The video has over a hundred thousand views."

The CIA surely didn't love Starfire outing MK-Ultra, but overall they were probably pleased with the video's popularity—thousands of people turned off to Gardner and his research. Cam smiled. "I'm lucky all I have to deal with is some two-bit blogger. Think about what poor Gardner had to endure."

"The whole thing is repulsive."

"And effective. It totally tarnishes Gardner's work."

"And we still have no idea why the CIA felt the need to target him."

"Randall has no idea either. That's why he's still digging around. He wants to see the big picture."

She shifted in her seat and exhaled. "All right, now your turn. What did you learn about the Mellon family?"

He took a swig of his soda and leaned forward. "No reptilian aliens, but some interesting stuff. I'll start with Paul Mellon and work from there. Paul was the son of Andrew Mellon, who made a fortune in banking."

"So Paul was born on third base and thought he'd hit a triple?" She smiled. "That's one of my favorite American expressions."

"Actually, no. Paul was a decent guy from what I read—he entitled his autobiography, *Reflections in a Silver Spoon,* which is pretty self-deprecating when you think about it. Now his son's a different story. But back to Paul. Born in 1907, went to Yale, then during World War II he was the station chief of the London office of the old OSS."

"OSS is the precursor to the CIA, right?"

"Yes. So that's our first clear connection: Paul was a big shot at the CIA."

She leaned forward. "As presumably were many of his mates from Yale. What else?"

"Connection number two: After the war, the CIA used a number of Mellon-funded foundations to funnel money to covert operations around the world. That continues even today—they help fund something called the Heritage Foundation, a conservative think tank."

"Okay, not surprising based on what we know of Paul Mellon."

"Later, in the 1960s, the CIA director, Richard Helms, spent a lot of time at the Mellon family estate in Pennsylvania. Weekends, holidays, that sort of thing. Apparently he and the Mellons were very close. Oh, and care to guess the name of the young CIA operative who first founded MK-Ultra just after the war?"

"Our boy Richard Helms?"

"Yup. So that's connection number three."

Cam looked down at his notes and continued. "You already know about some of the other stuff: Paul bought the Vinland Map and donated it to Yale. Later his son tried to make a trophy out of the Narragansett Rune Stone. And after Paul died, his second wife, Bunny, gave all that money to John Edwards to help bury the whole scandal with his mistress. Oh, and this Bunny was close friends with Jackie Kennedy and spent a ton of time at the White House in the sixties. So that's another connection to the government."

Amanda sat back and chewed her lower lip. "Some interesting connections, but nothing particularly earth-shattering. I suppose any family with that much money is going to do many of the things you just described.

"Except of course for stealing a rune stone."

"Yes, there is that."

"There's actually more than that." He smiled. "I've saved the best for last. And I think you'll agree this is not something most wealthy families would do." He took a deep breath. "The main focus of Project MK-Ultra was experimenting with drugs as a form of mind control. Pugh talked about that, how he and other Chinese nationals were used as guinea pigs in those New York experiments. Well, one of the primary drugs they were using was LSD."

"Okay."

"So they did a lot of lab experiments on convicts, students, immigrants, whatever. But when it came right down to it, nobody knew more about LSD in the 1960s than a professor at Harvard named Timothy Leary. He was part of the Beat Generation. At one point Nixon called him the most dangerous man in America."

She nodded. "I read about Leary. 'Turn on, tune in, and drop out.' LSD is still a big deal in England, even today. *Lucy in the Sky with Diamonds* and all that."

"So here's where it gets interesting. Our boy Paul Mellon has a first cousin named William Mellon Hitchcock. Billy, as he was called, owned a mansion north of New York City called the Millbrook Estate. He basically gave it to Leary, who moved in with all these counter culture poets and musicians. They spent five years there experimenting with LSD—it was essentially one giant acid trip."

"And you think the CIA was behind it all."

Cam nodded. "Wait. It gets better. Care to guess where Leary and his gang got their LSD?"

She shrugged.

154

"Cousin Billy. He bankrolled an illicit LSD manufacturing operation. Interestingly, the government never saw the need to shut it down."

Amanda pushed her chair back and walked toward the living room windows. She stared out over the lake for a few seconds. "You know, everything else you said about the Mellon family could be shrugged off as the typical actions of a wealthy family—friends in high places, donations of artifacts to universities, connections to the intelligence community. But this LSD business is different. I'm certain wealthy people use drugs. But donating a flop house to Leary? And operating a black market LSD manufacturing plant? What you're describing is on a whole other scale."

"Oh, and by the way," Cam said, "this was during the time frame when Richard Helms, the CIA director, was spending weekends at the Mellon family compound."

Amanda turned and looked at Cam. "Clearly, the Mellons didn't need the money. And nobody, no matter how wealthy, just gives up their home to strangers for use as a drug den for five years. I don't know what other conclusion you can reach: The Mellons were fronting for the CIA. Fronting for Project MK-Ultra so they could run their LSD experiments."

Stefan Antonopoulos sat and watched the tunnel walls fly by. Washington was a funny place. In many ways it was the most important city in the world, yet the local government was as dysfunctional as a Third World backwater—as his taxi last night crossed the border from Maryland into D.C. the road went from bare pavement to a thick layer of slush and slop. And it hadn't snowed in three days.

Thankfully, the Metro system was as modern and efficient as any in the country. He had no idea what was going on and the anonymity of public transportation fit his mood. He disembarked at Metro Center and descended to a blue line train. Six stops later he arrived at Eastern Market, a couple of blocks from the Hawk & Dove. He checked his watch. Three o'clock. Probably a good lull time to ask a few questions of the staff.

He entered and wandered around, hoping to see their waitress from last night. But no luck. He ambled to the bar and ordered a burger and beer. Was it worth concocting some story? He decided to play it straight. "Hey, I met a woman in here last night, upstairs. And like an idiot I didn't get her number. Tall, pretty, I think bi-racial. Long, straight hair. Name is Evgenia. Drinks Sam Adams. Any ideas?"

The bartender, a short, pony-tailed guy with a barrel chest and thick arms, eyed him. "I think I know the one." Aussie accent, maybe New Zealand. "She pops in every week or so. Fancies the hockey games."

"Boyfriend?"

"None that I've seen."

He smiled. "Good. Any idea how I might find her?"

"Negative, mate."

Antonopoulos thanked him and paid, leaving an extra twenty as a tip. "If you think of anything else, here's my card." He dropped another twenty. "I'd really appreciate it."

Evgenia sat at her cubicle, trying to fight off the mid-afternoon malaise. She desperately wanted a ten minute catnap. But she couldn't very well curl into a ball on the floor beneath her desk. Instead she opened the hockeyfights.com webpage and watched a couple of battles from last night's games.

Her father had not been a big fighter, but he explained to her that there was a code of honor the players abided by—you never fought a smaller man, never hit a guy once he was down, never waited for a teammate to fight your battles. And most of all, if you were going to knock out someone's teeth you better make sure they deserved it. Not that, as her mother liked to point out, sometimes the code wasn't broken. But for the most part it worked.

Awake now, she focused on the three red files in front of her, each representing a researcher the Agency had puppeteered—Fell, Whitewood and Glynn. Barry Fell's file sat on the top of the stack; she spread its pages across her desk. Fell, author of a 1976 bestselling book entitled *America B.C.*, was the most famous of the three. The book claimed that waves of pre-Columbian Europeans visited North America, including Irish Druids in Vermont and ancient Phoenicians in both the Great Lakes region and New England. Evgenia examined a photo of an inscription found at a site in New Hampshire called America's Stonehenge, which Fell described as an offering to the pagan god Baal, a deity worshiped by the ancient Phoenicians and their precursors, the Canaanites. Fell translated the inscription as, "To Baal of the Canaanites, This in Dedication."

Baal Stone, America's Stonehenge, New Hampshire

The Oath of Nimrod

The America's Stonehenge site also contained a stone slab called the Sacrificial Table; the Canaanites were known to offer human sacrifices to their gods. Evgenia peered closer. A grooved channel ran along the border of the stone slab, presumably to drain the blood away.

Sacrificial Stone, America's Stonehenge, New Hampshire

Fell's work piggy-backed on many other researchers, but because Fell was a Harvard professor his message resonated nationwide. Fell's problem—his button to push, as it were—was his massive ego. He based his research on his ability to read an ancient language called Ogham, which in many cases consisted of no more than a series of squiggly lines. Fell's ego apparently was such that he believed every marking on every stone was an ancient writing that only he could decipher. Some of the engravings were indeed ancient artifacts, but many others were nothing more than natural fissures or glacier marks in the stones. It had been a simple matter for an agent—in fact, a twenty-something Dr. Jag—to plant some promising-looking carved stones in the woods and wait for Fell to pounce on them and trumpet their import. Once the stones were revealed to be fakes, of course, Fell's reputation plummeted and his body of work became discredited. Evgenia shook her head. All his work had been dismissed—the world had no idea that much of it was legitimate.

Why, she wondered, did the CIA even care? Was Professor Fell some kind of threat to national security? Fell was discredited in the early 1980s, which was the height of the Cold War. But what did his research have to do with the Soviets?

As if on cue, Dr. Jag shuffled into Evgenia's cubicle. As usual, the pockets of his blue blazer were stuffed—keys, glasses, a phone, papers, pens, a pipe and, based on the smell of egg wafting off of him, perhaps even half a breakfast sandwich. "How did last night go?"

She quickly closed her browser. Dr. Jag would no doubt think hockey fights were barbaric; this from a man who regularly ordered his employees to ruin peoples' lives. "Fine," she answered. "Antonopoulos took the artifact, like we knew he would."

"Good. He suspect anything?"

"There's nothing to suspect yet." It was an odd question. "He set up a meeting to examine a carved rock and, well, that's what happened."

"Okay. So how you going to play him?"

She pointed at the red files. "Don't know yet. Hoping for some inspiration."

"I've got more if you need them."

"More files? How many people are out there researching this pre-Columbian stuff?"

He turned and left. "Too many."

She returned the Fell materials to their folder and quickly read the summary pages of the new files. Three stories. Three innocent men ruined. In many ways, three American tragedies. And now she was in charge of making sure Antonopoulos would be a fourth. She sighed. Perhaps this job didn't pay so well after all.

Perhaps it was time to take a page out of the hockey fight code of conduct and make sure Antonopoulos really did deserve getting his teeth knocked out.

Cam watched as Astarte worked at the kitchen table, turning a smart phone and old webcam lens into a microscope for a fourth-grade science project. Whatever happened to papier-mâché volcanoes?

Amanda stomped in. "Aargh, this is so frustrating!"

"What?"

"It is impossible to prove giants existed without the actual bones. But the NAGPRA law made it illegal to keep the bones—they've all been reburied. No bones, no bloody proof."

"I can't believe there's not a few skeletons still around in private collections." He paused for a second. "Maybe I should call Herm Gablonsky." A widower, Herm was the father of one of Cam's college roommates; he lived outside Boston, in Newton, and possessed a large collection of Americana documents and artifacts. Once things turned serious with Amanda, Cam had brought her to meet him and get his approval.

"But Herm doesn't collect bones."

"No. But he might know someone who does. He's been collecting for decades, and these guys love to show off their collections. If someone in the state has a giant skeleton, chances are Herm would know about it."

She nodded. "Fair enough. God knows I'm getting tired of looking at old newspapers."

"I'll call him." It was better than sitting around thinking about all the people reading on the internet what a racist idiot Cam was. "I'll offer to drive down tonight with a couple of pizzas and some Kimball's ice cream." Cam smiled. When he had moved back to Westford from Boston a couple of years ago, Herm had cursed him for leaving the city for farm country. *Are you going to keep chickens, Cameron? And read by the goddamn candlelight?* But Herm never turned down a gallon of homemade cherry vanilla chip. Luckily Amanda had stocked up for the winter.

"Wait, you're going to give him our last gallon?" Amanda pouted.

"You know we can't show up without it."

She sighed. "The sacrifices we make for science."

Stefan Antonopoulos stood outside the modern, glass-topped Eastern Market subway station. Periodically he ducked inside to get warm but only from the top of the escalator could he see everyone leaving the station. Evgenia would surely stand out in a crowd, but he didn't want to risk missing her amongst the sea of evening commuters.

He shoved his hands deep into his jacket pockets, wondering if he was just wasting his time. His flight home would have landed already and he could be a short drive away from a family dinner, a glass of wine and a Disney movie with the kids. What was he thinking?

He killed another half hour, bouncing and blowing on his hands to keep warm. At this point everyone looked alike—he started following a woman down the street only to overtake her and realize she was in reality a tall man with a long beige scarf.

It was approaching seven o'clock, and Antonopoulos was about to give up, when his cell phone rang. "Howdy, Governor." The bartender. "Your birdie just walked in. Watching the hockey game on the telly."

Herman Gablonsky was the type of American that Europeans often made fun of—loud, opinionated, gruff, even a bit crude. And Amanda adored every bit of it.

The Oath of Nimrod

Cam parked in the driveway of an expanded ranch in a quiet Newton neighborhood, ten miles west of Boston. Herm met them at the door, bear hugs for all. "And there's my Astarte," he boomed. "You better have a kiss for Uncle Herm!"

Astarte, rarely intimidated, planted a pair of wet lips on his cheek and pushed by him to roll on the floor with his Chocolate Lab, a half-sibling to Venus. "Hello, Benjamin Franklin," Astarte said, rubbing the dog's stomach. "Have you been a good boy?"

"Good?" Herm bellowed. "Hell no! He chewed up a letter signed by President Andrew Jackson." He faked a kick at the dog. "He's lucky I don't make him sleep in the garage."

Amanda was always surprised Herm was of only average size when she saw him—in her mind's eye he always seemed a hulking presence. Perhaps his large, bald head contributed to the illusion, or perhaps it was simply a function of his personality and thundering voice. Or perhaps, she concluded, it was because his living room was so stuffed with display cabinets and bookshelves that he seemed completely to fill the room.

Herm showed them some of his recent acquisitions, most notably George Washington's surveying compass, before they reheated the pizza. Herm cleared a stack of papers off the kitchen table; Cam had brought paper plates and plastic silverware, anticipating Herm would likely not have washed his dishes.

Herm made a face. "Is this Westford pizza?"

Cam grinned. "No. We swung by Brooklyn on the way here."

"Well, it's not bad for the boondocks. You guys ever see polar bears up there?"

Amanda saw her opening. "No, but we found a wooly mammoth buried in the ice."

Herm stopped mid-bite, cheese hanging from his chin, and smiled at Cam. "I like her. I really do. Sassy. Miss Sassafras." He shook his head. "Wooly mammoth."

Cam took her cue. "That sort of segues to why we're here, Herm." He explained Amanda's research on giants. "We were

162

wondering if you've ever heard of anyone with any giants bones."

Herm sighed. "Why you guys wasting your time on this stuff, Cameron?" He motioned to the living room. "We have so much fascinating history—this country was the first great experiment in democracy. And it worked, it succeeded! Why are you so focused on what happed before that? Who cares if the Phoenicians or the Chinese or the Greeks were here thousands of years ago. They came, caught some fish, maybe traded with the Indians, took a dump in the woods, and left. Yippee shit." He squared his shoulders. "Our Founding Fathers were some of the greatest men in the history of the world; they built something never seen before! Why not focus on them?"

Amanda knew that Cam knew this argument was coming—it always did. And Cam was ready. He put an arm on Herm's shoulder. "Because the truth matters, Herm. The truth matters."

Herm exhaled loudly. "The truth." He shook his head. "You are such a pain in my ass." He stood, found a leather address book in a drawer, and dialed a number. As it rang, he said to Cam, "Of course I know a guy; you think I don't?" He shook his head again. "But we're not going anywhere until we eat some of that country ice cream of yours."

Evgenia sat at the bar and sipped her Sam Adams. As soon as she walked in the bartender had motioned to her. "A bloke was in here earlier asking for you. Dark hair, about my height." He smiled. "Handsome bugger, just like me. Said he met you last night." It had to be Stefan Antonopoulos. But why?

Had he grown suspicious of her or Rachel? She was fairly certain the professor's intentions were not amorous; she had tried a couple of times to flirt last night and he had not responded. She replayed the evening in her mind: There was nothing that should have given him pause. They had a drink, he examined the artifact, he asked to keep it, Rachel agreed, they said goodnight. That was it. Vanilla.

She positioned herself near the far end of the bar. From there she could look at the television in the center area of the bar and also glance at the mirror beneath the TV to see the front door reflected in it. Half a beer later Antonopoulos edged through the front door, shook the water from his coat and, partially covering his face with his arm, pushed through a crowd at the far end of the bar. Obviously he did not want to be seen.

So what was proper procedure here? A mark was following her. She was an analyst, not a field agent—she had some basic training in hand-to-hand combat and in surveillance and avoidance, but she was no expert. On the other hand neither was Antonopoulos. She tried to recall her training. Priority one was her own safety. Priority two was not allowing her cover to be exposed. Priority three was to maintain the integrity of her mission. She sighed. None of these priorities told her what actually to do. Perhaps she should have called Dr. Jag while she waited, though he would have just told her to follow her training. She looked at her half-empty beer—whatever she did, getting drunk was probably not a good idea. She ordered a Diet Coke. And waited.

Twenty minutes later Antonopoulos was still hiding, hunched at the far end of the bar. Enough already. She dropped a twenty on the bar, grabbed her coat and strolled to the door, careful not to look in the professor's direction. She pushed out the door. Wanting him to show himself in the open, she jaywalked across Pennsylvania Avenue midblock, darting through traffic. When she reached the far side she ducked into a darkened storefront and waited.

Antonopoulos followed, his head on a swivel as he alternately watched for traffic and scanned for his prey. He had lost her already. He jogged to the corner and scanned the cross street; not seeing her he jogged back down Pennsylvania toward where she hid. She reached into her purse and took a deep breath. As he passed, she called out. "Professor, stop."

He spun toward her as she stepped from the shadows. Before he could react she held up a small canister and sprayed his face.

Herm sat in the front seat while Cam drove, with Amanda and Astarte in the rear. It was a cold night and the heat hadn't even kicked in yet when Herm said, "I actually do know something about these giants of yours."

Amanda and Cam exchanged glances, not sure if he was being serious or not. "Really?" Amanda replied.

"You know I'm a history buff, especially Colonial history. There's a monument down in Cumberland, Rhode Island called the Nine Men's Misery monument. Nine Colonists were ambushed, captured and tortured by the Native Americans during King Phillip's War in the 1670s. Brutal, nasty stuff. They identified the bones because one of the Colonists, a guy named Benjamin Bucklin, was supposedly almost eight feet tall and had a complete double row of teeth." He shrugged. "That's how they knew who they were. So maybe there is something to these giant stories."

Cam and Amanda exchanged glances again. They had not told Herm anything about double rows of teeth. "So what happened to the bodies?" Amanda asked.

"They were reburied, except according to an old book I have Bucklin's skull was given to the Rhode Island Historical Society in the 1800s. But they lost it."

"Of course they did," Amanda replied. "Do you know if by chance this Bucklin was part Native American?"

Herm shrugged. "Wouldn't surprise me. Especially down in Rhode Island a lot of the Colonists took Narragansett wives and mistresses." Herm switched subjects. "So anyway, I gotta warn you, this guy we're going to visit is an odd duck. Works at Boston College as some kind of archivist. Married into some old money, but the wife is a recluse, even more nuts than him—I think her father invented the stapler or the paper clip or something. Anyway, the big thing you should know is he's one of those guys who thinks the government is corrupt. You know, Big Brother and all that conspiracy crap."

Cam nodded, remembering the conference from a few weeks ago. "I know the type. So why's he letting us come over?"

"Because he owes me one. I'm the guy who hooked him up with the giant skeleton. But like I said, he's paranoid. I had to give him your names on the phone—I'm sure he spent the last hour checking you out online." He pointed. "Turn right here. Second house on the left."

Unlike Herm's neighborhood of ranches and Capes, brick Tudor-style homes dominated this area of town. "You know some of these things are selling for two million?" Herm said. "Who can afford that?"

Cam pulled into the driveway. "The same guy who can afford to own an ancient giant skeleton." He smiled. "People buy a lot of staplers and paper clips."

Herm snorted. "You got me there."

A thin, bookish, middle-aged man in a gray cardigan sweater met them at the door; Herm introduced him as Maxwell. The smell of cat urine greeted them as Maxwell guided them furtively down a dusty, dimly lit hallway to a set of stairs running down to the basement. "Please hurry, and be quiet," he explained. "My wife does not know you're here. She does not like it when I show my collection to strangers." He glanced over his shoulder and wiped sweat off his upper lift with the back of his hand. "She is the anxious type. She worries someone will rob us."

"Like I said, I can vouch for these guys," Herm said.

When they reached the bottom of the stairs, Maxwell handed them a canvas bag. "I must insist on no pictures. Please put your cell phones and cameras in here and I will return them when you leave."

The basement had been refinished at one point but was even dingier and darker and urine-scented than the upstairs hallway; most of the space was filled with file cabinets and

166

stacked storage bins. Cam wondered how much of what was in the bins and cabinets actually belonged to Boston College. In the middle of the room a pool table had been covered with various wooden and iron tools and implements. Herm said, "Maxwell has one of the most complete collections of Inquisition torture devices in the world." Cam stepped closer and noticed what looked like a thumb screw. Herm pointed to a second object, a brass metal orb that resembled a corkscrew. "That's a pear of anguish," he whispered. "It was inserted inside the anus or vagina and then expanded like flower pedals opening to tear the internal tissue."

"How barbaric," Amanda said.

Herm nodded. "The Church agreed. They liked to think of themselves as pious and holy. So they decreed no blood could be spilled during questioning. Instead they did things like hoisting heretics up to the rafters with their wrists tied and then dropping them, dislocating their shoulders." He raised an eyebrow. "But no blood."

Astarte took Cam's hand. "It looks like the Addams Family's house," she whispered, pointing to a wooden chair with scores of nails protruding up from the seat and seatback.

Cam pulled her closer. "Stay with me, honey." He smiled. "And don't sit down."

A pathway between the bins led to a gray steel door recessed into the back wall; Maxwell pulled a key from his pocket and unlocked it. He pushed open the door, moved aside and motioned for the others to enter some kind of storage closet tucked into the corner of the basement. Cam stepped forward first, Astarte in tow, followed by Amanda and Herm. The room was warm, the air thick, the room illuminated only by a streetlight shining through a single rectangular window atop the room's back wall. Cam glanced around, his eyes adjusting to the dark—more display cases and storage bins along with a few filing cabinets. Amanda wandered over to examine a large skull mounted in some kind of Plexiglas display case. "Cam, look at this. It's huge," she exhaled. "And it has a double row of teeth."

The Oath of Nimrod

Cam spotted a chain for an overhead light bulb, pulled it and moved to join Amanda. As he peered to examine the skull the steel door echoed closed.

"What the hell you doing, Maxwell?" Herm bellowed, pounding on the door. Cam froze and turned. What was going on?

"I'm sorry, Herm," came the muffled reply from beyond the closed door. "But I can't have government agents confiscating my collection." His voice rose in pitch. "They're everywhere, you know. Just waiting to come in and steal our property, steal our freedoms. It's only a matter of time."

Herm exhaled. "Maxwell, these people are my friends. They're not government agents. They don't want to take your stuff. Now let us out of here."

"I checked them out, Herm. They have friends at the CIA. They have friends who are Freemasons. They can't be trusted." He paused. "You should not have brought them here. Even if they don't work for the government, they will tell people about my collection, about my skeleton—Thorne gives lectures, that's what he does. They'll take my things, Herm." His voice was almost a shriek now. "I won't let them take my things!"

"Maxwell, calm down. Just listen to me." Herm placed his ear against the door. "Damn it, he's leaving." He pounded the door again. "Maxwell, come back!"

Nothing.

Astarte leaned into Cam. "It smells funny in here."

"And it's warm," Amanda added.

Cam sniffed. It smelled like a basement, sort of musty and furnace-like. He glanced around, searching for some kind of escape route. He rejected the window as too narrow, even for Astarte. Behind one of the walls, the furnace hummed. "Basements are often hot," he said.

"What does he mean to do to us?" Amanda asked.

Herm kicked at the rug. "Like I said, the guy's crazy. Paranoid." He looked at Astarte and shifted his speech pattern. "I have been privy to certain allegations regarding the subject in question, in which same subject was purported to have engaged in nefarious activities and experimentation with

168

certain implements of the Inquisition." Herm paused. He was a tough guy, a city kid—not one to be easily frightened. "Substantial financial consideration was conveyed in order to resolve these allegations."

Great. The guy tortured somebody and then paid them off to stay out of jail. "Well, I'm not planning to wait around to find out what happens next," Cam said. Especially with a room full of torture devices on the other side of this wall. He hoisted himself atop a filing cabinet and began to probe at the ceiling. "I think this is a drop ceiling. Above these tiles are the pipes and electrical wires." He pushed a tile aside. "There's about a ten-inch gap between the real ceiling and the drop ceiling."

"Maybe I can fit," Amanda said. Cam jumped down and Amanda, an ex-gymnast, removed her jacket and vaulted her way up. "Cam, come closer. Let me stand on your shoulders."

One leg on his shoulder, she pushed herself up so her head was in the crawl space. Cam said, "You'll need to crawl on top of the wooden framing. The ceiling tiles won't hold you."

Herm laughed. "Careful about the weight comments, buddy." But the levity was forced—Herm was apparently still thinking about Maxwell and the torture devices.

Amanda wriggled herself upward, her entire body above her thighs disappearing into the gap. Ten seconds passed, the sound of Amanda's movements filling the storage room. The wooden framing bowed a little and creaked, but it held her. Finally she scooched backward and dropped down, landing atop the file cabinet. She wiped her face with her sleeve. "I can fit, but then I get blocked by a pipe running across in front of me. I can't squeeze beneath it."

"Can you push it out of the way?"

"No. It's cast iron. Probably a drain pipe."

"I could fit," Astarte said. "I'm smaller than Mum is."

Cam looked down at the cobalt eyes staring up at him. The front of his head had begun to pound; he massaged it and tried to blink the pain away. "What do you think, Amanda?"

She swayed a bit atop the cabinet, caught herself and blinked before answering. "It might work. But then what? I don't want Astarte out there dealing with Maxwell by herself."

"I can sneak out and get help," Astarte said, her jaw out. "I'll just run to neighbors and bang on their door."

Cam looked up at Amanda. "I don't know if we have a choice. Who knows how long we could be stuck in here?"

She bit her lip. "Okay."

Amanda moved over as Cam lifted Astarte atop the file cabinet, from where Amanda hoisted her into the ceiling gap. "You need to stay on top of the piece of wood, just like a balance beam," Amanda said.

Astarte pushed off, squirming ahead, only her purple rubber boots visible. "Okay," the girl called, "I'm up to the pipe."

"Can you squeeze under it?" Amanda asked.

"I think so." Five seconds passed. "Okay, I'm past it."

"Stop there," Amanda said. Then to Cam: "The drain pipe was right above the wall between the storage room and the rest of the basement."

"Good," Cam said. "I think there's bookcase right beneath her. Tell her to move a ceiling tile aside and see if there's something she can drop herself onto."

While they waited for Amanda to give instructions to Astarte, Herm spoke. "Sorry about this." He yawned and sat on the floor, his back against a wall. "I'm going to kill Maxwell when we get out of here." He yawned again. "Must be getting past my bedtime."

Cam was about to reply when Amanda screamed. Not a shriek or a screech, but a full-fledged, terror-in-the-heart scream.

"What?!?" Cam said.

At the same time, Astarte called, "Mum, are you okay?"

"A bat! I saw a bat!" She flailed at her hair and leapt from the cabinet.

"Okay, calm down," Cam said. "I didn't see anything. It must have been in the ceiling. It's winter—he was

170

hibernating." And to Astarte: "It's okay, Astarte. Something scared Mum."

"But now it's up there with Astarte!" Amanda said in a stage whisper.

"Shh, keep your voice down. The bat is more afraid of us than we are of him. And we don't want Astarte flailing around."

"What if it's rabid?"

"If it were rabid it wouldn't be hibernating," Cam said.

Astarte called down, "I don't like bats."

Herm ended the conversation. With a shaking hand, he pointed up toward the giant skull. "Forget the freaking bat. I just saw the skull moving." His face had turned gaunt, his eyes wide. "I'm not shitting you, Cam, I saw it moving. He shook his head at me, back and forth." He pushed himself back to the corner. "It was as if he was saying, no way are you getting out of here."

Stefan Antonopoulos' entire body recoiled as the chemical engulfed his face. Eyes on fire, he tried to scream, but when he opened his mouth it was like breathing in flames. He fell to his knees, his hands clawing at his eyes, his face bubbling and boiling. "I … can't … breathe," he gasped.

Evgenia pulled him to his feet and guided him, surprisingly gently, into the darkened doorway from which she had appeared. "Just breath normally," she said. "And don't rub at your eyes; you'll only make it worse."

"Why?" he stammered, swaying as he dropped back to his knees. Coughing violently, he fought for oxygen as the chemical filled his airways.

"You mean why did I pepper spray a man stalking me on the streets?"

He had no good response to that, even if he could talk.

She pulled his hands behind his back and tied his wrists together. "You'll be able to see again in about fifteen minutes," she said. "Crying will help wash the spray from your eyes. In the meantime we're going to have a little talk." She rubbed snow on his face, cooling the burning a bit. "First of all, why are you following me?"

He was in no position to lie. "Gut feeling," he said as another coughing fit overcame him.

"Don't gasp; just breathe normally," she said. "What do you mean by gut feeling?"

In fits and starts he described how the grooves in the carving were too weathered, too smooth, too pristine.

"Doesn't that just mean the thing is old?" she asked. "Isn't that what you're looking for?"

He nodded.

"So you think somehow Rachel is trying to set you up? For God's sake, why?"

He shrugged. He tried to explain his other suspicions. As he verbalized them, he realized how flimsy they sounded.

Evgenia stared at him with disdain, like he was some kind of idiot. "Look, Rachel has an unlisted number because some ex-boyfriend has been stalking her. And if you got the sense she was holding something back last night, it's probably because she was going to ask you if you could sell the artifact for her; her mother really needs the money. But she felt … I guess the word is *cheap* … asking you to help her cash in on a piece of history. Frankly, she was embarrassed." She exhaled. "Like you should be."

What an idiot he had been. He should have been home now, the worst of his worries being a bit too much pepper on his dinner.

She continued. "So why didn't you just come talk to me in the bar? Why did you stalk me?"

Good question. He forced out a response. "I was just trying to get more information." His eyes still simmered and it felt like he was swallowing fire every time he breathed, but at least the excruciating pain had begun to fade. He spat. "Where you lived, where you worked, how to track down Rachel."

"Look, dude, you've been watching too many movies. You want to give Rachel her rock back, I'm sure she'll take it. And if you want to fly back to Maine and look at it in your lab, I'm sure that's fine with her also. But this James Bond stuff is bullshit."

Before he knew what was happening she untied his wrists. He heard her footsteps as she jogged off into the night. It hurt to talk, but the words tumbled from his mouth. "What a fucking idiot I am."

Astarte listened to the conversation on the other side of the wall from her. She had dropped from the ceiling onto a bookcase, then from there onto the floor. She must have banged her head while squeezing through, because the area above her eyes was throbbing. She blinked and took a deep breath.

But she knew there was no such thing as ghosts. Mr. Herm must have just been seeing things.

She tried the door to the storage room. Locked.

She put her mouth close to the keyhole. "It's locked. What should I do?" She glanced over her shoulder, ready to scurry under the display tables if anyone came after her.

Cameron replied after a few seconds. "Is that bag with our cell phones out there?"

She looked around. It was dark, and she didn't dare put a light on. "I don't see it."

"Okay, listen carefully to me Astarte. I remember there was a phone on the wall at the bottom of the stairs. It was on the right hand side as we came down. I want you to go find it and call 911." He gave her the address. "Tell the police we are being held prisoners in the basement. Then come right back here."

"Right," she said. There was more light near the staircase and she edged her way toward the landing. She scanned the wall, the right-hand side as Cameron said. There was nothing there—no phone, nothing. Not even a light switch. Just a flat wall. She checked the other wall, and even crept halfway up the stairs. No phone. Which was weird, because Cameron usually had a good memory for things like that.

Not knowing what else to do, she scampered back to the locked door. "Dad-Cam, I didn't see any phone." She waited. No response. "Dad-Cam? Mum?"

Finally, after what seemed like an hour, he replied. "Are you sure?"

His voice sounded funny, like he had just woken up. Her heart thudded. "Is Mum there?"

Another few seconds. "Yes, honey, I'm here."

She remembered something she read in a Nancy Drew mystery book about haunted houses. "Mum, have you seen the bat again?"

"Yes, honey, I've seen him twice more. But he's in here with us, so no need for you to be frightened."

"And Dad-Cam, have you seen the skeleton move his head again?"

"No. But Mr. Herm said he saw it again."

Skeletons heads did *not* move. She took a deep breath. This was very important. "You need to break the window. Now. Break the window."

Cameron's tired voice replied. "It's too small. We can't climb through. We'll wait for you to get help, Astarte. Go."

"No!" she barked. "Listen to me. You need to break the window. The room is filling up with…" What was that word? "Filling up with carbon oxide. That's what's making you tired. And making you see ghosts and bats." *Hallucinate*, it was called. "I read it in a Nancy Drew book. People thought they saw ghosts but it was just the carbon oxide making them hallucinate."

No response.

"Dad-Cam! Wake up!"

"We can talk about it in the morning, honey."

"Break the window," she sobbed. "Break the window!"

Cam dreamt.

A strange, disjointed dream about Astarte and Amanda and ghosts and bats and broken windows. There was something he needed to remember to do, but he was too tired. Maybe open the window. Or was he supposed to close the window? But so what if the window stayed open? He was too damn tired. Window open, window closed, whatever—it could wait until morning.

Suddenly Astarte knew what she had to do. Wiping the tears from her eyes, she retraced her steps back to where she had dropped through the ceiling. On her way she saw a long metal bar on the table with the other creepy Addams Family tools and grabbed it.

Climbing the bookshelf like a ladder, she pulled herself upward and slid the metal bar into the ceiling crawl area. Then, using all her strength, she pulled herself up through the hole, swung her leg up and rolled herself atop the wooden beam. Fearing the bat, but fearing what was happening to her parents more, she wriggled her way back under the black pipe and returned to her starting spot atop the storage room file cabinet.

She looked down. Three adults, sleeping on the floor. Her heart pounded. She wished there was a way to do this without making noise, but there was no time. Holding the metal bar like a sword, and covering her eyes with her free hand, she jabbed the bar at the window.

The window shattered, sending shards of glass along with gallons of fresh winter air tumbling into their prison.

But Astarte was not done. In fact, she suddenly realized the broken window might be her chance.

Without even waiting for Mum and Dad-Cam to wake, she snaked herself back under the black pipe for a third time and dropped through the ceiling hole just as the sound of footsteps came racing down the stairs. She crouched and watched as the man named Maxwell turned on the light and peered around the room, a black gun in his hand. She crouched lower as he walked slowly toward the storage room door.

Now was her chance. Crawling under the display cabinets, she crossed the room as Maxwell checked the door. Before he could turn she burst to her feet and sprinted toward the stairs. He called after her as she neared the top, and she could hear his footsteps in pursuit as she ran down the hall. But unless his smelly cats somehow were able to tackle her there was no way he was going to stop her from running out the door and getting help.

Amanda barely remembered being carried out of the basement, an oxygen mask on her face. The oxygen tasted like a tall glass of cold water after a long summer run. A young female paramedic told her the story on the way to the hospital.

"The girl saved your lives. Even with the window broken the carbon monoxide levels were pretty high in that room. Another ten, fifteen minutes and you'd all be dead," she said matter-of-factly. "The furnace was venting right into there. The outside vent was blocked by a snow bank."

A snow bank, how convenient. "Where is Astarte?"

"An officer is bringing her to the hospital. She's fine."

Amanda had seen Cam loaded into the ambulance next to hers; he had waved and given her a thumbs-up. "How is Herm?"

"The older guy? He'll make it. He was closest to the vent and furthest from the window, so he had it worst."

She closed her eyes, the movement of the ambulance making her nauseous. "Is this supposed to feel like the world's worst hangover?"

The paramedic smiled. "Exactly."

"Did they arrest Maxwell?"

"Not yet. He's claiming it was all an accident. Said you three wanted some privacy to look at some of his collection so he left you alone for a while. When he went back down to check on you were all passed out. Claims he figured it must be carbon monoxide poisoning so he broke the window to let in some fresh air. Says he was just about to call 911 when the police banged on the door."

"How does he explain the bloody locked door?" Amanda said.

"To the storage room? I was first on the scene with the cop—when we got there the door was opened. But he mentioned it gets stuck sometimes."

"So it will be the word of a nine-year-old against him?"

"Her and the neighbor's 911 phone call." The paramedic smiled. "Unless you can get that giant skeleton to testify."

Evgenia sprinted to the next corner, her heart thumping more from adrenaline than from exertion. She stopped and turned to make sure Antonopoulos hadn't followed. Her body shivered. They made these kinds of encounters seem so *uneventful* on television and in the movies and even in Agency training videos. But she was a mess. A shaking, shivering, gasping, raw-nerved mess.

But she had done well. She had protected herself, protected her identity, protected her mission. Antonopoulos, his instincts sharp, suspected something was amiss but he had no idea what. And her performance tonight probably convinced him he was being paranoid. Hopefully he would get on a plane in the morning and get on with his life.

177

Yet something he said resonated. He sensed Rachel might be setting him up, believed the carving to be too pristine. And he was, after all, the expert. She had covered for Rachel with the lie about a stalking boyfriend, but the reality was she didn't know anything about the girl other than what Dr. Jag had told her; he claimed to have vetted her, to have checked out her story about the artifact, but who knew what really went on inside that dandruff-covered head of his? Was there another game going on here, one in which Evgenia was a lowly pawn? It was one thing for Dr. Jag to compartmentalize things and keep her in the dark about certain aspects of her assignments. It was another to be lied to and manipulated....

And it still gnawed at her that she couldn't figure out why the Agency cared about Antonopoulos and his research. Perhaps there were some clues in the other files Dr. Jag had given her.

Walking quickly, her heart still pounding, she covered the six blocks back to her apartment and dead-bolted her door. Unlocking her briefcase, she spread the folders across the kitchen table. She grabbed a light beer from the fridge and began with the file for Frank Glynn, a postal worker from Connecticut. Reading quickly, she learned that in the late 1960s Glynn set out to prove the truth of the legend of Prince Henry Sinclair and the Westford Knight. The legend recounted the exploits of Sinclair, a nobleman from northern Scotland, who, following ancient Viking maps, island-hopped his way across the North Atlantic in the 1390s. Eventually Sinclair found his way to what is now Westford, Massachusetts, where a kinsman by the name of James Gunn died. Sinclair ordered that an effigy be carved into bedrock as a memorial to this fallen knight.

Evgenia pulled some photos from the folder and sipped her beer. She could clearly make out the pommel, grip, cross guard and upper part of the blade of the medieval battle sword:

178

David S. Brody

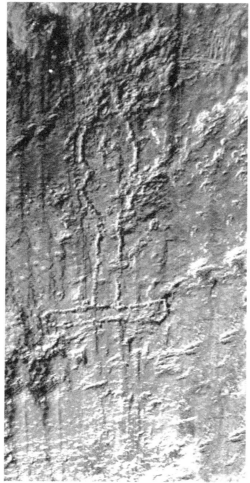

Westford Knight Sword, Massachusetts

The rest of the effigy seemed to have faded over time, though a rubbing done of the entire carving did clearly reveal the knight with his sword and shield:

The Oath of Nimrod

Westford Knight Rubbing, Massachusetts

"Pretty cool," she whispered. Not that it really mattered. How could Europeans have 'discovered' a continent that was already occupied by thousands of Native Americans?

In any event, apparently Frank Glynn spent many months cleaning and photographing the Knight carving. Eventually he began exploring surrounding areas in Westford, figuring there might be other evidence of the Prince Henry journey. He soon came upon the Boat Stone, a two-foot square rock with a medieval ship called a knorr, a crossbow arrow and the number 184 carved on its face. Interestingly, the technique used to carve these images—a pecking or punching motion using some kind of iron tool—was identical to that employed in the Westford Knight effigy carving.

Westford Boat Stone, Massachusetts

Gunn consulted with heraldry experts in Great Britain who suggested the Boat Stone may have marked Prince Henry's winter encampment site. Returning to the location the stone was found, and believing the arrow and number 184 may have been directional markers, Glynn paced 184 paces into the woods and stumbled upon the remains of a rectangular stone foundation. The foundation, located in an ideal location for a winter encampment site, did not appear in the historical town records. She read further: Apparently the custom was that the group's boats would have been turned upside down and placed on the low foundation stones to serve as the encampment's roof. Evgenia pulled a drawing of it from the file, along with a photo showing three of the walls:

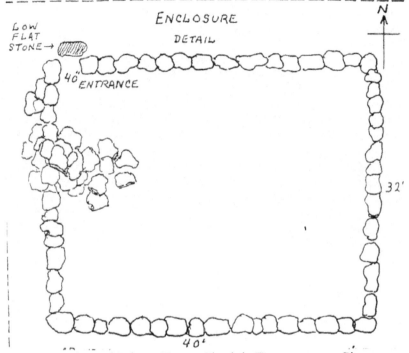

Drawing of Prince Henry Sinclair Encampment Site,
Massachusetts

David S. Brody

Foundation Stones of Prince Henry Sinclair Encampment Site

That summer Glynn conducted some preliminary archeological work—work that seemed to indicate the site dated to AD 1400—before falling ill. Then he did something that will forever remain a mystery to the outside world but which was explained in detail in the Agency file.

He sent a letter to the town historian explaining that he had recently returned to the site only to find it bulldozed over to make way for a housing subdivision. "Alas," he wrote, "the site has been destroyed."

The reality, Evgenia learned, was that Glynn had not returned to the site. Nor had it been bulldozed, though there had indeed been a new subdivision rising up nearby. Rather, an Agency operative had deceived Glynn and led him to believe that, while he was laid up in bed, another archeological team was snooping around, searching for the site and hoping to excavate. Glynn, jealous and protective of his find, had lied about the site being destroyed in hopes of discouraging other would-be diggers. Glynn never recovered from his illness and died that winter. The encampment site, to this day, remained overgrown and unexamined in the woods behind the subdivision.

Poor guy, Evgenia mused. So close to fulfilling his lifelong work, but stuck in his death bed imagining some other guy rushing in to steal the credit.

But, again, why did the Agency care? So what if some Scotsman had been running around Massachusetts in the late 1300s?

She tossed the file aside. Last file, and half a beer left. Daniel Whitewood. An only child from a wealthy family, Whitewood spent his life—and his parents' money— conducting archeological digs around New England, trying to find definitive archeological proof that European exploration of America predated Columbus.

By the time Whitewood reached his sixties he found himself insolvent with an elderly mother in a nursing home sucking away the last of his inheritance. But he had also finally hit pay-dirt: While digging beneath Rhode Island's Newport Tower in 2007 he uncovered a piece of seashell imbedded within some old mortar in the Tower's foundation—apparently in pre-modern times seashells, because they contain lime, were a key ingredient in making mortar.

David S. Brody

The Newport Tower, Rhode Island

Whitewood had the shell carbon-dated: It dated to the early 1400s, a result that tantalizingly seemed to tie the Tower construction to the Prince Henry voyage of 1399. Prince Henry or not, the find offered definitive proof that the Tower was built long before Columbus arrived in America. But before Whitewood could publicize his find, a wealthy collector contacted him and offered to purchase the mortar sample for one hundred thousand dollars under the condition Whitewood keep the find quiet until the collector was ready to announce the discovery. Whitewood—in need of the money and with no reason to doubt the motives of his benefactor—agreed. Six years later Whitewood died; his discovery had never been publicized and the mortar sample remained locked away in a safe somewhere. Evgenia shook her head. That 'somewhere' was likely Langley, Virginia.

But, again, why did the Agency care? Why the need to discredit or bury this research? The common thread connecting all the men, of course, was that their discoveries debunked the "Columbus first" ethos that American schoolchildren were taught in second grade. But if eight-year-olds could come to grips with the loss of Santa Claus and the Easter Bunny, surely they could survive the tarnishing of the Columbus image.

Of all the things for the CIA to focus on, of all the threats to national security over the decades, why was the Agency wasting time on ancient history?

She sipped the last of her beer and tossed the files back into her briefcase. The answers, she sensed, were not in any files.

CHAPTER 6

The walk from the Back Bay to the North End was about two-and-a-half miles as the crow flies, twice as long as it would have been from Randall's Chinatown apartment. But it was one of those rare winter mornings where the sun was shining and the temperature above freezing so Randall grabbed a walking stick, slipped into his winter garb and bounded out to Commonwealth Avenue.

Cameron had sent him a fascinating email late last night, outlining the various connections between the Mellon family, the CIA in general and Operation MK-Ultra in particular. He had been wise to bring the young researcher on—Cameron's fresh set of eyes and sharp instincts were clearly bearing fruit. The man would have made an effective Agency analyst.

The sun in his face, Randall pondered the Mellon connections. This was how his brain worked best, slowly sifting through the information, categorizing and compartmentalizing. Later he would begin to look for connections and then, hopefully, draw some conclusions. But for now he was content to stroll east along the avenue's tree-lined median called the Mall, dodging dog-walkers and baby-strollers and joggers, all of them funneled together by the snow banks intruding on the Mall's walkway. Boston was alive, and he happy to be alive in it.

Commonwealth Avenue ended and he entered the Public Garden. A pedestrian bridge spanned the frozen pond—would this be the last year he watched young families ride the Swan Boats and picnic and feed the ducks? He hoped not. He felt damn good for a man of eighty, but the insurance companies did not rely on the actuarial tables because they were *incorrect*. Smiling, he recalled a recent conversation he had with his brother:

The Oath of Nimrod

"The average life span for a man in this country is seventy-six," his brother had said. "So we are living on borrowed time."

"But the odds also state that one of us will live to eighty. So it behooves me to kill you now."

He had done some research and phoned his twin an hour later. "Your actuarial table may be accurate, but the statistics also indicate that if one reaches the age of eighty, the expectation is that one will live another eight years in addition to that."

Smiling at the memory of the exchange, Randall continued onto Boston Common. *Eight more years.* And if he lived to eighty-eight, then the tables gave him another four years after that. And so on. Perhaps he should go purchase a new suit.

The Common was a bit grittier than the Garden, especially in the winter, but a pleasant walk nonetheless. Just off the far edge of the Common stood the Masonic Grand Lodge, the third oldest Grand Lodge in the world and the oldest in the Western Hemisphere. Tonight he and Cameron and Amanda would be attending a lecture there given by a geologist from Bates College regarding pre-Columbian artifacts possibly connected to the medieval Knights Templar. Yesterday's blogger attack had convinced Randall that MK-Ultra was continuing to target Cameron—there was too much vitriol and passion in the post, and too little leading up to it, for the post to be random. One of the things Randall hoped to do tonight was question the professor to see if he had been targeted in any way himself. And of course he wanted to discuss the Mellon research with Cameron.

Ten minutes later Randall emerged on the far side of the Common and entered Government Center. This was his least favorite part of Boston, the hulking, Brutalist-style, City Hall building dominating a barren, wind-swept plaza like some kind of giant concrete harmonica dropped from outer space. The structure had once been named the ugliest building in America, which Randall thought was perhaps the kindest thing ever said about it. Randall lowered his head and plowed forward.

He lingered at the glass towers of the Holocaust Memorial for a few minutes before skirting the Haymarket produce market and crossing the Greenway to Hanover Street and the North End. He licked his lips; the walk had given him an appetite, but he'd wait until after his Copp's Hill visit to grab some pastries.

He checked his watch. Almost ten o'clock. Passing the Old North Church, he turned onto Hull Street and climbed the narrow way bordered by red-bricked buildings dating back to the early 1800s. The burial ground rose up on his right, one of the highest points in Boston. In the distance the sail-shaped Zakim Bridge loomed, its flowing white cables—meant to emulate the rigging of the nearby USS Constitution—in stark contrast to the rigidity of the neighborhood's Colonial architecture. Some people thought the bridge design too modern for Boston, but Randall loved the structure, especially at night when it was bathed in purple or blue or yellow light. And as a minority in a city with a racially-charged past, he also appreciated that the bridge was named for a civil rights activist. No doubt Prince Hall, one of the country's earliest Abolitionists, appreciated the civil rights memorial looming over his gravesite as well.

Randall passed through a wrought iron gate and followed a path to the back left portion of the grave yard. The sun had melted the snow in all but a few of the shaded areas of the cemetery. Much of the cemetery was in disrepair, with the slate grave slabs rising from the frozen ground crooked and chipped and discolored like a mouth full of neglected teeth. But the Prince Hall marker—an inscription carved into the base of an obelisk, the obelisk being a common motif in Masonic burials—stood polished and proud.

A splash of yellow caught Randall's eye as he approached. Too early for dandelions—perhaps a piece of trash had blown against the marker. He increased his pace, his eyes narrowing as he peered ahead. *Could it be?* A single yellow rose stood propped against the base of the grave marker, its golden pedals framed against the purple-black granite of the memorial. The flower seemed to shiver in the cold, even as it bravely stretched toward the sun.

He froze and stared, unable to accept what he was seeing. So many lonely nights, so many lonely years, so many lonely decades. All erased by a single yellow flower.

Finally he stumbled forward. Hand shaking, Randall lifted the rose. A single tear fell and landed on a rose pedal as he lifted the flower to his nose. He dropped to one knee, closed his eyes and choked out a single word.

"Consuela."

Cam recognized Randall's number on the caller ID and answered on the second ring. He, Amanda and Astarte had slept in after finally being released from the hospital well after midnight. He and Amanda still had splitting headaches and bloodshot eyes, but at least the nausea had passed and the doctors didn't believe they would suffer any long-term effects from the poisoning. Herm had not yet been discharged, but his condition had improved as well.

As if the headache was not bad enough, Cam was slogging through a particularly poorly-drafted Purchase and Sale Agreement. So he welcomed the late-morning interruption. "Mr. Sid. What can I do for you?"

"I am going to need to make a slight alteration of plans for tonight. I will meet you at the Grand Lodge at just before seven o'clock." The lecture began at seven, and the original plan was to meet at six so Randall could give Cam and Amanda a tour. Randall continued. "The tour will have to wait for another time."

"Okay. Is everything all right?" The old man was normally so … chipper. But he sounded lifeless this morning, sort of like the way Cam felt.

"Yes. As I said, something came up. My apologies. See you this evening."

They hung up and Cam returned to his real estate work. But his mind was on last night's events. He and Amanda had discussed it on the car ride home last night: Was Maxwell was just a paranoid, unstable collector, as Herm had warned, or was he put up to it by the CIA or someone else who wanted to stop their research? Cam sighed. As if they didn't have enough enemies already. At least this one was facing attempted murder charges.

He finally put aside his work and decided instead to focus on tonight's lecture. He had met Professor Antonopoulos a couple of times before, once at a conference and once when they both appeared as experts on a television documentary. He liked the man and, more importantly, liked his work—the best way to prove ancient explorers had come to America was with hard science. And he knew it took guts for Antonopoulos to challenge academia; for many researchers, questioning the Columbus-first dogma had been akin to committing professional suicide.

Cam was also anxious to ask the professor what he knew about the Bat Creek Stone. Cam had read that geological testing confirmed the stone had been in the ground for decades if not centuries when Emmert unearthed it. If that was indeed the case, those who accused Emmert of planting it would somehow have to reconcile the fact that Emmert had only recently arrived in Tennessee when he dug up the artifact.

Not that people like Vito Augustine cared about things like science or logic. He didn't seem like the type to let the facts get in the way of an otherwise perfectly good story.

Evgenia had arrived at the office at her usual eight o'clock time. She made sure to stick her head into Dr. J's door and give him a quick summary of last night's encounter with Professor Antonopoulos.

He had pondered her account. "And you think his concerns have been assuaged?"

Not the word she would have chosen, but yes. "Honestly, I think he feels like a fool."

"Good. Fools are easier to manipulate than professors. Make sure you file a report. And good work."

She started to turn away. "I'm not feeling great," she lied. "I think a bunch of that pepper spray got into my lungs. I have a few calls I need to make, but after that do you mind if I take the afternoon off and try to get some sleep?"

He waved her away. "Of course. See you on Monday. Feel better."

One of the most difficult things for an agent was remembering which lies were lies, which lies were truths, and which lies you told to whom. She exhaled and focused on clearing her head of any doubts about Dr. J and Rachel and their back story about the artifact. She needed to behave as if she trusted them completely. Even as she lied to them.

She phoned Rachel. After a bit of small talk, Evgenia said, "So, I ran into Professor Antonopoulos last night. He has some concerns about the artifact." She left it out there, dangling, to see how Rachel would respond. This is how an agent who trusted Rachel would play it—she would tell her of the encounter, but not the alarming details. Some lies were half-truths.

"Yes, he called me yesterday. He said the grooved areas were too clean." She laughed. "Turns out my mom put the rock in the dishwasher."

"Well, anyway, he mentioned he was going to be in Hartford on Saturday and wanted to ask your mother some questions." The file said Rachel's mother lived in Vernon, a suburb of Hartford. "I hope it's okay that I gave him her contact information—it was in the file and, as an old friend, I couldn't really claim not to know what town you grew up in. I think he plans to visit." Again, this is how an agent typically would have responded to the professor's request.

"Oh." A slight hesitation, but a quick recovery. "That should be fine. I'll call my mom and warn her. She's pretty busy, running around all the time."

Evgenia laughed, keeping it light. "I guess our professor wants to make sure anything he steals from your mother isn't a fake."

"Yes, a thief with standards. Thanks for the call; I'll warn my mom."

Evgenia stared at the phone. If her suspicions were correct, Rachel would be calling Dr. J now. He, in turn, would make a few calls, probably to a retired Agency operative or maybe a trusted military family. Within hours a house in Vernon, Connecticut would begin a makeover and its residents given a back story so that when the professor visited 'Mrs. Gold' on Saturday all would be in order....

Evgenia cleaned off her desk top and reached for her coat. By ten o'clock she would driving north on Route 95 in a friend's Toyota Corolla with a few hundred dollars in cash and another five hundred on a Visa gift card she kept on hand for emergencies. She wouldn't fly or rent a car or even use a credit card—she wanted to be off the grid for the weekend. She sensed there was more to this Antonopoulos assignment than she was being told. And since he was heading up to Boston, that's where she was headed also.

But not before making a stop in Vernon, Connecticut.

As had been agreed to so many decades ago, Randall's response to finding the yellow rose was to replace it with a stick of Juicy Fruit gum. He had been knocked so off-balance by the discovery of the flower that he had trouble regaining his feet. He staggered to the burial ground gate and hailed a taxi; three convenience stores later he finally found a pack of Juicy Fruit.

With a shaking hand, in the back of the taxi, he removed a stick of gum from the yellow five-piece pack and wrote on the inside of the wrapper: "Friday, 4:00 PM, Abbey Room, Boston Public Library." He refolded the wrapper around the gum as best he could, removed the other four sticks from the pack and slid the piece with the note on it back in.

He did the math in his head. Consuela would be eighty-two. Had she somehow made her way from Cuba to Boston? Hand still shaking, he opened a second piece of gum and popped it into his mouth. It tasted different than he remembered—sweeter and more tropical punch-like than the peach flavor he remembered from his youth. Then again, everything tasted different than it did in his youth.

He checked his watch. Just past eleven. Barely an hour had passed, an hour that in some ways seemed like a lifetime. He was tempted to wait at the cemetery for Consuela or whomever had left the rose, but he was too much of a professional to be careless after all these years. At four o'clock he would have some answers. And no doubt many more questions as well.

Amanda walked into to the living room to find Cam, Astarte and Venus watching an old *Scooby Doo* cartoon on TV. "Now this is some fine parenting," she said, her arms crossed.

"Don't blame me," Cam responded. "Venus insisted on it. I think she has a crush on Scooby."

Friday afternoon was the one time Astarte was allowed to watch junk TV. After a long week, it was her chance to sit with Cam and laugh and giggle. And after last night it seemed like a fine idea.

Amanda turned to Cam. "Any chance I can pull you away for a few minutes? I just found something extraordinary."

"But Shaggy is lost in the haunted house."

"Venus can tell you how it ends."

Astarte grinned. "Maybe it's not haunted. Maybe there's just a blocked furnace."

Cam ruffled her hair. "Very funny, smart girl."

Cam followed Amanda upstairs to their office. Sensing he was about to pinch her ass, she spun in time to slap his hand away. "Wow, impressive," he said.

"Perhaps you're just too predictable."

"Perhaps your ass is just too predictably pinch-able."

She nodded. "Well-argued." It was good to see him energized; they both were feeling better as the day went along, aided no doubt by an hour-long, post-lunch nap. Again, much like a bad hangover.

"So what is this extraordinary discovery?" he asked.

"You know how sometimes after you solve a puzzle you look back and all the clues were just lying there, waiting to be discovered?"

"Happens all the time."

"So for me, this giants research is the key to understanding everything." She clicked on an image on her computer. "Recognize this?"

Grave Creek Tablet, West Virginia

"Isn't that the Grave Creek Tablet?"

195

"Actually, a mold. The original has been lost. What do you know about it?"

"Let's see. Found in West Virginia in the 1830s. Some people thought the writing was Phoenician. But then the experts said it was just a mish-mash and decided it was a fake." Cam smiled. "Oh, I get where you're going with this. The stone was discovered in a burial mound."

"Yes, this one." She clicked on an image.

Grave Creek Burial Mound, West Virginia

Cam nodded. "And inside burial mounds are buried … skeletons. Let me guess, the skeletons were a bit oversized?"

"Almost seven-and-a-half feet. Not as gigantic as some, but still quite an aberration. A small giant, if you will."

"I've never heard about a giant skeleton being found with the Grave Creek tablet."

She handed him a page from an old book. "That's because you've never read this. It's from an 1879 book. It's amazing what you can find now that these old books are on the internet." She pointed. "There, at the bottom."

Cam read aloud. "*The engraved stone was found in the inside of a stone arch that was found in the middle of the mound, and in that stone arch was found a skeleton that measured seven feet and four inches.*" He looked up at her. "You know, you may be onto something. Does it seem likely to

196

you that a *fake* ancient artifact would be found buried with a *fake* giant skeleton?"

She rolled her eyes. "Hardly."

"So let's go back to the script. Is it really a mish-mash?"

She shook her head. "No. That's another of those mistaken conclusions that took on a life of its own. At the time it was found many linguists believed it to be a Phoenician-style script. Only later, with experts working from inaccurate copies of the inscription, did questions arise about the script's validity." In fact, one set of critics claimed the inscription was random markings while another set claimed the inscription was copied verbatim from a book containing ancient Phoenician writings. Apparently the experts couldn't even agree on why exactly the inscription was fake—it was either too authentic or not authentic enough.

"And does the age of the burial mound sync up with the Phoenicians?"

She nodded. "Perfectly. The mound dates back to the Adena Culture." Amanda and Cam both knew that the Adena Culture described a group of Native Americans who lived in the Ohio River Valley around 1000 BC to 200 BC; by comparison, Phoenician culture and exploration peaked around 800 BC and their language survived for centuries thereafter.

"So we have more ancient explorers from the Middle East. This wouldn't be too much earlier than the Bat Creek Stone."

"Fancy that. Ancient explorers who actually *explored*."

He smiled. "So the stone is not a fake?"

"I know this will come as a shock to you, but no, I think not."

"Amazing."

"What *is* amazing is how you Americans managed to build a nation, what with all of your early Colonists spending so much time carving and burying fake inscriptions. It seems to have been quite a national obsession." She sighed. "If we Brits had known how preoccupied you all were, we might have chanced another invasion."

"So what's the bottom line?"

She bit her bottom lip. "I don't know. On the one hand we have over a thousand accounts of giant skeletons unearthed in burial mounds, all of which have now disappeared. On the other hand we have a couple of dozen ancient inscriptions that have all been called fakes by the experts."

"And now both hands have come together, in the same mound." Cam clapped, illustrating the imagery.

"Yes." She took a deep breath. "An ancient inscribed stone was buried alongside a giant skeleton two thousand years ago. Are the stone and the giant related?" She shrugged. "The giant can no longer speak. But perhaps the stone can."

Randall arrived at the library a full hour before the appointed four o'clock time. The minutes had been dragging by all afternoon so finally he washed his face, combed his hair, brushed his teeth, put on a clean sweater-vest—yellow and green in honor of the flower—and walked the four blocks from his brother's apartment to Copley Square.

He had chosen the Boston Public Library as a meeting place because it was a locale that a visitor to Boston might innocently choose to visit. Within that vast edifice, the Abbey Room might afford a bit of privacy. The space was called a 'room' like the gilded mansions of Newport, Rhode Island were called 'cottages'—at over two thousand square feet, the ornate room was larger than many homes and was often used for large weddings. In any event, at four o'clock on a Friday afternoon the spacious hall would likely be empty. And if not empty, then he would have a good idea of who might be tailing them.

Some of his favorite art work adorned the Abbey Room's walls. A series of richly-colored murals, painted by American artist Edwin Austin Abbey, depicted the legend and history of the Holy Grail. Many scholars believed the medieval Knights Templar, closely associated with the Freemasons, were the guardians of the treasured cup which had held the blood of Jesus and there was much in Abbey's murals that hinted at this guardianship. Randall loved to examine the paintings for clues.

But even the Holy Grail could not distract him today. He was about to meet with Consuela, or at least someone extraordinarily close to her. His last direct contact with her had been in the summer of 1959, just after Castro took power and a couple of years before President Kennedy's ill-fated Bay of Pigs invasion poisoned U.S.-Cuban relations for the next fifty years. But in 1959 he had been a young man in love, visiting a beautiful woman in an exotic city, caught up in the heady euphoria of building a utopian society.

Somehow over fifty years had passed. How had it happened? And more importantly, how had he allowed it to happen? He read once that God gave us memories so we might have roses in our winter years. Well, he had his memories, at least, of a heavenly summer in Havana. And, on this day in the winter of his life, he had his rose as well. Randall carefully pulled the flower, which he had wrapped in wet paper towel and sealed in a plastic bag, from his jacket pocket. He closed his eyes, breathed in the flower's fragrance, sighed, and dried the corner of his eyes with his sleeve.

When he looked up she stood in front of him. Somehow he had not seen her enter.

He reached out with a shaky hand. It was Consuela, but not Consuela. Consuela made older and somehow also made younger again. Reddish-brown hair streaked with gray. Age spots atop the freckles on her nose and cheeks. A bit of sadness within her deep brown eyes.

"Hello, Papa," she whispered. "My name is Morgana. Mama sent me."

His eyes filled with tears as he took her in his arms. "I did not know," he sobbed. "God forgive me, I did not know."

She pulled away gently, her hands still clasping his. She looked deep into his eyes, disengaged her right hand and tapped the side of his forehead with her fingertips. "You did not know *here*," she said. She moved her hand down and rested her fingers on his chest. "But I think you have always known *here*."

Evgenia skirted Hartford just after four o'clock, missing the worst of the afternoon rush hour. She had made good time, pushing eighty and stopping only once to gas up and grab an energy bar and ice tea for lunch. She squirmed in her seat, trying to loosen her back. Even though it sometimes made it hard to find eligible men, she considered her height an asset. But while traveling—and of course planes were worse than cars—there never seemed to be enough leg room. Ten miles to Vernon, followed by another hour-and-a-half to Boston. Then park the Toyota in some garage and be done with it for the weekend.

She exited Route 84 north of Hartford, where she grabbed a poppy bagel with lox from the famous Rein's Deli for a late lunch. As she ate, her GPS guided her to a gridded neighborhood south of the highway. She easily found Scott Drive and drove by Rachel's mother's house. Or what supposedly was Rachel's mother's house—a beige raised ranch with a one-car garage attached to the side and a fake wishing well in the center of the front yard, shaded by a single oak tree. Anyplace, America. A pair of vehicles sat in the driveway, an unmarked white van and a red pickup truck. Odd choice of vehicles for a middle-aged woman. But faded gold-colored lettering that spelled 'Gold' adorned the mailbox, which was a point in favor of authenticity. Rachel drove by, circling the block.

On her second pass a clean-cut young man carried a cardboard box from the van into the home. She didn't dare make a third pass so she parked a couple blocks away, rubbed the poppy seeds from her teeth, buttoned her coat and walked back toward the house. Wishing she had a dog, she walked slowly as she approached, her face angled toward the winter sun. The dull thud of hammering cascaded from the home. As she reached the driveway the same clean-cut guy bounded out the side door toward the van. She waved and smiled. "Howdy. You moving in?"

He smiled and shifted his weight. "No. Just bringing in some boxes."

She considered asking about Rachel, but that might tip them off. "I remember when I was a kid they always had the best Halloween decorations here." The guy was about her age, probably a young agent just cutting his teeth on a grunt assignment. She would need to be careful not to make him suspicious. She offered her best smile. "Used to scare me half to death."

He shrugged. "No Halloween decorations in the boxes. Just pictures and stuff." He slid another box from the back of the van.

She smiled again, her eyes locked on his. She leaned forward playfully, counting on his testosterone to trump his training. "I bet there's a spider or ghost or something in there ready to jump out at me."

"No," he grinned. He tilted the box toward her. "See, just pictures. Nothing to scare you."

She feigned relief. "Well, all right then. Thanks." One final smile. "Have a great day." She turned to continue her walk and suppressed a shiver. In many ways the framed photo of Rachel in that box was more frightening than any spider or ghost.

Randall and his daughter had moved into the reading room adjacent to the Abbey Room. They sat across from each other at a table in the corner, their heads bent forward. *A daughter, named after me.*

He exhaled. "Are you certain you have not been followed?" Randall asked, more concerned for Morgana than for what might happen to him.

She nodded. "I am certain. I am here as part of a cultural exchange program with a music group." She smiled. "I am a singer."

He met her smile with one of his own. "That is an honorable profession, bringing joy to peoples' lives."

Laughing, she replied. "Singing is only a hobby. I am a pediatrician."

He sat up. "A doctor. Just like your mother." He nodded. "You have done well. Your mother has done well."

Morgana grinned. "And you have a grandson who will soon graduate from medical school as well." Her English, like her mother's, was near-perfect. She showed him a picture of a dark-haired young man with a kind smile. "His name is Ricardo."

Randall fingered the photograph. *A grandson.* He was not sure if he wanted to laugh or to cry. "The worst form of loneliness is to have memories but nobody to share them with," he whispered.

She took his hands again. "I am sorry, Papa. Mama is sorry. Many nights has she wept for your loneliness."

A few seconds passed. "Did you know Mama was the Minister of Public Health for many years?" Morgana asked.

He shook his head. "We do not get much news out of Cuba." Plus Consuela had stopped writing soon after his return from Havana. He guessed the position was akin to Surgeon General in the U.S. A good job for her. Randall recalled a debate they had one night over a pitcher of sangria. "In Cuba," Consuela had argued, "our poor are guaranteed the right to medical care. In America, your poor are guaranteed the right to complain when they can not afford medical care. You tell me which is the better system." Randall smiled. Often he let her win these types of arguments because he wanted to take her to bed; this time he had been truly defeated. It had been the first time he appreciated and understood what Castro—and Consuela—were trying to accomplish....

"She loves to tell the story how she first won Fidel's confidence," Morgana said. The Cubans had a strange custom of calling their leader by his first name. "It was just after the Bay of Pigs invasion, and Fidel held hundreds of American soldiers as prisoners. Mama convinced him to trade the prisoners for baby formula."

Randall chuckled. "I remember that. It made a lot of Americans respect Castro, made him seem more humane. We invaded his country and instead of taking a pound of flesh he chose to feed his children." Randall had been a young CIA operative at the time; the invasion's failure, coupled with Castro's public relations coup, had demoralized the Agency. "Of course I did not realize that had been your mother's idea—how could I?" He smiled. "Though it does sound like her."

She squeezed his hand, anticipating his unspoken question. "She never married, Papa. She told me all about you, showed me pictures. Your photograph still stands next to her bed."

"I am glad—"

The words caught in his throat. He took a deep breath and tried again. "I am glad to know this." He pulled out his wallet and flipped it open, revealing a faded photo of Consuela sitting on a beach, and angled it toward Morgana. "Please tell her I carry her picture with me always."

He took another deep breath. He could not take his eyes off her. Off his daughter. In some ways it was like looking at Consuela all over again. "You have your mother's eyes," he finally said.

"And she says I have your sharp tongue."

He smiled and checked his watch. "The library closes in half an hour. Will you join me for dinner?"

She frowned. "I am sorry, I cannot. My group expects me back—I do not want to raise any suspicions. We are leaving tomorrow already." She brightened. "I was worried you would not find the flower. For three days I have been waiting. I would have been so disappointed ... heartbroken ... if I did not see you. And Mama also."

"How is she?"

Her eyes clouded. "Not well. I think that is why she wanted me to see you—she wanted me to meet my father before she died."

He swallowed. "She is sick?"

"Very." Morgana shrugged. "The details do not matter. But she has had a good life. She has helped many, many people. The revolution has truly worked, Papa, even with America opposing us at every turn. Cuba is not perfect, but everyone is educated, everyone has medical care, people care for each other. Cuba is not Russia or China, with all their corruption and greed. In Cuba the great experiment has succeeded. Mama is very proud. And, now with us meeting, she will be at peace, I think."

Randall sighed. He was sad to hear about Consuela. But he was also angry, bitter that fifty-odd years had passed and she had hidden his daughter and grandson from him. He pushed the anger from his mind—it was done, and there would be plenty of time to be melancholy later. "Please give her my love. Tell her I have missed her. All these years, I have never stopped loving her."

Morgana's eyes brimmed. As hard as it was for Randall to learn he had a daughter, it must have been infinitely more difficult for Morgana to grow up knowing she had a father who would never be part of her life. "I will tell her, Papa," she whispered.

He swallowed. "Did she tell you why … she never informed me about you?"

"Yes, she did." Morgana had the same forthright way of speaking as did her mother. "As you know, soon after you left Cuba, the U.S. government broke off relations. Mama feared things would be hard for Fidel, hard for Cuba. She loved you very much, but she loved the revolution more. She was worried if she told you about me you would want to join us in Cuba." Morgana looked down. "And she thought you more valuable to the revolution here." She took his hands. "She had no way to know the hostilities would last a lifetime."

So his daughter knew. Knew the truth about him. Knew he was a sleeper agent, imbedded deep inside the American intelligence community. *But never awakened.* He slapped the table with his hand, causing a few heads to turn. He fought to keep his voice low. "Why was I never activated?" he hissed. When he left Cuba, the plan was for him to get a job at the CIA for a few years, wait for instructions, and eventually rejoin Consuela in Cuba. But a few years had turned into more than half a century, a half century of waiting for a single yellow rose that never appeared. "It is bad enough I have wasted away my life. But to miss watching my daughter and my grandson grow up *for no reason*?" His shoulders dropped. "How futile it has all been."

Her wide brown eyes engulfed him. "That is why I am here, Papa. Cuba has not forgotten about you. The Cuban people, *your people*, need you now. You have been activated. You have a very important mission."

He sat back. "I am eighty years old and retired. What can I possibly do?"

She lifted her jaw. "You can save Cuba."

Now, after all these years? "How?"

"You must prevent Webster Lovecroft from being elected President, Papa. If he is elected, he will invade Cuba." Her eyes moistened. "Our society is good and honest and just. It is *humane*. But this Lovecroft has promised to send modern-day Crusaders to destroy us. In the name of religion, he will crush everything we have built."

He sighed as she held his eyes. "Please, it is up to you, Papa. You must stop him."

"We should get ready," Cam said, walking into the upstairs office. "The lecture starts at seven. You said you wanted to make a stop first? And I want to swing by and visit Herm for a few minutes—he's doing okay but they want to keep him for another night." He had just dropped Astarte off at a friend's for a sleepover birthday party, after eliciting from her a promise to go to sleep no later than ten. They all needed a good night's sleep.

Amanda looked up from her computer. "I do need to make a stop. And of course let's go see Herm. How is he?"

Cam smiled. "Ornery and pissed. He's already contacted some of his drinking buddies. They're going to make Maxwell pay, one way or another."

She nodded, her jaw clenched. One of the few things they disagreed on was vigilante justice. Cam was fine with Herm exacting some revenge if for some reason the legal system let Maxwell walk—as a lawyer Cam knew the system was far from perfect. But he sensed even Amanda wouldn't argue this one too much. The guy had tried to kill her entire family.

"I'm almost done here," she said. "I'm trying to find a good translation of the Grave Creek Tablet."

"A *good* one? You mean there is more than one choice?"

She dropped her hands into her lap. "This stuff can be infuriating. But here's a rough translation: *Burial mound in honor of King Tasach. His queen caused this Tablet to be inscribed.* Apparently Tasach is the name of the giant skeleton."

"And his wife, the queen, built a burial mound for him and put the carved stone in it."

"Yes."

"So who is this King Tasach? And why does he speak Phoenician?"

"Before I get to that, fancy this: There's another burial mound in West Virginia called the Criel Mound. It was excavated by the Smithsonian in the 1880s. Care to guess what they found?"

"Another giant?"

"Seven-and-a-half feet tall. Another king, based on the decorations and ornaments he was buried with. Adena Culture, same as Grave Creek."

"Would you consider seven-and-a-half to be a giant?"

"I'm guessing they shrunk over time as they inbred with the natives. And there are still plenty of skeletons well over eight feet. So, yes, I would still call them giants."

"Fair enough. Especially when you consider the average height back then was just over five feet."

Amanda continued. "And there's more. A mound in Ohio called the Miamisburg Mound—a skeleton over eight feet tall unearthed nearby. Again, Adena time period." She gestured to her computer. "I found dozens, all in Adena burial mounds. And here's something nobody talks about; listen to this." She read from her computer screen. "Burials of chiefs were accompanied by a great ceremony. Like the Egyptians, their bodies were buried with items such as pottery, projectile points, beads, and pipes." She looked up.

"Like the Egyptians," he repeated.

She nodded, chewing her lower lip. "And the Phoenicians were known to adopt Egyptian burial practices." Cam looked at her expectantly; Amanda had a remarkable ability to play connect-the-dots with various data points and come up with a narrative that made sense. "So tie it all together."

Amanda took a deep breath. "Okay, let's start with the Book of Mormon."

Cam smiled. "Do we have to?" Neither of them believed Joseph Smith's claim that he found golden plates, written by prophets of God in a language called 'reformed Egyptian,' that contained the third part of the Bible, after the Old and New Testaments. But they did not dismiss the Book of Mormon entirely. Based on their research, they believed that Smith wrote the Mormon narrative himself after finding a copper scroll written in an ancient language—probably Phoenician—that told of Middle-Eastern explorers traveling to America in the millennium before Christ.

Amanda ignored him. "So why did Smith write about a war between Middle-Eastern explorers and Native Americans?"

Cam replied. "Probably because that's what the scroll said. Always base your legends on a foundation of truth."

"Right. A Phoenician scroll, in all probability. Now let's turn to the Old Testament. The Bible talks about a race of giants who lived in ancient Phoenicia, Goliath being the most famous. I found a Phoenician funerary inscription from 500 BC that makes reference to Og, who the Bible tells us was king of the giants. The point of all this is that if the Phoenicians came to America to mine copper, who's to say they didn't bring giants with them?"

They had done extensive research over the past year at a site in New Hampshire called America's Stonehenge showing that ancient Phoenicians, whose ships dwarfed those of Columbus, sailed to America. Many scholars believed the Phoenicians came to mine copper in New England and the Great Lakes region to meet the insatiable need for the metal during the latter part of the Bronze Age.

"The Phoenicians," Cam said. "All roads always lead back to the Phoenicians."

"How so?"

"It's just that every site and every artifact we find can be traced back to them. They came here first, and others followed."

The Phoenicians were accomplished navigators and boat-builders, and possessed advanced maps and charts. Centuries later, the Templars used old Phoenician maps they found in the Middle East to navigate the Atlantic.

"I read where some bloke is going to sail a replica of a Phoenician ship across the Atlantic."

Cam nodded. "The Phoenicians sailed around the tip of Africa, so why not across the Atlantic?"

Amanda shifted. "To my point: With giants on board."

"Okay. And if the giants came, they could have stayed. Gone native."

"Yes. And your Native American tradition confirms this— a race of giants living in the Ohio River Valley that drove the Cherokees and other tribes south."

"And you know what else confirms it? The Sacrificial Stone at America's Stonehenge." Researchers had long wondered what, exactly, was being sacrificed atop the stone slab. "Phoenicians back then worshipped Baal. To please Baal, they offered human sacrifice—usually children captured in battle, but sometimes their own babies."

Amanda wrapped her arms around herself. "Giants and children being sacrificed. Sounds like a Grimm fairy tale. It's a wonder children ever fall asleep." She focused back on her computer screen, to the translation of the Grave Creek burial inscription. "So you think our boy King Tasach was a Phoenician giant?"

Cam nodded. "Or a descendant of one. In fact, the name 'Tasach' is a derivative of the Semitic name, 'Isaac.' And whoever Tasach was, he and his family brought with them their burial customs, which explains all the burial mounds and the Egyptian-like burial practices."

"And all the giant skeletons." She stood. "I don't know if we have the story right, Cam, but the dates work and the idea of King Tasach and the other giants coming from Phoenicia holds together. It explains the mounds, the skeletons, the inscriptions, the funereal objects, the Native American legends, the Book of Mormon, the Sacrificial Stone, everything."

"Not everything." He smiled. "It doesn't explain the coverup."

Randall and his daughter walked hand-in-hand through the library, past the pair of giant marble lions standing guard on the grand stairwell, and out onto Boylston Street. "May I walk with you a bit longer?" he asked. He did not want to let her go.

"Is it safe?" she asked.

He shrugged. "Either we were followed or we were not. I doubt another ten minutes together will change anything."

She smiled and slid her arm around his and leaned into him. "My group is meeting at Quincy Market for dinner." She turned to him. "I must say, you Americans do eat well. So many choices!"

"Yes. And the Romans ate well also, just before their empire fell. I fear we spend too much time feeding our mouths and not enough feeding our brains."

He guided her down Boylston Street, past Trinity Church and the Hancock Tower. She stopped to snap a picture. "I love the way the reflection of the old church is captured in the mirrored walls of the office tower. Boston is a beautiful city." She turned to face him. "And I would like a picture of you, if that is okay." She smiled. "The one Mama has is a bit old."

He nodded, straightened his hair and lifted his chin. Then he in turn took her picture with his cell phone. They continued along, taking a right on Commonwealth and retracing his steps from this morning. Eight hours had passed; in that time he had gained a daughter, a grandson and a mission.

"This assignment of mine," he said. "Are there any specifics?" His mind had already begun to focus on his task; his first step would be to plumb Cameron Thorne for information about the friend he mentioned who worked on Lovecroft's campaign.

She exhaled. "No. We leave it up to you."

He nodded. At his age it might be asking a lot for him to assassinate a Presidential candidate; on the other hand, it was not like he would be sacrificing a bright future if he got caught. What was that expression? *You do not need a parachute to skydive. You only need a parachute to skydive twice.* In some ways old age could be liberating—he could take some risks, pursue this mission without a parachute.

Randall questioned his daughter. "Regarding Lovecroft, do you really feel he would invade Cuba?" He had made the comment a couple of decades ago, as a young Congressman—perhaps his position had changed or the man had tempered his passion as he aged.

Her hand tightened on his forearm. "Obviously this is not my area of expertise. But the Cuban government believes the threat is real. Lovecroft used the words, 'modern-day Crusade.'" She made a face. "As if we poor Cubans need our souls to be saved by some ... *American politician.*"

Randall smiled. He wasn't sure what was worse in Morgana's mind—the American part or the politician part. "Politicians often say things they do not mean."

David S. Brody

She stopped and looked up at him. "Yes, that is true. But I think this Senator Lovecroft said exactly what he meant to say. Since then, he has been more careful. But his words tell us what is in his heart. And his heart is black."

Not black so much as misguided. Did Lovecroft really think forcing religion down Cuba's throat was a wise strategy? Had he not studied history? How many people had died in the name of God? If Lovecroft did not understand this, perhaps he was not smart enough to be elected in the first place. Or perhaps, more likely, Lovecroft was playing the Cuban invasion card as a way to curry favor with certain groups of American voters. But there was no sense in getting into a philosophical discussion now with his daughter.

Randall nodded. "I understand he is a danger."

"Perhaps he will not act on this threat, Papa. Perhaps he will change his mind or not be elected in the first place." Her eyes smoldered, just as Consuela's did when she felt passionate about something. "But we can not take that chance. It is like the 1962 situation in reverse: President Kennedy could not risk Khrushchev pointing nuclear missiles at him from so close by, no matter how unlikely it was he would use them. It is the same for us."

She took her hand off Randall's arm and stepped back. She held his eyes for a few seconds before speaking. "We can not risk having a crazy man who wants to invade Cuba sitting in the White House."

Amanda kissed Cam at the corner of Tremont and Boylston, in front of the eight-story granite Masonic Grand Lodge, one of the more venerated Masonic structures in North America. They paused for a few seconds to admire the mosaic murals adorning the exterior walls. "You sure you don't want me to come with you?" Cam asked.

211

"No. It's only half a block up. I think I'll have more luck alone." She smiled. "You know, the helpless girl approach."

"I'm not so sure about helpless. Just ask Chung. Call me when you leave and I'll come out and meet you."

Both of them looked gaunt and colorless after the previous night. But at least they were stylishly haggard, she in a black evening gown, he in a tuxedo. Apparently the Freemasons liked to dress up. She kissed him again. "Shouldn't be more than a half hour."

The wind whipped across Boston Common as she walked up Tremont Street, her overcoat pulled tight around her. She checked her watch: a few minutes before seven. Based on a call she had made, Dr. Anoosian saw his last patient at 6:30. Assuming every appointment lasted at least a half hour, she should catch him before he left for the weekend.

She rang a bell in the foyer and was buzzed through a fingerprint-marked glass door. A faded label, 'Artun Anoosian, DDM, 4th Floor' directed her—she punched at the buttons of an old, cramped elevator and ascended, shaking and bumping along the way. A cheerful male voice called out as the door opened: "To your right, end of the hall. Have a seat in the waiting room."

The room was tired and cramped but clean. Also empty, the receptionist presumably having left for the day. The sound of a drill, accompanied by an occasional moan, wafted from behind a closed door. Five minutes later a pimply-faced young man wearing an Emerson College sweatshirt loped out from behind that door and passed through the waiting room, followed by a plump, smiling man with bushy gray eyebrows, olive skin and an appropriately bright dentist's smile. "I am Dr. Anoosian." He eyed her gown. "Is there an emergency?" He had an accent which, if exaggerated, would sound something like Count Dracula in a low-budget horror film.

She stood. "No, Doctor, no emergency. My name is Amanda Spencer-Gunn." She held out her hand and he shook it stiffly. "I was hoping I might ask you a few questions. I promise it will not take much of your time."

He glanced at his watch and sighed. "My wife is waiting for me for dinner." He eyed her like a man who knew that the company of a beautiful young woman would be preferable to that of his wife, but who wondered also whether it was all worth the risk. He sighed again. "Very well. How may I be of service?" He leaned against the receptionist's desk a few feet to one side of her.

She pulled a copy of the old dental journal article from her purse and handed it to him. "I believe you wrote this."

He glanced at it, nodded and rubbed his eyes. "I was wondering when this would happen. You are a reporter, I assume? No doubt part of the liberal media?"

She tilted her head. Why did he think that? "Reporter? No. I simply wanted to ask you a few questions about hyperdontia."

He eyed her suspiciously. "Very well. I will do my best to answer them."

She took a deep breath and smiled, trying to ease the tension in the room. "I was just wondering if this type of hyperdontia—an entire second set of teeth—is common?"

He frowned. "If you read the article, you know the answer to this question already. It is very rare."

"Yes, of course. Otherwise there would have been no reason to write about it." This was not going well. She took another deep breath. "You noted in the article that your patient was almost seven feet tall. Do you think his height is in any way related to the hyperdontia?"

His eyes narrowed. "I do not believe you said what your interest in this subject is? I can see you do not suffer from hyperdontia yourself. And I do not believe you are a dental student, or you would have mentioned this fact already."

She lifted her chin. "I am merely doing research, and I came upon your article."

"Yes, doing research." He stood and handed the article back to her. "As I suspected, you are a reporter. I am afraid I cannot help you. You are asking me to divulge confidential patient information." He gestured to the door.

Why did he think she was a reporter? She stood to leave. This had clearly not gone well. "I am sorry to have bothered you. Thank you for your time."

He nodded and turned away. Sadly, almost as an afterthought, he spoke over his shoulder: "I feared this day would come. There are no secrets when you run for President."

As Cam entered the Grand Lodge foyer, Randall, wearing a tuxedo and Masonic apron, strolled over to greet him. Randall's Arlington Lodge was using the Grand Lodge to host tonight's event. "Welcome to the Grand Lodge of Massachusetts, chartered in 1733, making it the oldest Grand Lodge in North America." Randall smiled wryly and gestured up a couple of stairs to a high-ceilinged room filled with dark woods and plush furnishings that Cam usually associated with the waiting rooms of some of Boston's old Brahmin law firms. Unlike the law offices, the room smelled like cigars and wet wool. "Notice the quiet elegance of our lobby," Randall continued.

"Quiet elegance?"

"That's another phrase for stodgy." He pulled Cam aside. "And you must not laugh when the Brothers address me as 'Most Worshipful.'"

"Most Worshipful?"

"Yes. As in, 'Most Worshipful, can I hang your coat?' It took me a while to get used to it as well. Because my brother was once Grand Master, he retains that title. And, of course, as far as anyone knows, I am my brother."

Cam's eyes had been drawn more to the alternating black and white square floor tiles. Every Masonic Lodge he had ever been in had the same floor pattern. "Okay, Most Worshipful, you're not going to tell me this floor has nothing to do with the Templars, are you?" The Templar flag, the Beauseant, featured the same black and white pattern, as did the floor of King

Solomon's Temple. Despite the countless overlapping rituals and iconography between the Freemasons and the Templars, there were still some historians who doubted the two groups were connected.

Randall spread his hands. "We are not a secret society. We are a society of secrets."

Cam shrugged off the typically unresponsive response and explained that Amanda would be joining them in a few minutes. There was a flush to Randall's cheek that Cam had never seen before and his full head of cottony- white hair, normally so neat, was disheveled. Perhaps he had had a glass of wine with his Brothers. "Have you met Professor Antonopoulos yet?"

"No. I was detained this afternoon and only just arrived myself."

A steady stream of tuxedo-clad men, many with wives or girlfriends, passed through the lobby toward the elevator. Cam had lectured here a couple of years ago; he guessed the professor would be speaking in the Gothic Hall upstairs. It looked like he'd have a good crowd.

Cam made small talk with a couple of the Brothers. He mentioned the Phoenicians in passing, and one of the Brothers informed him that Hiram Abiff, the most prominent historical figure in Freemasonry, was a Phoenician. "He was an architect. King Solomon hired him to build the original Temple in Jerusalem."

Cam tilted his head. "Wait, wouldn't you want Jewish builders building a sacred Jewish temple?"

The man nodded. "You would think so. But apparently this Hiram Abiff was something special."

Or, Cam mused, perhaps the Masonic-Templar ties to the ancient Phoenicians went deeper than just a few navigational charts and maps. For Solomon to hire—and the Freemasons to venerate—a pagan like Hiram Abiff made no sense unless there was more to the story. As he and Amanda had discussed earlier, all roads seemed to lead back to the Phoenicians.

Amanda strolled in, interrupting his thoughts. She shook her hair loose and took his arm. "How did it go?" he asked.

"Not well," she sighed. "He thought I was a bloody reporter."

"Why? Who cares about some guy's teeth?"

"That's what I thought. But I think I might have figured it out."

"What?"

She lowered her voice. "I think the patient, the bloke with the double rows of teeth, was Senator Lovecroft—"

Randall appeared out of nowhere, interrupting Amanda. He greeted her, bowing and kissing her hand, as Cam pondered Amanda's discovery. Could that mean Lovecroft descended from a race of giants? Even if not true, the mere allegation, accompanied with the dental article, was not the type of thing likely to win him votes....

"Cameron claims you do not have a sister for me," Randall crooned. "Pray tell me he is mistaken."

She laughed lightly. "No sister. But I have an older brother, and also a hideously obese old aunt."

"Alas, I will just have to win you away from Cameron." He released her hand and offered his arm in its stead. "Come, my dear. The lecture begins in five minutes." After a few steps he turned and sighed. "And I suppose you might as well join us, Mr. Thorne."

Evgenia had long ago learned that disguises did not work for her. She was tall and striking and bronze-skinned—it was tough to disguise herself as anything besides a runway model or beach volleyball player. So instead she turned her looks to her advantage.

Dressed in a hip-hugging black cocktail dress, she sauntered over to the middle-aged Masonic Brother seated behind a desk in the foyer checking off names. She bent low, revealing a generous amount of cleavage. "Is this where Professor Antonopoulos is lecturing?" she asked with a smile.

"It sure is."

She exhaled and swung her hair. "Oh, thank goodness. I've been so lost. I am one of his ex-students and he invited me to come hear him speak tonight...."

A few more smiles and white lies and she had talked her way in.

Based on what she had seen in Connecticut, she was not the only puppeteer pulling the professor's strings. She assumed she was being used as a kind of distraction—Antonopoulos would be so preoccupied by Evgenia framing him for selling an artifact he did not own that he would overlook the too-perfect weathering patterns of the carving. So far, she had to admit, it was working.

But if she was the "other agent" in this spy triangle, that meant another operative, perhaps even Rachel, had been assigned to Antonopoulos as well. And that agent might be in attendance tonight. Evgenia needed a way to stay close to Antonopoulos without being seen.

She rode the elevator to the seventh floor. She had taken a few minutes to research the layout of the Grand Lodge, so she expected Gothic Hall to be decorated in a "cheerful red tone," but she hadn't expected solid, deep red to dominate the floor, the walls, the seats and the stage curtain. She had a friend once in middle school who talked her parents into letting her paint her room purple; then she went out and bought purple sheets and a purple area rug and purple curtains. A few days later she confided to Evgenia, "I hate my room. My head hurts every time I go in there."

Evgenia surveyed the room from the entryway. The performance hall was laid out more like a Victorian theater or playhouse than a meeting room, with a stage and a curtain at the far end and stadium seats facing them. Perhaps half the seats were filled; Antonopoulos fiddled with a projector aimed at a screen on the floor in front of the stage. Apparently the professor would speak from the floor and then afterward autograph books on the stage, where a table and chair had been set up for him, meaning anyone who wanted to talk to him would have to approach him on stage. An idea came to her: If she could hide behind the stage curtain, within earshot of the table....

Crammed together in the elevator, Randall's face a mere inches from Amanda's breast, they ascended. The warm musky scent of her filled Randall's nostrils. He had never paid less attention to a beautiful woman.

His mind was on Consuela and Morgana and the revolution and Senator Lovecroft. Nothing else mattered.

Including Project MK-Ultra. Suddenly he no longer cared what the CIA was doing, why the program continued to exist. He had a more important mission.

But he could not just cast Cameron aside. If nothing else, the man would become suspicious, which could be a liability— Thorne knew Randall and his brother had switched identities. More importantly, Thorne and his fiancée were his best, in fact only, connection to Lovecroft. So he needed to continue to cultivate the relationship. And what was this Amanda said about a double row of teeth....

They entered Gothic Hall. "My Lodge is technically hosting this event, so I will need to sit in the back in case something is needed," Randall said. "As much as I hate to return Amanda to you, I suggest you find a seat closer to the front." The truth was that Randall needed time to think and did not want to have to make small talk.

The lights dimmed and Professor Antonopoulos began his PowerPoint presentation. He began lightly, showing an image of a humorous rock formation. "I call this "Rock Bottom," he said, smiling.

Rock Bottom Formation

"I sometimes wonder if it wasn't the work of some ancient explorers, hoping to moon those that came after them. But more likely it is a natural formation."

As the crowd laughed, Randall rose and exited the performance hall. He needed to figure out a way to convince Cameron to set up a meeting with Lovecroft. The obvious approach would be to interest Lovecroft, who chaired the Senate Intelligence Committee, on the activities of Project MK-Ultra. But interesting Lovecroft in MK-Ultra was not a plan, it was a goal.

A passageway ran up the length of the performance hall, allowing private access to the stage area. Randall paced this hallway, deep in thought. He checked his watch. A half hour had passed. He cracked open a side door and peered into the performance hall; all seemed to be in order. As he turned away a movement caught his eye from behind the stage. Through a gap in the curtain he was certain he saw something move. There were only two ways to access the area behind the curtain: from the stage and from the hallway he was standing in. He dried his palms on his trousers.

The Oath of Nimrod

Moving quietly, Randall crept to the end of the hallway and pressed his ear against the door leading directly to the backstage area. Nothing. He dropped to the floor and peered under. No light, no movement. Assuming the door would be well-oiled to prevent noise during a performance, he slowly turned the knob and eased his shoulder into it. The door moved a half-inch; he froze and waited. Nothing. Another couple of inches, another wait. A third push and he turned his body sideways and slid through, entering a rectangular storage area running front to back alongside the stage; dimly lit from the hallway, the room was filled with tools, cleaning supplies and stage props.

He crossed to the far side of the storage room and waited. The thick curtain blocked whatever lights remained on in the performance hall. Randall counted to thirty, allowing his eyes to adjust. Crawling like a baby, keeping his head low, he ascended a short staircase to the raised stage and peered in. *There.* In the folds of the curtain, only fifteen feet away, a woman sat cross-legged on the floor, her back to the stage. He studied her, wondering what she could possibly be doing. Was she Antonopoulos' girlfriend, waiting for a post-lecture tryst? But why sit in the dark?

It was too dark to make out her features so Randall waited. Five minutes passed, then the woman opened her cell phone and lifted it to her face, presumably to check the time. The glow briefly illuminated her face. Randall swallowed a gasp. He knew her.

In fact, he had trained her.

Randall sunk back down the short staircase and exhaled quietly. What a day for surprises. A daughter he never knew he had. A mission he had waited a lifetime for. And now a student come back to face-off against her mentor. But that was not fair:

220

Did Evgenia even know why he was here? More fundamentally, did Evgenia even know why *she* was here?

His brain, normally so efficient, struggled to sift through today's avalanche of information. As far as he knew, Evgenia still worked in the MK-Ultra division. Which meant it was likely she had been assigned Professor Antonopoulos, presumably to discredit him just as the blogger was trying to discredit Cameron Thorne and he himself had discredited Laurence Gardner. And that meant...

"Hello Mr. Sid." He jumped as a hand touched him lightly on the shoulder. Evgenia, crouching, smiled at him in the dim light. "Why are you hiding behind the curtain, one spy said to the other?"

He tried to bluff his way out. "I am sorry, do I know you?" His brother would have no idea who she was.

"Nice try. Like I could forget those piercing eyes."

This was unfortunate. As far as the Agency knew he was on a cruise around the world. With his new assignment, the last thing he needed was to be subjected to heightened scrutiny. He tried a different tack. "The second spy said to the first, I am behind the curtain so that nobody can see me."

She lifted her chin and laughed quietly. "That's better. So, are you assigned to Antonopoulos as well? I thought you were retired."

"I *am* retired." He had always liked Evgenia, appreciated her spunk and good humor and raw intellect. Plus, of course, they shared a biracial heritage. He shrugged. "I am here because I am a member of this Lodge. And I saw movement behind the curtain."

She shook her head. "And I don't believe you." Her tone was light, but her dark eyes shone intently in the dim light. She gestured her head toward the stage, where the professor was discussing a rock carving found in Vermont. "There's something about that rock carving that smells funny. I'm being played, as is the professor, and I have a feeling you're the one doing the playing."

The Oath of Nimrod

Life was so unfair when, on the rare occasions when one was being honest, one was thought to be a liar. Randall knew nothing about any rock. He shifted his weight and edged further down the stairs, toward the storage area. "We can't talk here," he whispered, "come with me."

Without waiting for an answer he descended the final two stairs and edged into the storage room. There. A hammer. He slid it off the shelf and concealed it behind his hip. Evgenia seemed to hesitate a second, but then followed. Clasping the hammer in his right hand, Randall waited. She glided toward him. "Shh," he hissed. "I thought I heard something."

He gestured with his chin back toward the stage. As she turned to look, he took a deep breath and lifted the hammer. *Could he do this?* His training told him he must. If he did not, Evgenia would include him in her report, which would raise suspicions in the Agency and seriously jeopardize his mission. And the mission was really all he had. The mission, Consuela, Morgana, Ricardo—he must be true to them. Otherwise what had the past fifty years meant? But the hammer would not fall. This was a woman he knew, trained, even had called a friend.

A sound wafted toward him. A voice. Consuela's voice. "You must," it whispered. "You must, my love. Duty is knowing when there is a need to take action, and taking that action. Cuba needs you. I need you." Tears in his eyes, he gritted his teeth. As the smell of Juicy Fruit gum filled his nostrils, he flung the hammer forward, aiming at the dark curls on the back of Evgenia's head only inches above his face. *To a man with a hammer, the whole world is a nail.* She crumbled silently. Randall caught her around the waist before she fell to the ground; as he did so the crowd in the performance hall erupted into applause.

A single sob bubbled out of Randall's mouth as he dropped to his knees, the hammer clanking to the floor. The show was over. Another was about to begin.

Cam and Amanda hung back, waiting for Professor Antonopoulos to finish chatting and signing books. "Where's Randall?" Amanda asked.

"Last I saw him he was out in the hallway. He was pushing a garbage cart around. He joked that his brother's job was to take out the trash, so now he's stuck with it."

"There he is." Amanda pointed as Randall came through a side door.

"Good. And the professor is finally alone."

They climbed the stage and exchanged greetings with Antonopoulos, who stood to greet them. Randall explained that he was a retired CIA agent and that they had reason to believe the CIA might be trying to discredit researchers like Cam and the professor.

Antonopoulos' face fell. "Oh my God. That explains so much."

Randall nodded. "I thought it might. Perhaps we should go someplace private."

Randall led them down a back staircase to a private meeting room where they sat in easy chairs around a rectangular coffee table. He seemed to have his run of the place; he opened a cabinet along the side wall and poured them each a glass of cognac. Cam thought Randall's hand shook as he took the first sip. "Now," Randall said, swallowing, "please elaborate on your last comment."

The professor explained meeting Rachel and her friend in Washington and examining the artifact under his microscope. "The artifact was almost too perfect—there were runes and Hebrew letters and Goddess symbols on it, everything you'd hope to find if you were trying to prove medieval explorers were here. And the weathering was amazing; all the grooves were clean, like they'd been out in the elements for hundreds of years." He shrugged. "It seemed too good to be true."

Randall nodded. "This friend of Rachel's. Can you describe her?"

"Tall, mid-twenties, bronze-skinned, pretty."

Randall nodded again. "As I suspected. Her name is Evgenia. I trained her."

Antonopoulos' eyes widened. "Yes, that was her. Evgenia." He chuckled. "She's CIA? That explains how she kicked my ass." He recounted how he had followed her until she ambushed him and tied him up. "So what does the CIA want with me?"

Randall gestured toward Cam. "Same thing they want with him. For some reason they are trying to discredit researchers like yourselves."

Cam jumped in. "My guess is they were going to wait until you went public with this artifact, claiming it was authentic, and then it would come out that someone had carved it in their basement a few years ago."

The professor sighed. "Right. Some kid probably carved it as part of a Dungeons and Dragons game."

Amanda asked, "Is it possible to make something modern look ancient?"

"Sure, if you wanted to. You could put the artifact through a car wash a bunch of times, use a power-washer, sandblast it, freeze and thaw it, bury it for a few months, stuff like that. If you knew what you were doing you could make it look really old." He swallowed. "So what should we do?"

Cam turned to Randall, who seemed deep in thought, staring out a window over Boston Common. Finally he spoke. "Cameron, I believe you mentioned at one time that you had a friend who worked on Senator Lovecroft's campaign."

"Yes."

"Do you think you could set up a meeting with him? He seems like the type who might be interested in hearing what the CIA is doing to innocent American citizens."

At last the Grand Lodge was empty. Just Randall and a still-warm corpse.

David S. Brody

He eyed the bottle of cognac. *Later, when your task is complete.* It had been such a long day, such an emotional day. And it would be hours before he slept. Or, more likely, tried to sleep. Decades had passed since he had killed someone—and that person had deserved it. Such a shame. Evgenia was a bright, talented woman with her whole life in front of her. She just happened to be in the wrong place at the wrong time....

After putting a plastic bag over her head to make sure she was dead, he had wrapped her body in an old tarp and stashed it, along with her purse, backstage under some blankets behind a plastic garbage cart. Now that the last of his Brothers had finally staggered out of the basement bar where they had congregated after the lecture, Randall began the tedious task of covering up his crime. Hand shaking, he locked and alarmed the Lodge door and returned to the seventh floor. Using a hand towel, he wiped the banister and hammer clean of any fingerprints. Next, grasping Evgenia under her arms and standing on a footstool, Randall lifted the body, spilled her into the garbage cart and tossed the blankets on top in case anyone happened upon him. He rolled the garbage cart to the elevator and descended to the first floor, the wheels squeaking in the quiet, empty Lodge. Earlier in the night he had brought a couple of garbage bags out to the alley behind the Lodge, so he knew where the security camera was mounted. Now he wheeled the cart into the kitchen, tipped it on its side and rolled the body out. Disentangling the corpse from the tarp and the blankets, he removed her jewelry and ripped a corner of her dress. He had previously retrieved her coat from a rack in the coat room; sitting on the floor, he wrestled first one arm and then the other into their sleeves. Maneuvering the body had exhausted him—she probably outweighed him by fifty pounds and she was, sadly, dead weight. He wiped the sweat from his eyes, tried to ignore the tears mixed with the perspiration. He took a deep breath and gulped some water from the sink. *Almost finished.*

Staying in the shadows, he walked back to the foyer and disabled the alarm before retracing his steps to the kitchen. He

225

cracked open the alley door and peered outside—a few red-eyed rats stared back at him accusingly, but otherwise the alley was empty. Crouching, he dragged the body to the door and slid it over the threshold. A dumpster shielded him from the security camera as he maneuvered the body fully into the alley and propped it in a sitting position in the corner formed by the dumpster and the Lodge's exterior wall. He rubbed some dirt on her knees—gently so, as if treating the corpse with respect would somehow minimize his crime. He removed one of her shoes, stuffed eight twenty-dollar-bills in the sole and wedged her foot back into it. He surveyed his work: A dead woman in an alley with a head wound, no jewelry, purse or ID, and signs of a struggle. The cash and the dirty knees should point to a prostitute being attacked while on her knees servicing a client. At some point someone might wonder who she was and how she got there, but for a few days at least the police would probably treat it as a sexual encounter gone bad. And even if the police dug deeper there was nothing to tie Evgenia back to him.

He touched her lightly on the cheek and swallowed a sob. "I am so very sorry," he whispered. He stared at her—even in death she was a beautiful woman. He wanted to tell her she had died for a worthy cause, but he knew doing so would be both trite and untrue. The cause was worthy to him, but Evgenia did not give a damn about Cuba.

CHAPTER 7

"Are you sure?" Cam asked, sitting with Amanda at the kitchen table on a snowy Saturday morning. Hoping to sweat out the last of the carbon monoxide, they had just finished working out together in the basement and were still in sweats; Astarte was upstairs taking a shower while Venus barked out the window at a cat that dared to venture too close.

Amanda nodded. "The dates work—Lovecroft was a divinity student at Harvard at the time. And the dentist came right out and said the guy he was writing about was running for President. How many six-foot-ten Presidential candidates who went to divinity school in Boston in the seventies are there?"

"Okay, so Lovecroft had all these extra teeth. So what?" Cam had connected the dots already himself, but he wanted to test his theory by learning what Amanda thought.

"Not just extra teeth. A complete set, upper and lower. Just like the giants in the burial mounds."

"Which means you think Lovecroft is … a giant?"

She turned her laptop screen to him. "Look. It says here Lovecroft is one-eighth Cherokee. And the Cherokee legend is that a race of so-called giants interbred with them. So, yes, I think it is possible Lovecroft has some giant blood in him. Even likely. The extra row of teeth is probably one of those recessive gene things that pops up randomly every so many generations."

"For the record, I agree with you." Cam smiled. "And I think we should call Georgia. I'm sure she can craft a whole campaign around this. How about this: *Lovecroft: A Giant Among Men.*"

"And he can choose the bearded lady from the circus as a running mate. My guess is that Georgia wants nothing to do with this."

"So do you think he knows? Lovecroft, I mean."

Amanda sipped her coffee. "I don't know. Perhaps he suspects. Since he apparently believes in the Bible literally, he presumably believes in giants."

"So then here's the next question. Does his candidacy have anything to do with why the Smithsonian has been trying to keep this quiet?"

She shook her head. "I don't see how. This coverup has been going on for decades, long before Lovecroft came along."

"Still, it seems like an odd coincidence."

"Yes. And now Randall has suggested we set up a meeting with Lovecroft." She hesitated. "It's all a bit … queer."

Cam nodded. "Or not." He stared out the window. He couldn't see the far shoreline through the swirling snow. But he knew it was there.

Randall slept late, awaking at eight. 'Slept' was actually the wrong word—he slumbered, drifting in and out of consciousness as guilt and regret and images of shattered skull fragments bounced around inside his head like popcorn in a hot-oil pot. Finally he shuffled out of bed and into the shower, skipping his regular yoga routine; he might never get *over* the guilt he felt for Evgenia's death, but he needed to try to at least to get *past* it. He had read something once, something about guilt being a useless emotion—it was seldom strong enough to prevent one from taking an action, but often strong enough to render one useless afterward.

The act was done; he must not allow the guilt to make him useless.

As the hot water cascaded over him he sifted through the items the analytical part of his mind had digested during the overnight, thankful to be able to distract himself if only for a few minutes. First, Amanda had seemed excited about her discovery that Lovecroft had a double row of teeth; in fact, apparently she made a special visit to some dentist to investigate this. Normally a Presidential candidate's bicuspids were not fodder for the Sunday morning political roundtable discussion. So why was this different?

Second, Evgenia suspected that Antonopoulos' carving was a fake but did not know for certain; in fact, she thought she was being played. So obviously this went beyond a simple discrediting of the professor—why use a second agent, Evgenia, if a first agent, for now unknown, had already discredited Antonopoulos? It was redundant and unnecessary. Something else was going on here.

Third, whatever was happening with Project MK-Ultra—and there seemed to be plenty, including active operations targeting both Cameron and Professor Antonopoulos—may be just the opportunity he needed to get close to Senator Lovecroft. As Randall had mentioned last night, the Senator, as Chair of the Senate Intelligence Committee, would be interested to learn of a covert operation targeting innocent American researchers.

Fourth, there was little tying Randall to Evgenia's murder, other than they once worked together. If the police did investigate, they might find a witness who saw her enter the Lodge. But even if so, the main suspect would be Professor Antonopoulos, whom Evgenia was tracking and apparently trying to discredit and with whom she had had a physical altercation in Washington a night earlier. Yet at some point the police might come to suspect Randall, which meant he needed to complete his mission quickly.

Fifth, he needed a strong cup of coffee.

Morgana tossed her clothes, unfolded, into her suitcase and dropped a couple of dollars—the last of her U.S. currency—onto the dresser for the chambermaid. No doubt the capitalists did not pay the hotel workers enough to survive.

"Our plane can not depart soon enough," she said, speaking to her roommate in Spanish.

Lucia, a middle-aged soprano with droopy eyes and a pair of watermelon breasts, sighed. "I would not mind staying another few days, Morgana—"

"Oh, and how I hate that name," She interjected. "Once we get back to Cuba I never want to hear it again—"

Lucia continued as if she had not been interrupted. "The people here are nice and the food is so good."

"The people are *not* nice—the ones you meet are kind to you because they want your money. That is all they care about. And the food is only good because they give you too much and they fill it with preservatives." She glanced at Lucia. "In fact, you look more yellow than you did when we arrived. No wonder everyone in America dies of cancer."

"Are you going to contact him before our flight?" Lucia asked.

"No." She spat. "I am done with the fool." She preferred not to confide in her simple-minded roommate, but Lucia's father was her boss and Lucia was technically her partner on this mission. Lucia's father, a distinguished-looking gentleman with fine manners, perfectly exemplified an old Cuban saying: *Since light travels faster than sound, some people appear bright until you hear them speak.* Lucia, on the other hand, had not even been blessed with the appearance of intelligence. "It is best we get on the plane and let him continue to think I am his daughter."

"My father did not think the plan would work."

She fought to keep the edge from her voice. "And my mother knew it would. She knew Sid was a foolish old romantic." She rolled her eyes. "As if my mother would remain unmarried for fifty years because of a summer fling!"

"And you are certain he believed you?"

She guffawed. "He practically broke down and sobbed." She mimicked him. *"My daughter, my daughter!"*

Lucia lowered her voice. "And do you think he will take on this mission?"

"Oh yes, he will take it on. But he is old and frail and weak." She rolled her eyes again. "Yet the Americans are so arrogant and stupid it just might work. They would never expect someone like him to be an assassin."

Cam allowed the hot water to run over his body. There were few joys that surpassed a hot shower on a cold day after a long workout. He smiled to himself, recalling Amanda's and his spirited lovemaking session last night after returning from the Grand Lodge. "*Few* joys ... not *none*," he muttered.

His cheerful mood turned as he banged his injured pinky against the soap dish while reaching for the shampoo. Had it been only one week since Chung and his sons abducted him? The Bat Creek Stone bracelet was locked away in the safe deposit box and the restraining order seemed to be keeping Chung away. But maybe Cam should check in on Pugh....

Thinking about the old Chinese man jarred something in Cam's mind. He had meant to do some research on Leonard Carmichael, the man Pugh said had been in the office with the Cornell professor, Wolfe, when Pugh stole the Bat Creek Stone bracelet. Carmichael was, at the time, the Secretary of the Smithsonian Institution; prior to that Carmichael had been a behavioral psychologist and later President of Tufts University. The intersection between the Smithsonian and Project MK-Ultra had intrigued Cam, even more so now that it appeared that agents of MK-Ultra were using ancient artifacts normally housed at the Smithsonian to discredit researchers like Antonopoulos. Was this just another coincidence? Cam rinsed off and grabbed his towel.

Ten minutes later he was dressed and in front of his laptop at the kitchen table. The click-clack, click-clack of a ping pong ball echoed from the basement where Amanda and Astarte had descended. Cam would join them later, but for now he felt compelled to jump down the Leonard Carmichael rabbit hole....

First he rechecked the dates, confirming that Carmichael was indeed the Smithsonian head at the time Pugh and the other Chinese immigrants were being experimented upon in New York. It made sense—how else would Carmichael come to possess the Bat Creek Stone, which he apparently brought to New York to show Dr. Wolfe?

Next he did a Google search combining the terms "Leonard Carmichael" and "MK-Ultra." He didn't expect much—it was one of those shots in the dark that rarely amounted to anything. Which is why he nearly fell off his chair when the search yielded over two hundred hits. *What the—?* Reading quickly, he learned that Leonard Carmichael, though apparently not employed by the CIA, was one of the founding directors of Project MK-Ultra—they called their group, in a fine example of government-speak, the 'Human Ecology Society.' Cam rubbed his eyes and let the words sink in. *Leonard Carmichael helped found MK-Ultra?* Could this be just another coincidence?

Carrying his laptop, Cam ran down the basement stairs and snagged the ping pong ball out of the air just before Amanda could slap it. "Hey," she cried.

"Sorry. Point for Astarte. But look at this."

Amanda's eyes moved across the page. "Bloody hell. This is the bloke who headed the Smithsonian, right?"

"And also the bloke who Pugh stole the Bat Creek bracelet from."

"Were he and Mellon mates?"

"Good question." He tossed the ball to Astarte. "If Mum says 'hell' again, you get the point."

Cam raced back upstairs with his laptop and, fingers fumbling on the keyboard, Googled the words 'Mellon' and 'Carmichael.' Sure enough, Carmichael and Paul Mellon served on many boards and committees together in Washington.

Certain he was onto something, Cam dug further. Carmichael, it turns out, had been mentored in the 1920s by a

Brown University psychologist by the name of Edward Delabarre. Delabarre was renowned not only for his work in psychology but also for his research on Dighton Rock and other mysterious and presumably ancient stone carvings found in New England. Exposure to Delabarre's research probably first sparked Carmichael's interest in early American history, setting him on the path to eventually running the Smithsonian. And it was another piece to a puzzle that was becoming increasingly discernible.

Cam kept at it, searching for more connections linking Carmichael, the Smithsonian and Project MK-Ultra. A 1958 article in the New York Times further tied things together. The article stated: "Soviet advances in brain research and the possible advent of pharmacological warfare were cited last night by an eminent psychologist in a plea for a greater American effort to penetrate the secrets of the mind." The psychologist called for "the development of novel methods for altering human behavior" in order to meet the Soviet threat. Cam read the words again and shook his head: *the development of novel methods for altering human behavior.*

And who was this eminent psychologist calling for advancements in mind control? Leonard Carmichael, then Secretary of the Smithsonian Institution. The next question was obvious: Why was the guardian of the nation's historical artifacts calling for advancements in mind control? And, more importantly, what was he prepared to do about it?

Georgia's cell phone rang as she meandered around the supermarket's bakery section, searching for a fresh loaf of multi-grain bread. Did people really still eat white bread? Apparently in Kansas that was pretty much all they ate....

"Sorry to bother you on the weekend, Ms. Johnson, but the Senator is helping paint a church this morning and doesn't want to be disturbed."

"What is it, Mary?" Mary had been Lovecroft's personal secretary for decades.

"There's a dentist from Boston who keeps calling. He insists on talking to the Senator directly. He won't tell me why, but he says it's confidential doctor-patient information. Why would a dentist in Boston be calling? The Senator hasn't lived there since the 1970s."

"Perhaps it was just a reminder call—forty years is a long time to wait between cleanings."

"Yes. Yes, I suppose it is."

Nobody out here seemed to get Georgia's sarcasm. Georgia walked her cart into a corner of the store. These kinds of calls were never good news. "If you give me the dentist's number, I'll call him."

Georgia spent ten minutes on the phone with Dr. Anoosian, alternately charming and cajoling and bullying him, but he would not violate the doctor-patient confidentiality. Eventually she gave up, paid for her groceries and tracked down her boss, paintbrush in hand, atop a ladder in a church reception hall in a rundown neighborhood on the outskirts of Wichita.

"Can I steal you away for a few minutes?" She explained the dentist's call.

"Did you say his name was Anoosian?"

"Yes."

He nodded. "Very well. I will call him. I have a feeling this will turn out to be important."

"Do you want some privacy?" she asked.

"On the contrary, I think you need to hear this." He led her to an unoccupied office and closed the door.

Georgia put her cell phone on speaker and the dentist, once he confirmed it truly was the Senator on the line, explained the reason for his call. "I'm pretty sure she was a reporter. She knew all about the second row of teeth."

Georgia looked quizzically toward the Senator. "I'll explain later," he replied. To the dentist, he said, "What did you tell her?"

"Nothing. But she had the article from the dental journal, so she didn't need me to tell her anything."

"Not to cast blame here, doctor, but you assured me when you wrote this article that my identity would remain confidential."

"Yes, well, the information didn't get leaked by my office, I can assure you that."

Lovecroft thanked the dentist, ended the call and turned to Georgia. "It seems as if the Good Lord is going to put us to the test." He smiled sadly. "We have a problem. And I'm guessing it's not one you've ever dealt with before."

She returned his smile. In an odd way, she welcomed whatever challenge the Senator was about to describe—navigating a candidate around obstacles was what made politics so fascinating to her. "Staying with the dentist theme," she said, "I have a feeling you're going to tell me we may have bitten off more than we can chew."

"So if you are correct," Amanda said as they finished lunch, "then for some reason the Smithsonian has been helping the CIA with MK-Ultra. Seems like strange bedfellows."

Cam nodded and finished chewing his sandwich. Astarte had cleared her plate and was outside with Venus getting the mail. "We knew they were, as you say, bedfellows back in the 1950s. And it looks looks like the CIA spends a lot of time worrying about ancient history, which is not exactly at the top of the list of threats to national security. So there's something funky going on."

Amanda smiled. "I heard another of your quaint American expressions the other day: 'When there's that many beer cans lying around, there's probably been some drinking going on.'"

"So who left the beer cans?" he asked.

She shrugged. "That's what Randall and Georgia are supposed to be helping us with."

But they had both hit dead ends. "There is one other possibility."

"What?"

"Vito Augustine, our intrepid blogger. How hard could it be to get him to tell me who's paying him?" Cam smiled. "The snow is stopping. Might be a nice day for a drive to New Hampshire."

"Are you intending to just knock on his door and he'll invite you in for tea?"

"No. But it's really easy to be a jerk by email or in a blog. It's a lot harder when you're meeting face to face." He shrugged. "If he won't talk to me, I'll just drive home."

Amanda locked her eyes on him. "They all have guns up in New Hampshire, Cameron. And they have that silly slogan on their license plates—*Live Free or Die*. He might just shoot you."

Cam tried to lighten the mood. "You know who makes those license plates? The jail inmates." He smiled. "So much for living free or dying."

"They're probably in jail for shooting at blokes like you."

Despite Amanda's protestations, half an hour later Cam was driving north in the light snow, his four-wheel drive Equinox having no trouble gripping the road. Fortunately the name 'Vito Augustine' was a unique one and, using the internet, Cam had located an address for him in Franklin, New Hampshire, an hour north of the Massachusetts border. The great orator Daniel Webster was born in Franklin—perhaps Augustine imagined himself a modern-day version of the famous wordsmith.

Cam found a 1980s rock station and turned up the volume, singing along with U2. Out of habit he checked the rearview mirror to make sure he wasn't being followed. A dark sedan with Connecticut plates had been on his tail for the past ten miles, but that probably was just because of the slippery roads. As if on cue, the sedan took the next exit; Cam exhaled and belted out the words to "Sunday Bloody Sunday." He hoped Saturday would be blood-free. Especially his own.

236

He exited Route 93 just before two o'clock and followed the GPS directions up a hill to a neighborhood full of small, Colonial-style homes that looked like they had been built just after World War II. Many appeared not to have been updated since, including number 92.

Cam parked on the side of the road, took a deep breath and trudged through the snow to the front door. Four or five inches had fallen here, yet nobody had bothered to shovel the walk, so Cam followed a couple of sets of footprints that had recently preceded him. In the movies they always made it look like no big deal to confront someone in a hostile situation, but Cam's fingers tingled and there was a tightness in his chest as he rang the buzzer.

A pasty-faced young man wearing an open flannel shirt and a pair of dark sweatpants opened the door. Taller than Cam by a couple of inches but pear-shaped and wheezy, he eyed Cameron silently.

"I'm Cameron Thorne."

The man nodded and shifted his weight from one foot to the other. "What do you want?" His bottom lip drooped, showing a set of graying teeth. Cam actually felt a little sorry for him—it was rarely a good thing when your skin was whiter than your smile.

Cam had expected surprise, perhaps even fear. "I want to come in and talk to you. Assuming you're Vito Augustine."

Vito glanced to his side, to something blocked by the open door, before shrugging. "Suit yourself." He stepped aside, turned his back and began shuffling toward the back of the house.

Cam kicked the snow off his boots and followed Vito to the kitchen. A sour smell wafted off the younger man and his blondish hair hung limp and darkened with grease. Vito sat at the kitchen table, his back to the window, and motioned for Cam to sit opposite him.

"Why did you write that stuff about me?"

Vito shrugged. "Because it's true. I think you're wrong." He glanced up once in a while in Cam's direction but never actually made eye contact. "You're not a true historian and your conclusions are flawed."

"That may be so. But what you wrote was personal. You came after me. I want to know why." He paused. "Actually, I think I know why, but I want you to confirm it."

"Confirm what?" Again, Vito focused not on Cam but on a point over Cam's shoulder.

"That you are working for the CIA. They told you to come after me. Like I said, I want to know why."

A deep voice from behind Cam responded just as a massive arm encircled his neck in a choke hold while a second set of hands grabbed his arms and pinned them behind the chair back. "If you want to know why, we can tell you."

Cam thrashed and kicked but almost instantly the vise-like bicep around his windpipe sapped his strength. He felt himself losing consciousness, the deep-voiced words traveling a great distance before finally reaching his brain. "But you're not going to like the answer."

Amanda tried not to imagine the worst. Cam had texted almost three hours ago that he had parked in front of Vito Augustine's New Hampshire house and was going in. Nothing since. Her calls went straight to voice mail, her texts unanswered.

She stared out over the frozen lake and jabbed at the redial button as the late afternoon light faded to gray. Voice mail again. Venus rubbed her head against Amanda's thigh and whimpered, sensing her anxiety.

Not knowing what else to do, Amanda dialed the Franklin, New Hampshire police and explained the situation. "I know he's only been out of touch a few hours." The story needed a bit of embellishment. "But there is bad blood between Cameron and this Vito Augustine, and I'm concerned things might have turned violent."

David S. Brody

A sympathetic desk sergeant agreed to send a squad car over, probably just to kill the boredom. He phoned back fifteen minutes later. "No sign of Mr. Thorne. Augustine says he arrived around two, they talked for ten minutes, then your fiancé left. No signs of violence. My officer then drove around the block but didn't see Mr. Thorne's vehicle." He sighed. "Sorry, lady, there's nothing else I can do for you. My guess is his phone died and he'll be home in time for dinner."

Amanda bit her lip. If Cam only stayed for ten minutes, he'd have been home two hours ago. Under normal circumstance perhaps he wouldn't have checked in, but since the Chung abduction they had agreed to maintain constant contact. She dialed Georgia's number.

"There are very few people's calls that I'd answer at the moment, Amanda," Georgia said. "I'm having a shitty day."

"Me also." She explained the situation. "Is there any chance the CIA is involved with this? If they are tracking Cameron, and he confronted their hired pen, perhaps they intervened."

"I'll look into it right away, Amanda, I promise." Georgia paused. "But after he's found I'm going to need to talk to you about this research you're doing on giants."

Cam woke up on a narrow bed in the center of a square, windowless, white room illuminated by an overhead fluorescent light. His head throbbed and his neck and throat hurt when he moved or breathed or swallowed, probably because his windpipe had been compressed to the diameter of a drinking straw. Unlike in many movies he had seen, it did not take Cam time to remember what had happened—he had been abducted while in Vito Augustine's kitchen, probably by the CIA. They must have somehow accessed his computer, seen his internet search for Augustine's address and laid in wait for

239

him. He had a vague memory of being carried into a van, and later of a needle being pressed into his thigh.

"Over sixty years, and you're the first person to put the pieces together." The voice came from behind him. Cam sat up slowly and turned his head. An angular, middle-aged man in a blue blazer sat in a banquet chair, his smudged glasses resting unevenly on his nose.

Cam blinked. "What pieces?" He felt lethargic and listless, disconnected from this body. Almost as if he was dreaming.

"When you entered the terms 'MK-Ultra' and 'Leonard Carmichael' into your search engine, Mr. Thorne, you set off some loud alarms. And left us no choice but to bring you in." He swallowed, his Adam's apple bobbing. "You may not realize it—yet—but you have wormed your way deep into the bowels of this nation's intelligence community."

"I was wondering what that smell was."

The man pushed his glasses up his nose. "And like a tape worm, you must be expunged before you do serious damage to internal organs." He shifted in his chair. "But, first, we must determine what you know. Then, and only then, will you be free to go."

Actually, Cam suspected his captor had skipped a step—at some point during his captivity Cam's mind would be wiped clean like the marker on those whiteboards. He looked around, trying to focus. A pair of overhead cameras panned the room, no doubt watching and recording. He thought about trying to overpower the man in the blue blazer, but then what? "And what if I refuse?" he responded. He hoped the words sounded braver than he felt.

The man shrugged. "Refusal, cooperation, subterfuge— none of it matters. We have drugs that do our work for us very efficiently, sophisticated drugs that have taken many years and millions of dollars to develop."

Cam sat up and turned to face his captor. "I'm glad I've been paying my taxes." He was just verbally fencing, trying to buy time until he could figure something out. And the adrenaline had begun to kick in a bit.

The man offered a cold smile. "Mr. Thorne, there are two ways this can go. First, you can cooperate and tell me what I need to know. Or we can use those drugs I mentioned." He shrugged. "The choice is yours."

"I have a third option. I can assert my rights as an American citizen and demand a lawyer."

"Unfortunately for you, and fortunately for us, the laws enacted after 9-11 have abridged some of those rights. We are holding you here at Langley as a threat to national security."

Cam sniffed. He was scared, but equally so he was outraged. Whatever he was, he was not a threat to national security. "You know what? Fuck you."

The man sighed. "I understand your anger, Mr. Thorne. And I apologize for bringing you here. But I promise you, we do what we do for the good of the country." He shifted in his chair. "You and I will be spending a good many days together, Mr. Thorne. Some of our time, frankly, will be unpleasant. But there is no need for it to be personal." He stood and offered a bony, ink-smeared hand. "My name is Dr. Jagurkowitzky, and I look forward to working with you. People here call me Dr. Jag."

Cam stood slowly and reached across to clasp the offered hand, feigning more unsteadiness than he felt. As their fingers touched, Cam grabbed the man by the wrist, spun his captor around and, bending low to gain leverage, yanked back Dr. Jag's middle finger until he heard it crack. "That's payback for my finger." Actually, Cam wasn't even sure the CIA had been behind that, not that it mattered now. Dr. Jag screamed in agony as a pair of uniformed guards burst into the room.

Instead of fighting them or trying to flee, Cam lifted his hands in surrender and sat calmly on his bed. The guards stood by, unsure what to do now that Cam no longer posed a threat. Cam waited until Dr. Jag, grasping his finger, stood and eyed him. "You may get what you want from me," Cam said. "But let's get one thing straight: This is *very* personal."

The Oath of Nimrod

Randall had just nodded off in front of an old Bette Davis movie when his cell phone rang. He slapped his face and answered the call. "Ms. Spencer-Gunn. A pleasure. What can I do for you?"

She explained that Cameron had driven to New Hampshire to confront the hostile blogger and had not been heard from since. Randall sucked in his breath. "I wish he had informed me. I would have been pleased to accompany him on his excursion. Are you aware that the most popular wintertime activity in New Hampshire is *ice fishing*?" He shuddered. "Not the kind of territory a man should venture into alone."

"Yes, well, I am concerned."

"As you should be." The Agency would not take kindly to Cameron questioning the blogger, who could hardly be counted on *not* to reveal whom he worked for. And if, somehow, the Agency had already learned Evgenia had gone rogue, they would be even more skittish—an agent was missing, and a secret operation in danger of being revealed, perhaps embarrassingly so. Things were moving more quickly than Randall had anticipated. Too quickly. "We have been poking around the hornet's nest for quite a while, Cameron and I. We cannot now be surprised when we are stung."

"As far as I can tell, only Cameron has been stung."

"Yes, quite." If Cam really had been abducted, it is likely he would be brought to Langley for questioning. "In any event, I suspect we might soon find ourselves journeying to Washington, D.C." He made a rough plan in his head. "I suggest you pack a bag and make arrangements for your daughter. We will travel by automobile. You will need to bring ample cash." He paused. "And Amanda, one additional item."

"I am listening."

"Cameron is in grave danger. He has told me of your friend working for Senator Lovecroft. We may need the Senator's assistance in order to save your fiancé."

Amanda knew she needed to be strong, knew that Astarte would smell any fear on her like a cat on the prowl.

She knocked on the girl's bedroom door; Astarte was playing with her dolls on the floor as Venus napped in a box of sun by the window. "Honey, I need you to pack an overnight bag. You are going to sleep over at Julia's house tonight."

Her cobalt eyes looked up. "Why?"

"I need to go to Washington, D.C."

She nodded. "Dad-Cam is in trouble, isn't he?"

How did she know? "Yes, I think so."

Astarte nodded again. "Okay then." She stood and gave Amanda a tight hug. "He'll be okay, Mum. It seems like people are always trying to hurt him, but they never really can."

Holding his finger aloft, Dr. Jag snapped the end off a wooden ruler, found some medical tape in his desk drawer and taped his throbbing middle finger and the ring finger next to it to the ruler span. He popped a couple of Advils, dropped a handful of ice cubes into a sandwich bag and returned via elevator to the detention room in the subbasement of the sprawling CIA complex in Langley, Virginia, the ice bag on his hand.

He was not angry at Cameron Thorne as much as he was angry at himself. He should not have been alone with his prisoner. But Evgenia had gone AWOL and Thorne had somehow connected MK-Ultra to the Smithsonian through Leonard Carmichael—he had hoped to earn Thorne's trust and cooperation with a personal, one-on-one approach. His discolored and swollen finger made it clear the personal approach had been the wrong one.

243

As he rode the elevator he replayed the Evgenia series of events in his head. She had been spotted by an agent in Vernon, Connecticut, where she presumably ascertained that her Agency boss had been lying to her about the Vermont stone carving. She would be angry, Dr. Jag knew—she would figure she had earned the right not to be played and manipulated. And she was right, under normal circumstances. But normal had given way to abnormal, and abnormal was well on its way to yielding to crisis. No doubt disaster was not far behind.

Crisis or not, one of his agents was missing. Yesterday afternoon in Connecticut was the last anyone saw of Evgenia. But Thorne had attended Professor Antonopoulos' lecture in Boston, and it seemed reasonable to assume Evgenia had been there also. Yet there was no sign of her. That would be the first of his questions for Mr. Thorne.

It was one of those Catch-22s that Cam would normally find fascinating, but for the terrifying reality that the conundrum involved him: No doubt there was a law banning the CIA from giving prisoners drugs to erase their memories. But if the Agency ignored the law, and the prisoner had no memory of his memory being erased, how then would anyone ever learn of the crime? It was like a tree falling deep in an empty forest. Except Cam was a lab rat caged deep in the bowels of the most sophisticated mind control operation since the Nazis and Josef Mengele....

On that happy note he slid off his bed and did twenty-five jumping jacks to try to clear his head. He knew that part of the mind control game was sensory deprivation—they would keep him alone in a colorless, noiseless cell, provide as little stimulation as possible and prevent him from sleeping. Bread and water only. The uncertainty and boredom and isolation and lack of sleep would weaken him, make his mind malleable. Exercise would help, as would keeping his brain sharp. For some reason the prisoner sentenced to solitary confinement in the old movie, *Papillon,* popped into his head. Emulating the prisoner, Cam pounded out fifty pushups on the floor, then tried to estimate exactly how many foot-lengths in width his cell was. His guess of eleven-and-a-half was three-quarters of a boot shy. He'd save the length and diagonal for when he got really bored.

The door opened and Dr. Jag ambled in, surprising Cam—he figured it would be hours before he had a visitor. There must be something they needed in a hurry. "A doctor is on his way to examine you. Before we can give you the drugs we need to make sure your body is strong enough to take them."

Leaning against his bed, the only piece of furniture in the room, Cam smiled. "Your finger can attest to that."

Dr. Jag ignored the comment. "Do you have any drug allergies?"

Delay, always delay. At some point help will come. "Why should I make this any easier for you?"

His captor adjusted his glasses. "It does not matter to *me* if you break out into hives."

"Sure it does. You need me alive to answer your questions. Not to mention even the CIA can't just go around killing U.S. citizens."

"We won't let you *die*, Mr. Thorne. We are not amateurs." He lifted his clipboard, as if that somehow proved his point. "I'm simply trying to save you some discomfort."

Cam remembered something he had read about CIA mind control experiments. Feigning resignation, he said, "I'm allergic to Dramamine."

Dr. Jag flinched slightly. "I see. Are you certain?"

"I puked my whole way through a Caribbean cruise because I couldn't wear one of those seasickness patches."

Holding his pen with thumb and index finger only, he made a note on the clipboard. As he did so, his sleeve pulled up and Cam caught a glimpse of his watch—9:37, presumably in the evening. "Very well. Anything else?"

Delay, delay. He was over five hours late returning home. Hours ago Amanda would have assumed the worst and contacted Georgia and probably also Randall. "I don't like beets. Food shouldn't be that color."

Dr. Jag tapped the board with his pen. "Any other *drug* allergies, Mr. Thorne?"

Why not? The more he could come up with, the harder it would be to start injecting him. He had chosen Dramamine because one of its active ingredients was also used by the CIA as a mind control drug. "Aspirin and ibuprofen. I have something called Stevens-Johnson syndrome." It just popped into his head, a memory from an ex-girlfriend. "And I'm allergic to most kinds of nuts." Let their doctors try to figure out a safe way to inject him.

Dr. Jag eyed him skeptically. "You know, this would be much easier if you would just tell me what we want to know."

Delay. Cam furrowed his brow. "Best I can remember, you haven't asked me any questions yet."

"All right, then. Answer this: Where is Evgenia Samsanov-Johnson?"

"Who?" Cam didn't even try to mask his surprise.

"One of my agents. Tall, biracial, attractive. And missing."

So that's what this was about. "I have no idea. Maybe she defected—I hear the Russians pay well these days." Again, delay.

"Are you also going to claim you don't know Professor Stefan Antonopoulos?"

Cam saw no reason to lie. "I saw him last night at a lecture in Boston. Did he defect also?"

Dr. Jag was growing irritated by Cam's jabs; apparently the man was not used to be being treated disrespectfully. He took a deep breath. "Why were you at Vito Augustine's house?"

"The guy rips me on his blog for no reason, what do you expect? I wanted to know why." Cam shifted. "A better question is why were *you* there? Which leads to a whole bunch more questions, such as why are you doing everything you can to sabotage our research? Me, Professor Antonopoulos,

246

Laurence Gardner." This last name caused Dr. Jag's eyes to flicker—Cam had hit a nerve. He turned his palms up. "I don't get it. It makes no sense. Go chase terrorists or something."

"Thank you for the career advice, Mr. Thorne."

Buy more time. "You're surprised I know about Laurence Gardner, aren't you?"

Dr. Jag swallowed, considering his response. Apparently he had concluded that Cam wouldn't remember any of this conversation anyway. "Yes. Discrediting him had been one of our most difficult tasks."

Cam played another card. It was the last hand of the night, and he was way down anyway. "I also know about the Mellon family."

Cam's mention of Laurence Gardner had surprised Dr. Jag; the mention of the Mellon family caused outright consternation. Dr. Jag strode toward him, his face reddening. "*What* exactly do you know about the Mellon family?"

Locked in a cell in the basement of CIA headquarters, about to be drugged and tortured and brainwashed, Cam somehow was enjoying himself. "I know they helped fund Project MK-Ultra. I know they produced the LSD you used to experiment on soldiers and students and prisoners. I know they helped you bury and discredit research proving there were waves of Europeans here before Columbus—sometimes rather clumsily." Cam paused. "What I don't know is why."

"Let me answer your question with a question, Mr. Thorne: Have you ever heard of war games?"

"Of course. Armies have been playing them for centuries."

"And rightfully so. How else do you prepare for actual battle? It is the same in the intelligence community, especially in the field of PsyOps and mind control: We need war games. We need to prepare our agents to go out in the field in the real world and do their jobs."

"I'm not following you."

Dr. Jag closed his eyes and massaged his forehead. "Think, Mr. Thorne. How would you design war games for the

CIA? How would you give our agents practice in the real world, a dress rehearsal if you will?"

Cam considered the question. "Honestly, I don't know. You can't just go around brainwashing people you pull off the street anymore—Congress put an end to that. So it would be difficult."

"Exactly. Difficult, but crucial. We needed to come up with a Petri dish, a laboratory, a venue in which our agents could ply their craft."

"I'm still not following you." It was true. And better yet, this conversation was killing more time.

Dr. Jag stared him for a long beat. "*You* are the bacteria in that Petri dish, Mr. Thorne. You and all the other self-important, sanctimonious, ego-fueled researchers in your field. Barry Fell, Laurence Gardner, Scott Wolter, Daniel Whitewood, Stefan Antonopoulos. You all think you are smarter than the historians, smarter than the history books. You all think you have a monopoly on *truth*, of all things. But there is no truth. Truth is whatever we believe to be real. It is a perception."

Cam nodded. He understood. "Whatever you can convince people is real, becomes reality. Mind control. You used us as your lab rats. If you could suppress us, if you could convince the country that Columbus really was first, then you had won."

"Not won, Mr. Thorne. But proved we *could* win, when the stakes became real. We don't care what people think about Columbus or the Vikings or Prince Henry Sinclair. But we need to train our agents, to test our methods, to determine if mind control works in the real world. And when I use the term 'mind control,' what I am really talking about is behavior modification, of course. That is the ultimate goal: Can we change what people believe or think, and thereby alter their behavior?"

"So for, what, sixty years, you have been discrediting researchers, destroying careers, covering up the true history of this country—all for some kind of dress rehearsal?"

Dr. Jag nodded. "The truth is we have done very little real harm. A few careers have been damaged, that is true, but don't you think it remarkable that we have been able to operate such a large-scale experiment for so many years with such impressive results and so little collateral damage?" He shook his head. "It is truly one of the great accomplishments in modern intelligence." He smiled smugly. "We have convinced an entire nation to believe a history that is false, despite the best efforts of brilliant and devoted researchers like yourself, Mr. Thorne."

The whole thing was obscene, reeking of Big Brother. And it was wrong. Yet it explained so much—Cam had always sensed that opposition to pre-Columbian research was fueled by an almost religious zealousness, that there had to be something more behind it than a simple disagreement regarding the evidence. That something, it turned out, was the full weight of the federal government. "So that's how Leonard Carmichael got involved? He was a behavioral psychologist who happened also to have control of the nation's historical artifacts, which gave you the tools you needed to run your little experiment."

"Exactly. Had Carmichael been the chair of, say, the Library of Congress rather than the Smithsonian, perhaps we would have used the card catalog as our Petri dish. But it just so happened that Carmichael had the keys to the country's attic. In the end, it was a marriage made in heaven. You and your fellow researchers have been tenacious and skilled over the decades in your efforts to rewrite history—worthy adversaries for our agents and our methods. Barry Fell almost won the day back in the 1970s; were it not for his large ego we may not have been successful in discrediting him."

Cam's mind raced. What this meant was that all of the artifacts and sites that had been debunked over the years—the Kensington Rune Stone, the Newport Tower, the Westford Knight, the Tucson Lead Artifacts, the Bat Creek Stone, dozens of others—were probably authentic. An entire chapter of America's history had been whitewashed away. Just as Cam's memory was about to be...

As if on cue, the door opened.

At least the snow had stopped. Amanda weaved Randall's Ford Taurus through traffic on the George Washington Bridge, fighting to get clear of the Saturday night New York City crowds for the second half of their run to Washington.

"You drive rather … fast," Randall said.

"As fast as is needed." It was just after nine-thirty, three hours after they departed Westford. She smiled sideways at her white-haired, white-knuckled passenger. Cam was in danger, and the elderly, retired CIA agent next to her was her best bet to rescue him. And he seemed to like to flirt. "If we get pulled over, I shall claim we are eloping to Atlantic City."

His dark skin may have blushed a bit. "Yes, well, at my age it is probably wise to hurry."

Early in the trip Randall seemed in no rush to talk about how he planned to rescue Cam. Instead he spent the few hours feeling her out, gauging her intelligence and character. He had asked about her giant research—apparently the Biblical giant Nimrod played an important part in Freemasonry, which had sparked Randall's curiosity in the subject.

She accelerated past eighty-five as they crossed into New Jersey and looped south. Absent some accident, the bridge should be the last of their traffic problems, which should put them in McLean, Virginia a few minutes after midnight. She pressured the accelerator and watched the gauge edge up to ninety.

Randall cleared his throat. "If we die in a fiery crash, we cannot be married." He turned to look at her. "Or help Cameron."

"It was your suggestion to drive rather than fly."

"Yes, because no doubt they will be watching for you on the planes and trains and buses. We have very few weapons at our disposal. The element of surprise is one of them." He cleared his throat. Now, apparently, it was finally time to discuss the rescue. "Speaking of which, I will need to wear some kind of disguise to avoid being recognized. You will introduce me as an attorney, as is Cameron's right." He smiled slyly. "Even at Langley, the Constitution can not be totally ignored."

She nodded. He was correct about the element of surprise. The other possible weapon they had was Senator Lovecroft. Georgia and the Senator were flying to Washington now, scheduled to land at Dulles within the hour. Georgia had promised that the Senator would make sure they would get to see Cam as soon as they arrived.

"You know these people," she said. "What are they doing to Cam?" She almost hated to ask.

"The Agency prefers not to abduct American citizens, as it can create quite a mess. If they did abduct Cameron, it is because they view him as a serious threat or because he has vital information they require. In either case, standard operating procedure calls for a three-step approach." He held up his index finger on his left hand. "First, they will conduct a medical examination to ensure that he is healthy enough to survive an interrogation. Second, they will administer drugs that render him incapable of withholding information. And third, they will administer more drugs that block his memory of the entire episode."

She drove in silence for a few seconds. "If they have these drugs that turn people into ... zombies, why do they bother with all this mind control silliness?"

Randall puts his hands together in front of his chest, like a person praying. "Because a zombie can follow instructions, but only up to a certain extent. I could drug you, for example, and order you to withdraw money from your bank and give it to me. But if a policeman arrived and asked if you were in distress, you would be unable to strategize an appropriate response. If, on the other hand, I convinced you it was in your best interest to withdraw funds for my benefit, you would smile at the kind officer, offer a few reassuring words, and send him on his way." He raised his eyebrows. "Zombies are of limited use, whereas puppets are invaluable."

She swallowed. "And the drugs they use. Are they safe? Are there any side effects or repercussions?"

"The drug *du jour* at Langley is scopolamine. It is sometimes referred to as Devil's Breath." He paused, seeming to expect a response.

"Is it foul-smelling?"

Randall shook his head. "On the contrary, it is odorless. It gets its name from the way it is often used in Colombia, where it is most prevalent: Criminals blow a handful of scopolamine powder into a victim's face, removing the victim's free will. The active ingredient is the same as in the belladonna plant, used in ancient times as a love potion." He paused. "Many victims have no recollection of what they have done while under the drug's influence."

He had not answered her question. "Yes, but is it safe?"

"Usually so. But it can cause powerful hallucinations." He raised his eyes to hers and shrugged. "And in some cases it can be fatal."

Georgia and Senator Lovecroft's flight from Kansas City landed; a member of the Senator's staff met them at the Dulles terminal when they disembarked.

"Where to, sir?" the young aide asked, taking Georgia's overnight bag.

"Straight to Langley, Jason. And I'll carry my own suitcase, thank you." It was just after ten at night.

The Senator bent forward as they walked through the terminal, stretching. He insisted on flying commercial, and even refused an upgrade to first class. "You know," Georgia said, "when you get to be President you're not going to be able to fly United."

"Yes, well, I suppose my back will thank me. But if Lincoln can make the trip from Illinois to Washington by stagecoach, who am I to complain about a two hour flight?"

The Senator did not often openly compare himself to Lincoln, but Georgia knew he idolized the sixteenth President and strived to emulate him.

The twenty-minute ride east across northern Virginia passed quickly. Jason dropped them at the main entrance to the modern, sprawling, glass-and-chrome CIA headquarters building. The arched glass entrance always made Georgia feel she was about to step onto an escalator and descend to an underground subway platform. As it turned out, after clearing security they were indeed escorted by elevator into the subbasement of the complex.

The new building boasted the latest in sophisticated technology and security. But it never smelled right to Georgia—instead of shoe leather and old smoke and dusty files the building smelled sterile and cold, like a rental car with its air conditioning turned up too high.

The deputy director of the CIA waited for them in a carpeted conference room. Ming Wang was the number two man at Langley, a man who probably knew more American secrets than any person who had ever lived. Yet most Americans had no idea he even existed. In his mid-seventies, Wang had worked his way up in the Agency after arriving from China in the late 1940s as a college student just before the Communist takeover and taking a job with the CIA a few years later. Sharp, hardworking and fiercely patriotic, he had overcome the cultural bias against Asians in the intelligence community—the prevailing belief was that Asians, for cultural reasons, would always remain loyal to their homelands—to serve under a dozen administrations. As far as Georgia knew, had accomplished the almost impossible task in Washington of having never made an enemy.

He stood and greeted them cordially, his thin gray hair combed neatly across the top of his head. "Senator Lovecroft, Agent Johnson, a pleasure to see you both." He bowed his head to each and introduced a few underlings sitting around the table. "Dr. Jag is with Mr. Thorne in the interrogation room.

He will join us shortly." He spoke slowly, enunciating each word, as if aware his accent made him difficult to understand.

The Senator cleared his throat. "That is why we are here," he said, still standing. "We do not want him to be interrogated." He looked apologetically toward Georgia. "At least not yet."

Wang nodded. "I understand your concern. In fact, I happen to have a certain amount of fondness for Mr. Thorne myself."

"You?" Georgia blurted out. "How do you even know him?"

Wang smiled, his teeth browned by a lifetime of pipe smoking. "I assume he informed you of the Bat Creek Stone bracelet he found in a bag of Chinese food?"

"Yes. Then he was kidnapped." She leaned forward, wondering where this was going.

"Thankfully I am not yet too old to go out into the field. Mr. Thorne knows me by the name Pugh Wei. I delivered his Chinese food."

Georgia's eyes widened. "You?" This was exactly the type of convoluted plan the CIA would come up with to suck someone like Cam in. Why just knock on his door and give him the bracelet when you could instead manipulate him through lies, fear and torture?

Wang smiled again. "Mr. Thorne is a good man. One can usually tell by the way a man tips when nobody is watching."

A thirty-something woman in a light blue lab coat strolled into the interrogation room carrying a black medical bag. She nodded to Dr. Jag and smiled kindly at Cam. "I am Dr. Smith."

Delay. "Dr. Smith?" Cam sighed. "What, Jones was taken? Are you really even a doctor?"

"Johns Hopkins," she said humorlessly. "Top of my class."

Even in glasses and with her hair pulled back, Cam noticed she was attractive. Why he noticed this, he had no idea—obviously he wasn't going to ask her out. But it was somewhat comforting that she didn't look like the Kathy Bates character in that Stephen King movie, *Misery.* He glanced around. "I see you're on quite a career track. Perhaps someday you can be in charge of water-boarding."

"This is not torture, Mr. Thorne."

"Easy to say when you're on your side of the needle."

"I see you are a diabetic. When was the last time you checked your blood sugar levels."

"It's been a while. I should probably eat something."

She handed him a granola bar. "Start with this."

She asked him to strip to his boxers. He thought about resisting, yet that would just mean a couple of grunts would come in and do it for him; better to bide his time and attempt something less futile later. But he was running out of time. The thought of his captors crawling around inside his head and learning his most private secrets reminded him of the despair he had felt as a young boy when a bunch of neighborhood bullies barged into his house and ransacked his bedroom. The bedroom had been permanently and irreversibly violated; he finally convinced his parents to let him switch to a spare room in the basement. But he couldn't very well switch to another head.

The doctor gave him a quick physical, checking his pulse, blood pressure and respiration as he sat on the bed. She glanced at Dr. Jag's clipboard. "You really allergic to all this stuff?"

Buy time, wait for help to arrive. "Yup."

She sighed. "Give me your arm." She swabbed a handful of different solutions onto his forearm and then lightly pricked each of them with a needle.

Cam knew how this worked—if he was allergic, there would be some kind of reaction on his skin within fifteen or twenty minutes. But that was fifteen or twenty minutes more of a delay. "Can I get dressed?"

She shook her head. "Negative."

He knew this was part of the process, the dehumanization of the prisoner. Cam slid off the bed, reached down and pulled his jersey over his head. Then he stepped into his jeans. A small act of rebellion.

Dr. Jag didn't seem to care. He said, "After we inject you with the scopolamine, I will be asking you a series of questions. You may be surprised to know that I will be asking you a number of questions about giants."

"Why are you telling me this now?"

"Because we have found that the scopolamine can make subjects lethargic, sometimes even dimwitted. Forcing subjects to focus on certain material beforehand allows them to recall more information under the effects of the drug." He smiled. "You know the old childhood game, where someone tells you *not* to think about pink polar bears and, of course, that's all you can think about? Well, Mr. Thorne, please do not think about giants."

"Fee-fi-fo-fum," Cam retorted. But he was curious: Why giants?

The doctor took a long needle from her bag. Suddenly Cam didn't care about giants.

"Wait, so you set this whole thing up?" Georgia asked, looking directly at Deputy Director Wang. He was technically her boss, but she didn't really care about offending anyone at the moment. "You intentionally put Cameron and Amanda in danger as part of some mission?"

Wang put up a hand defensively. "Please allow me to explain." He sighed. "Perhaps it would help if I were to give you some history on Project MK-Ultra," Wang said, still articulating every syllable. "You may know its original mission was to develop mind control techniques during the Cold War. Today, it is more concerned with behavior control. But the intention is the same: To surreptitiously change behavior. Often this is accomplished by changing beliefs."

"And I know for some reason you have chosen the field of pre-Columbian history as your testing ground," Senator Lovecroft said.

"Correct. Our agents use various tools and strategies developed at MK-Ultra to undermine and discredit research in this field—if we can, for example, convince American citizens that Columbus was here first, then we can use these same strategies to, say, convince Afghani villagers that the Taliban is evil." He shrugged. "We have nothing in particular against pre-Columbian research or researchers; it is simply that Dr. Carmichael's position as Secretary of the Smithsonian gave us control of the artifacts in this field." He paused. "And controlling the artifacts allowed us to control the debate."

"When you say *controlling the artifacts*, what you really mean is tampering with the evidence. You buried artifacts that didn't support your claims, and you altered others so they did. You cooked the books."

Wang didn't seem to take Lovecroft's comment as a criticism. "Correct. For example, we arranged to have the Vinland Map donated to Yale so we could control who was allowed to study it. But we did not focus on just the artifacts themselves—we built up or tore down the reputations of many researchers in the field. And it worked." He arched an eyebrow at the Senator. "To this day there is not a single textbook—cooked or otherwise—that recognizes European exploration of the United States prior to Columbus."

"I'm sure George Orwell would be very proud of you," the Senator said. "Continue."

"In early 2011, just after Fidel Castro stepped down, we received some disturbing intelligence from a senior Cuban official who lost a power struggle with Castro's brother." He waved his hand in the air as if the particulars did not matter. "The intelligence was that a Cuban sleeper agent had infiltrated the CIA. Our source did not know many details, but one thing he did say led us to believe the agent likely worked on the MK-

Ultra program." Wang sighed. "As you might imagine, we have been striving to learn the identity of this sleeper agent."

Georgia interjected. "And, of course, to use this information to your advantage."

"If possible, yes. But primarily to neutralize any threat. We can't have a Cuban agent lurking inside Langley."

"But what does any of this have to do with Cam and Amanda?" Georgia asked.

Wang nodded. "I'm getting to that. One of the agents we suspected might be the sleeper was a young woman named Evgenia Samsanov-Johnson. Her father was a Russian hockey player who played in Detroit. We thought perhaps her heritage would make her sympathetic toward Cuba, an old Soviet ally."

Georgia sat forward in her chair. "Wait, Cameron told me about her. She's the one who tried to discredit that professor with the fake rune stone."

Wang bowed his head. "Yes, she was trying to discredit the professor. But she knew nothing about the fake rune stone. We were playing her, testing her—we wanted to get her out of the office and into the field, so we assigned her to Professor Antonopoulos." He lowered his voice. "As it turns out, we may have been wrong to suspect her. She is dead."

"Dead? How?" Georgia asked. It was rare for a CIA agent to be killed on American soil.

"We do not have many details; I just received the call a couple of hours ago. The Boston police found her body outside the Masonic Grand Lodge. Presumably she was tracking the professor." He paused and rested his dark eyes on Georgia's. "But your man Thorne was at the Lodge last night also. Which is one of the reasons Dr. Jag is so anxious to question him."

Georgia doubted Cam had anything to do with the agent's death, but she also knew an agent was dead and that everyone would be considered a suspect until proven otherwise.

Wang's phone rang, interrupting her thoughts. The deputy director listened for a few seconds and then to Georgia and the Senator: "Thorne's fiancée is here, with a lawyer."

The Senator nodded. "This is still the United States of America. Have them brought down."

Amanda cut off Georgia before she could finish the introductions as they stood in the doorway of the conference room. She appreciated the efforts her friend was making to help, but this was not the first time she and Cameron had been targeted by overzealous federal authorities. "Not to be rude, but where is Cameron?"

Randall interjected. Dressed in a three-piece suit and carrying a leather briefcase, he would not have looked out of place addressing a jury. "My client is correct. You have no right to hold him, and I am prepared to obtain a writ of *habeas corpus* if necessary. The Sixth Amendment demands—"

Senator Lovecroft cut him off. "We are familiar with the Constitution, sir. And I don't think you'll have much luck finding a judge at midnight." He turned to the older Asian man. "Nonetheless, it hardly seems as if Mr. Thorne is a threat to national security. I see no reason to further deprive him of his due process rights. I suggest you take us to him."

The Asian man nodded. "Very well. But, Senator, if I may first have a brief word with you and Agent Johnson, that would be appreciated."

Randall and Amanda waited in the hallway outside the conference room as Senator Lovecroft, Georgia Johnson and Deputy Director Wang huddled together, their backs to the hallway window. It seemed to Randall as if Wang was doing most of the talking and, from their body language, it seemed as if what he was saying was important. Randall hoped they were not talking about him.

This was the most dangerous part of tonight's mission. If somehow Wang recognized him, or doubted he was an attorney, the whole thing could blow up. The three-inch lifts in his shoes had helped, as had the heavy-rimmed glasses. And he and Wang had never met. But Wang had not become the number two man at Langley by being an idiot.

"What are they talking about?" Amanda asked.

Randall guessed this might be a stall to allow whatever drugs they were giving Thorne to kick in, or perhaps they were waiting while someone checked on Randall's bona fides. But he could not verbalize either possibility to Amanda. "Probably figuring out a way to deny this ever happened if it blows up in their faces."

Randall bent over to tie his shoe; surreptitiously he removed the shoelace from his wingtip and dropped the black lace into his pants pocket. He had hoped to dislike Senator Lovecroft, but he found the man honest, steadfast and, most of all, humble. The Oval Office could use some humility. But it would be with someone other than Lovecroft sitting behind the famous Resolute Desk if Randall had any say in the matter.

After ten minutes the three conferees stood and entered the hallway. "Thank you for your patience," Wang said. "We will take you to see Mr. Thorne now."

Randall exhaled. Wang led the group down the hallway, Randall in the rear working to stay balanced atop his lifted and now lace-less left shoe. They stopped in a vestibule area where a half-dozen monitors sat on a shelf against the long wall of the room. A pair of guards with holstered sidearms, along with a woman in a lab coat and a couple of white-shirted men, eyed them as they approached. Randall glanced at the monitors—each displayed a sole figure of a man slouched in a banquet chair in the middle of a square white room. Amanda gasped as Randall recognized a dazed-looking Cameron being interrogated across a banquet table by an angular man in a blue blazer. Randall's heart dropped. It was Dr. Jag—he would surely recognize Randall.

Randall thought quickly. He raised himself up. "I demand to see my client. Immediately. And alone." He pointed at Dr. Jag. "And I demand that man's full name and address. He is conducting an illegal torture interrogation in violation of both federal law and the Geneva Convention. We plan to hold him fully accountable for his crimes."

"Mr. Thorne is heavily sedated," the woman said.

"Even more reason why I demand to see him."

"As for the gentleman with Mr. Thorne," Wang said, "I am afraid we will not be able to comply with your request." He turned to one of the white-shirted men. "Please escort our associate out the back door of the interrogation room." And to Randall. "You may meet with your client once they have departed."

Amanda interjected, her voice shaky. "I'm coming in also."

Randall touched her arm, relieved he had successfully handled the Dr. Jag problem. He was so close now. "Please, Amanda, let me handle this." He leaned closer. "I am not sure you want to see him like this." Louder now, so everyone could hear. "And I need you to make sure our conversation is private." The monitors, for now at least, did not project any sound. "Please bang on the door if our conversation is in any way audible."

Amanda nodded. "Very well then."

Randall turned to the Senator. "I rely on your assurances, sir, that this conversation shall remain entirely private."

Lovecroft nodded. "You have my word."

Randall turned and almost stumbled before pushing open the door and striding through. Exhaling, he sat opposite a pale and lethargic-looking Cameron Thorne. He had always liked Cam, and he hated seeing him doped up, but this was not the time for sentiment. He covered his mouth with his hand so that nobody could read his lips. Later—perhaps only hours so—someone would come in and try to piece together this conversation. But for now it needed to remain private. "Cameron, do you know who I am? Do not use my name—merely nod if you recognize me."

Cam squinted at him and, lolling in his seat, nodded slowly.

"Very good. I am here with Amanda. We are here to help you. You need to trust me. Is that clear?"

Cam seemed to sit up a bit at the mention of Amanda's name. He nodded again.

"They have drugged you. Do you know the name of the chemical they have used?"

Cam opened his mouth, closed it again, shook his head, blinked and then finally stuttered a response. "Scop ... scopolamine."

The Zombie Drug. As he suspected. And hoped. "Excellent." This next part was crucial, and Randall needed to be sure. "Cameron, I need you to give me the password to your ATM account."

Cam mumbled his response.

"Good." Randall didn't care about the ATM, but he wanted to make sure Cam really would follow instructions. He gave him another test. "And please now put your hand on the table. I am going to take my pen and stab you in the palm. You must not move."

Cam nodded and stuck out his hand. Randall pulled a retractable pen from his briefcase, clicked it open, made a point of showing the tip to Cam and, clenching the pen in his fist, held it a few feet above the table. "Remember, do not move," he said.

Randall stabbed the pen downward like a deranged being in some old horror film, smashing the pen into the table a few inches from Cam's hand. Cam flinched but did not withdraw his hand, even as the plastic pen splintered and pieces flew about the room.

Satisfied, Randall took a deep breath and again shielded his mouth with his hand. "Excellent, Cameron. Now I need you to listen carefully, and to do exactly as I say. In a few minutes a very tall man—his name is Senator Lovecroft—is going to come into this room." He spoke quickly, fearing the pen stunt might cause Wang to cut their meeting short. "He is an evil man. He is trying to hurt Amanda, and Astarte, and you, Cameron. He is trying to destroy America." Randall bent closer to Cam. "I am going to shake your hand as I leave. When I do so, I am going to give you a shoelace. But this is not a normal shoelace. Inside the fabric is a sharp metal wire. The shoelace is a kind of garrote. Hide the shoelace until Senator Lovecroft comes into the room. When he comes over to examine your feet, I want you to wrap the garrote around his neck, twist the wire, and strangle him." He looked into Cameron's placid eyes. "You must not fail, Cameron. You must kill him. Do not stop squeezing until he is dead."

Amanda met Randall as he passed through the door from the interrogation room into the vestibule area. She desperately wanted to push ahead to go see Cameron, but Randall had explained that people under the influence of Scopolamine could suffer permanent emotional scarring if emotionally traumatized. There would be time enough to see him once the effects of the drug wore off.

"How is he?" she breathed.

Ignoring her, Randall edged past and confronted Senator Lovecroft, the top of his head barely reaching the Senator's chest. Upset as she was, Amanda appreciated the skill with which Randall played his part—his anger and outrage were evident in his clenched jaw and pulsating forehead. "Sir, I must appeal to your sense of decency. An American citizen—an *innocent* American citizen—has been abducted, detained, drugged and tortured—"

The female doctor interjected. "Tortured? That is not so."

Randall spun angrily. "Yes, *tortured*. The soles of his feet have been bludgeoned, like in some fascist police state. What next, electric cables on his nipples?"

"What?" Amanda gasped. She staggered and had the vague sense of Georgia guiding her to a chair even as the anger rose in her throat.

Wang stepped back, hands spread. "I assure you, Senator, there has been no torture—"

Randall cut him off. "Go see for yourself, Senator. Ask to see the bottom of Mr. Thorne's feet. He tells me he has been beaten repeatedly with a baseball bat."

Lovecroft strode forward. "Open the door," he said to one of the guards. Without looking back, he marched into the interrogation room. The door closed behind him.

Randall knew every second was crucial. A garrote could kill a man almost instantly, but if Randall blocked the door and gave Cameron another ten or twenty seconds, that would ensure the job was done. He watched as Wang and Georgia moved to the monitors on the far side of the room; even the guards edged closer, their eyes on the video screens. Randall pulled a chair away from a wall, surreptitiously positioned it partially to block the interrogation room door, sighed and dropped into it.

"I hope all your houses are in your spouses' names," Randall said to the room, "because this is going to be one hell of a lawsuit."

The monitors showed the Senator entering the interrogation room and sitting opposite Cam. After a brief conversation, Lovecroft pointed to Cam's feet. Still seated, Cam nodded, bent over mechanically and removed his sneakers. Senator Lovecroft stood, rounded the table and dropped to one knee in front of Cam. Bending low, he ducked his head almost to the ground and peered up at the bottom of Cam's right foot. As he did so, Cam reached into his pocket and removed a black shoelace.

One the guards reacted. "Hey, what's that?"

Even as his eyes were glued to the monitor, Randall braced himself to block the door. Cam, no longer moving sluggishly now that he was following specific instructions, looped the lace around the Senator's neck and twisted.

Time froze. It seemed to take forever for anyone to understand what was happening on the monitor—finally Georgia screamed and the guard who had first reacted to the shoelace jumped toward the door.

"Move!" he yelled to Randall.

Randall clenched the arms of the side chair and braced his legs against the wall, wedging the chair into place. The guard grabbed the chair and tried to shove it aside, but Randall fought him, treasuring the delay, counting every precious second as a victory for Cuba, a validation of his lifetime of service, a testament to his love for Consuela.

Finally, something that gave meaning to his life. *For you, Consuela!*

Once the guard realized Randall was fighting him, he hurled him aside and barged through the door. Randall lay crumpled against a wall, his wrist turned at an awkward angle and his head throbbing. But he smiled. At least ten seconds had passed. There was no way anyone could survive a garrote around their neck for that long. He focused on the monitor, on the lifeless body of the obscenely tall, war-mongering Senator sprawled on the floor at Cam's feet.

Randall closed his eyes and smiled. Mission accomplished.

CHAPTER 8

Cam relaxed his grip, pulled his hands away from the Senator's neck. He had never strangled anyone before—it was easier than he thought. He shook his hands, trying to get the feeling back into his fingers. The garrote, gripped so tightly, must have restricted his own blood supply as well as that of the Senator.

He exhaled. It had been a long day. A very long day. Maybe they'd finally let him go now. He shook his hands again, pulled his foot out from underneath the Senator's body...

"Well done," Dr J said, bounding into the room from a back door.

"Thank you," Cam responded.

"Easy for you to say." The Senator sat up and rubbed his neck; a few drops of blood reddened his hand. "You were the *strangler*, not the *stranglee*."

"Did it work?" Cam asked.

Dr. Jag responded. "Perfectly. Mr. Sid is out in the vestibule, a self-satisfied smile on his face. Senator, perhaps you should wave to the camera? I'm sure at some point the smug old bastard is going to look back at the monitor."

"Gladly." Lovecroft smiled. "I know this may sound un-Christian, but I sure would like to see the look on his face when he sees me standing here."

Cam held Amanda close as she sobbed against his shoulder. The guards had marched Randall away and everyone had left Cam and Amanda alone in the interrogation room for some privacy.

"You didn't know?" Cam asked, his lips against her hair.

"No. I thought you really had been turned into a zombie, really were strangling the Senator." She exhaled. "Thank God it was all a ruse."

"It all came together pretty quick. Maybe they didn't have time to tell you."

She nodded. "I've been with Randall every moment." After a few seconds she added: "More likely they didn't trust me to keep the secret."

"I have to tell you, I was really scared." He shook his head and smiled. "One minute I'm about to be drugged up and interrogated, the next minute our delivery guy walks in and tells me he's the deputy director of the CIA."

"Wait, the guy who delivered our Chinese food?"

Cam nodded. "Yup, Pugh Wei." He smiled. "I half-expected him to hand me an egg roll."

"I don't understand."

"I don't know all the details yet either." He had dozens of questions, which the deputy director promised to answer after a good night's sleep. "But I guess at one point, I think when Pugh and I were in the hospital waiting room, I asked him if Randall Sid gave him the bracelet to give to me. I had just met Randall and I figured the two things might be related."

"Which, it now seems, they were."

"So, Randall was already on their radar. When you arrived with your so-called lawyer, Pugh or Wang or whatever his name is figured Randall was up to something. They thought he might be the Cuban sleeper agent. Lovecroft had made some aggressive comments about Cuba, so it sort of all added up. They decided to try to set a trap. I was the cheese." He smiled. "The hardest thing was not flinching when Randall stabbed the table with the pen. I wasn't sure, at his age, how good his aim was."

She sighed. "It was a good plan. Randall ordered you to kill Lovecroft, figuring he'd never get close enough to do the job himself."

"And this way, he would never have to take the fall: The zombified Cam kills Lovecroft while Randall waits in the other room."

She touched his cheek. "So they didn't drug you? You're not an automaton, programmed to simply obey?"

"No."

She sighed, frowned and backed away. "How disappointing." And then a bright smile, as much with her eyes as with her mouth. "It seems I drove all this way for nothing."

Cam and Amanda spent the night in a suburban Virginia hotel, much of it discussing their crazy week. Exhaustion, and the knowledge they had an early morning meeting, finally brought on sleep.

When they awoke the storm front had passed, replaced by a warm southwesterly breeze. Cam did a quick twenty minutes on the hotel elliptical to get his blood flowing while Amanda texted with Astarte; they left the hotel at 7:30 and easily found their way downtown. By eight o'clock the temperature was already pushing fifty and a bright sun reflected off the quickly melting snow in Meridian Hill Park, due north of the White House on 16th Street. A few joggers and dog-watchers were about, but otherwise the city slept.

They parked and ascended a set of wide, steep stairs running alongside what in the warmer months was a cascading water fountain. "You know," he said, "I really liked Randall. Or Morgan. Or whatever his name is."

"And you trusted him," Amanda replied. "He must have been quite an adept liar. You usually have a keen sense for these things."

"I don't think he was lying to me. At least not until the very end. From what Wang told me last night, they think he had only been activated for a day or two—he spent time Friday with a Cuban tourist. Before that he had been dormant for decades." He frowned. "But I guess that could be said for all sleeper agents."

She slipped her arm into his. "Even so, I know you liked him. It hurts to be betrayed."

Senator Lovecroft, along with Georgia, Deputy Director Wang and Dr. Jag, waited for them on a concrete bench, the three men in dark overcoats and Georgia in a black leather motorcycle jacket with a fur collar and a pair of tattered blue jeans, as if she had awoken and decided to distance herself from the Agency in any way possible this morning. The Senator unfolded himself and stood as they approached. "Good morning. I brought coffee and some muffins," he said, gesturing, his neck discolored from where the garrote had chafed against it. "I'm sorry I didn't have time for something more elaborate."

Amanda, after her initial relief that Cam had not been brainwashed, had spent much of their time in the hotel room complaining about fascists in the U.S. government. "We didn't come for food. We came for answers."

The Senator nodded. "And you shall have them, along with an apology."

Georgia greeted them with a hug, Wang and Dr. Jag with a nod.

Amanda didn't waste any time. "We now know it is official policy for the American government to kidnap and torture its own citizens. Does that also include attempted murder of innocent children?"

Wang looked her in the eye. "We had nothing to do with the attack on you in Newton."

She flared. "And I'm supposed to believe that?"

"At least give us credit for being more ... proficient than that. Quite honestly, if we wanted you dead, you would be dead. From what I have learned, Mr. Maxwell is a deluded, paranoid collector who felt threatened by you. Again, we had nothing to do with it. I trust the court system will handle it appropriately."

"What about the witch of a social worker at Astarte's school asking inappropriate questions?"

Wang turned to Dr. Jag.

"That's us," Dr. Jag said. "It's a possible pressure point against Mr. Thorne."

Wang exhaled and held his eyes closed for a couple of seconds. "End it, please. Immediately."

"Unbelievable," Amanda hissed.

As Amanda worked her jaw, Cam cleared his throat. He preferred to take the conversation a little slower. He wanted many things explained, and an angry exchange of accusations and denials would make it difficult to get answers. "I'm assuming we're here in a park rather than in one of your offices so that you can later deny this meeting ever happened."

Wang pursed his lips. "It is not a question of denial so much as privacy." He smiled. "Later today the park will be filled with drummers and dancers. It is a Sunday tradition. But at this hour we can talk freely. There are not many places in Washington anymore where that is true."

"Speaking of true," Cam said as they stood in a small group, "were you really part of the MK-Ultra experiments in New York City?" Or was that another lie?

The Chinese man smiled sadly. "I was. And I am sure you are wondering why then I would work for my torturers—"

"It does seem odd."

"The honest answer is, compared to what the Nazis did and what the Communists in China and the Soviet Union were doing, the CIA programs seemed almost … benign. I suppose you could say I chose the lesser of two evils." He spread his arms. "The United States is far from perfect. But compared to most others…."

Nobody said anything for a few seconds, until Lovecroft spoke. "I suggest we walk." The Senator walked with his hands behind his back, bent slightly at the waist. Cam and Amanda strolled with him, while Georgia, Wang and Dr. Jag followed close behind. "Did you know," the Senator asked, "that President Jefferson wanted the Prime Meridian relocated to Washington? This park was originally built to mark it. The

270

Washington Monument was supposed to mark it as well, but the ground was too unstable to support such a massive structure so it was moved a few hundred feet to the east. Nonetheless, the meridian line runs from the Jefferson Memorial, due north through the center of the White House, through the Andrew Jackson statue in Lafayette Park, up 16th Street to the Scottish Rite Masonic Temple, and then to this park. Hence the name Meridian Hill Park."

"Why the Masonic Temple?" Cam asked. He knew Lovecroft was trying to ease into things after the volatility of last night.

"Indeed, why the Freemasons again?" The Senator smiled. "If Mr. Sid were here, he could no doubt respond. But he is otherwise detained this morning." He eyed Cam. "In any event, I think we both know the answer to your question, Mr. Thorne."

Cam nodded. The entire layout of Washington, D.C. tied into Masonic ritual, imagery and belief.

"So why is the Prime Meridian still marked at Greenwich?" Amanda asked, trying to be civil but a bit of edge still in her tone.

Lovecroft smiled again. "Well, you know how touchy you Brits can be about things like that. I'm guessing we decided not to force the issue."

She rolled her eyes. "How bloody generous of you."

Cam found himself liking the Senator. He wasn't nearly as stiff and humorless as the press portrayed him. But Cam still wanted answers. "So, what the hell is going on?"

Lovecroft's eyes flashed. Cam knew the Senator objected to cursing, but Cam was beyond caring. "Yes, well, that is why we are here," Lovecroft said. He turned to Wang. "Deputy Director, I think you should be the one to explain things."

Wang slid forward to walk with Cam and Amanda as the Senator lagged behind with Georgia and Dr. Jag. "Much of this you have already pieced together, Mr. Thorne."

"Yes. Lucky me. My prize was a night in a man-cave with the fun-loving Dr. Jag."

Wang ignored the barb. "The marriage of MK-Ultra and the Smithsonian was originally one of convenience, brokered if you will by the father of one entity and the custodian of the other, Leonard Carmichael. As often happens, the union proved beneficial to both parties. The Smithsonian benefited from a close relationship with the CIA—never a bad thing in Washington—while the CIA used the Smithsonian and its archives as a testing ground. Dr. Jagurkowitzky, I believe you use the term *Petri dish?*"

"Yes," Dr. Jag said, stepping forward. "A self-contained environment within which we could conduct experiments. Very few people outside the world of pre-Columbian research care about this stuff, so the fallout was minimal and containable."

Cam had heard this before, but Amanda and Georgia had not. "So," Amanda said, "the CIA got to train its agents without having to use real bullets. If MK-Ultra could control what Americans believed about their history, then it could control what, say, the Vietnamese believed about their government."

Wang smiled wryly. "Viet Nam is probably not the best example, but the concept is correct. Over the past couple of generations there have been a number of talented researchers trying to prove the 'Columbus-first' doctrine was outdated and wrong. But it is still taught in all our schools, which is a testament to the success of MK-Ultra and its agents."

Amanda replied. "You should be very proud of yourselves. You have mastered the art of deceiving the people you serve. At any moment the Statue of Liberty is going to break loose from her pedestal and jump for joy."

Again, Wang ignored the jab.

Cam asked something that had been bothering him. "So why give me the Bat Creek Stone bracelet if you're trying to suppress this research?"

Wang nodded. "Fair question. And, honestly, a decision I may come to regret. But we knew we had a mole inside the Agency, and were looking for a way to smoke him or her out. In order to do so, sometimes one needs to start some fires. You, Mr. Thorne, were one of those fires. You and your research."

It was a convoluted plan. But that's how these guys' minds worked. Wang didn't know which of the MK-Ultra agents was the sleeper agent, so he had to assume any of them might be. So his plan was to put the whole operation on steroids, get everyone in the field and running around and out of their comfort zone. People only make mistakes when they need to make choices. The fake rune stone planted on Professor Antonopoulos was another fire, as was the Mormon parody video of Scott Wolter and Vito the blogger attacking researchers and the billionaire stealing the Narragansett Rune Stone and probably a dozen other things no one would ever know about. For these guys it's all about manipulation and deception and misdirection. And what was a broken finger and a few bruises weighed against the task of making the world safe for democracy, which was what these guys saw themselves doing? Cam smiled wryly. "To a man holding the puppet strings, the whole world is their Pinocchio." Deception and lies.

Dr. Jag, like his boss, ignored Cam's jibe and instead responded directly to Wang. "Give yourself some credit, Deputy Director. You set into motion a series of events that allowed us to capture the sleeper agent. That never would have happened without your decision to involve Mr. Thorne."

Wang closed his eyes and bowed slightly in acknowledgement of the praise, which Cam saw as mostly kissing up to the boss. Wang addressed Cam. "If the price for catching our mole was allowing you, Mr. Thorne, to prove the Bat Creek Stone was authentic, so be it. We would gladly pay it." They had circled the open area at the head of the cascading fountain and began walking back downhill alongside the dormant waterway. Wang continued. "But your involvement had an unintended consequence, Mr. Thorne. Another price to pay. A dear one."

"Yes. I nearly had my memory erased." Cam shot an angry glance back at Dr. Jag. Despite the lies and subterfuge, Wang seemed like a decent guy. But Cam's sense of Dr. Jag was that he was one of those soulless bureaucrats that made so many people abhor governments.

"I am referring to Ms. Spencer-Gunn's giant research," Wang said. "We had not foreseen this. In fact, we believed the question of ancient giants had been resolved decades ago. We planted a few fake skeletons which, predictably, had the effect of poisoning the entire well—no reputable anthropologist would risk his reputation by even examining a giant skeleton." He pursed his lips. "It is not a question we wanted to reopen for debate."

"Why?" Lovecroft asked. "Why is her research such a 'dear price,' as you say?"

Wang stopped and turned, the group stopping with him. "Because of you, Senator. Because of you."

The Senator's mouth opened but no words came out. He swallowed, shifted his weight and swallowed again. Finally he spoke. "What do you mean?" Lovecroft glared down at Wang and Dr. Jag. "Out with it, one of you. Stop beating around the bush."

Wang responded in a measured tone. "As you know, officially the CIA does not interfere in American politics. And, in fact, in my decades at the Agency I am proud to say that this policy has for the most part been followed. But this election is different."

"How so?" the Senator responded.

Wang raised himself to his full height. "Because, Senator, the senior staff members at the Agency are in unanimous agreement that this nation needs Webster Lovecroft as its next President."

"Needs?" Georgia said. "Not wants. Not prefers. *Needs?*"

Wang nodded. "Our country is at a crossroads. We are becoming a nation divided. Rich and poor. Republican and Democrat. Red state and blue state. More and more we are defining ourselves by our differences rather than by our similarities. The CIA sees this. We all see this. We need a President who can bring us back together, who can unite this country."

Lovecroft nodded. "Very well. And I am flattered by your confidence in me." He bent forward and spoke slowly, like a parent to a stubborn child. "But you still have not answered my question."

The deputy director responded. "To be blunt, Senator, we are concerned that research on giants could impact the election. Specifically, it could torpedo your chances."

"So that's it." Lovecroft sighed. "You think I am a giant, or at least have giant blood in me. And you think the American public will not elect me because of it."

Wang nodded. "We know about your double row of teeth, and about your Cherokee bloodline, and about your shoe size. What we don't know is whether the American public is ready to elect someone ... different than themselves ... as their President."

Georgia weighed in. "It's a fair point. Romney lost in 2012 largely because people were not convinced a Mormon was *normal* enough." She looked up at the Senator. "Imagine how easy it would be for your political opponents to paint you, to be blunt, as some kind of freak, perhaps even un-human." She turned to Wang. "But this is all academic anyway. Some reporter already has the story. So unless you plan on silencing her, you're too late."

Wang gestured toward Amanda. "Meet your reporter."

Georgia's jaw fell. "What? Amanda?"

Amanda angled her head. "I did go visit the dentist. And he thought I was a reporter." She shrugged. "But I'm just me."

It took Georgia a second to process everything. "Wait, that's great news. So the press knows nothing about this second row of teeth." She turned to Lovecroft. "Your secret is safe," she grinned.

But Lovecroft did not seem to share her joy. His face darkened as he turned on Wang and Dr. Jag. "So the CIA has been suppressing research on giants just because you're afraid of what people might think?" He did not wait for a response. "This is America, darn it. People have a right to think what they want, whether the government likes it or not. If Americans don't want a giant as their President, don't want me as their President, so be it. That is their choice."

The Senator glared at Wang and Dr. Jag. "Your actions are a fundamental betrayal of everything this country stands for." He turned to Georgia. "Please call a press conference. I will be releasing all my medical records. *Including* my genealogy and dental records. The American people have every right to know who they are voting for."

He glared again at the two CIA operatives. "And I expect this is the end of MK-Ultra. The American people also have every right to know the truth about their history."

Amanda and Cam ambled through the park back to their car. The temperature had continued to climb and the morning sun glistened off the thin layer of remaining snow. "Well," she said, "that was interesting."

"Lovecroft was really pissed."

"He's an interesting bloke. I don't know many other politicians who would offer up their medical records like he plans to do. He may be torpedoing his own campaign." She smiled. "As the saying goes, there are some skeletons in his closet. Rather large ones."

"I'm glad you waited until now to point that out. I don't think Lovecroft would have appreciated the humor."

She shrugged. "Honestly, after what they put us through, I'm past caring."

"Back to your original point, I do give him credit for, as you say, opening up his closet. You've heard of 'What would Jesus do?' I think for Lovecroft, it's 'What would Abe Lincoln do?' That's how he looks at things."

"Yes, well, Lincoln didn't live in the internet age. Things are sure to get nasty and ugly."

They walked in silence for a few seconds. "This is the piece Randall Sid could never figure out," Cam said. "The big picture. In the end, the CIA knew all paths eventually led back to the Phoenicians. Back to the giants." He smiled. "And they couldn't have people stumbling upon beanstalks and giants if they wanted Lovecroft to win."

"And it explains what Randall said, about how in the past year MK-Ultra had redoubled its efforts against researchers like us. There's a researcher out in western Massachusetts, a bloke named Jim Vieira. He started looking at the old stone chambers in New England and it led him back to some fascinating research on giants. He did a lecture that was posted on the internet—then out of the blue the host pulled it, claiming it was too controversial."

"Too controversial for the internet?"

She chuckled. "I'd wager the CIA was behind it. They couldn't have anyone sniffing around so close to the election."

Cam took her hand as they crossed the street. "But you messed them up. You didn't follow the bread crumbs back to the giants. You *started* with the giants." He grinned. "You cheated."

"You mean I figured it out before you."

"Because you cheated."

She elbowed him in the ribs. They walked silently for a few seconds. "Seriously, I don't know if it's a question of where you start," she said. "I think all of this is interconnected. You started with the Templars and it led you back to the Phoenicians. I started with the giants and it led me back to the Phoenicians also. People who study America's Stonehenge and Burrows Cave find the same thing. Apparently all roads lead back to the Phoenicians." She smiled. "At least all ancient roads."

"So your instincts were right about the giants. Spot on, as you say. Now you're finally going to be able to dig in."

"Not just the giant research. All the pre-Columbian artifacts can finally be studied and honestly evaluated. Without the Smithsonian hiding artifacts and the CIA intentionally souring the milk."

"Souring the milk?"

"You know, poisoning the research."

"Like cheating, you mean."

She leaned over and kissed him as he opened her car door. "You know, being smarter than you is not cheating." She went in to kiss him again and instead poked him in the chest as he closed his eyes. "It's just being smarter than you."

David S. Brody

EPILOGUE

"Wow. There sure are a lot of reporters here," Cam said as he and Amanda found seats in the back of a Marriott Copley Place meeting room. Six rows of chairs were filled with men and women wearing press badges on their lapels while a half-dozen shoulder-mounted cameramen formed an arc behind them. In addition to the local stations, he saw cameras from CNN, CNBC and Fox. "Must be a slow news day."

"Lovecroft promised a major announcement," Amanda said. "They probably think he's going to officially announce his candidacy. Or maybe receive an important endorsement." She smiled. "But they'd be mistaken."

Cam slipped his arm around her. The last time he had been in a hotel conference room was a month ago, listening to the alien reptile speaker Autier and then meeting Randall—or, rather, Morgan—Sid. It was nice to relax a bit and not worry about people trying to brainwash him. Or worse.

The Senator emerged from behind a curtain and strode to the dais as camera flashes bathed him in white light. A dark-haired man with bushy gray eyebrows walked by his side, eliciting a buzz amongst the crowd. "Is that the mayor?" a reporter a few seats away asked in a stage whisper.

His companion sneered at him. "The mayor's a Democrat, you idiot. What would he be doing here?"

"So who is it?"

"Dunno."

Lovecroft held up his hand to silence the crowd as he blinked away the flashes, After raising the microphone, he made a point of unfolding a piece of paper that presumably contained prepared notes before exhaling and tossing it aside.

"Nice effect," Amanda whispered. "Makes him look unrehearsed."

279

"That's the thing about Lovecroft. I don't think he did it for effect. I think he is unrehearsed."

Always a dynamic speaker, Lovecroft today spoke with a restrained fury. "Thank you for coming today. Standing to my left is Doctor Artun Anoosian, DDM. When I am done speaking he will answer any questions you might have."

Georgia peeked from behind the curtain as the Senator sipped some water. Cam noticed bags under the candidate's eyes which had not been there two weeks ago in Washington—experts say running for President aged a man a full decade. But above the bags his hazel eyes smoldered.

"When I was a divinity student at Harvard in the 1970s, Dr. Anoosian removed a complete second set of teeth from my mouth. This condition is known as hyperdontia. There is some evidence to suggest hyperdontia is a genetic trait left over from a race of oversized humans—what most people would call giants—who lived in North America in the distant past. Given my height, and the fact that I am one-eighth Native American, I felt that this information should be known to the American people." He scanned the audience, a looming presence atop the dais, as if daring any of them to challenge him. "Politics in this country being what they are, no doubt at some point my opponents will try to use this information to call into question my qualifications for higher office." He paused. "I will therefore be releasing today complete copies of my medical and dental records. I will let the American people be the ultimate judge as to its importance and relevancy. Thank you."

A woman near the front instantly stood. "Senator, are you saying you descend from a race of giants?"

Georgia stepped forward from behind the curtain to stop the question, but the Senator froze her with a quick glance. He looked the reporter in the eye. "I honestly do not know the answer to that. None of us can. But I will say that I believe in the Bible, and the Bible recounts numerous tales of giants living during Biblical times, Goliath being the most obvious example."

She followed up before Georgia could intervene. "Are you disclosing this now because your political opponents are threatening to out you?"

Lovecroft shook his head. "I am one of God's creatures, created in his image and with his infinite love. When you use the term, 'threatening to out me,' you are implying that there is something for me to be embarrassed or humiliated about." He shrugged. "But who are we to question God as to in what form or size or color he chooses to create his children? We are all as God created us. Myself included."

Georgia raised her hand to prevent more questioning, though many reporters shouted queries to the Senator as he slowly walked away, flashbulbs again illuminating the room. "Dr. Anoosian will answer any questions you have about hyperdontia," she said, "but the Senator will not be taking further questions today."

"That's too bad. This was getting interesting."

The voice came from behind Cam. He turned and froze for a second, before instinctively stepping in front of Amanda. His fingers tingled as he fought to process what was happening. "You're supposed to be locked away, rotting."

The short, elderly man smiled. "You mistake me for my brother. I promise you, I am harmless."

Cam squinted, studying the smiling man in the white dress shirt and gray slacks. Randall, but not exactly. The same curly white hair, the same wrinkled forehead. But the features were fleshier and less sharp and the shoulders and chest less defined. In all, a softer version of his twin. This was the real Randall, while his brother Morgan sat in jail in Virginia awaiting trial.

Amanda broke the silence. "Harmless or not, what are you doing here?"

"I came to watch the spectacle." He was less charismatic than his twin, but his dark eyes shone with the same sharp intellect. He had more of the typical Boston accent, unlike the Brahmin twang his brother affected.

"Why not just watch it on the evening news," she said, motioning to the row of cameras. "It starts in just over an hour."

"Because it's not going to be on." He shrugged. "At least not the 'spectacle' parts of it."

"Of course it will," Amanda challenged.

He shook his head. "No, it will not."

"Look at all these reporters. How can you be so sure?"

Randall held up his hand and showed a gold ring with a black triangle mounted on it; inside the triangle was a gold number 33.

"What does being a 33rd Degree Freemason have to do with anything?" Cam asked.

He smiled, showing a row of even, gray-tinted smoker's teeth that again reminded Cam of President Obama. "If you'll let me buy you a drink, I'll explain."

They were planning to have dinner with Georgia, but she would be busy with the press for the next hour. Cam and Amanda exchanged a quick glance—how could they not hear him out? They followed him in silence down an escalator to the lobby bar; he chose a table far from other patrons where they ordered drinks.

"First of all," he said, "I suppose I owe you an apology."

Cam shrugged. "You didn't do anything."

"Well, that's not totally true. I traded identities with my brother. Clearly there were consequences." He grimaced. "And I realize buying you a drink doesn't make us even. But answers—I'm guessing you're looking for some answers. Maybe I can give you some." He shrugged and smiled sadly. "Though none about my brother, unfortunately."

"I thought you were sworn to secrecy," Cam said, referring to Randall's Lodge Brothers rather than his biological one.

"Our initiates are sworn to secrecy, and our members are held to that as they progress up the ranks. But once you get to the 33rd Degree, the rules change a bit. I am authorized to speak candidly to you; we felt we owed you that much." He smiled. "Though I will of course deny it later."

Amanda leaned forward. "Let's start with why you're so certain this story is not going to run tonight."

"Okay." He took a deep breath. "It starts with Nimrod. Though today his name is associated with being inept, Nimrod was one of the most powerful kings in the history of the Middle East. So powerful, in fact, that he directly challenged God by building the Tower of Babel."

"Wait," Amanda said, "your brother mentioned something about this in our car ride to Washington. He said Nimrod used to be venerated in Freemasonry, but they pushed him to the background because he was closely associated with Baal and pagan worship."

"Yes. But Morgan had just scratched the surface. It goes way past Nimrod. Have you ever heard of Jahbulon?"

They shook their heads.

"Freemasons going through the Royal Arch Degree are taught that Jahbulon is one of the names of God. Each of the three syllables stands for an ancient god worshiped in the Middle East. The first stands for Jehovah, the God of the Bible. The second stands for Baal. The third is an old name for Osiris." He didn't have the same affected way of speaking as his brother, but he was clearly educated and intelligent.

Amanda nodded. "Makes sense. Those were, indeed, the three ancient gods of the Middle East."

Randall responded. "The issue is that we continue to use this name Jahbulon in our rituals today. So we open ourselves up to accusations that we are giving equal status to Baal and Osiris alongside the Judeo-Christian God." He shrugged. "The truth is that none of the Brothers have any idea what it means—it's just part of some ritual we memorize and parrot back..."

Randall paused as a waitress brought their drinks—a Shandy for Amanda, a Sam Adams for Cam and a scotch on the rocks for Randall.

The Oath of Nimrod

Amanda waited for the waitress to leave. "When you start talking about Baal, you start getting into the area of devil worship and human sacrifice, usually children."

Randall sipped his drink. "So now you are beginning to see our problem. People today tend to be opposed to child sacrifice."

Cam said, "I read that some churches in the South won't accept Masons into their congregations."

"Not just some, but many." Randall smiled wryly. "Nobody wants a family of devil-worshipers in the pew next to them. It's the biggest problem we face nowadays. If you go on the Internet, every other site is some conspiracy theory about how the Freemasons are devil-worshipers and that we are trying to take over the world. Hell, the Catholic Church's official position still is that you can't be both a Mason and a good Catholic."

"I suppose it doesn't really matter if any of it is true," Amanda said. "If people believe you really are devil-worshipers, the perception becomes the reality."

"And this gets back to what I said earlier," Randall said, "about the biggest challenge and danger for Freemasonry today is being thought of as un-Christian. Our membership numbers have been declining for decades, and now we are finally beginning to reverse that trend." He paused, waiting until they both looked him in the eye. "To be blunt, we can't have stories about devil-worship in all the newspapers." He sat back, as if having played his last card, and again sipped his drink.

Cam replayed the words in his mind. *Can't have stories about devil-worship in all the newspapers.* He looked at Amanda; she, too, had connected the dots. Cam took a deep breath. "I think what you're saying is that if people start investigating Lovecroft and giants, it almost inevitably leads back to Nimrod and accusations that the Freemasons are devil-worshiping child-sacrificers."

Randall smiled sadly and lifted his glass to them. "And now you know why that story about Lovecroft being a giant is not going to run. We don't control the country, despite what people think. But we do have many powerful friends who agree with our core beliefs and who think it is important to protect us."

"What do you mean by core beliefs?" Cam asked, taking advantage of the rare opportunity to get candid answers from the Freemasons.

Randall sat forward and folded his hands under his chin, his Masonic ring gleaming in the light. "At it's most basic level, we believe man is essentially good. Organized religion and big government believe the opposite, that man is fundamentally evil and needs to be controlled or policed."

Cam had never heard it summarized that succinctly, but it resonated with him. He reflected on it for a few seconds. "There's a striking irony to this, isn't there?"

Randall smiled, apparently pleased Cam had teased it out. "Yes."

Cam expounded on his thought. "All the conspiracy theorists think the Freemasons are trying to take over the world, trying to build this whole New World Order. The reality is you guys don't trust government."

The older man nodded. "And we never have. That is why our forefathers built this great nation with so many safeguards and an emphasis on individual rights." He shrugged. "But why let the facts get in the way of a perfectly good conspiracy theory?"

Amanda brought the conversation back to the present. "Speaking of conspiracy theories, so you do admit it is the Freemasons who are putting the kybosh on the Lovecroft story?"

"Honestly, I'm not sure the story needs to be kyboshed. It's rather outlandish—seafaring Phoenicians came here thousands of years before Columbus; they brought giants with them; the giants bred with our Native Americans; one of their descendants is now running for President; we know this is true because he has extra teeth." He shrugged. "Who's going to put their name to a story like that?"

Amanda shook her head. "But that's not the story from today. The story from today is a simpler one: A prominent

Presidential candidate held a press conference saying he might descend from a race of giants."

Randall shrugged again. "Fair point."

"And you are saying that story won't run."

"Not in that form, no. At least not in the mainstream press. A few fringe sites may pick it up and run the story next to the latest Elvis sighting."

Cam replied, "And to be clear, this has nothing to do with the election, with you guys favoring Lovecroft over some other candidate?"

Randall made a face. "He is a bit too religious for our taste, as we just discussed. Our concern is that the press not start digging around in our old rituals and add to the chorus of voices accusing us of devil-worship."

Cam was beginning to see shapes in the mist. "There are two trails of breadcrumbs here. They're parallel; they lead to the same place. One starts with giants—if you follow this back, like Amanda has been doing, you end up stumbling onto all these old ties between Masonic ritual and paganism."

Randall nodded.

"And the other trail," Cam continued, "is the one I've been following. You start with ancient artifacts like the Bat Creek Stone and the Sacrificial Stone at America's Stonehenge and follow it back. It has nothing to do with giants but, again, you end up back in Phoenicia and run head-first into ancient ties between the Masons and paganism."

Randall nodded again, this time more slowly.

Cam leaned forward. "So if you don't want us to follow one trail, isn't it fair to say you don't want us to follow the other either?"

Randall didn't need to nod again. He merely offered a long blink. "Your logic is impeccable, Mr. Thorne."

Cam followed the reasoning to its natural conclusion. "So the CIA and the Smithsonian weren't blocking research of pre-Columbian artifacts merely to give MK-Ultra a forum to practice mind control. It goes beyond that. You had an ulterior motive."

"You are correct," Randall conceded. "As you say, research like yours eventually leads back to the Phoenicians. To a certain amount of … ugliness. For that reason, decades ago we made clear our preference that research in pre-Columbian history be discouraged. And our friends in the government agreed to assist us."

Amanda lifted her jaw. "The whole partnership between the Smithsonian and the CIA never totally made sense to me. There were easier ways for the CIA to train their agents and experiment with mind control—they didn't need to ruin the careers of so many researchers. But this makes sense. Suppressing the research served a secondary purpose as well."

Randall shrugged and smiled. "Some would argue that protecting Freemasonry was the primary purpose, and that supporting MK-Ultra was in fact secondary. But either way, you are correct."

"So Deputy Director Wang lied to us," Cam said.

Randall shook his head. "I don't think so. I think policy decisions like this are made above his pay grade. And, more importantly, this decision was made generations ago, in the 1950s when Project MK-Ultra was begun by President Truman. Truman, perhaps you know, was a 33rd Degree Freemason."

"That's a bloody surprise," Amanda said, setting down her drink loudly.

Cam weighed the implications of this. He had a good relationship with many Masons, and had never felt they opposed his research in any way.

As if reading his thoughts, Randall said, "This all happened, what, sixty years ago. It's just pretty much been on auto-pilot since."

Cam nodded, "So if they do shut down MK-Ultra as Wang promised, does that mean the Freemasons—or your friends in government—will no longer block our research?"

Randall sat back. "Our policy on this is evolving. Old-timers like myself are being replaced by a generation who don't see the need for all this cloak-and-dagger stuff. In fact, blocking today's Lovecroft story may be the last hurrah for my generation—going forward, we are going to focus on scrubbing our rituals clean so they aren't tainted by the old pagan beliefs. But to answer your question, we will not encourage research in this area, but nor will we work to obstruct it." He shrugged. "As one of the younger guys said, in the age of the internet, it's not practical to think the free flow of ideas can be suppressed."

As if on cue, the television above the bar began to run the five o'clock news, with the Lovecroft news conference as the lead story. Cam, Amanda and Randall leaned forward to listen as a thirty-something man in a blue blazer reported from the Copley Marriott lobby:

"Senator Webster Lovecroft, believed to be strongly considering a run for the Republican nomination for the Presidency, held a press conference today in Boston. The Senator released his medical records and called for all other candidates to do the same. The Senator's spokeswoman also said the Senator would be releasing ten years worth of tax returns. In a prepared statement, the Senator said: 'I believe in full disclosure and complete transparency. The American people should know as much as they can about a candidate before entering the ballot box.'"

And that was it.

Randall cocked his head and shrugged. "As I said, no story." He stood and dropped a twenty on the table for the drinks. "Again, I'm sorry for the trouble my brother put you through. But at least I can promise the Freemasons won't block your research. Good luck to you."

Cam chuckled and shrugged as Randall walked away, his Masonic ring catching the light from the bar. "The twenty's not even going to cover the drinks," he said to Amanda.

Amanda took his hand. "Yes, but think about his promise. It's invaluable. I don't think the Smithsonian is going to be putting giant skeletons on display, and I don't think anyone is going to be rushing to rewrite the history textbooks." Her green eyes sparkled. "But at least for the first time in decades, the fix won't be in."

THE END

AUTHOR'S NOTE

Inevitably, I receive this question from readers: "Are the artifacts and historical sites in your stories real, or did you make them up?" The answer is: If they are in the story, they are real, actual artifacts and sites.

It is because they are real that I have included images of many of them within these pages—I want readers to see them with their own eyes, to be able to make at least a cursory judgment as to their age, origin and meaning. Are they authentic? Do they evidence ancient exploration of this continent? I hope readers will at least consider the possibility that they do.

Just as the artifacts and sites displayed in this book are real, so too are the other images—the works of art, the newspaper clippings, the maps. In short, if something is displayed within this book, it exists in the real word.

Likewise, the historical references are accurate in a general if not specific sense. Project MK-Ultra did, indeed, exist, although of course I take some liberties with the historical record within the pages of this novel.

For inquisitive readers, perhaps curious about some of the specific historical assertions made and evidence presented in this story, I offer the following substantiation (in order of appearance in the story):

- Leonard Carmichael was, as I wrote, the President of Tufts University before becoming the Secretary of the Smithsonian Institution. According to some sources, he was—through his involvement with something called the Human Ecology Board—one of the founding members of Project MK-Ultra. http://scientific-misconduct.blogspot.com/2008/05/lsd-and-corruption-of-medicine-part-iii.html. Prior to his tenure at Tufts, he was a professor at Brown University, where he worked closely with Edmund Burke Delabarre, an expert on Dighton Rock and other ancient stone carvings of New England. http://www.brown.edu/Administration/News_Bureau/D atabases/Encyclopedia/search.php?serial=P0450. However, while it is true the U.S. government recruited Nazi scientists and doctors after World War, there is no evidence Carmichael traveled to Argentina or otherwise was involved with the recruiting of Nazi doctors as I write in the Prologue.

- Project MK-Ultra was an actual program. This Wikipedia description is a fair summary of it:

> Project MK-Ultra — sometimes referred to as the CIA's mind control program — is the code name of a U.S. government human research operation experimenting in the behavioral engineering of humans. Organized through the Scientific Intelligence Division of the Central Intelligence Agency (CIA), the project coordinated with the Special Operations Division of the U.S. Army's Chemical Corps. The program began in the early 1950s, was officially sanctioned in 1953, was reduced in scope in 1964, further curtailed in 1967 and officially halted in 1973. The program engaged in many illegal activities; in particular it used unwitting U.S. and Canadian citizens as its test subjects, which led to controversy regarding its legitimacy. MK-Ultra used numerous methodologies to manipulate people's mental states and alter brain functions, including the surreptitious administration of drugs (especially LSD) and other chemicals, hypnosis, sensory deprivation, isolation, verbal and sexual abuse, as well as various forms of torture.

The Oath of Nimrod

The scope of Project MK-Ultra was broad, with research undertaken at 80 institutions, including 44 colleges and universities, as well as hospitals, prisons and pharmaceutical companies. The CIA operated through these institutions using front organizations, although sometimes top officials at these institutions were aware of the CIA's involvement. As the Supreme Court later noted, MK-Ultra was concerned with "the research and development of chemical, biological, and radiological materials capable of employment in clandestine operations to control human behavior." The program consisted of some 149 subprojects which the Agency contracted out to various universities, research foundations, and similar institutions. At least 80 institutions and 185 private researchers participated. Because the Agency funded MK-Ultra indirectly, many of the participating individuals were unaware that they were dealing with the Agency.

Project MK-Ultra was first brought to public attention in 1975 by the Church Committee of the U.S. Congress, and a Gerald Ford commission to investigate CIA activities within the United States. Investigative efforts were hampered by the fact that CIA Director Richard Helms ordered all MK-Ultra files destroyed in 1973; the Church Committee and Rockefeller Commission investigations relied on the sworn testimony of direct participants and on the relatively small number of documents that survived Helms' destruction order.

In 1977, a Freedom of Information Act request uncovered a cache of 20,000 documents relating to project MK-Ultra, which led to Senate hearings later that same year. In July 2001 some surviving information regarding MK-Ultra was officially declassified. [citations omitted]

http://en.wikipedia.org/wiki/Project_MKUltra

- Researcher Jim Vieira has documented over 1,500 accounts of giant skeletons found in North America. A Facebook page he maintains references many of these accounts: https://www.facebook.com/pages/Stone-Builders-Mound-Builders-and-the-Giants-of-Ancient-America/556606251021542. Many of the giants listed by Amanda in the story come from Mr. Vieira's research. Many of the skeletons in these accounts are reported to have double rows of teeth. The references in the story to giants in the Bible are accurate ones.

- A good summary of the Bat Creek Stone research can be found here and in the sources cited therein: http://www.econ.ohio-state.edu/jhm/arch/batcrk.html

- The history of Nimrod—both his role in the Bible and his role in Masonic ritual—is as I describe it in the story. See *Encyclopedia of Freemasonry,* by Albert C. Mackey, at page 181.

- As in the story, the Vinland Map was purchased by Paul Mellon (of the Mellon banking family) and donated to Yale University. Also as in the story, the Narragansett Rune Stone was allegedly removed from the water by an abutter in 2012. The Providence Journal identified Timothy Mellon (son of Paul Mellon) as a possible suspect in this removal: http://www.providencejournal.com/breaking-news/content/20130706-as-theories-of-its-origin-abound-what-does-future-hold-for-narragansett-rune-stone.ece . For the assertions that a Mellon-family

Millbrook estate was used by Timothy Leary for LSD experimentation and that William Mellon Hitchcock financed an LSD manufacturing operation, see generally *Acid Dreams: The Complete Social History of LSD: The CIA, the Sixties, and Beyond*, by Martin A. Lee and Bruce Shlain.

- For more information on Judaculla Rock, see here: http://www.judacullarock.com

- For a good explanation of the Burrows Cave map stone and the changing course of the Mississippi River, see William and Marilyn Kreisle of the Midwest Epigraphic Society here: http://www.midwesternepigraphic.org/sMap01.html

- Laurence Gardner was a prolific author who, in *Genesis of the Grail Kings,* postulated that the Jesus bloodline could be traced back to ancient aliens. He died in 2010.

- The Vermont Rune Stone is an actual stone carving that, after study, was found to be the work of local youth and/or young adults as part of a fantasy role-playing game.

- The Stefan Antonopoulos character is fictional.

- Geologist Scott Wolter is an actual researcher and author. He hosts the History Channel series, *America Unearthed.* The parody video referenced in the story is real: https://www.youtube.com/watch?v=iQ8C8rTM0yc&feature=player_embedded

- Barry Fell is an actual researcher and author, as described in the story.

- The Baal Stone and the Sacrificial Table can both be found at the America's Stonehenge site in North Salem, NH.

- Frank Glynn is an actual researcher, though the report about him dying under the belief other researchers were digging at the Encampment Site is fictionalized. The research I describe him doing on the Westford Knight and Boat Stone (and Encampment Site) is real.

- The Daniel Whitewood character is fictional, though the carbon-dating research I describe him doing on Newport Tower is real. See *The Hooked X*, by Scott F. Wolter, at page 86.

- The Grave Creek Burial Mound of West Virginia did indeed contain both an inscribed tablet and a giant skeleton. See *Ancient American Magazine*, Volume 16, Issue Number 95, at page 37. The translation of the tablet inscription offered in the story is one possible translation.

Out of all this, then, comes a story that hopefully both educates and entertains. Did giants once roam the American countryside and, if so, are they related to the Biblical giants? Has our nation's government for some reason been working to hide this history from the American people? Can the answers to these questions be found in ancient Masonic ritual and custom? These are the questions that fascinate me. Hopefully you've found both some enlightenment and some entertainment in them as well.

PHOTO CREDITS

Images used in this book are either in the public domain and/or are provided courtesy of the following individuals (images listed in order of appearance in the story):

IMAGE OF MAP SHOWING GIANT LOCATIONS
Courtesy Cecilia Hall, USOKS

FOUNDATION STONES OF PRINCE HENRY SINCLAIR ENCAMPMENT SITE
Courtesy Kim Bacik

ROCK BOTTOM FORMATION
Courtesy Karla Aikens

ACKNOWLEDGEMENTS

Researching these novels is a ton of fun—and also a lot of work. Thankfully, I have fellow researchers who enjoy joining me as I ferret around in the dark, dusty corners of our history. Thanks to (in alphabetical order): Michael Carr, Matthew Cilento, Richard Lynch and James Vieira. For insights into Cuba and the changing political climate, thanks to Jay Goober and Amy Halpern Degen. I am grateful to you all.

I also want to thank my team of readers, those who trudged their way through early versions of the story and offered helpful, insightful comments (listed chronologically): Michael Carr, Debra Scott, Spencer Brody, Matthew Cilento, Jeanne Scott, Paul McNamee, Renee Brody and Richard Scott.

For other authors out there looking to navigate their way through the publishing process, I can't speak highly enough about Amy Collins and her team at New Shelves Distribution—real pros who know the business and are a pleasure to work with.

Lastly, to my wife, Kim: Thanks for your unending patience and support. To the extent any of my novels is a success, it is because of your keen eye and wise counsel.

Made in the USA
Coppell, TX
20 July 2021